ORDER OF TRUTH

THE ORDER SERIES, BOOK 4

LISA CAVINESS

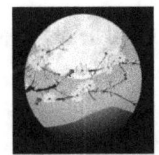

To Mom and the sisters...

Chapter 1

Lila Caldwell had seen death before.

She stood for a moment, taking in what little she could see of the rainy Dallas skyline through the floor-to-ceiling windows of her law mentor, Jack Struthers's penthouse apartment. Her gaze shifted to the white marble floor, which gleamed even in the dull light of the cloudy day. A table in the center of the wide foyer held a gold vase filled with purple orchids. The serene nature of the flowers tickled something in the back of her brain. She stepped farther in the penthouse and any hope of having a good day evaporated as her body stilled. The unmistakable scent of blood settled into her nostrils, taking hold of her senses. Her body shook as past images of lifeless bodies surged in her mind.

It's my imagination. Nothing to fear.

She tried in vain to believe that, but after getting a late start due to another terrifying nightmare, which, ironically, had dead bodies littered at her feet, Lila's ability to embrace the sunny side of life resembled the rainstorm raging outside—gray and foreboding. She forced the ghastly images out of her thoughts and attributed her off-kilter sense of smell to her runaway imagination.

"Jack. It's Lila Caldwell," she called. "I have the Abbington files for your review." She shivered again as her voice bounced off the ecru colored walls, and she inhaled another scent, a faint acrid odor of smoke, as if someone had extinguished a fire in the fireplace or something else hot that she couldn't quite discern.

After no answer, she called his name again. Could he be in the shower or still sleeping? After a quick glance at her watch, she sighed. Jack was always on time. She ambled a few steps into the living room and noted the scent of blood grew stronger. A chill tickled her spine. This time she couldn't push aside her senses. She clutched her bag, wishing the weapon she'd left in the car was inside.

Beige-colored sofas and chairs sat in front of her. A large kitchen with dark walnut cabinets and an expansive bar occupied the left side of the open room. As she neared the kitchen, she jolted as the burnt odor became more pronounced.

"Jack!" She stopped when she spotted what she believed was the back of Jack's dark blond hair evident above a chair, facing the large windows. She didn't want to embarrass him or startle him awake so she called his name again but in a softer tone.

She moved around one of the sofas as the earthy aroma of blood bombarded her. When she stepped in front of the chair, her mouth dropped open, but no sound emitted. She stared at the blood saturating the once-white polo shirt. A bullet had ripped into Jack's chest. His torso resembled cherry gelatin, and she wondered if he was even still alive. A moan escaped as if he emitted the sound to confirm his existence.

"Jack." She let her briefcase slip from her grip as she leaned over the injured man. Her heart thrummed, and her mind raced. Would CPR help? His chest had almost caved inward. Where would she put her hand to do chest compressions? *I can't just let him die.* "Don't try to talk." She glanced toward the door. "Help!" The name of the doorman who'd escorted her up to the penthouse escaped her. She fumbled inside her purse in search of her cell phone.

"You have to get the files." Jack's wide eyes were focused on her. His voice raspy and just above a whisper. Each shallow breath gurgled with blood.

"I have the files right here, Jack. I'll take care of them. Don't worry." Where the hell was her phone?

He grasped her hands, smearing them with sticky, warm blood. "No, get the files. But don't tell anyone. Be careful. They are powerful."

"I'll handle it. But now I've got to get help. Henry!" She remembered the doorman's name at the same time she recalled she'd placed her phone in her raincoat's pocket. Thrusting her hand inside the pocket, she drew out the phone but before she could punch any buttons, she was stilled by Jack's surprisingly strong grip.

"Listen!" His brown eyes burrowed into hers. "Must get the files." He grimaced.

"What files? I don't know what you're talking about." Lila gripped Jack's hands just as hard as he held on to hers.

"Don't tell anyone. Take the files and hide them. They killed me because of what's in them. Very powerful people." His eyes closed and what was left of his chest quivered.

"Jack!" She shifted, and the movement jerked his eyes open.

His mouth fell open, revealing bloodstained teeth. "Get the files. Please."

She'd never witnessed the powerful Jack Struthers so weak and vulnerable. "Yes, but right now I have to get help."

He pulled her closer. "Intel important. Don't let them fall into wrong hands. Tell Cheryl and the kids I love them." He coughed, sputtering blood on her face and arms. "Location of files..." he paused and closed his eyes again.

"Jack!" Lila held onto his hand. "Don't die."

His gaze lifted to the photo sitting on a nearby table of Jack, Cheryl, and their two teenaged boys. Her heart thundered. They were about to lose their foundation, and she couldn't do a thing to stop this death train. The family would be shattered, a horror she knew all too well.

"What do you want me to do?"

He opened his eyes and raised his head; his voice was so soft she had to lean closer to hear his words. "Find 7011 and Jennings. Docs important."

Lila's mind spun with questions she had no time to ask. "I'll take care of it, Jack. Don't worry."

He nodded, and his head fell back against the chair. "They killed me. They...are...dangerous. You're in danger. I'm sorry." More blood sputtered from his mouth then his gaze fixed on her.

"Jack. Jack!" Lila shook his arm, but he didn't respond.

The door opened.

"I heard screaming. What's wrong, Miss?" the doorman said.

"He's been shot!"

The man rushed to her side. "Oh, my goodness! Mr. Struthers!"

As Jack's hand went limp, Lila stared at the lifeless eyes of a man she'd once believed immortal. Jack's death was a price too high, but for what? "Call 911. My boss has been murdered."

Chapter 2

"Please gather your desk possessions and meet me in Building 5, Hallway 3A. Tomorrow, 8 A.M. You've been reassigned."

Cody stared at the email he'd received the previous day from Bill Jessup, a human resource officer at Veridian Technologies, one of the most powerful tech companies in the world. *Reassigned.* He'd only been at the company six months, each day pounding away as a software engineer programmer on a virtual reality project team.

Closing the email, he shoved the phone back into his pocket. Although the email didn't mention the nature of his role, Cody's gut told him this was what he'd been waiting for. Shifting the small box filled with personal items from his cubicle, he stood under bold letters spelling out the words, Restricted Access.

"Green, what are you doing here?" Paul Munson said as he rounded the corner.

Cody suppressed a groan and choked back an expletive. He and Paul had started at Veridian at the same time, and the guy thought he rode through life on a golden chariot. *Pompous know-it-all* was too nice a description. Although Cody had no intention of competing with Paul, he hated that the guy insisted on always trying to one-up him.

"I suppose the same thing you are. Any idea what this is about?"

"Not a clue. But we're in Building 5, the most secure, top-secret place on the Veridian campus. B5 houses a lot of the top-secret program teams. Been here six months and they are inviting me to the heavy hitter team." Paul set a box twice the size of Cody's on the floor. His expression grew serious. "I'm up for the challenge. But whatever this is, it's only temporary. I will be in executive management before you know it." Paul's nod emphasized his point.

Cody ignored Paul's inflated comments.

"Glad you two found the place," Bill Jessup said, humping down the hall. "Not many people get this far, even though we are still technically in the all clear zone." He thumbed toward the RESTRICTED ACCESS sign.

"Why are we being reassigned?" Cody asked.

Jessup beamed. "Not reassigned, promoted. This is a special team comprised of a select group of experts considered to be the best of the best. You two were handpicked. We had our eyes on you both from the beginning, but we wanted to test you in other, less critical roles, first."

Jessup slapped them each on the back as if they were his sons who just received A's on their report cards. "Believe me when I say this is an excellent opportunity. Shows someone has noticed your potential. This is a big deal. Many of our scientists and engineers are dying to get on these upper-level project teams. Major coup for you. This is a level-fifteen clearance. There are only twenty levels, and I don't even have clearance that high."

Paul puffed his chest. "I won't let you down."

Cody remained silent. This could be the break he'd been hoping for, the reason he accepted a job with Veridian.

The door swung open, and a short man, wearing jeans and a white polo shirt with the Veridian logo on the chest, emerged. "Cody Green and Paul Munson?"

"Paul, here." The jerk stepped forward.

"Rick Brawley. I'll be your team leader."

Rick, who stood about five feet eight, studied them, his gaze shifting from their heads to their feet. With his slicked-back, dark hair and gold pinkie ring, the man reminded Cody of Lance Sinclair, the current leader of The Order. They had reason to believe Lance was interested in taking over Veridian, which would give him untold wealth, power, and access to intelligence. Something about Rick rubbed Cody wrong but he needed this lead.

The Order, a covert organization was started in Virginia by Russell Sinclair in reaction to his dissatisfaction with his lack of progression in the Free Masons. Over time the organization change from a simple social group to a powerful assembly of people led by a Grand Commander from the Sinclair family with strict rules for loyalty. Murder, blackmail, torture were common staples for Order business. Lance Sinclair, Russell's grandson, now headed the organization which boasted members from every walk of life, including government, business, and law enforcement.

"Nice to meet you." Cody shook Rick's hand, who offered a quick, loose, pump before giving Cody a feeling that the man considered himself superior. Rick and Paul should get along great.

"Good luck, guys," Jessup said, turning and retracing his steps down the hall.

"Follow me. You are about to enter what we call the *hive*. You'll see why." Rick swiped his badge across a security panel which unlocked the door. They entered an anteroom with five monitors and a row of lockers. "This is where you're stripped."

Paul's mouth dropped opened.

Cody didn't react but continued to eye Rick.

He grinned. "Just kidding. Sort of. Gentlemen, you are about to embark upon entry into one of the world's most secured offices, rivaling the high-tech Situation Room in the White House. We do not allow personal cell phones or any electronic devices past this point. You will see your name above your assigned locker. This is where we strip you of your personal devices. Please deposit them inside."

Cody hated the idea of not being connected. After he placed his cell inside the locker, he froze. In an instant he made the decision. Removing the chain from under his collar, he cut a glance at Rick.

When the man turned toward the security monitor, Cody tucked the silver necklace with a compass pendant under his phone. Probably best not to chance Veridian monitors detecting the hidden GPS device inside the compass.

"Green, what are you doing? Saying a fond farewell to your phone. Let's go." Rick stepped up to a station and placed his head in front of a panel. Seconds later, another door unlocked. "We use a series of biometric security measures. These are retinal scanners. Our first task will be setting up your access credentials."

Cody followed Rick through a heavy door similar to a bank vault which led into a large, windowless, two-story room. The upper loft area had several stations with large computer monitors and rows of network servers tucked inside hexagonal inlets. Underneath were rows of computer equipment and more servers. The entire setup resembled a beehive, hence the *hive* moniker.

Rick stopped and waved a hand upward. "We set our equipment inside those inlets to keep them cool. You probably noticed a definite drop in temperature. We like to keep it about sixty-eight degrees in here. You won't be actually working in this room on a daily basis, but everything here is essential to our work and completely segregated from the rest of the company. We're like our own sovereign island." He laughed, then pivoted. "This way."

After a short walk down the hall, they arrived at an unmarked door. Rick placed his handprint on a wall screen and the door swung open. They were greeted by a middle-aged woman with short dark hair and large square glasses.

"Our new recruits." Rick rocked back in his expensive loafers. "This is Tally Unger." He waved at the woman and then motioned for them all to sit.

Cody entered the windowless office and sat in one of the soft-cushioned chairs in front of the desk. Bare white walls and a steel-gray carpet gave the room a clinical atmosphere, as if someone were studying them from a secret location. Cody didn't see any evidence of a two-way mirror, but he did observe a small orb in the corner of the ceiling indicating a camera. They *were* being watched.

Paul took the chair next to him.

"Ah. Paul Munson. Twenty-seven years old, hails from Stamford, Connecticut, matriculated from University of Connecticut. Parents, Jerome and Tanya." Tally crossed her arms and stood behind her desk. "Jerome is head of the grounds crew at UConn, and Tanya works for an insurance company. Two siblings, older brother Jerome, Jr. or JJ and younger sister, Debbie. JJ's girlfriend Crystal is pregnant. Debbie is a senior at UConn, majoring in business. Your parents are considering a cruise for the next vacation, probably in March or April."

Paul's eyes widened.

"I won't ask if I'm right because I already know I am." Tally chuckled. "All the information is out there for me to retrieve."

"Yes, it's all true," Paul's voice was thick.

Tally turned to Cody. "You are a bit of a country-music sad song straight out of Virginia. Grew up in a lower-class neighborhood without a father. Mother works at the Sparkle Nail Salon. Brother, Holden, was dishonorably discharged from the Army. Spends time boozing and getting high, and basically ignoring his three-year-old son. You managed to get yourself to MIT, then on to Purdue for your graduate degree." She cocked her head. "Well done, Mr. Green."

Cody tensed. How much did this woman know? Cody considered his allegiance to The Alliance, the covert FBI group formed to combat The Order, a dangerous, almost cult-like organization with tentacles extending into the highest levels of government, business, and law enforcement. The Alliance had been careful not to leave a digital footprint of anything. Cody's connection with The Order had been avoided at all costs on social media and even in emails and texts.

She continued. "Worked for a start-up software company outside of San Francisco before moving here six months, two weeks, and four days ago. After breaking up with your girlfriend, Abby Burnham. A schoolteacher. Third grade." She perched on the side of her desk. "Mr. Moneybags here"—she lifted her chin toward Cody— "bought a house while his poor diabetic mom is still living back home in a tiny house in desperate need of repairs. How's that?"

"Thorough." Cody didn't want to say much more.

"Yes, I am. I rely on impeccable intelligence. I can find out virtually anything I want about anyone. We are riding the wave of the future. The public has a thirst for social media. They lap it up like a man happening upon water in a desert. We're like drug dealers with a new highly addictive substance. One sniff and they are hooked. Veridian takes them on a ride, but like any drug they need more and more to achieve that high. That's where we come in. We study them, figure out their motivations, and what it will take to get to that next high. Welcome to the Deep Dive Initiative, DDI as we like to call it. Now, let's get your biometrics set up."

The rest of the day, he and Paul were forced together. To Cody's consternation, Rick set them up in a small conference room inside the unit but just outside the hive where he and Paul spent the afternoon reading introductory material. Cody found the documents rudimentary and nothing of a confidential nature. This time he had to agree with Paul, who labeled the activity "busy work." Nevertheless, Cody was certain the DDI project would yield him intelligence.

At the end of the day, Cody retrieved his personal belongings from his locker and headed out. He jumped on to his prized possession, a silver-and-black Ducati motorcycle. The rain of the morning had dissipated making conditions much better for his ride home. As he pulled into the garage of his suburban home thirty minutes later, the buzzing of his phone rattled in his pocket. Cody set his helmet aside and answered. "Reid, just the person I wanted to talk to."

Chapter 3

When Lila stepped out of the police station, she shielded her face from the last glimmers of sun before night settled in. She huffed out the stale air of the police headquarters' interview room and inhaled a sweet aroma, thanks to a light breeze and the pink flowers from the desert willow trees bordering the parking lot. Even in the urban setting, the crickets chirped, and a few fireflies lit the sky. Pulling her purse close, she rushed toward her car. As she rounded the vehicle, she saw a black sedan roll to a stop and the front driver's side window slowly lowered.

"Ms. Caldwell."

The voice, a thick southern drawl, belonged to Walt Talcott, senior partner of Hirst, Talcott, and Painter. With dull brown eyes the color of oolong tea and a ring of matching brown hair circling his half-bald head, the man pivoted toward her.

"Mr. Talcott." Lila's voice rose. Her head pounded, and her stomach picked the wrong time to growl. She hadn't eaten since breakfast, over ten hours ago.

"I'd like a word. Get in."

Although she'd worked for HTP for two years, she'd yet to have a conversation with him. She'd been in the room when he addressed the young associates, but he'd never spoken to her personally. The fact he even knew her name shocked her. She pictured him consulting the firm's website to find her attorney picture and profile.

A brown tendril of hair blew across her face. She tucked the wayward strand behind her ear and climbed into the passenger side of the car. With her bag between her and Talcott, she settled into the smooth leather seat.

Talcott parked in the open spot next to her eight-year-old SUV. He kept the engine running as he tapped his meaty fingers on the steering wheel. His platinum wedding ring made a thudding sound against the leather wrapped helm. "We're all saddened by the news of Jack's death. However, the firm cannot waver in its commitment to our clients, just as you mustn't waver in your allegiance to the firm. You are to consult with me on any matters related to Jack's death, even police inquiries. Hilary Foster, as you are aware since she accompanied you during your interview, will represent you in any legal matters, although we don't expect you're much more than an unfortunate witness."

Tensing, she bristled at his dismissive tone. What about the well-being of Jack, his family, or her? She shouldn't have been surprised as she waded through the dog-eat-dog world of working for a large law firm. She could have opted for a less intense environment, but HTP was the top firm in Texas and one of the top five in the US. The on-the-job training she'd received had been invaluable and probably more educational than all three years of law school. Despite the acco-lades attributable to HTP, she'd come to the firm for other reasons.

Her father had asked her more than once to consider joining his expanding restaurant business as vice president under his chief legal officer. Although Lila wanted to gain some experience separate from her father's company, she hadn't ruled out the possibility of joining her him in a few years.

She turned her attention back to Talcott, disgust washing over her. One of his fellow legal partners was just murdered and another of his attorneys witnessed his death. Yet the man displayed not an ounce of sadness for Jack or even a modicum of compassion for her.

She'd learned one thing from her years in foster care—if you don't care about yourself, no one else will. Thanks to reuniting with her father, after her mother abandoned her, she'd escaped more lonely years. Shifting in her seat, she forced herself to look Talcott in the eye.

The round-faced man continued, "I dispatched Hilary Foster to guide you through the police interview because I don't want any mistakes on our part or theirs."

Hilary, a criminal defense attorney, was a fearless litigator. Prosecutors groaned at the prospect of facing off against her, defendants paid through the nose to have her represent them, and she walked on water at HTP. Her tough exterior did not escape her underlings as she taught them the secrets of being a top litigator with passion.

"Thank you, sir." She'd been both relieved and alarmed when Hilary presented herself as her attorney. The first rule from a criminal defense attorney was never speak to the police without an attorney present. But did Talcott or Hilary believe she *needed* an attorney for more serious reasons? She'd witnessed the death of a man, not the actual murder so she couldn't offer much to the investigation.

"Did you see anyone curious at Jack's residence?" Talcott asked, cutting through her thoughts.

She shook her head. "No. Other than the doorman, I was alone in the penthouse. At least to my knowledge. I didn't see or hear anyone else." The idea that the killer might have still been lurking hadn't occurred to her until the detective had asked hours later. She'd only spent a few precious moments with Jack before the silence of death took over.

"Good. You didn't see anyone?"

"No. When I entered the penthouse, Jack was slumped in a chair, bleeding and barely hanging on to life." Images of his bloodied body played before her. How long had he suffered?

What about the killer or killers? A receptionist monitored the front entrance, and Lila had been escorted to Jack's penthouse by the doorman, leading her to believe building security was a priority. She would expect cameras to be mounted throughout the building. The murderer couldn't have escaped unnoticed. Or could he?

"Was Jack able to communicate with you?" Talcott's dark gaze bore into hers.

Her heart kicked up a notch. She hadn't divulged the entire conversation she'd had with Jack moments before his death. Without any idea if what Jack had said was him talking out of his head or the actual truth, Lila made the decision not to disclose this bit of information to anyone. During the interview with the detective, she summarized the conversation as Jack giving her instructions about work and messages of love for his family. When prompted, she told the detective Jack hadn't disclosed who his killer was. All true, so technically, she provided an honest answer, just as she would to Talcott. "He wanted me to tell his wife and children he loved them. Also, he told me to stay on our cases." She wrapped her hands together. "That's it."

Talcott clamped his jaw then nodded. "You are not to grant any media interviews or speak of this matter with anyone outside of me, Hilary, or anyone else *we* deem appropriate."

"Understood." Exhaustion clung to her like a weighted tarp. She could have uttered some polite and completely insincere thanks, but she didn't have the energy for such niceties. As an attorney, she'd learned to perfect distortions of truth. How could she be grateful for support purely designed to cover their asses? Any potential for negative news about the firm was met with hypervigilance. HTP even employed a media relations specialist.

"Report to my office in the morning. As I've already stated, do not talk to anyone regarding Jack, his caseload, or the circumstances of his death. In the morning, we will brief you in further detail on the firm's stance regarding Jack's death as well as our plans to cover his clients." Talcott gave her a brief smile then clicked open the door locks. "Say, eight A.M., sharp."

Lila cleared her throat and placed a hand on the door handle. "I'll see you in the morning." She gripped her bag with one hand and opened the door with the other, thankful her hands were occupied, and she was unable to pummel him. Warm, humid air mixed with the car's cool blast stirred around her as she balanced for a second between two worlds.

As soon as the door shut, Talcott gunned the European export out of the parking lot.

Turning, she trudged to her vehicle, car keys jangling in her hand. She glanced in the backseat before unlocking the door. Her car had been sitting in the station parking lot for several hours and the late-summer Texas heat had baked the inside. Despite the heat, Lila shivered and slid into the driver's seat. She gave in to the urge to check her backseat again, then started the car. Glancing in her rearview mirror, she spotted several empty parking spaces but no one directly behind her. Returning her gaze to the front, she eyed another car pulling into a space a row ahead. She blew out a breath when a harried sandwich delivery guy jumped out and ran into the station with several bags of food.

As she angled out of the parking lot, another glance behind her told her no one followed, but to be safe she decided to take a round-about route to her house.

Lila didn't turn on the car's air conditioner right away, which helped to ward off the chill invading her body. For the next minute she counted, a technique to settle her nerves. When she reached eighty, she felt her shoulders loosen. The day had been a jumble of emotions, but she couldn't afford to lose control.

Could Jack's murder have been an isolated event having nothing to do with her life or The Order? Jack said she was in danger. Could his warning be true?

Lila rooted in her purse while keeping her eyes on the road. Grasping the secured phone she always carried, she drew out the device.

Her cousin answered right away. Born Sloane Sinclair, she made the painful decision to change her name to Carson Maxwell and flee her cruel family. "Lila, I'm so glad you called. Adam and I are having a disagreement about the wedding cake. I want red velvet and... What's wrong?" Carson's voice grew serious.

After gushing out the entire explanation of what happened, Lila drew in a breath.

"Are you hurt?" Carson asked.

Lila angled on to the highway ramp and headed toward home. "No, but Jack said I was in danger. He could have been delirious. I can't be sure. Is everyone okay?"

"We're all safe, but based on what you told me, I'm concerned about you. Do you mind if I put Adam on?"

Adam Forrester was not only Carson's fiancé but also an FBI agent in the Boston office. "Lila, what's going on?" Adam asked.

She gave him the short version.

"We haven't had any threats, but I don't want you to go home," Adam said. "Get to the safe house. Remember the procedure we discussed? Do you have your weapon and go-bag?"

The words "safe house" ignited her pulse to a gallop. The attack hadn't been on her, but Jack's warning replayed. Lila made a U-turn and headed away from her house. "I know what to do. I'm prepared."

"I'll talk to Reid and check again on threats. We know Lance is in New York right now."

"But that doesn't mean he hasn't sent his thugs after me or anyone else." She sighed. "I don't know that Jack's death is related to Lance or The Order, but we can't take any chances."

"I'm here, Lila," Carson's voice filled her ear. "Adam is going to contact Reid and the Alliance task force leader. Would it help if I talked for a little longer?"

"Yes." Lila nodded, even though Carson couldn't see her. The Alliance always made her feel safe. The group was an organized covert task force led by Reid Patterson, who was also her uncle and an FBI agent, along with one of his trusted colleagues, Yvonne Hill. The special group was formed as a secret operation to respond to the number of federal officials compromised by The Order. All of her dear friends had suffered through near-death experiences with the cult-like organization founded by her great-grandfather, Russell Sinclair. They'd all been read in as consultants to this special task force. Now, with Lance at The Order's helm, the Alliance believed the danger had more than tripled.

"I spoke to Marissa this afternoon. Justin was at the hospital as usual and little Isabella was talking up a storm. She's such an adorable two-year-old. They love Virginia, but both Marissa and Justin plan a vacation after the wedding." Carson kept her voice calm and spoke to Lila as if they were having an everyday conversation.

Lila pictured cute little Isabella, her curly brown pigtails framing her angelic face. She couldn't live if something happened to that little girl or her parents.

"I also had lunch with Holly this afternoon," Carson continued. "Her private practice is going well and she's doing wonders for the kids she counsels. Reid makes it a priority to spend as much time with Holly as possible, but he's focused, as always, on bringing down Lance." She paused. "And Cody, he—"

"I don't want to know about Cody right now. Thanks for talking. I'm good now." Lila gripped the wheel tighter. The clanging of her heart every time someone mentioned Cody Green's name only increased her nerves. Purging his image from her mind, she took the next exit.

"Okay, honey."

"We're scheduling an emergency meeting." Adam came back to the phone.

"Please call us when you get to the safe house," Carson added.

Gray clouds curled into the creamsicle colors of the setting sun. Soon, darkness and maybe a storm would arrive. She hated being caught in the darkness. Pulling into a gas station, she glanced at the SUV's instrument panel as her main cell buzzed. Gia Vidal, her best friend and fellow second-year HTP associate, was calling for the third time.

"I've been worried about you," Gia said.

"I've had better days."

"I'm coming over and bringing dinner. And wine."

Gia's voice full of concern, made her smile. "Thanks, Gia, but all I want to do is climb into bed. I have a meeting with Talcott and Hilary in the morning. Let's meet for lunch after."

"I'm holding you to that. If you change your mind about me keeping you company, call me."

Glancing at the inky sky, she shivered as she filled the gas tank. A low growl of thunder moaned in the distance. She jumped back into her car and picked up speed out of the station. She should be used to fleeing monsters in the dark.

Chapter 4

The soft dinner music drifting through the large ballroom slowly ended as Lance Sinclair climbed the stairs to the dais. He turned, gave his practiced grin, and waved at various business leaders, celebrities, and politicians. Standing in front of the podium, Lance adjusted the microphone. "Welcome to the Sinclair Foundation Annual Gala." He swept a glance over the room, landing on a familiar brunette. He'd met the raven-haired beauty, Katarina Yurkov in St. Petersburg five years ago. Although she wasn't his date for the evening, he'd invited the New York City Ballet's principal dancer to Manhattan for the evening's festivities.

Katarina flashed a pearly smile, the wattage matching her silver sequined gown. She lifted her chest as if offering him a preview of things to come.

Lance tore his gaze from the woman and slipped into his compassionate millionaire persona. "We're the lucky ones. We're able to be here tonight. Right now, children are struggling against a beast called cancer. Tonight, I'm proud to say my foundation, thanks to all of you, will be making a $1.5 million dent in childhood cancer research. I've set the tone for this foundation, and my team has delivered. I...*we* are one step closer to curing childhood cancer."

With the room erupting in thunderous applause, Lance soaked up the glory as he lingered at the podium. Power, like an electric current, flowed through him. *My father could never accomplish what I have, even the FBI wouldn't dare come after me.* Lance smiled, drinking in the adoration of the crowd. Strolling off the dais, he shook hands and kissed several women then stopped in front of Katarina.

"You look beautiful tonight." He planted quick kisses on each of her prominent cheekbones. From the moment he'd first laid eyes on her at the small café on the shores of the Baltic Sea, he couldn't shake her from his thoughts. During that trip, he'd invited her to his table where they'd shared ice-cold shots of vodka and savory bites of caviar on *bliny*, buttered bread. During the meal, he'd learned she was a ballet dancer, during the night he'd learned she exuded passion. He'd become her benefactor and spearheaded her audition to the New York City Ballet. While he'd been prepared to guarantee her acceptance into the exclusive company, the move proved unnecessary as her talent had exceeded expectations.

"Thank you, Lance." Katarina beamed and placed her long thin fingers on his arm. Dark hair, twisted in an elegant chignon, emphasized her sensuous neck currently encircled by a sparkling diamond-and-ruby necklace. Warm memories of kissing that neck and more flooded his thoughts.

Another voice broke the spell. "Lance. It's good to see you."

The memories faded as he turned toward the voice and clasped hands with the CEO of Pilotscope Media, one of the top news media companies. "Lewis. Glad you could make it."

Lewis Schultz, a committed Order member, had been instrumental in rehabilitating Lance's somewhat sullied reputation after his recent legal wranglings. After the Department of Justice dropped all the charges against Lance, Lewis suggested he sit for a number of television and print interviews. The interviews had included flowing accounts of Lance as a boss and business partner while painting him not only as a grieving son heartbroken over the deaths of his parents, but also as a devastated victim of a sinister plot. He'd blamed escaped convict Joe Wagner, for killing his father, Ivan Sinclair. Yet, the real truth was that he and his mother, Pia, had determined Ivan needed to die. Ivan made a weak Grand Commander of their family's powerful organization, The Order. Pia and Lance had believed their goal of more power and money would fall short without someone at the helm who was capable of making ruthless, sometimes deadly, decisions to move them toward the target.

After a meal of chateaubriand, lobster tail, root vegetables, and tiramisu for dessert, Lance worked the room. With a tulip-shaped glass of cognac in hand, Lance schmoozed with his rich and famous friends and colleagues. He danced with a few other women before requesting a dance with Katarina.

She nodded and took his hand.

Once he had her on the dance floor, he held her close. "Have I told you how beautiful you look tonight?" His hand splayed across her bare back as he stared into her captivating blue-gray eyes.

She lifted her head to gaze at him and emitted a throaty chuckle. In her sexy Russian accent, she said, "You've already said as much. But I haven't told you how handsome you look. You were born to wear a tuxedo." They swayed in cadence to the smooth notes from the orchestra.

"Thank you." He pulled her tighter, enjoying the gentle swell of her hips under his hands. He leaned in close. "Come to my Tribeca apartment tonight." Cognizant of the looks from other women, many of whom he'd bedded, he loosened his embrace. He could have any woman in the room, single or married. The power he yielded, both in business and on a social level, was unparalleled. Women desired him, and men were envious. The target on his back proved a constant reminder he stood atop the pile, exactly where the Sinclair heir and current Grand Commander of The Order should be.

She flashed another smile and gave a subtle tilt of her head.

Once the music ended, she stared up at him. "Thank you for the dance, Mr. Sinclair."

He dipped his head and whispered, "Your beautiful dress will look lovely on my floor." He rubbed a thumb across her back before stepping away. The crowd parted to allow him to reach his table, front and center in the room. His carefully chosen tablemates rushed to engage him in conversation when he took his seat at the most visible location at the table.

Twenty minutes later, his assistant, Casper Halvorsen, approached. Also clad in a black tuxedo, Casper leaned toward Lance. With his dark blond hair slicked back, the severity of his jagged features stood even more pronounced. "Mr. Sinclair. I'm sorry to interrupt your evening, but your presence is required upstairs. It's urgent, sir." Casper met his gaze then moved away with the stealth of an electric eel.

Lance stood and buttoned his jacket, scraping his hands across the emerald cuff links at his wrist. "Please enjoy the evening. Excuse me."

Minutes later, he stepped into the elevator with Casper by his side. "We have a secured video uplink set up in the suite," Casper said with a clipped German accent.

Lance nodded. "Excellent." When the elevator doors separated, he breezed into the room and approached a man sitting at the end of a shiny black boardroom table.

Casper stood by the door, rigid and alert thanks to his years in the military Special Forces.

The man at the table swiveled in his chair. "Lance, we're waiting on your go-ahead."

Turning to the screen on the large wall monitor, Lance settled into a chair and stared at the warehouse scene splayed out before him. The setting almost appeared like a still photo until one of the three handcuffed men standing in the middle of a large plastic tarp shifted. Lance narrowed his eyes and nodded.

The man pressed a button. "This is Peter Shaw. In our business we don't tolerate leaks. You knew that and took the gamble anyway. Guess what boys, you lost."

One of the men puffed out his chest. "Shaw, you're nothing but a hired thug. The FBI's trash. I may die today, but you'll get yours." The man, covered in bruises and cuts, spat toward the camera.

Peter chuckled. "I'll take your pathetic attempt at bravado as the sentiments of the rest of you." He leaned back in his chair and allowed the men on screen to stew in the grips of their last moments. Finally, he cleared his throat. "Proceed."

Gunfire erupted, and the three men lay crumpled in a heap. One of the shooters approached them and after inspecting their bodies, he nodded toward the camera. He scuttled backward as another man with a flamethrower stood wide-legged in front of the dead men. A swooshing sound exploded, then a bright orange fireball mushroomed in the building.

Lance smiled and stood. "Good work. How's our other campaign?"

"Complete and successful. Sends a serious message to others considering stepping out of bounds." Peter gathered his briefcase from the floor.

"Good work, Peter. I'll expect a full security briefing in the morning. In the meantime, grab a drink downstairs. The liquor is flowing, and the women are primed." Lance patted Peter on the shoulder as they headed for the door.

Casper opened the door and stood aside.

"I think I will." Peter smoothed back his light-brown hair and sauntered into the corridor.

"Casper, have my driver bring the car around. I'm headed to my Tribeca property for the night." Visions of Katarina naked on his bed danced through his head as he approached the elevator.

Casper stepped closer to his boss. "Sir, you have a phone call."

Lance shook the cuffs of his designer jacket. "Who is it?"

"Your wife, sir."

Chapter 5

Cody cursed again as he tossed the useless phone on the passenger seat. A crackle of lightning charged across the sky. Cell service was down, probably because of the storm. He cut the headlights, coasted into the driveway, and drove to the back of the house. The house appeared quiet, but he spotted a light on.

He inhaled. An hour after he'd given Reid an update on his new position, Reid and Adam called back. They informed him about what happened with Lila and asked if he'd join her at the safe house. He'd already planned to check on the surveillance setup, but still, his heart thundered at the notion she could be in danger.

He grabbed his laptop bag and backpack and climbed the steps to the back door. Punching in the code, he waited as the lock clicked. When he stepped into the kitchen, he noticed the light under the microwave mounted over the stove giving off the only illumination.

"Don't make a move."

"Lila?" Cody stilled and shot his hands skyward. He stepped closer. "It *is* you." Part of him wanted to wrap her up in his arms but the more logical part of him remained rooted. She just might shoot him, and he couldn't blame her.

"Cody? What are you doing here?" Her eyes narrowed as she glared at him.

"Reid called. He told me what happened and that you were headed to the safe house." He shifted but kept his arms up. His gaze swept over her. Lila was even more beautiful than the last time he saw her. She'd let her hair grow longer and the now flowy brown waves cascaded over her shoulders. Gray sweatpants molded to her figure and a red shirt with THE RANCH printed in the center, fit snugly over her breasts. Her casual look reminded him of their time spent studying together during college. Lila at Harvard, and he close by at MIT, had been a dream come true for the both of them. Then one day their relationship ended.

"You can tell Reid I'm safe."

He nodded. "Do you think you could lower your weapon?"

She raked her teeth over her lower lip. The gesture was sexy as hell, but all Cody could do was swallow.

Lowering the gun, she stepped back, maintaining her glare. "I didn't think it could get worse." She let the comment hang in the air before adding, "But I can take care of myself. What are you doing here?"

"I told you Reid called—"

"I mean what are you doing in Dallas?" She remained cemented to her spot between the kitchen and living room.

"I came to work on the network." He glanced at the surroundings. The Alliance hadn't had the house for long. Cody had promised Reid he'd make sure the secured VPN, virtual private network, was set up on house's computer as well checking on the other safety mechanisms inside and around the house.

"You traveled all the way to Texas to work on the network?" She tugged on the hem of her T-shirt as she waited for his answer.

Cody took a deep breath. "Not exactly. Lila, I live here now. I've been in Dallas for six months, working as a software engineer."

A crack of lightning and a deep grumble of thunder highlighted her shocked expression. "You live here, in Dallas?" She swallowed.

They once shared an amazing bond, so strong that her shock that he'd moved appeared foreign. They'd shared inside jokes, their fears, and dreams. Now she didn't know where he lived. The idea was like a gut punch.

"Great." Lila stepped back. She stalked across the room, stuffed the gun into her purse, and swung the strap over her shoulder. "This is Alliance property. You don't need my permission to stay. I'll take the first bedroom at the top of the stairs."

Her footsteps retreated punctuated by the closing of a door. He'd been so worried about Lila's safety that he hadn't stopped to consider her reaction to seeing him. They'd run into each other at Alliance meetings but to spare her feelings, he'd stopped attending in person and conferenced in. Now, for the first time in five years, they would sleep under the same roof.

He checked the lock on the kitchen door, then every window and door in the house. The storm intensified, but so far the power remained on.

With his secured phone, he contacted Reid. "I'm at the safe house. Lila is okay but mad as hell to see me here."

"Her safety is more important right now," Reid said. "The death of her law mentor may be unrelated to Lance or The Order, but until we know for sure, we can't take any chances. Keep an eye on her."

"Will do. Even though she's pissed at me, I think she's glad to have someone around."

"I'm arranging for the entire group to meet in Dallas in a day or so."

"Good. I'll check in later." Cody powered off the phone and headed into the office.

An hour later, Cody's head snapped up from his laptop when the lights went out. He drew his weapon from the holster and reached for a flashlight near the counter where he'd been working.

The power outage was likely due to the weather, but he couldn't take any chances. Suddenly, he remembered Lila hated the dark. He bounded the stairs two at a time, arriving upstairs in record time. "Lila!" He rounded the corner and ran into her just outside her bedroom door. For a second his flashlight illuminated the panicked look on her face before she cast her gaze downward.

"Cody." She expelled a sigh and tucked her weapon back into the purse she'd slung across her body. "Is it the weather?"

He detected a slight quiver in her voice as he shifted his flashlight to the dark hall. "Probably." He wanted to take her hand, but he didn't dare.

With the additional light, Lila's shoulders relaxed. "I think the circuit breaker box is in the laundry room."

Cody peered out her bedroom window. "Looks like a few other houses lost power but let's stay away from the windows. Just in case." He turned. "Stay here. I'm going to search the house and then check the circuit breaker."

Lila glared at him, her hazel eyes blazing. "If you weren't here, I'd be handling this myself." She pulled out the gun again.

The heat in the room jumped a few degrees. Cody doubted the nonfunctioning air conditioner was completely to blame. He followed her out the door. In silence, they searched every room in the house and found nothing alarming. Once in the laundry room, he checked the circuit breaker and found it had been tripped. "Must be the storm. I'll turn on the generator."

She nodded and wrung her hands together.

Cody prayed the generator was in working condition. More than anything right now he wanted to bring her light to ward off the dark shadows.

Chapter 6

Rubbery legs threatened her rigid stance as her stomach flip-flopped. The flashlight beam illuminated a set of candles on the fireplace mantle. She lit them and set one candle on the coffee table and the other on an end table. Sitting on the edge of the sofa, she continued to sweep the room with her flashlight beam. Another crash of thunder made her jump. "Just a storm," she said under her breath "Do you need any help?" she called.

"No, we should have lights in a sec," Cody replied.

She settled back against the sofa. When she got up that morning, she never imagined she'd be huddled over Jack's dying body, and by night, holed up in a house with Cody. The last time she'd seen Cody he'd been a guilt-ridden boy. The person who rushed to her room when the lights went out was a man, a jaw-droppingly handsome man. Wide shoulders led to ripped biceps which trailed to a slim waistline, and muscular legs. He'd built some muscle, *a lot* of muscle in all the right places. His dark brown hair swept up on top with the sides cut short created a visual reminiscent of a male fitness model. Stubbly facial hair rounded out his manly appearance. Definitely not the same Cody she'd known, at least on the outside.

A few select lights came back on as Cody burst into the room.

"The generator will power the essentials like the furnace, AC, stove, refrigerator, and certain lights."

"I'm glad we don't have to sit here in the dark all night." She jumped when another crack of lightning lit the sky. "I'm going upstairs."

"I think it would be best if you stayed down here. The lights won't be on in the bedrooms." Cody sank onto a chair across from her, placing his laptop bag on the floor. One small lamp lit in the corner didn't offer much light.

Lila hesitated, then stalked to the bookshelf when she saw more candles. She lit the wicks and placed them on the coffee table. The room swirled with an amalgamation of scents—vanilla, lavender, and cinnamon. The flickering flames created romantic feel they didn't need, but at least they weren't in the dark.

"Just a power outage," she said under her breath.

"I guess not every bad thing is the fault of The Order." He offered her a slight smile.

"Guess not."

After a few awkward minutes, Cody cleared his throat. "Are you hungry? I can see what's in the kitchen?"

"No, but feel free to help yourself. I only intended to stay overnight so I didn't check the pantry but I'm sure you'll find something."

"I'm sorry about your law mentor. Finding him in that condition had to be a shock," Cody said.

Had his voice changed? Could it really be deeper? Cody had been in his early twenties when they parted, well past the squeaky-voiced puberty stage. She nodded, unwilling to engage in a conversation. Yes, she was being juvenile, but his presence had thrown her.

Cody rubbed the stubble along his cheek. "Look, I don't mean to make your life more difficult right now. You've had a helluva day. If my being here makes you uncomfortable, I can move to that corner and you can pretend I don't exist."

Before she arrived at the safe house her father, Dan Caldwell, had called, worried about his oldest daughter. She'd brushed over his concern and rejected his offer for her to come stay with him and her stepmother, Patty. The last thing she wanted was to expose her family. Her stepsister, Jenna, was away at college but Brent, was a high school senior and still at home. Instead, she'd called a hotel and made a reservation.

After parking her SUV in the lot and checking in, she spent a few minutes inside the room then went down to the bar and ordered an iced tea. Lila had forced herself to sit for twenty minutes before she told the waitress to charge her room for the beverage. Escaping to the ladies' room, she had changed into jeans and a loose hoodie. Her dark hair covered with a short blonde wig, she'd slapped on a TEXAS RANGERS baseball cap. Slipping out a back door of the hotel, she had walked three blocks to a parking garage. With her weapon in the pocket of her hoodie, she'd raced to the third floor, parking space number twenty-seven. After finding the key in a magnetic box under the bumper and settling into the drivers' seat, Lila had clicked the door locks and expelled a loud sigh. Then she'd started the five-year-old white sedan and made the thirty-minute drive to Hinko Lake and the safe house.

She blew out a breath. "It's been a rough day. I didn't expect to see you, and I don't know how to deal with all this right now."

Cody nodded. "That's fair. I'll be up front with you. I won't let anything happen to you while I'm around. That may be weird for you, but that's the way it is. We have a past and we don't need to deal with that now."

"Thank you." She managed a wan smile. "I really don't mean to be an ass."

Cody chuckled as he stood, walked into the kitchen, and returned with two bottles of water. "So, you work for a big law firm. How do you like it?" He handed her the bottle.

She stared at the bottle, amazed by the gesture. He was kind of being wonderful, but she couldn't forget what he put her through. As she accepted the bottle, their hands touched. The lightning-quick contact resembled the electricity charging through the night sky, extraordinary and intense. "Thanks," she said, her voice thick. "My job is good."

"If you want to get some rest, I'll..." Cody stared at the front window. "Get down!"

A second later the living room window exploded, and a bullet slammed into the chair next to Lila.

Cody dove, pushing them both to the floor and covering her body with his. "Stay down." He lifted his head and drew out his gun, belly-crawling to the window. "Looks like two shooters. It's too dark for me to be sure." He ducked as another bullet slammed into the wall behind him before returning fire.

More gunshots riddled the house.

Crouching against the wall on the other side of the window, Lila pulled out her weapon. She knocked out what remained of the window, aimed and fired her weapon.

"I told you to stay down!" Cody grimaced as he gave her a quick glance.

"I'm not a damsel in distress." She unloaded several more rounds.

A man stepped out of the tree line and the moon illuminated him for a second. Lila and Cody capitalized on his mistake.

Lila aimed and fired. A scream indicated she'd hit him.

Seconds later, Cody hit the remaining shooter.

When the gunfire ceased, Cody scrambled over to her and took her hand. "We're getting out of here."

Lila grabbed her purse and backpack and they ran to the back of the house.

"Stay behind me." Cody, his mouth set in a grim line, scooped up his own backpack. "We'll take my SUV."

She nodded as she gripped her gun.

He peered out the door before stepping out. Scanning the dark yard, he didn't see any intruders. The gunmen had been shot, but he couldn't be sure if they were dead or the extent of their injuries. He and Lila needed to move. Thankful he'd parked just outside the back door, he ushered her inside. He slid into the driver's spot and gunned the SUV around the garage and out the back drive. Tree branches scraped against the vehicle as Cody raced down the narrow road. Glancing in the rearview mirror, he said, "We're good, but I don't know for how long."

"How did they find us?" Lila held on to the door, casting a glance behind them.

"I don't know, but our safe house has definitely been compromised." Cody grimaced as he took a hard turn on to the main road. The streetlights were still out due to the storm but after a mile the road splayed out with limited illumination.

"Someone must have called in the gunfire." He eyed two sets of red and blue strobe lights approaching. "We need to stop them. The last thing we need is to be wanted by the police." Cody blinked his lights while he told the 911 operator who he was and where he was coming from.

The officer must have received a message from the dispatcher as one of the police cars pulled over. The other cruiser continued passed them.

Cody angled the SUV to the side of the road, lowered his window, and nodded to Lila's firearm. "Keep your hands on your lap. Is your gun registered?"

"Yes. I have a carry license," Lila replied.

A young officer with large round eyes approached. "Were you the folks who called 911 about a shooting?"

"Yes." Cody peered closer. "Officer Allen."

Another cruiser slowed and pulled to the side of the road. An older officer alighted from the car and swaggered up to the group. "I'm Officer Riley." He placed a hand on his service weapon. "Please step out of the vehicle and keep your hands up."

Cody informed them they both were carrying.

After their weapons were secured, Office Riley said, "Want to tell us what's going on?"

Cody and Lila explained how the shooting started and that they had returned fire to protect themselves. The police continued to question them, until suddenly Riley stepped away. He bent his head low as he listened to the radio positioned on his shoulder.

Cody eyed the officer. *Something is going on.*

Lila cut a quick glance at Cody, and he felt her stiffen next to him

Officer Riley approached them again. "Allen, let's go. You folks are free to go. We'll board up your windows but get on the repairs ASAP."

Allen gave him a quizzical stare, then shifted back to his professional demeanor.

Lila stepped forward. "Did you catch the shooters?"

"Investigation is closed. I suggest you move on," Riley said.

"But people shot at us."

Officer Allen stood wide-legged. "Miss, Officer Riley says it's done. Move on." He motioned for them to return to their car.

Cody took her hand. "Let's go." Something definitely was going on.

Once they were inside the SUV, Cody released a sigh. "Weird."

"The police have no interest in investigating a shooting? Someone shut it down." Lila leaned her head back. "My life was okay. I was doing okay. Now this."

Cody pulled into the roadway. "I don't know what happened there, but I want to put some miles between us and them."

"Someone shut down the investigation. Why?" Lila's voice held a tremor of fear.

"I don't know. But we're not going back to your house or mine. I have a friend we can trust. We'll go there for tonight."

An hour later, they pulled into the small drive of a two-story house on the outskirts of the city. Cody led her to the back of the house. As they climbed the stairs, they halted when the back door opened, and a familiar face waved them inside.

Stepping into the kitchen, Cody inhaled a faint aroma of bacon. "Thanks for letting us crash here for the night." He clasped the man's hand before turning to Lila. "Do you remember Jeb Barker?"

The older man wore a khaki button-down shirt, jeans, and black cowboy boots. He resembled a cross between a safari guide or a rancher but Jeb's life involved animals of a different kind.

"Of course. Thanks for letting us stay here." She reached out to shake his hand.

"Nice to see you again, Lila." Jeb then pumped her hand. "I retired from the force and now I'm in private detective work."

Cody crossed the room and pulled apart the curtains. He scanned the yard. A rusted grill, a few lawn chairs, and a shed with a huge padlock sat in the fence-enclosed perimeter. Thankful he didn't spot any gun-toting criminals, He let the curtains fall back in place.

"What happened tonight?" Jeb motioned them to the kitchen table.

Cody glanced at Lila. "We can trust Jeb. He knows about the Alliance." Jeb had once dated his mother back in Virginia. When his mother decided to move on to what she thought were greener pastures, Cody, who'd developed a connection with Jeb, couldn't understand. Jeb was the first and only father figure in his life. To Jeb's credit, he continued to visit and spend time with Cody until he moved to Dallas to take over his buddy's detective business.

Cody gave Jeb the rundown of what happened.

Lila collapsed into one of the kitchen chairs. "We think someone heard the gunfire and called the police. Then they shut down an investigation before it even started."

Cody took a chair opposite her. "Only one person we know has the power to do this. Jeb, can you check your sources? Maybe you can get a bead on what happened."

"That won't be a problem. Do you think you hit either of them?" Jeb asked.

"I think so. They didn't pursue us when we left."

Jeb pulled out his phone and left the room.

"I wish I could tell you not to worry. We'll call Reid when we get more information from Jeb." Concerned washed over him. Lila appeared shell-shocked, but he'd been impressed that she tamped down her emotions when they were under fire. Now that the danger had dissipated her emotions appeared raw. He hated Lance and The Order for what they'd done to her.

Lila nodded and rubbed her eyes.

Cody's heart lurched. She masked her concern and exhaustion well, but Cody knew fear had slithered in and wrapped its ugly tentacles around her. He understood more than he cared to admit. Her safety had always been his number one concern. This out–of-control situation had him off-kilter, too. Memories of her being dragged away flooded his mind. No time for what-ifs or sad trips to the past, he had to gain some clarity in order to keep her safe. He'd hurt her, and the guilt of his actions would stay with him forever. The least he could do was keep her out of harm's way.

Jeb returned. "Here's what I discovered. Someone did report hearing shots. Two cruisers were dispatched. They didn't find any bodies. If the gunmen were hit, they got away, but not before the house was ransacked. The investigation didn't get far before the Chief shut it down. My source tells me the call came in via the Justice Department." Jeb scratched his bald head. "Very strange."

"That's what I was afraid of." Cody rubbed his chin.

"Did either of you get a look at the shooters?" Jeb asked while he stuffed snacks into a bag.

"It was too dark." Lila folded and unfolded her hands in her lap.

Jeb glanced at his watch. "I have a case requiring surveillance tonight. Help yourselves to anything in the kitchen. Cody lived here for a few weeks before he moved into his house. He knows where everything is." Jeb picked up a huge thermos, put his hat on, and headed for the door. "It's good to see you again, Lila. Wish it was under different circumstances. Call me if you need anything."

Cody reached for the phone.

Before he could punch in the number, Lila stood. "I need a minute." She stalked to the bathroom. Seconds later Cody heard the rush of water. He cursed under his breath. *I can't screw this up.*

Chapter 7

The sound of the gunshot rang Lila's ears, piercing her insides as if she'd been shot. She turned and in front of her lay the recipient of the bullet. Blood oozed from a hole in her head as her long, blonde ponytail spiraled around her neck. Her pale eyes resembled the stillness of calm waters. The dead woman looked at her, a slight grin stamped on her face.

Mother.

LILA RIPPED AWAY the covers and bolted up. Ragged breaths bounced off the shadowed walls as her body trembled. *Where am I?*

The still form of a man asleep in a chair across from her sent her pulse into overdrive. She jumped up and reached for her weapon. But she wasn't at her home. Everything appeared wrong.

In seconds, the man was by her side. "Lila. It's me. Cody."

As her vision and memory cleared, she released a breath. "Cody."

"We're at Jeb's house. Remember?" Cody gathered her in his arms. "You're safe."

A shudder traveled the length of her spine as the nightmarish images continued to play in her mind. Blood had seeped from the wound in her head and trailed down her face. Bright blonde hair the color of whipped butter had been stained with streaks of red.

Lila blinked, urging the image of the dead woman to vacate her head. Swallowing, she stared at Cody's chest, his bare chest. Reality slammed into her and she skittered out of his arms. "I'm sorry." She shook her head. "I didn't mean to..."

"To what? You had a nightmare. I know this isn't the first time, and you've handled nightmares on your own, but I'm here now." Cody's eyes held a gentle softness.

She hated him more for looking at her like that. Turning away, she glanced at her watch. 4:16 A.M. "I need a shower." Lila scooped up her bag and rushed out the door.

Sinking to the bathroom floor, Lila wrapped her arms around her knees and began to count backward from twenty, exhaling after each number. When she reached zero, her body continued to shake. With one more breath, she stood. She turned on the shower, then splashed water on her face at the sink. Standing in front of the mirror, she repeated, "I'm okay. Everyone's safe."

Steam swirled inside the bathroom. With the water as hot as she could stand, Lila stepped into the large claw-foot tub with a wall-mounted shower and stood under the spray as her thoughts drifted away from gory nightmares to Cody. Why had fate allowed them to meet at such a vulnerable time in her life? No one in the Alliance had warned her that Cody had moved to Dallas. Of course, whenever his name came up, she reminded them that she'd rather not know, unless the information was life or death. Scrubbing harder at her reddened skin, she cursed herself for allowing Cody to catch her with her defenses down. Fresh thoughts about Jack's death had triggered a boatload of other crap floating in her head, which likely spurred this latest nightmare. Not that she needed much to trigger a nightmare.

TWENTY MINUTES LATER, she entered the kitchen carrying her backpack and purse. The scent of coffee stirred her stomach.

"Good morning," Cody said, turning away from the counter.

She felt his gaze sweep over her. In an instant, she was trans-ported back to the days when Cody had been her world. They were in sync, enjoying their youth, love, and happy visions of the future. She loved the way he used to look at her. They had their own special language; generally, with one glance, she understood his thoughts.

Cody wore jeans and a Purdue T-shirt. Nothing fancy but Lila marveled at the finely sculpted man in front of her. She chewed her lip and forced the traitorous thoughts out of her head. Thankful she'd stuffed work clothes in her large backpack, she pulled at her pale blue blouse. Maybe the wrinkles would fall out.

She moved farther into the kitchen which appeared brighter and lacked the dark shadows from the night before. Light wooden cabi-nets juxtaposed against beige tiled floors created a calming atmosphere. On the edges of her mind, she considered that maybe being in Cody's arms, even for a few seconds, had calmed her. Reaching into a cabinet, she found a travel mug and filled it with black coffee. "Thanks for making coffee. I need to get to work. The storm, power outage, and everything else put me behind."

"They expect you to come in today?" Cody scratched his ear and pivoted toward her.

"Work never ends and we have important issues to discuss regarding Jack's caseload. My job could be on the line." She needed to keep her job, not only because she needed the salary, but also because the Alliance was counting on her.

"I've got to get to work, too. I'll drop you off on my way. Jeb and I will go back for your car later." He pulled opened a cabinet door before turning back to her. "If that's okay with you."

Lila yearned to be back in her own home with her own car in the garage. She didn't do well being dependent on someone else. Jeb hadn't returned so she couldn't ask him for a ride. She considered calling Gia or her father but explaining how she ended up with Cody and staying overnight at Jeb's didn't appeal to her. Spilling that news when she hadn't had time to sort through everything would only bring more anxiety. "That's fine." She expelled a sigh.

"I'm not trying to be a jerk. I'm thankful for Jeb and for your help driving away those shooters. Alone, I might not have been successful."

"You held your own. I was impressed." Cody placed two pieces of bread into the toaster. "I don't know how Lance found us but we're obviously on his radar now, which means we need to be careful."

"I will," Lila sipped her coffee as the conversation stalled.

The toast popped up and Cody slathered the bread with butter. "I hadn't intended to impede upon your life. Staying away from you had been my goal when I moved to Dallas." He put the toast on a paper towel and turned toward her. "I always want the best for you. If there's ever anything I can do..."

Lila's heart lurched as electricity sparked. She nodded and held tight to her purse.

He stepped closer.

Happy memories flooded her as she detected the familiar scent of his soap. Half of her wanted to run toward him and the other half screamed for her to push him away.

"Lila, I'm sorry about...everything."

She nodded. "We don't need to go down that path. It's all in the past." She scooped up her bag and headed to the door.

A FEW MINUTES after six A.M., Lila arrived at the office, coffee in hand. On the way into the office, she'd glanced several times behind them but found nothing of concern lurking. Despite the lack of bad guys, her nerves were still on edge.

When Cody pulled to the front of her building, he'd placed his hand on her arm. "Give me your phone."

She cocked her head then handed the device over.

He added his cell to her contacts then returned the phone. "Call me if you need anything, see anyone weird, or need me to come back sooner than we agreed upon. Safety first. I added my work phone because you won't be able to reach my cell while I'm inside."

She furrowed her brows, then nodded, before exiting the car. The brief skin-to-skin contact had obliterated her nerves even more.

At this early hour, either the grunts were passed out at their desks or she would encounter an empty office. As she stepped off the elevator and onto the twenty-first floor, a quiet hush blanketed her. Jack's parting instructions dominated her thoughts. *You are in danger.*

Security guards patrolled the building twenty-four hours a day, which offered some comfort. She passed the empty receptionist desk and angled to the right. Most of the first- and second-year associates were housed on the twenty-first and twenty-second floors. Senior associates and junior partners occupied the next two floors, while the senior partners occupied floors twenty-four and twenty-five. An accounting group, a brokerage firm, and several smaller businesses occupied the remainder of the twenty-five-story building.

She rushed through the empty hallways, passing attorney offices on the right with window views and support staff cubicles and offices on the left. Most attorneys left their doors open at night and so far, each open office she passed remained unoccupied. Lila bypassed the firm's library, which all junior associates got to know well. Today, only a few lamps were lit, casting shadows on the empty space.

When Lila arrived at her office, she deposited the coffee, the muffin she'd purchased in the lobby café, and her bag on her desk. The room had one window overlooking the parking garage below, which sat next to a pond dotted with a few weeping willow trees. Focusing on the lone car parked at a slant on the top level of the garage, she inhaled. Could someone be watching her? After observing the car for a few minutes, she pulled her gaze away.

Jack's tortured face flashed before her eyes. He deserved better than a horrendous death. Perhaps his last words were the ramblings of a man on the precipice of death, but something urged her to take his request serious. If she chose to accept his last assignment, she'd also have to assume his warnings were legitimate. Sipping the hot coffee, she weighed her options with the full understanding she could be wading into dangerous waters.

Scooping up her uneaten muffin, Lila dashed out of her office.

She raced along a back corridor, slowing as she reached the end of the hall. Blue lights from computer monitors filtered out of an opened door. Lila knocked, and then stepped inside.

"Hey Lila. What's up?" Marshall Radley said, twirling around in his chair to face her, sporting hip square glasses and a Dallas Cowboys hat he always wore flipped backward. He'd been working as the firm's IT guy for three years. Lila had gotten to know him when she first started and needed help setting up her computer. He'd told Lila that he played guitar in a band after hours. Today, the driving music of Prince played in the background.

"I need a huge favor." She stepped closer, thankful Marshall was the one on duty and not the other, less friendly, IT guy. The huge room housed the firm's servers, IT equipment, and security cameras. During the day, three techs worked the room, managed the help line, and performed any other tasks necessary to keep the firm secured and the employees productive. "I'm sure you've heard about Jack's death."

"Yea. Horrible. I liked the guy. He wasn't as stuffy as some around here." Marshall tossed an empty microwave dinner tray in the trash.

She eyed the three rows of monitors featuring footage from the multitude of security cameras mounted throughout the office. "Have you noticed anyone up on twenty-four?"

Marshall reached over to the control panel and the music quieted. He consulted one of the computers before turning back to her. "One of the assistants was up there moving some boxes, but she left about half hour ago."

Lila blew out a breath. After hours, everyone was required to use their badge to operate the elevators and get into the office. Lila assumed Marshall checked the database for the twenty-fourth floor. "I have a meeting later this morning with Talcott and Hilary. I need a document out of Jack's office to prepare my report." She glanced around the room, although she understood only one IT person worked the overnight shift. "Do you think you can switch the security cameras off on twenty-four, especially around Jack's office, for say, five minutes? I don't want them to see me creeping into his office. I misplaced a document. I don't want to involve Jack's assistant by asking her for it. Besides, I need it right away and she's not in. Now that Jack's gone, I can't afford a screwup."

Marshall tapped his fingers together and nodded. "Got it." He glanced at the clock. "You have seven minutes." He grinned. "Lila the badass."

She smiled. "Undercover badass." Devious acts weren't usually her modus operandi, but if she had any hope of retrieving the files, she'd have get comfortable in spy mode. "Thanks, Marshall. You're a lifesaver, but please take this to the grave." She handed him the muffin. "Breakfast is on me."

She loped from the twenty-first to the twenty-fourth floor using the firm's interior staircase. Marshall said the floor was vacant, but she opened the door a fraction and listened for sounds of life. No bits of conversation, music or scuffling of feet met her ears. The absence of sound, however, didn't mean the floor was empty. Lila pushed open the door and stepped through. Glancing from her gray pumps to the shiny wooden floor, she slipped off her shoes.

Lila headed right and made a turn into the copy room in the center of the floor. Dashing through the workroom, with four large printers, stacks of copy paper, and shelves of office supplies, Lila exited on the opposite side of the room. Two offices down without detection and she'd be golden, for the moment. Jack's office, located at the midpoint along the hall, had double the square footage of hers.

A gold-plated wall plaque reading JACK R. STRUTHERS greeted her. A lump grew in her throat. Inhaling, she twisted the knob, pushed open the door, and gasped. Jack's essence had already been sucked out of his office. Dark cherry furniture remained, but his desktop had been cleared. Boxes were stacked on top of each other. Floor-to-ceiling bookshelves, which had been bursting with law text-books and journals, now were empty. The photos of family ski trips through the years that Jack loved discussing were missing from his credenza. All evidence of someone who'd built a career, spanning almost twenty years, had been reduced to blank walls and empty drawers.

Why would they clean out his office so soon? Was someone else at the firm aware of Jack's suspicions, and were they out to ensure no else knew what he knew? Perhaps other partners had been targeted. Her breathing settled when the notion occurred that the police had cleared the office to hunt for evidence of Jack's killer. No, the conclusion didn't make sense. Jack's office contained mounds of confidential material. Handing over those documents en masse to the police would violate the firm's commitment to their clients. A search warrant would be necessary, narrowing the scope of materials law enforcement could obtain. None of that could be done so quickly, could it?

She shivered under the blast of cold air, even colder in the vast emptiness of the office.

Lila ran a hand over the smooth wooden desk surface. If the files had been in his office, where were they now? She pulled open his lap drawer. Empty. She shut the drawer and moved on to one of the side drawers. Nothing. Just as she pulled open the last drawer, she froze when the office door thrust open.

"What are you doing here?"

Chapter 8

Cody set his cell phone inside the locker and then aligned his eyes in front of a retinal scanner. The light flashed green and he moved to the door. He settled his hand on the cool screen then watched the door slide open. *Guess I'm legal*, he mused as he stepped into the hive.

Cody held in a groan as he stepped next to Paul.

"Ready to get outshined," Paul wore a white Veridian polo shirt. He double clicked his company pen, crossed his arms and stood wide-legged as if surveying his kingdom.

"Sure, you'll look spiffy clean after I've wiped the floor with your ass." Cody dismissed Paul as he moved farther into the room.

Rick entered. "Glad you two made it in. Everyone in the bullpen!" Rick led them to an open conference area with whiteboards, huge computer screens, and funky electric blue seating. A large acrylic table occupied the center. Rick stood near the whiteboard while he sipped a cup of tea as everyone assembled. Once the group had settled, Rick cleared his throat. "I want to welcome Paul and Cody to our team." As he explained everyone's roles it became evident to Cody that the man knew his stuff.

"Glad to be here, boss," Paul said, rubbing his hands together, a wide grin plastered across his face.

Rick cut a side glance at Paul before turning back to the group. "Before we continue, remember the Veridian benefit this evening. We're all expected to be there, that includes Cody and Paul. It's black tie, so look nice."

Several groans rumbled through the group.

Rick rolled his eyes. "Many people would kill for an invitation. Consider yourselves lucky." He turned to Paul and Cody. "Stop at the company dry cleaners before you leave today. We've arranged to have tuxedos in your sizes delivered."

Cody's skin prickled as he considered how they determined his suit size. But they knew his mother had diabetes so figuring out his suit size wouldn't be too difficult.

"We're a small group, compared to other project teams but I think you'll find us fun to work with." Rick crossed his arms. "Bear with me, everyone, as I give an overview of DDI to the two newbies. Veridian is committed to the future and pushing the bounds of technology. Everyone knows AI, artificial intelligence, is next the frontier in intelligence and while millions, perhaps billions of people will find their jobs no longer necessary, we'll always be relevant as the masterminds of the future. We're pushing past AI and pressing toward ASI, artificial superintelligence."

Cody hated the notion of being responsible for the extinction of jobs and heralding in computers to take the place of humans. As a young kid, he envisioned helping people and enhancing lives. He hadn't considered the ethics of advanced technology. As a college student, he'd been forced to grapple with his own battle lines. For the moment, he'd have to put those ethical arguments aside.

"DDI is the most sensitive project we have going at Veridian," Rick continued. "Imagine knowing people better than they know themselves. Our basic questions are: *What if we can anticipate your every need? What happens when all of your needs are taken care of?* You have more time to think, to evolve, to be. We have several secondary studies running within the larger project. One of those studies involves monitoring a group of test subjects. We're mapping their every movement, keystroke, website visit, and document they create or edit, even at their jobs. We know where they are at any given moment. We know if they have a doctor's appointment, and we subsequently know if they're healthy or have some underlying condition. With our new search engine technology, we will have deep, personal intel about the user. We are involved in testing the limits of a new social media platform which also includes using drones not only as delivery vehicles but as an eye in sky. Imagine if we can anticipate whether someone is thinking about committing a crime? Your tasks are to collect and evaluate pieces of data, and to gather the intel by any means possible."

Cody shifted in his seat as farfetched movies and books of the past were now not so improbable. "You said one of those studies involves test subject, does that mean other studies use simulations?"

After sipping his tea, Rick tapped his forefinger on the table. "Most of the people are real but it will be up to you to determine the authenticity of the data."

"I'm ready to get started," Paul said.

Leaning on the table, one of the engineers addressed Cody, "Moby Patel, here." The man gave him a quick wave.

Moby, who Cody estimated to be around his age, had unkempt black hair, a strand falling into his left eye, and a faded wrinkled dress shirt he paired with jeans.

"This is cutting edge stuff. People will crave what we create." Moby tapped his green Veridian pen on the table.

Next to Moby sat a middle-aged man with thick, round glasses which made him appear as if his DNA had been crossed with a common housefly. This man nodded with such vigor even his sparse splattering of white hair shook. "Name's Stanley Walls." He extended his hand to Cody, then Paul, before settling back into his seat.

A petite woman with a pencil jutting from her black hair, smirked. "Newbies. Don't get caught up in the ethics. You have to look at this opportunity like the scientists we are, on the hunt for a blockbuster breakthrough. We're providing knowledge for the future. You'll get used to the way we do things."

Rick nodded. "That's right, Sher." He reached over and pressed a button on a nearby computer. The screen populated with photos. "These are Veridian drones. We're using the technology to map various aspects of the lives of our test subjects. As you can see, these drones are small, giving us the ability to monitor the subjects in an unobtrusive manner."

For the next two hours Cody learned about the unique and secret nature of the project and his role on the team. The more he learned, the more concerned he became. He suspected he'd just landed in the snake pit of Veridian.

LILA JUMPED and tore her hand away from the drawer. With eyes wide, she stared at Jack's assistant. "Naomi, I didn't know anyone was here." Her heart thundered as if a hundred racehorses trekked across her chest. "I...I just wanted to step into Jack's office. We are, I mean we were working on several cases together."

Naomi frowned, her crow's feet accented her dark eyes. "You shouldn't be in here." She leaned out into the hall before straightening. "Mr. Talcott asked me to pack up Jack's office yesterday afternoon. I worked until after eight o'clock to get everything organized." Her gaze swept the room as if assessing the office.

Lila nodded as her heart steadied. "I needed important files for cases Jack and I were working on."

"Of course." Naomi's eyes softened. "I'm so sorry. Jack was a good man and a brilliant attorney. But I don't have to tell you."

"Yes, he was. I'd like to make him proud and continue his work. If the partners see it that way."

"I think Jack would like that." Naomi folded her arms across her white blouse. "All files have been placed in banker's boxes in the work room, and I've already sent his personal belongings home. If you need something, Mr. Talcott has instructed me to get authorization from him."

"Of course. I have a meeting with Mr. Talcott later this morning so I'm sure we'll work through all of the client logistics." Lila forced herself to move slowly toward the door to avoid the appearance of being caught with her hand in the cookie jar. She cast an exaggerated gaze toward Jack's desk and sniffled. "I'll really miss him."

Naomi's hands fluttered around her neck. "Of course. I apologize if I seemed insensitive. You poor thing. Jack's death has to be very upsetting. He thought of you as a rising star. I'm so sorry."

Lila hated using emotion to steer this interaction. Although Jack's death had impacted her, and she felt genuinely sad, she exploited those feelings to elicit sympathy. Wiping her eyes, Lila inhaled. "I'm so embarrassed."

Naomi moved next to her and patted her shoulder. "This will be between us."

"Thank you." Lila gave her a weak smile and ambled to the door.

Naomi's low black heels muffled against the thick carpet as she followed.

A click of the light switch shrouded the room.

"Looks like you've got the office all packed up." Lila glanced around the room, this time with an honest sense of loss for her mentor and friend. For the hundredth time she wondered who'd want to kill him?

The fiftyish-looking woman nodded and glanced around the office as if to ensure she hadn't left so much as a piece of paper. "I can't understand the rush, but I've learned not to question when Mr. Talcott requests something."

Lila pushed down the rising panic. What if the documents ended up in the wrong hands? Even if Jack had been talking out of his head, she owed it to him to at least try to find the documents, although she had no idea what they entailed. And if she found them, then what?

With a last sweep of the office, Lila stepped into the hall. "Probably best not to anger Mr. Talcott." The thought Jack had done just that entered her mind. If his death had been an inside job, could she be next?

Naomi sighed. "Mr. Talcott has been on edge lately. I witnessed him on a rampage. He was screaming up a storm at his assistant last week." Naomi shook her head. "If looks could kill, her family would be shopping for a casket."

~

TWO HOURS LATER, Lila once again opened the door to the twenty-fifth floor. Emerging from the stairwell, she stepped into the hall and glanced over the railing at the library four floors below. Several attorneys and staff personnel were either browsing the stacks or sitting at various sized tables in the center. The firm had spent millions renovating each floor. The library now had lots of natural light and greenery. Every time Lila caught a glimpse of the vines flowing over one wall of the library, her body jolted. Memories flooded back of another vine-clad wall simulating the Hanging Gardens of Babylon. She shook off the memory of The Order's, now-abandoned, Virginia headquarters, Babylon Hall. Today wasn't the day to parade down that terrifying trail of memories.

Barb, master gatekeeper for all partners on this floor, eyed her from behind the circular reception desk. Even as an associate, Lila couldn't simply walk into senior partner's office, aside from Jack's, which is what made his different. Lila approached the desk, rearranging her ID badge photo side outward. "Hello, Barb. Mr. Talcott is expecting me for an eight A.M. meeting."

Barb glanced up and removed her half-moon glasses. The older woman always appeared impeccable from her fresh from the salon dark hair to her array of sophisticated suits. The gatekeeper flashed a smile. "They are in conference room C. Please head on back."

"Thank you." Nerves surfaced, and she pulled her notebook to her chest, hoping the status report she'd emailed would help save her job. Would the partners be satisfied with her summation of cases? She angled around the corner, her gray pumps tapping along the dark wood floor. Her heart thumped at the closed door and thick walls surrounding the room. Was she about to get fired? As she inhaled, she admonished herself. Creating more drama than necessary would serve her no good. *I'm a damn good attorney.* She usually saved the positive affirmations for mornings as she prepared to come to work but today required an additional reminder. After another deep breath, she knocked, and a few seconds later, the voice of Talcott granting her entrance wafted through the door.

"Ms. Caldwell. I appreciate your punctuality." He extended his hand in a combination handshake and means to draw her into the room.

"Thank you." Her gaze landed on the other two partners seated at the glass table, Hilary Foster and Steve Dorman. "Good morning."

"Please have seat, Ms. Caldwell," Talcott said. "May we call you Lila?"

"Please do." She took the seat Talcott waved her toward, which was immediately across from the Dorman and Foster. Talcott sat in the head chair.

Placing the black folder on the table, she clamped her hands on top.

"I asked you here to discuss the terrible situation with Jack and your role going forward. I'll turn this over to Hilary."

Hilary, tenacious in the courtroom, commanded respect from colleagues and clients, alike and elicited fear from her opponents. Rumor indicated her expensive suits were procured from her yearly trips abroad. Up until eight years ago, she was married to a heart surgeon. She spoke little of her husband and even less about the divorce.

The gray skirt and white blouse matched Hilary's salt-and-pepper-colored hair. She clasped her brown hands together and cocked her head sideways. "First, let me repeat how sorry I am about Jack's death. He was a personal friend and stellar attorney. Jack had a brilliant legal mind and was always well prepared. I'm especially thankful for that attribute today because I read an assessment of you he'd prepared to submit next month."

Lila swallowed as her mind reeled backward in search of any minor hiccups in her work and steeled herself in preparation to defend them. Jack hadn't indicated being dissatisfied with her work, but she'd learned never to take anything for granted.

"You've done exemplary work. You have the makings of a great attorney." Hilary nodded before adding, "In Jack's words."

The momentary thrill that had zipped through Lila fell flat as she braced for more.

"I also read the status report you put together." Hilary pointed toward the file on the table in front of Lila. "I'm assuming that's a hard copy in case we needed to consult it during this meeting."

"Yes, it is," Lila said.

Hilary crossed her legs. "Jack taught you well. Always be prepared. Why did you go into law?"

The question took Lila by surprise. Her job interview skills hadn't been necessary in the last couple of years. "I could say I'm fascinated by how laws are written, enforced, and interpreted. And I can tell you that I hadn't thought corporate law was my calling until after my first summer internship at a New York law firm. In reality, I like defining and creating the best argument to win."

"Good answer." Hilary nodded. "You will now be working with Steve, who will be assuming all of Jack's largest and most important clients. The smaller cases will be split between a couple of junior partners."

Lila wanted to release a loud sigh but instead concentrated on the people in the room. Why was she so nervous? Jack's last words barreled into her thoughts. *Don't trust anyone.* Did he mean the people around this table, as well? She straightened in her seat as the lull in the room was meant for her to fill. "I appreciate the confidence you have in me."

Steve cleared his throat and adjusted the large college ring he wore on his right hand. His left hand remained bare. A confirmed bachelor, Steve carried the title with flair. Lila had often heard women around the firm swooning over his wavy brown hair and sexy black facial hair. He appeared to be in his late thirties and was one of the youngest partners at the firm. He, somehow, successfully navigated between the old, moneyed attorneys and the younger associates. "Since Jack and I headed up the corporate law group, I am familiar with your work, Lila. I took the liberty of also polling a few of your clients and they all gave glowing praise."

"I will also be assisting Steve with a couple of the most important clients, particularly Veridian Technologies," Hilary said. "As you know our work with Veridian is in the early stages from the corporate law perspective, but you will remain with this client. Steve will lead a conference call this afternoon to discuss the case status. I expect you to attend."

"I'm glad to be working with you both." Not exactly true, but what else could she say? Hilary concentrated on criminal and product liability law. Why would she partner with Steve to supervise a corporate matter? Although Hilary knew her way around a courtroom, she had the reputation of being cutthroat. Gia, who worked under Hilary, had spent enough time complaining about the woman's rough exterior. Lila's mind churned with possibilities, the primary thought being Hilary wanted to keep an eye on her. Perhaps, they were considering firing her and as managing partner she'd be responsible.

Lila had no idea what to expect, but the tectonic plates of her working life shifted when Jack died. Her new world had yet to be determined.

Hilary pursed her lips and crossed her arms. "This should be a seamless transition from Jack to Steve. Also, you'll be expected to attend the Veridian benefit ball as planned."

Steve clapped his hands together. "As head of the Corporate division, I want to welcome you to my team." He scooted back in his chair and stood. "Excuse me. I have a client call in ten minutes. I'll see you and Hilary in my office at two this afternoon."

After Steve left, Talcott leaned back in the black leather chair. "You've made our job easier by your good work." He inhaled then tapped his fingers on the table. "As I advised you last night, do not engage in conversations about Jack's murder. We recognize that the police may have more questions. Please cooperate but consult with us before any interviews. As you already know, Hilary will be assisting you in a legal capacity, should the need arise."

Lila nodded, unsure what she could say.

"I understand the scene was...unpleasant but I'm asking you to tell me once again about events that occurred." Talcott steepled his fingers as Hilary's gaze burrowed into her.

Once again Lila relayed everything she'd witnessed from the time she entered the apartment to Jack's death—minus his instructions. *Don't trust anyone.* Jack's mantra played through her head.

"So, Jack was still alive when you got there?" Hilary leaned forward on the conference table.

"Yes. I found him slumped in a chair."

"And what, if anything, did he say to you?" Hilary settled into litigator mode.

Lila straightened in her chair. She wasn't on trial so why did she feel like a witness? "He said to take care of his clients. I urged him not to talk, to save his energy. I tried to stop the bleeding, but it was just too much."

Hilary nodded. "Did he say anything else?"

Hilary, who'd been present for the police interview, had heard everything Lila reported, so why this additional questioning? Were they attempting to trap her or find a crack in her story? "He said to tell his wife and children he loved them. Then he was gone."

Talcott cleared his throat and stood. "Lila, are you certain Jack didn't say *anything* else?"

Jack's warning now took on a deeper meaning. These two were nervous about something. *What is going on here?* "No, nothing else." She decided to take a chance. "Jack was murdered. Who would do something like this? I'm not aware of any disgruntled current clients. Could there be an unhappy client in his past?"

Talcott and Hilary exchanged a quick glance.

"We haven't received any threats to the firm, and I'm quite sure Jack would have informed us if he had any concerns." Talcott placed a hand on her shoulder. "We trust you will maintain the same level of communication Jack displayed. We have high expectations for you.

Someone with your legal abilities can go far in this firm. Don't give us a reason to doubt our confidence." He gave her shoulder a squeeze.

Bile rose in her throat as Talcott touched her. Had he actually just threatened her? Lila concentrated on remaining still, but the urge to put this dude in a chokehold created a tough choice. She could end her legal career with one jab to those flabby jowls. For the first time, she considered if she wanted a future here. She'd been excited and eager to learn under Jack's tutelage, but now that he was gone, this shiny mecca of legal brains didn't appear so bright.

Hilary rose and pasted on a smile. "Thank you for your time. I'll see you this afternoon in Steve's office."

Lila scooted out of the chair and grabbed her folder. "Thank you."

"Lila, we want to help the police find Jack's murderer, but we also have to balance that with client confidentiality. My door is always open. If you remember anything, even the slightest tidbit, I expect you to be forthcoming. Here's my card with my personal cell." Mr. Talcott extended his hefty arm toward her.

Lila accepted the card. "Thank you."

After escaping the conference room, she made a beeline for the ladies' room. Slamming the stall door, she leaned against the wall. Something told her life as she knew it had taken a dangerous turn and that the key to survival might be in Jack's files. She needed to talk to the Alliance. After two years at the firm, she may have finally garnered more than legal experience.

Chapter 9

While Paul was busy sucking up to the other team members, Cody slipped out. Rick had let them leave early to prepare for tonight's event. Once he had possession of his cell phone, he made the trek from Building 5 to the main building containing the dry cleaners. Cody entered the massive lobby atrium, which always reminded him of an over-the-top Las Vegas hotel. In addition to a dry cleaner tucked in an out-of-the-way corner, the lobby also included a post office, bookstore, gift shop, and restaurant. The center of the lobby featured a five-story waterfall surrounded by lush foliage with an illuminated Veridian logo embedded in the greenery. After picking up his tux, he traced his footsteps back to the main lobby. As he crossed in front of the water, he heard his name being shouted over the rush of water. Turning, he spotted his friend, Angie Nelson, a classmate from graduate school.

The petite woman jogged up to him, her long braids flopping around her brown face. "Hey Cody, looks like you got invited to the fancy kiss-up party tonight." She placed her hands on her hips and stared at him with her intense brown eyes. Somehow, they both ended up at Veridian, although Angie had been an employee for two months longer than him. During their last year of graduate school, she'd been his roommate for a brief time after her live-in boyfriend hit her in a drug-infused rage. She broke up with him on the spot, and as platonic friends, Cody urged her to move in with him until she found other accommodations.

"Yes. Not looking forward to this event either. It's for charity so at least it's a party for a good reason." Cody flung the suit bag across his shoulder.

"This charity event will make the rich upper executives feel like they're doing something good with their money aside from buying expensive cars and vacations. And Veridian will get a huge tax break."

Cody stared down at her. "You're so jaded. Kids without enough food will benefit. I don't know why we have to do this with glitz and glam though."

"I plan to take full advantage of the glitz and glam. Just wait until you see me in all my bling." She smirked. "But I suppose you'll be preoccupied with your new team. Still irks me that I've been with the company longer than you and haven't received one freakin' promotion."

"You've only been here two months longer."

She raised her hand to silence him. "Still calling bullshit. Numbers don't lie, I have seniority."

"It may not be all it's cracked up to be. Time will tell." Cody started off toward the parking garage.

Angie kept pace. "Aww. I'll bring out my tiny violin."

Cody grinned. When he'd told Angie he'd been offered the Veridian job, her reaction was pure joy. Although she gave him a hard time, he trusted her. "Where are you parked?"

"Your good guy routine is killing me, but if you insist on walking me to my car, it's this way." She sauntered off.

Angie was a great programmer, with a brief stint into hacking. The Alliance could benefit from her skills. He'd talk to Reid about her.

After leaving Angie, Cody took the outside walkway to the parking garage nearest Building Five. He hopped into his SUV, slid his gun from under the seat, and holstered the weapon. He'd stop at home before picking up Jeb, then retrieve Lila's vehicle from the hotel where she left it in hopes of avoiding being trailed to the safe house. Both he and Lila had taken precautions so how was the safe house compromised?

Cody coasted into the garage of his single-story bungalow, cut the SUV's engine, and ambled past his prized black-and-silver Ducati motorcycle. "Sorry, won't be able to take you out tonight." His usual Friday evening treat involved a ride on his bike, weather permitting. As soon as he stepped into the kitchen, his blood stilled.

Someone had been here.

His gaze swung to the security panel near the kitchen door. The even hum alerted him that he had sixty seconds to disarm the system before it engaged and alerted the police. Cody punched in his code, then drew his gun from his holster. Although the kitchen appeared undisturbed, a faint scent of perspiration penetrated his nose. A slip of paper listing items he needed from the grocery that had been tacked on a corkboard near his refrigerator now lay on the floor. Cody moved past the note and entered the living room. His gaze zeroed in on the bookshelf. Three books on astronomy, one of his favorite subjects, were displaced. As he glanced around the room spotting more small nuances, like the pillows on the sofa. He'd left them angled and facing east. Two of the pillows were turned in the opposite direction, as if someone lifted them to dig into the sofa.

Even with these small things, Cody didn't spot anything missing. He searched the rest of the house and counted eight examples of items moved or not positioned as he knew they were when he left for work a day earlier.

He holstered his weapon and expelled a sigh. Had they found him?

Calling the police would create a report but without a theft he was likely to be labeled paranoid. More alarming than anything was the fact the intruder had evaded his security system. As a computer engineer, he understood most any system could be hacked but everyday criminals didn't have the know how or desire to go after a target that took work.

Who'd been inside his house?

Cody logged on to his computer and twenty minutes later discovered an unknown IP address. He traced the IP address back to his security system provider. He rubbed his eyes. If the company had his system down for maintenance, which was unlikely, then the intruder picked the one time his house was vulnerable. Someone either hacked into the security company or was really good with masking their system intrusion. Whatever occurred, this turn of events concerned him.

The next two hours, Cody performed a thorough inspection of his house. After running a malware scan on his computer, he disconnected his WiFi. He pulled out wires, checked outlets, smoke alarms, lights, and objects he noticed were out of place. He probed the usual places for tiny listening devices and searched for unfamiliar USB devices. Finding nothing, he swept the house again, this time using a radio-frequency detector. He ran the device over every inch of the house, even over his clothes and vehicles in search of transmitters and GPS tracking devices. When nothing turned up, he switched to a nonlinear junction detector, which would pick up semiconductor electronics. Lastly, he checked for hidden cameras. The house appeared to be in the clear.

On his last sweep of the exterior, he came across two sets of footprints outside the patio floor. Thanks to the recent rain and Cody's sloppy attempts at gardening, a swath of soil lay in front of the patio pavers. Stooping he studied two set of footprints. Measuring his foot against the prints, he concluded the intruders were men. Zigzag shoe treads reminded Cody of his hiking boots. He snapped several photos of the footprints then headed into the house.

Cody swiped at the thin layer of whiskers sprouting from his cheek as he entered his bedroom. He and Lila had already destroyed their secured phones from last night to be safe. In the back of his walk-in closet, Cody squatted and opened a hidden panel near the bottom of the wall. A shiny black safe sat behind the wall. After placing his finger on the recessed slot, he grunted in satisfaction when the door popped open. Cody grabbed another secured phone, another gun, and shoved a couple thousand dollars into his backpack already containing more clothes and toiletries. He'd learned from the Alliance about preparing to be on the run. He suspected Lila had prepared in the same way. Closing the safe and wall panel, he pulled shut the zipper and stalked out of his bedroom. After reengaging the alarm, which now seemed useless, he slid into his SUV and drove to Jeb's house.

"You okay?" Jeb adjusted his cowboy hat as he jumped into the passenger side of the SUV.

"I need to check out the safe house before we pick up Lila's car." Cody pulled away from the curb. "Someone has been inside my house. Nothing is missing but they definitely were there looking for something." Cody shoved his phone at Jeb. "Take a look."

Jeb slapped on his eyeglasses and studied the photos. "Looks like two men. By the size of those prints, I'd estimate one of them to be around six feet tall, the other a little shorter." He lifted his gaze from the photos. "You think this is related to The Order?"

"I checked my security cameras and swept the entire place. The footage had been erased but the house was clear. Whoever broke in knew what they were doing."

"You didn't call the police?" Jeb removed his glasses.

Cody shook his head. "No. Given that they shut down any investigation into the attack at the safe house, I don't have much faith in the authorities, regardless if it's a different jurisdiction."

"Have any idea what they were looking for?"

"No. Lance Sinclair, his family, and that ridiculous Order ideology have caused enough pain for several lifetimes. I want Lance put away for good, but he's been quiet for a few years." Cody banged his fist on the steering wheel.

"Maybe the man doesn't have it in him anymore. He's married to that actress and is running around in his expensive tuxedoes hosting one charity event after another. Sometimes old dogs just don't bark anymore."

Cody shook his head. "Lance isn't old, and I'm not willing to chance he's changed his spots. Lance and The Order *will* be back."

Cody glanced at Jeb. "But maybe the break-in at my house isn't The Order but Veridian. My new assignment is...different." Describing his new job proved to be difficult but he explained what he could.

"I've always said all this computer stuff is a double-edged sword." Jeb nodded. "Sounds like both you and Lila ended up in the crosshairs of someone." He cast a glance at Cody. "Based on the way you were looking at Lila, I'd say your feelings for her are still in play."

"I didn't expect to see her."

"Don't know how you would be. Every time I saw your Mama, I was thrown. Tina was beautiful and exasperating. I didn't know which way was up. A real head scratcher." He glanced at the passenger side mirror.

Cody angled the SUV on to the highway. "Lila pulled a gun on me when I walked in."

Jeb reared back, emitting a hearty laugh. "That's rich. She had you shaking in your boots."

Cody grimaced. "Wasn't funny at the time. I thought she was going to shoot me thinking I was an intruder. Then when she saw who I was, I still thought she'd unload on my ass."

"She was madder than a wet hen. Where you able to state your case?"

"No. I wasn't the only one in shock. She didn't want to say much, even when I asked her about her mentor's death." Cody sighed. The memory of Lila standing wide-legged holding that gun sent his mind in a dangerous direction. He shut down the illicit thoughts. No use going there when she hated his guts. He turned back to Jeb. "Did you have a chance to look into the Struthers murder?"

"Lila arrived with some work documents for one of the firm's partners and found him full of bullet holes. My source tells me the firm has gone on lockdown. Not one employee has agreed to say a word about the dead man on camera."

"That's weird."

"Damn straight. Jack Struthers was a partner in one of most high-falutin' law firms in Texas, probably the country, and no one is saying anything? Not a secretary talking how he great he was as a boss or another attorney talking about his prowess in the courtroom." Jeb shook his head. "According to my police source, the hit appeared professional. No leads so far. The killer searched the bedrooms and office of the penthouse but none of the bullet casings were found."

"Did anyone hear the gunshots?" Cody sat straighter.

"No." Jeb adjusted his hat. "Those fancy apartments have sound-proof walls and the attorney had the only occupied unit on that floor. Lila was lucky."

"She could have been seconds from walking into a murder in progress." Cody blew out a breath as his heart thundered with dread.

Forty minutes later, Cody slowed as the safe house came into view. As the officers had said, they'd boarded up the two front windows shattered in the shootout. Cody followed the drive to the back of the house and cut the engine.

"I want to check the car Lila drove here." Cody opened the garage, which sat about a hundred yards from the house. He stepped inside, approached the front of the white sedan and inspected the under-carriage.

Jeb started at the rear. Seconds later he straightened. "Bingo."

Cody raced around the car and fell to his knees. He detached the tracker, jumped up, and slammed the device with his foot. "Now we know how we were exposed."

When they approached the back entry, Jeb studied the door. "No splintered wood or torn hinges but with the busted-out windows from the gun fight we know they had easy access."

"These locks are the best money can buy." Cody entered the code and the door clicked open.

They stepped into the kitchen and destruction greeted them. Every cabinet and drawer had been emptied out. The pantry demol-ished with canned goods and staples scattered on the wooden floor. Plates and glasses had been shattered and cookware scattered on the floor.

"The Alliance recently obtained the house, but this is the first breach of any of our safe sites." Cody pointed to a set of footprints embedded in spilled flour. "Looks like at least one of them was a huge man."

Jeb bent to inspect the footprints. "Judging by the tread, I believe this guy was wearing hiking boots. I'd estimate at least a size 12 boot. Could be the same guys who rooted around your house." He rose and studied the chrome drawer pull on one of the drawers now discarded on the floor. "I'm willing to bet they left no prints. I'll check the rest of the house."

Cody continued through the kitchen and into the living room. Similar destruction met him. Couch stuffing lay in puffy clouds around the room. Books, pillows, and various knickknacks lay in fractured pieces. The Alliance had been careful to avoid anything personal in the safe houses and went to extreme measures to mask the identities of all members. Cody punched in the code to the hidden data center. Unlike the rest of the house, he was relieved when he discovered the room remained intact.

A whistle sounded from the door twenty minutes later. "You guys are serious about security." Jeb entered the room. "They searched the rest of the house. Even picked up all the bullet casings. Since the locals don't have a desire to investigate the Feds might be able to pick up some evidence." Jeb ambled around the room. "These guys were looking for something."

Cody sank into one of the chairs and logged on to the computer. "They didn't find anything. I'm sure of it. We're careful not to leave any sensitive information. I was here working on implementing even more secured measures."

Cody hated the thought that Lila could have been alone in the house when the gunmen arrived. Although she knew how to handle a weapon, she might not have been able to hold the gunmen off. Then what? Were they sent to kill her? Take her prisoner? They were obviously looking for something when they invaded the house, but her death could have been a secondary task, performed when their main goal had been thwarted. Someone had been snooping around his house, so he could have also been the target, as well.

Jeb leaned over him as Cody pulled up the security camera footage. After forwarding through the gun battle which showed both he and Lila were lucky to have escaped without injury, Cody hit the Play button when two gloved men dressed in black materialized on the screen. They climbed through the front windows shattered during the gunfight. Once inside, one man went through the house searching through drawers, shelves, and closets while the other collected all the bullet casings. After twenty minutes, one of the men made a call. He nodded, hung up, then slammed a vase against the wall in apparent frustration. That's when they began destroying furniture and anything within their grasp. Then suddenly they stopped and fled the scene.

"They were pissed their mission failed and probably heard the police coming and hightailed it out." Jeb continued to stare at the screen. "They're wearing bulletproof vests. Your bullets just stunned them. They work for someone, and my theory is these guys are in big trouble."

"Just like Lance to put his foot on the necks of his flunkies." Cody watched as the men climbed out of the window. The exterior cameras caught them jogging back down the street. "They must have parked somewhere down the road."

"They knew you'd have cameras. Yet they didn't make any attempts to destroy them once they were inside." Jeb scratched his forehead. "Either they were stupid, or they wanted you to see this."

Cody sighed. "You're right." He made a copy of the surveillance footage and logged off. "Let's get Lila's vehicle at the hotel. I have a party to get to."

Chapter 10

ind 7011 and Jennings. Docs important.

F Lila stared out of her office window at the traffic below, her thoughts on Jack's dying request. *Find 7011 and Jennings.* She turned away from the window and slid into her desk chair. She didn't recognize the name Jennings as an employee of HTP, but with over a hundred attorneys she didn't know everyone. Swiping her phone from the desk, she pulled up the public website for HTP and searched the attorney listing for a Jennings. She came up empty.

Damn.

No attorneys had the last name Jennings but perhaps the name was a client. She hit a key on her keyboard and her monitor awoke. HTP had a database of clients. Attorneys, paralegals, and assistants consulted the database prior to taking on a new client to ensure there were no conflicts with existing clients. She could run a search for Jennings, but she'd leave a footprint. If she logged into the system and scanned the database, she doubted anyone would notice. Seconds later, the database populated her screen. She sorted to put the client names in alphabetical order. A quick scan of the data came up empty.

She shifted gears and searched the database for client number 7011. She couldn't imagine documents as important as Jack indicated would be housed in HTP's database, but she had to try. Perhaps Jack hid them in plain sight. Using the same method of scanning the database she scrolled to the 7000s. Seconds later, she stared at the client *FoxSt7011*, with the word *church* in the industry column. Her heart clanged inside her chest. *Fox St?*

Fox Street Christian Church? The same Fox Street Christian Church where she spent countless volunteer hours with their tutoring program?

She dared not open the file. Based on the general information contained next to the client number, she noted this file had been initiated several years ago. If that were the case, then these files should be in the file room. She'd have better luck at cloaking herself with hard copy files than on the system. She hit the X in the corner and logged out of the system.

The cadence of her heartbeat ticked up. Jack was the church's attorney? She'd never heard him talk about representing the church nor had she ever assisted him. In the two years she'd work under him, she'd never known him to represent any religious organization, not that his services wouldn't have been appropriate in some capacity.

A knock interrupted her thoughts. Lila crossed the small office and opened the door. "Is it lunchtime already?"

Gia gave her a hearty hug. "Yes. Do you want to eat here or—"

Lila grabbed her purse. "Not here." Lila didn't say much as she led the way across the street to a coffeehouse. They ordered tea and salads, then took a booth in the back.

"I've been worried about you." Gia stirred sugar into her tea.

Lila, sitting across from her, leaned in close. Talcott's warning not to talk entered her mind but she dismissed the admonition. She could trust Gia. She explained how she'd found Jack. "I tried to save him." Lila shook her head. "His poor family. I have to go see them, deliver his last message. It's the least I can do."

"I'm sure Jack was comforted that you were there. Do you want me to go with you?" Gia covered her hand.

"No. I should do this alone." She focused on her salad, sliding the tomato wedges to the side.

"Was the police interview awful?" Gia's eyes were wide.

"No, not too bad. Hilary showed up as my attorney during the interview. I went along with it, especially since I don't know anything. I didn't see the killers."

"How was your meeting with Hilary and Talcott?" Gia munched on a bite of her salad.

Lila shrugged. "I still have a job. I'll be working with Steve Dorman. Hilary is working with us on Veridian cases."

"They can't fire you because your mentor died. They wouldn't dare!" Gia's eyes narrowed, as she held her fork in midair. "How does Hilary have anything to do with corporate cases?"

"First, they *can* fire me for any reason, but I'm glad they didn't. Second, Hilary has a good relationship with the senior executives at Veridian, and HTP feels her presence will help us secure the rest of their outside counsel work." Lila's gaze shot up as two people passed their table. The man and woman slid into a booth three tables away. Thankful Gia agreed to meet her after the rush of the lunchtime crowd, Lila was able to relax a little in the half-full restaurant.

Gia scrunched her nose. "Good luck working with the ice queen. I can't imagine the rumors are true that she's having an affair with some bigwig and has to keep it secret."

Lila shrugged then leaned forward and whispered, "Gia, you can't repeat any of this. Talcott has warned me not to talk to anyone. They are clamping down on everyone, but especially me since I'm now involved. I don't know who killed Jack or why but Talcott and Hilary, maybe even others, are very nervous."

"They don't want any bad press, but this seems a bit overboard." Gia sighed. "You have my word. Do you want to stay with me for a while?"

The swish of bullets flying past her filled her mind's eye. Cody could have been killed and despite her anger at him, she would have been devastated if something had happened to him. For most of her life she'd felt like a pariah, too toxic to be around anyone. Carson's best friend Nina Prince had almost been murdered because of Lance's vendetta against his sister. In his mind, he had reason to come after any of the Alliance members. No one was safe. Lila shook her head. "No, I'm staying at a safe house. That's as much as I can say." Lila folded her napkin, as the food suddenly took on the flavor of sawdust.

Gia nodded. "You know I understand but it won't stop me from worrying about you."

When her relationship with Gia had deepened to best-friend level, Lila had told her about some of her past. She'd wanted Gia to make the decision whether to be in her life or not. Gia hadn't hesitated, promising, "I won't toss my friendship with you overboard because you have a dangerous past."

"Thanks, Gia. We better get back. I have a Veridian conference call. And we both need to get ready for the charity benefit this evening."

Gia smiled. "I can't wait for Jimmy to see my dress. Maybe he'll get the hint and propose."

Lila laughed as they exited the restaurant. It was nice to talk about something other than death and danger.

LILA ENTERED Steve's office five minutes before the conference call. The dichotomy between Jack's and Steve's offices stood out like a red marble sitting atop a bucket of white ones. Jack's office had been understated and filled with images of family life and his hobbies such as fishing and hiking. Steve's office was an ode to himself. Photos of him smiling with the rich and famous of Dallas were plastered on his walls. Lila's heart stilled. A photo of Steve, a woman she didn't recognize, and Lance, hung at the top of a conglomerate of other photos. Steve knew Lance, her cousin, the Grand Commander of The Order?

Steve slithered up beside her as she stared at the photos. "I like to donate to various charities. These benefits and balls are not only for noble causes, but they're also great for business. I've met some interesting people and have built quite a client base."

Perspiration tickled her neck. How well did Steve know Lance?

Did he know about their familial connection? Her thoughts twisted and heaved as she conjured wild possibilities. She didn't believe Lance would allow her and the rest of those who railed against him to live a safe life. He would retaliate.

Hilary breezed into the room with a leather notebook in one hand and a coffee cup in the other. She tapped her watch. "It's two." She took a chair at the round worktable tucked into a corner of the office and spread open her notebook.

Steve motioned Lila to the table, then punched in the conference call number. Moments later, Steve introduced everyone in the room to Robert Gumfrey, Chief Legal Officer of Veridian.

"Hilary, it's great to talk to you," Robert said. "What are you doing prowling around this subject matter? Are you jumping ship from the criminal division?"

She laughed. "Robert, you know I live to defend all those poor unfortunate souls who find themselves accused of some heinous act or another. In light of Jack's death, we've had a few personnel changes. As one of our most important clients, you get the star treatment."

"A little client management from the top of the glass ceiling." He chuckled, then turned serious. "Condolences to HTP and Jack's family. He will be missed."

Lila had seen photos of Robert Gumfrey and had limited interaction with him, but his sentiment didn't appear sincere.

For the next hour, they discussed three companies available for takeover. Robert indicated that the patented technology they would usurp would take a few of their classified projects to the next level. By the end of the discussion, Lila and Steve had mapped out their legal tasks. Before ending the call, Mr. Gumfrey reminded them of the charity ball hosted by Veridian at their headquarters. "I look forward to seeing all of you this evening."

Steve nodded and grinned. "You can count on my team, including Ms. Caldwell, being there. Thanks for the invitation."

Lila, once again, bristled at the notion that Steve would accept an after-hours invitation on her behalf, but as the junior associate she couldn't renege on an important client function.

The call ended, and Steve pumped his fists. "This is a major coup. My goal is to become the go-to firm for everything Veridian. I don't want them taking a shit without calling us. It never fails that this social media crap will one day land them in hot water, and we'll be here to save their asses."

Hilary rose and shot Steve a glare. "Veridian has been on our radar and within grasp for a while now. As a full-service firm, HTP can handle anything Veridian needs. We'll bring millions to the firm. We expect a decision after this event. Please be on your best behavior." She ambled to the door and turned back. "Steve, I know you and Jack had some sort of testosterone-fueled rivalry going, but we need everyone to bring their best. We can't let Jack's death derail our goals."

Lila clamped her mouth closed. So much for everyone being broken up about Jack's murder.

SHE WAITED until late afternoon to leave her office. HTP had given everyone the option of taking the afternoon off in response to Jack's death. The majority of the support staff had left and only a smattering of attorneys on her floor were still working. Banking on not being disturbed, Lila made her way to the library where she weaved through the stacks and stopped in front of a door. A panel was mounted next to the door. After entering her unique code, the panel turned green and the door clicked open. Automatic lights switched on when she stepped inside. Rows of banker's boxes were stacked high on shelves lining the large room. Four tall tables sat on one side of the room, providing a working area for those wishing to review the contents of the boxes. Lila had spent a few weeks working in here during her first year. Filing tasks were assigned to familiarize new associates with the firm's system, but the project was viewed as a bit of a hazing tactic for new attorneys.

Numbered signs above each aisle pointed to the client numbers stored in that row. Lila located the aisle which contained client files numbered 7000 through 7050. Running her hand along the boxes, she spotted the block letters spelling out FoxSt7011. She pulled out the box and opened the files.

The first document verified Jack Struthers had been the attorney of record for Fox Street Christian Church. She discovered that the church purchased a few abandoned houses on either side of their property to make way for the parking lot expansion six years ago. Jack helped them with the transaction, performed on a pro-bono basis.

Returning to the file, she continued reading. When she reached the end of the file, she'd learned nothing other than the church had made a land purchase. If the number Jack had given her corresponded to this client number, how would the church's simple land acquisition figure into his death? Could the number 7011 Jack mentioned, and the church client number simply be a coincidence? Since she didn't believe in coincidences, she figured there had to be another angle.

On the last page of the file, she came across a memo. The note to file included information regarding the church leadership. She read through the three-page document. When she got to the last page, her heart dropped.

See documents (re LS) located in storage closet 3B inside Fox Street Church.

She stared at the initials. Could LS be Lance Sinclair?

The firm's copier would record a duplicate of any document she copied and the last thing she needed was to create a paper trial. Instead, she used her phone and snapped photos of each page, just in case there were more clues.

The door clicked, and Lila jumped. Someone was coming. She replaced the files and shoved the box back on the shelf. With nowhere to hide, she scurried off to an aisle containing files for an old client she'd represented with Jack. Pulling down a box, she whipped open a file.

Seconds later, Steve Dorman rounded the corner. "Lila, what are you doing?"

She turned and smiled. "Research. I wanted to check something in relation to the Veridian case." She returned the folder to its original spot and stuffed the box back on the shelf. "Dead end."

"Now you know my secret."

Her blood stilled. Steve's usual upbeat demeanor turned serious, almost creepy.

He leaned in closer. "Sometimes, I come in here to work in quiet. There are so many distractions when I work in my office with the phone ringing or people popping in. The file room is like a sealing yourself off from the world. Like a tomb."

Lila nodded. "I can see how you'd find solitude here." She had no idea where this conversation was going.

"You know Jack had it right—buying a condo near the office where he could get away." Steve glanced around the file room. "Did he show you around his penthouse?"

Her mouth went dry. "No. He wasn't able. I'd never been there. The day I found him was my first time." Lila studied Steve. He'd worked with her, Jack, and a few other associates on big cases, but she'd never had an opportunity to have a non-work-related conversation. Did he know something about the documents? Since she'd received Jack's warning example after example had popped up emphasizing her need to heed that advice.

Steve's expression clouded then he flattened his lips and nodded. "Right. Jack had been pumped with lead by the time you arrived." He moved behind her and stared up at the box she'd just re-shelved. "Dead end. What an appropriate word for Jack."

The room vents swooshed in cool air tickling the back of Lila's hot neck. Perspiration trickled down her back. *What had gotten into Steve?* Even though she didn't know him well, she found his behavior unusual. She stood wide-legged, ready to use her martial arts training if necessary. Stepping out of Steve's reach, she readied to run or fight. "I need to get going. You know, the Veridian event this evening."

He nodded. "Lila."

She turned before reaching the end of the aisle.

"Be careful."

She cocked her head sideways.

"Since they felt it necessary to put Hilary as my overseer, I felt I should warn you. She's a task master. Jack's dead and I'd hate to lose a second attorney. Working for her can be a real killer."

Chapter 11

When Lila emerged from the building and climbed into the SUV, Cody expelled a sigh. Setting eyes on her relieved some of the worry about her safety, but as he shot a glance over his shoulder, he knew danger still lurked.

She snapped closed her seatbelt. "Thanks for picking me up."

"Everything okay?" He shot a quick glance her way. Judging by her furrowed eyebrows and crossed arms, Cody suspected something didn't go well.

"Just another day at the office." The warble in her voice belied her words but he didn't push.

Cody pulled into traffic. "Jeb and I went back to safe house. We found a tracker on your car."

"Damn. In my haste to away I didn't check." Her face reddened. "We could have been killed."

"Don't beat yourself up. We survived." Cody shot her a concerned gaze. "The shooters searched the house, but they didn't find the data room. I'm certain they didn't find anything."

"Did you get the surveillance tapes?"

Cody explained what he and Jeb found on the tapes.

"This has Lance written all over it." Lila rubbed her forehead.

"I also discovered that someone had been snooping around my house. They didn't take anything or trash the place but two guys were inside." Cody shifted his gaze to the rearview mirror. He almost expected to see black-clothed men following them.

"Are you sure nothing was taken?"

"No, but they were looking for something." He caught her worried expression. "I'm glad you decided not to stay in your house the other night."

Lila rubbed her forehead. "I have a work event this evening that I can't get out of. I need to go home."

Cody headed toward her house. "I'm going inside with you then I'll take you to your work thing. It's too dangerous for you to go alone."

"I appreciate your help, but I can manage." Lila said, irritation laced her voice.

"That's not a good idea right now," Cody said.

"I'll call a car service. I'm not going to let you Uber me around town." Her voice rose with anger.

"Something happened to make two guys try to kill you. An attorney has already been killed and your background suggests this all could be related to your family. Don't take foolish chances."

With a defeated sigh, Lila nodded. "You're right. Take the next right."

"I know the way." Cody winced. Any hope she didn't catch that he knew the way to her house was dashed when a curious glare met him.

When Cody pulled up to her house, he placed a hand on her arm. "Let me go in and check it out."

When she bristled, he shot her an exasperated look.

She nodded but then pulled out her weapon. "You're not going in without me." Jumping out of the SUV, she simply gazed at him.

Sighing, he joined her.

They entered her house and with guns drawn, checked every room. After determining there was no danger inside, Lila rushed to her bedroom pack her things.

Cody stood in the living room, taking in his surroundings. Everything screamed Lila. Pale blue walls juxtaposed with dark wood floors graced every room. A tan rug with streaks of blue and light yellow covered the center of the living room floor. Bookshelves holding novels, candles, and various knickknacks graced two sides of the room. What she didn't have on her shelves or walls were photos of her family. Cody understood. If someone should break in, she didn't want to highlight her family or friends as another way to get to her. Even though that information could be obtained, Lila wouldn't want to make it easy. It was a sad consequence of being an enemy of powerful people.

"I'm ready," Lila said as she rounded the corner. She stopped as their gazes met.

"I like your house." The compliment sounded stupid, and Cody wanted to flinch.

"Thanks." She breezed past him with small piece of luggage and a blue garment bag.

When they were back in the car, Lila folded her hands in her lap. "I appreciate you doing this for me. I spoke to Reid earlier and he's working on getting everyone here. If I need any more help, there will be someone else available."

"Sounds like I'm getting fired." Cody raised his eyebrows and shot her a glance.

"I meant you no longer have to endure this awkwardness." She chewed her lip.

"It has been awkward as hell. I don't mean to make you uncomfortable." Cody cranked up the engine and shifted into reverse.

"You've already told me that."

"I meant it. I won't let anything happen to you." The air thickened and sweat erupted along Cody's shirt collar.

Lila nodded. "Jeb will drive me to the event tonight so you're off the hook."

"Damn," Cody said softly under his breath.

Chapter 12

Lila smoothed her sapphire colored dress and stepped into the Veridian Technology headquarters. The sounds of a jazz band belting out tunes suitable for a James Bond movie, wafted throughout the massive lobby. She had the urge to ask for a martini—shaken not stirred.

"Come on Cinderella, time to get our asses in gear." Gia looped her arm through hers.

"Do I have to?" Lila groaned as she trotted along with Gia farther into the room. Her irritation dissipated when she glimpsed the surroundings. The main hall had been decked out in green, blue, and white decorations. Tall palm trees twinkled with white lights. Brilliant blue water flowed from a five-story waterfall, splashing into a pond filled with koi fish and surrounded by tropical plants. Waitstaff circulated throughout the room with silver trays of stuffed mushrooms, bruschetta, and mini quiches. Long dessert tables, filled with cakes, pies, and cookies, sat on both side walls of the room while several portable bars had been wheeled out and placed throughout. How ironic they were in a room filled with decadent, expensive food all under the guise of raising money for starving kids. Lila loved her work as a corporate attorney but the occasional required attendance at these types of events weren't high on her list.

"I think we've landed in a Hawaiian paradise." Gia swiped a stuffed mushroom off the tray of a passing waiter. "And I thought the HTP offices were nice."

"It's clear why Hilary wants to ensure we handle the Veridian account well. They are paying us big bucks." Lila eyed a waitress circulating with some type of alcoholic beverage. As the woman approached, Lila opted for water instead. Probably best not to indulge on such an important night. Hilary and Steve had made a point to emphasize the team needed to make a good impression.

"There's Brandon." Gia knocked Lila's elbow.

Lila turned to see Brandon Pfluger, a third-year associate on the corporate team. For months, Gia had been trying to set her up with Brandon. She and Brandon had gone to lunch a couple of times, but she'd made it clear she wasn't interested in getting involved with anyone from work. "Not going to happen. He's nice and cute, but not for me."

"You need to get out there." Gia's voice held a note of concern. "I'm worried about you."

"I'll be fine. I just can't concentrate on a relationship right now." Lila turned to Gia. "Where's Jimmy?"

Gia leaned in closer and pointed. "There. He was parking the car. Isn't he handsome in his tux?" She smiled as she watched her long-time boyfriend, Jimmy Kenison, saunter toward them.

Lila smiled at her friends. Gia and Jimmy had an enviable relationship, and they never made her feel like a third wheel when they all hung out together.

Jimmy planted a kiss on Gia's cheek. "Ladies, you both look beautiful." He wrapped an arm around Gia. "Want to dance?"

Gia nodded. "Let's go."

Lila's thoughts drifted back to the note in the file pointing her to a closet inside Fox Street Church. What would she find there? How was the church connected to Jack's death? Although she wanted to ditch this party, Lila would have to wait.

"Beautiful," Brandon said as he approached.

The voice shook her from her thoughts. "Hi, Brandon. Yes, it is. I've never been to Veridian, but their offices are nice."

"Yes, this place is great, but I was referring to you." Brandon stepped closer.

Lila tamped down an urge to retreat. "Thank you." She smoothed her floor-length dress. The feel of his eyes combing over her, didn't set well.

"Should be a great evening. Our team has a table down front. I saved a seat for you next to me." He smiled.

Brandon had dark hair and eyes. He had a penchant for dressing as if he were a runway model for Ralph Lauren. Tonight, in his tuxedo, Lila could see why so many women around the firm had crushes on him.

"Oh, well that's great." She wanted to get away. "I'll meet you at the table. I need to head to the ladies' room." She weaved her way through groups of people, spotting a sign pointing to her destination. Lila entered an area off the lobby set up for the silent auction. After escaping to the ladies' room, she let out a breath. Somehow all this pageantry seemed disrespectful to Jack. His body hadn't even been put to rest and all of his team members were at a party. While she understood this was business and that life continued, she hated the apparent collective shrug Jack received from HTP.

After pretending to check her makeup, she emerged and ran straight into Steve.

"Lila, you look very nice." Steve, holding an empty glass in his hand, gave her a quick hug.

The gesture seemed appropriate for the setting but would have been taboo at the HTP offices. Nevertheless, the move sent warning signals through her. "This is an amazing event," she said, moving a step away from him as she inhaled the scent of alcohol on his breath.

"There are some great items at the auction. I've already put bids in for the Dallas Cowboy tickets. Even though the firm has box seats, I figured a couple extra stadium tickets would be nice for our less important clients."

Lila plastered on a smile. "Good thinking."

Steve grabbed a glass of white wine off the tray of a passing waiter, tossing his empty glass on the tray. "Let me show you a few more items. We have a few minutes before we need to be back at our table."

Lila wanted to flee but instead nodded and matched pace with him. They perused the tables scattered with Cowboys memorabilia, quilts, trips, concert tickets, and more.

A tall man facing an adjacent table, stepped back and collided with her. "Excuse me," he said, turning.

Lila glanced up and her heart slammed against her chest. "Cody?" She swallowed. "What are you doing here?"

"Lila. I-I didn't expect to see you." Cody placed both hands on his hips.

Swallowing hard, Lila's gaze traveled over him. Within twenty-four hours, she'd found herself close enough to touch Cody again and once again she marveled at the change in his body. His dark tuxedo jacket molded to his frame. She clamped her hands together, resting them in front of her. Although his body wasn't as she remembered, his scent transported her back to their college days. Cody wore the same cologne he'd always used for special occasions. The hint of citrus and musk always lingered after he left her dorm, and Lila felt comforted as if he'd remained with her. She shook away the memory. Inexperience and naïveté had caused her to make many mistakes back then and she wouldn't make them again. "I'm here on business. This is the work event I mentioned."

"You work for Veridian?" Cody asked, his gaze locked on her. His voice contained a deeper tone. Everything about him seemed, more defined, more masculine.

"Uh, no. I work for Hirst, Talcott, and Painter, a law firm." She swallowed then remembered Steve beside her. "This is Steve Dorman. He's a partner at my law firm."

Steve shook Cody's hand.

"Cody Green. Lila and I knew each other in high school and college."

She wanted to say they were more than casual acquaintances until one night when it all crashed down but instead, she bit her lower lip. Her gaze traveled to Cody's ear where she could still spot the small scar from a skate-boarding accident one snowy Virginia day when he'd decided to try his luck on an icy sidewalk. After spending almost twenty-four hours with him this was the most she'd actually looked at him.

Steve downed the remainder of his drink and handed her the empty glass. "Wonderful! I'll give you two time to catch up." Steve waved at someone in the distance. "Lila, I'll meet you back at the HTP table. Make sure to get back soon. You want to be seated for the special video announcement." As he strolled off, he said, "Nice meeting you, Cody."

"Likewise," Cody said before he turned back to her. "I never expected to run into you. I mean, I didn't know you'd be here."

"I'm just as shocked. I had no idea *this* was where you worked."

"I guess we didn't take time to talk about the specifics of what we've been up to." Cody shifted his gaze. "The company I worked for in San Francisco was bought out. I got an amazing offer from Veridian so here I am." He shoved his hands in his pockets. "My intent had been to stay away from you. Clearly that didn't happen."

Her insides flip-flopped, and her heart stalled for a second. *Isn't that what she wanted?* In this moment, she had no idea. Despite happy memories swirling in her mind, she urged them away like pulling rubber glue from paper. "You haven't been around, so I didn't know you'd moved."

He nodded. "I know. With moving and the new job..."

As part of the Alliance, they both adhered to guidelines, which included not discussing their disdain for The Order in public. But Cody hopefully understood that she referred to his absence at their monthly Alliance meetings, usually conducted via a secured video connection but sometimes in person. Their strained relationship had made the meetings uncomfortable. Then Cody had stopped attending in person, ignoring her objections that his presence didn't bother her. But everything about Cody bothered her, from what happened in Hawaii during their college graduation trip to the effect he had on her now. She hated that he still got to her despite telling herself on several occasions she was over him. "Veridian seems to be a good company. Good luck."

He glanced around. "Jury's still out on whether I made a good move."

"Veridian is a highly respected company, which is why my firm has us all here—to show we're committed to the company. It's all work for me." Emotions surged as she straddled wanting to hit him and wanting him in her arms. Tossing out both options, she took a step back. "Umm, well, have a nice time. And, Cody, I didn't mention it earlier but happy birthday." Memories of celebrating their birthdays reminded her of happier times. In a lot of ways, those were the best times. She turned to leave, or more likely flee.

"Wait!"

She whipped around, part of her angry that he would ask anything of her. He'd broken her heart, and although she longed to make sense of her twisted life, she couldn't do the noble thing and forgive. Not now. Even though, he *had* been integral in helping her escape the shooters earlier. Her mind whirled with confusion and indecision. She stared at him, her heart thumping so fast she hoped he couldn't hear the effect he had on her.

Cody's mouth dropped opened but no words tumbled out. He swallowed then said, "Thanks for remembering my birthday. Have a great evening."

She nodded, then turned back toward the main party area, heading toward the HTP table. Although she tried to keep her mind occupied, she couldn't keep Cody out of her thoughts. Her skin prickled as if sensing every fabric fiber of her dress. And had the music grown louder? She swiped a hand over her forehead, creating a temporary barrier to the blue and green lighting some event coordinator thought would create a warm atmosphere. Her senses were operating in overdrive.

Lila approached the table at the same time as Brandon. Seated at the round table were several attorneys from HTP, including Steve and Hilary.

Hilary was dressed in a black gown with a sparkling ruby necklace accenting her salt-and-pepper-colored hair. "Brandon Pfluger, Lila Caldwell, please meet Robert Gumfrey, CLO of Veridian."

"I'm glad to meet you." Brandon pumped the man's hand.

"So nice to meet you in person, sir." Lila shook his hand, too.

Robert smiled, deep lines forming at the corner of his eyes as the lights bounced off his white hair. "Putting a face to a voice on a conference line always makes for a better working relationship. And what a beautiful face it is, Miss Caldwell."

With someone as important to her livelihood as Mr. Gumfrey, how the hell was she supposed to respond? Tamping down her desire to punch the grin off his wrinkled face, Lila took the open seat Brandon had pulled out for her in between him and Steve.

Hilary glared at Mr. Gumfrey. "Now, Robert. It's comments like that which will call for my expert legal services. Ms. Caldwell is a very capable attorney, regardless of her outward appearance, beautiful or otherwise."

Robert clamped his hand around a glass of bourbon and grinned. "Hilary, can't a man show appreciation for beautiful women, such as yourself, without being hauled into a courtroom?"

Mr. Talcott shot a quick glare at Hilary, then softened as one of the Veridian VPs at the table struck up a conversation with him and Mrs. Talcott.

Before Hilary could respond, the band stopped playing and the lights dimmed. The crowd quieted as everyone took their seats. Veridian's CEO, Don Ingalls, approached the podium and stepped into the spotlight. Lila, thankful for something else to focus on, turned her full attention to him.

In CEO-speak, Ingalls droned on about Veridian striving to always be a good corporate citizen. He explained how much Veridian did for the community, Texas, the country, and the world. Listening to him, one would have thought life would collapse without Veridian Technologies.

As Mr. Ingalls concluded his speech, he segued into the introduction of their top donor. "This man is a true philanthropist who uses his money to help fund several important charities, many of which benefit children. He is known not only for his business mind but also his generosity. On behalf of Veridian and all of its employees, please welcome tonight's honored guest." He paused as a video screen lowered behind him. "It's my pleasure to present, Lance Sinclair."

The crowd erupted in applause while Lila clamped shut her mouth. *What the fuck?* Her pulse raced as she gripped the edge of her chair. Lance? Did she really hear his name?

A video materialized in front of her and Lance appeared. She'd seen him with his fancy Hollywood wife and wondered how Delphine Renaud could hook up with someone like Lance. And she was pregnant with his child.

Her blood stilled as Lance flashed a bright smile. The close-up featured him sitting in a room with gold walls adorned with patterns of white puffy clouds. He wore his dark tresses slicked back. "Greetings! I'm coming to you from sunny Los Angeles. I wish I could be there with you tonight, but happy circumstances prevented me from traveling. I'm thrilled to announce, for the first time, my wife Delphine and I have welcomed a new addition to our family. Lance Sinclair, Junior, a beautiful, strong healthy son." The camera angle widened to show Lance holding a baby swathed in a white blanket, tiny fingers were the only part of the infant visible. "Prevention of childhood hunger is a cause I'm extremely passionate about. I could spout off a million reasons for supporting this cause but, for me, this baby, my son, is my number one reason. He's lucky and will never want for food. I want the same for every child in this world. I've made a personal donation in the amount of $500,000 to the Kids Soar Foundation. I hope I can count on you all to make that number swell." He swept a loving glance over his son before returning his attention to the camera.

As the crowd erupted in applause, Lila caught Cody's gaze from across the room. He shrugged, and she gave a slight shake of her head. She had no idea Lance was the featured benefactor tonight.

During their last Alliance meeting, they'd discussed the potential connection between The Order and other large companies, including Veridian, but so far, they had no concrete proof. The theory had been that Lance would try to amass more wealth and power by gobbling up important companies. Although Lance's appearance at the Veridian benefit was for charity this could be a clue that he had a deeper connection to Veridian. Turning back to the screen, she caught one last look at her cousin before his image faded.

The band resumed playing and Brandon stood. "May I have this dance?"

Lila groaned inside and hesitated. She didn't want to dance with Brandon or anyone else. The affair had been sullied by Lance's disingenuous plea for charity money. She wanted to flee this party and go home. Grabbing a drink from a passing waiter, she gulped half the glass. "Let's dance."

As Brandon wrapped his arms around her, Lila mentally implored the song to end. Moving to the beat, she glanced over Brandon's shoulders spotting Cody taking the dance floor with a pretty woman with long braids. Her body stiffened as she watched Cody and the woman dance. Were they dating or perhaps more? She'd told the rest of the Alliance she didn't want to know anything about Cody, and after years of attempting to soften her heart about him, their efforts had slowed. For all she knew, this woman could be his girlfriend, fiancée, or perhaps even his wife, although she knew Holly, Carson, or Marissa would have told her if Cody was that serious about someone. Lila pushed away memories of being in Cody's arms and thoughts of how she'd feel to be back there. He'd probably moved on, and she'd do well not to travel down that path.

"You look gorgeous tonight," Brandon whispered in her ear.

His minty breath drew her back.

"Thank you. You look nice tonight, too." Once again, her gaze drifted to Cody, but this time, he stared back at her. His brown eyes drew her in like a huge welcome sign to her past. After she'd walked away all those years ago, she hadn't spoken to him. He'd left one voice mail message, and from that point on their interaction occurred with the occasional greeting at Alliance meetings. Then nothing when Cody stopped attending.

"Lila?"

She pulled her gaze from Cody. "Yes?"

"I'm sorry about Jack. I know you two were tight."

"He was my mentor, so yeah."

Brandon nodded. "I guess things finally caught up to him."

He had her full attention now. "What does that mean?"

Brandon shrugged. "Jack worked hard. Probably made a lot of enemies."

"What are you saying, Brandon? Jack was a dirty lawyer?" Lila knitted her brows and stopped moving.

"I'm not saying anything other than in this business we have the potential for making enemies. It's a risk we're all taking. We're representing one side and the other side may be passionate enough to kill." Brandon cocked his head and stared down at her.

"We're not criminal attorneys. Do you know something? Was there a threat against Jack?"

"I don't know who killed Jack, but I urge you to watch your back. His clients are yours, too, and although we aren't in the criminal defense area there's still the potential for working with bad people. But you're in good hands tonight." He winked.

Lila balled one of her fists behind Brandon's back then relaxed. Whaling on his ass in an evening gown didn't make for a good look. Besides, he had a point. Jack's enemies could now be hers.

The band's lead singer began vacillating between singing and talking. "Beautiful people, let's have some fun!" She swayed to the music.

Brandon had good moves and shuffled her around the floor. When she allowed herself not to think, she enjoyed the dance, an activity she hadn't done in a long time.

At the halfway point of the song, the singer called for the everyone to change partners with the couple nearest them. Did the singer think they were in junior high? But the crowd whooped and laughed, playing along.

Lila groaned. Why couldn't she just finish this dance with Brandon and get off the floor without all these antics? As Brandon let her go, she twirled around to face Cody. Her mouth watered at the sight of him. The facial stubble only made him sexier. "Oh, hi." She hoped her thoughts didn't show. Even though years had passed, she wasn't ready to move past the hurt.

The woman Cody had been dancing with shuffled into Brandon's arms, and they moved away.

Cody shrugged and opened his arms. "I guess we should cooperate."

Lila's heart raced as she moved closer and stepped into his embrace. When his arms encircled her waist, her breath caught. Years melted away and yet the old hurt lingered on the edge. As the soft jazzy music wafted, Lila let herself to float in Cody's arms, moving to the beat. How long had it been since she'd been this close to him? As she glanced at him, she could have sworn he was even taller.

Cody leaned down and whispered. "Crazy to see Lance, even if he was only on a screen. Are you okay?"

"Yes, it was, but I'm fine." She didn't want to get into a deep conversation. Truth was the entire night had shaken her. Cody's presence had exploded her nerves, and she'd had no idea Lance would be appearing at the event.

Cody's expression hardened, and he voiced her exact thought. "I'm not buying Lance's good guy routine. Even the birth of his son won't change his ways. He's no more worried about childhood hunger than a shark is about chowing down on a sea lion."

"I don't think that sentiment is shared by the masses." She wanted to run. This evening was supposed to have been a simple task where she did her duty, donated a few bucks to a worthy cause, and then went home. Now, her plan had all gone to hell. Aware of her hand on Cody's shoulder, she fought to control the chills running rampant up and down her body. A glass of wine, a long bath, and good book would be perfect now.

"You're coming back to Jeb's tonight, right?" Cody whispered into her ear.

"Yes, but only for tonight. I'm thankful he allowed me to borrow one of his cars, but I can't keep putting him out." She also couldn't continue to live under the same roof as Cody.

"Good. Everyone will be here in the morning, so we can strategize."

One long minute later, the music ended and she stepped away as if Cody were a live electrical wire. "I really do hope you have a good birthday."

He flashed a sexy grin. "That's bullshit, but okay." Cody leaned down and brushed a feathery kiss on her cheek. "I'll see you back at Jeb's." He pivoted and walked away.

She stood frozen before she forced herself to saunter away, instead of running like a crazy woman out of the room. Her faced flushed as heat from Cody's lips seared her skin. Tiny droplets of perspiration dotted her neck.

Lila spotted Gia across the room and made a beeline to her friend.

Gia grinned. "Who was that hottie you were dancing with?"

Lila signaled to a passing waiter. She swiped a glass of white wine from the tray. After draining half the clear liquid, she met Gia's shocked gaze. "Just someone I used to know."

"Must have been a damn good dance to get you all riled up." Gia nodded at Lila's half-empty glass before smoothing her dress. "Did you know Lance Sinclair was the featured donor?"

"First, I am *not* riled up." She crossed her arms then unfolded them again. "Secondly, hell no. I wouldn't have come had I known about Lance," she whispered.

Lila and Gia smiled at one of the Veridian VPs as she crossed in front of them.

When the woman passed, Gia elbowed Lila. "So, what's up with you then? Brandon is really into you tonight."

Lila huffed out a sigh. "I told you I'm not dating anyone from work."

Gia turned up her lips. "I suppose I understand."

Lila spent another hour of smiling and making the obligatory small talk with Veridian employees and other VIPs. Steve appeared to be in his element. He encouraged her to stick close, so he could introduce her to various important people. Everyone expressed sadness at Jack's death, and in keeping with Talcott's demand not to discuss the murder, both she and Steve accepted the condolences then moved off topic. In between her duties, she stole glances at Cody. He drifted around the room for a while, talking to various people before rooting himself at a back table with the dark-haired woman.

As people migrated in to see the results of the silent auction, Lila stepped outside. She couldn't wait to get away, and after putting in a few hours, she could now escape the party. She pulled out her phone to call Jeb to pick her up when a woman suddenly shoved a microphone in her face.

"Ms. Caldwell, you are a witness in the murder of Jack Struthers. Can you identify his murderers?" The reporter hovered close as her cameraman angled for the best shot. Other reporters jumped out of their news vans and raced toward her.

"I'm not giving interviews, so please, step out of my way." Claustrophobia blanketed her as reporters and cameras surrounded her.

Steve rushed up, taking her arm. "We have no comment." He steered her back inside. "Get those reporters out of here!" he yelled at the guards.

Brandon, along with Gia and Jimmy raced to her side.

"We saw the press gathered outside. Are you okay?" Gia went to place her hand on Lila's back but then retracted it.

Lila appreciated her friend's restraint, recognizing she hated feeling pitied or made to feel victimized.

"The police were *supposed* to keep my name out of this. How did they find out?" Her pulse raced. Mr. Talcott and Hilary had been adamant she refrain from making any public comments. She'd been more than willing to oblige. Even before Jack's murder the thought of granting an interview about anything had her tongue in knots. She couldn't afford to have her name out there. Granted, Lance could find her, probably without much trouble, but she didn't want to make it easy. Lance had already made an appearance tonight, and although it was via a live video feed, she still felt exposed, as if he knew she sat watching him. Maybe he *did* know her every move.

Now that the press had her name as the previously unidentified witness to Jack's murder, she couldn't hide. Had she now been exposed to more danger?

"Reporters can be scum. How the hell did they even know where you were?" Steve blew out a loud sigh. "I suggest you report this to Walt and Hilary. They'll want to hear from you. The attempt to interview you will probably make the evening news." He grimaced. "Leave it to Jack to cause a mess."

Lila gripped her clutch purse. "Jack was..." She stalled, unsure if Steve meant the barb as a joke.

"A decent man," Steve finished her thought. "Just trying to lighten the mood. Of course, I'm just as upset about Jack's death as everyone. He was a good attorney and a great guy. His death is a huge loss for this firm." Steve pulled out a business card and scribbled something on the back. "Please text me when you're home safely. I'd follow you home, but I'm having drinks with Robert and a few others in a bit. Hilary will also be meeting us." He handed her the card. "Don't worry. I go a long way back with some of these guys so it's nothing you're actually missing."

"I'll be glad to take her home," Brandon said.

Lila shook her head. "That won't be necessary, but thanks." She didn't want to deal with Brandon and his romantic notions. "A friend is picking me up."

"Great." Steve backed away, already heading back inside.

Brandon tightened his jaw. "I guess I'll head back in, as well. I saw a law school buddy I want to catch up with before I leave. Take care, Lila."

"Sure. Thanks again, Brandon." As he slunk away, Lila couldn't help wishing it were Cody who wanted to drive her home.

Chapter 13

Relief greeted her after the back door of her father's restaurant slammed shut. Jeb remained in the parking lot, content to wait outside.

Her mood had grown somber after Cody arrived just as Jeb pulled up. He wanted to follow her back to Jeb's, but she had other plans. Tensions erupted, and they argued. She told him she needed to see her parents in case things got bad, then jumped into Jeb's car and slammed the door. As they drove off, the hurt and concerned expression on Cody's face stabbed her heart with surprising force. If they were in for their next battle with The Order, she wanted to see her parents one last time before she sealed herself off from them.

A large party of executives had booked one of the private rooms, so her father would be working late. With the go-bag in hand she'd placed in Jeb's car earlier, she entered through the back entrance passing the pristine kitchen and food preparation area. Peeking into the main dining room, she glimpsed the restaurant still over half full despite the time ticking closer to closing time. An unwritten rule of staying open until the last patron left would keep her father at the restaurant tonight until the last car exited the lot. The Ranch restaurant exuded quiet sophistication. Rich, dark wood matched modern wall designs made of matching material. In the colder Dallas months, several fireplaces added warmth and ambiance. Lila followed the back hall to her father's office and knocked on the opened door.

Dan stepped out of the wine closet in a corner of his office where he kept his most expensive bottles. He had brown hair with a hint of gray, giving the fiftyish man an old Hollywood debonair appearance. Many times, Lila had witnessed her father rebuffing the advances of women patrons. At least she could count on her father to cherish his relationship with his wife.

He whistled as he held two bottles of wine. "You look beautiful." He stepped closer. "You okay, honey?"

Lila rubbed her temples and breathed for what felt like the first time in hours. "It's been kind of a rough few days."

Dan Caldwell's eyes shaded. She and her father shared the same hazel eye color, which darkened when angry or under duress. He waved to the restaurant manager passing by the office and handed him the bottles. "Make sure the Smith party gets another bottle of pinot. And please ask my wife to come to the office." Placing his hand on Lila's shoulder, he said, "Let's talk."

She held up her bag. "I'll change first." Fifteen minutes later, she emerged from her father's office bathroom in sweats and a T-shirt, the weight of her fancy dress lifted along with some of the angst of the evening. Lila sank onto the couch and pulled her feet under her.

"Has Lance threatened you?" Her father remained standing, his eyes full of concern.

"No, but I have news." She expelled a sigh.

"About the Struthers' murder?"

"Not exactly."

Dan held up a finger, then exited the room. A few minutes later, he returned with a glass of iced tea.

"Thanks, Dad."

"It's the Sinclairs, right? I wish I could remove the danger they hold over you." He sank onto the sofa next to her. "I kick myself every day for even getting involved with April. But I can't be totally upset because if it weren't for her, I wouldn't have you." He wrapped an arm around her shoulders.

Lila leaned against her father, warmed by the knowledge he'd always wanted her in his life. Vivian, her grandmother, and April, her mother, had conspired to keep him away, by convincing the authorities that Lila's father wanted nothing to do with his child. By threatening his parents and brother, her father had been forced to sign away his parental rights. But as soon as he could, he jumped at the chance to reclaim her as his daughter.

"April was very beautiful," Lila said, unwilling and unable to call the woman Mother.

Dan nodded. "That she was. I'll never forget the day she walked into the restaurant."

Lila's stepmother, Patty, burst through the door, her brown skin clear of any wrinkles. The fifty-year-old woman had light-brown hair and a trim figure. "I'm sorry I got delayed. We've been busy all week and tonight we had two big parties going on at the same time. I managed to get a peek at you in your gown, Lila. So beautiful." She stopped talking and stared from Lila to Dan. "What's wrong?" She sat on the other side of Lila and gave her a hug.

"I wanted to speak to you both. The press showed up at the Veridian benefit tonight. They were asking me all kinds of questions about Jack's death. My name is now out there, and they may start sniffing at one of the restaurants or try to get quotes from my family."

Dan emitted a loud sigh and stood. "I thought your name wasn't to be released to the press. How did this happen?" He splayed open his hands then crossed the room to shut the office door.

Lila shrugged. "No clue." She shifted in her seat. When she came to live with her father, one of the first things he told her was she could tell him anything. He made sure she felt comfortable talking about her mother and the Sinclairs. As she grew older, Lila always briefed her father when she could about Lance and The Order. Due to the sensitive nature of their FBI taskforce, she couldn't disclose everything. But both Lila and her father understood the danger they could

face. She continued telling them about Lance's video presentation at
the charity event that evening.

"I can't believe the nerve of that guy," Dan said.

"I feel sorry for his wife and that baby." Patty shook her head.

Lila nodded. "I'm sure he feels very manly about fathering a new
son to take the reins of evil, but I hope this child takes after his Aunt
Carson and turns away from The Order." Although Lila freely spoke
about her past with The Order, she remained mum about her nightmares and panic attacks. She hadn't wanted to worry anyone.

Patty placed her hand on Lila's arm. "Why don't you pack some
things and come stay with us? Since we're in a gated community, we
can let security know not to allow in members of the press. Your Dad
and I will both feel better."

Patty never fit the evil stepmother image. She'd always been
warm, welcoming, and caring. and treated Lila like her own, far
better than her biological mother. When their kids came along, first
Jenna, who was now twenty, and then Brent, now sixteen, Lila was
thrilled to be a big sister.

"Patty is right. Come back to the house."

Putting her family at risk had always driven Lila's decisions on
how much time she spent with them. Even starting her career in
Dallas had been an agonizing decision. In the end, she decided she
could watch over them better by being close. Now that the press had
found her, she hoped her refusal for interviews would be enough to
send them elsewhere, but with Lance's appearance tonight, and her
encounter with Cody, her nerves were raw.

"I'm staying with a friend tonight. I'll try to come by this weekend." She hated lying.

Dan crossed his arms. "That determined expression tells me I
won't succeed in talking you into coming home tonight, but I'm
holding you to this weekend. Besides, I have some contracts I want
you to look over."

Lila grinned. "You're moving forward with the new restaurant?"

Dan's business had grown from one restaurant in New York to ten
from coast to coast. He had plans not only to add new restaurants but

also to expand into the resort industry. Ever since Lila graduated from law school, he'd been clamoring for her to join his company. But Lila wanted to make it on her own and not be granted breaks because she was the boss's daughter. She hadn't, however, ruled out joining DBC International in the future.

"I have the final papers to sign right here." He slapped his desk. "It will be great to have a presence in Las Vegas."

Patty beamed. "Did you tell her the news?"

Dan shook his head. "We're contracting with a major hotel on the Strip."

"Wow, Dad. I can't wait to see the designs."

Patty stood and hugged her husband. "I'm so proud of him. In fact, I'm proud of my entire family. Jenna made the dean's list last semester, and Brent is doing well with football and school."

"All great news. I'm looking forward to catching up." Lila scooted off the sofa. As Lila reached for the doorknob, she glanced at her parents, and her heart constricted...if anything ever happened to them...

Concern washed over her father's face and he strode over and hugged her. "Text me when you get to your friend's." He leaned back and looked into her eyes. "And make sure to lock your doors."

"You be careful, as well, Dad." Lila left the restaurant thankful for the love and support of her parents. They wanted her behind the safety of their gated home, but Lila knew a fence wouldn't stop Lance.

Chapter 14

Muzzle flashes lit the dim tunnel. Lila crouched against the cool wall searching in vain for a way out. A bullet slammed into the concrete splattering her with chips of rock and dust.

They were outmanned. She counted at least ten men, all with guns. Reid couldn't hold them back forever. The wall and several vintage vehicles provided a modicum of cover. Her pulse raced, and her muscles tensed. How would they survive?

Holly screamed. "Lila!" She beckoned her toward the truck she and Cody had taken cover behind. Metal pinged, and sparks flew as bullets blasted into the vehicles. Lila's eyes teared as she searched through the smoke for a path toward her friends. The odor of gunfire seared her nose and spurred bouts of coughing.

Another bullet ripped by like a firecracker exploding around her. She screamed and fell to the floor.

"Lila, follow my voice!" Cody's voice cut through the battle sounds.

Her gaze locked on his as he inched toward her.

"I'm coming!" Cody stood and raced toward her.

"No, stay back!" She couldn't let her friends be killed trying to rescue her.

But he lunged forward.

Before Cody could reach her, she screamed when a rough arm clamped around her, lifting her up. She twisted and struggled against the grip of the strong, unknown person.

Cody's eyes were huge as he stared at her. "Lila!"

Gunmen formed a barrier between her and the people she loved. Reid, Holly, and Cody stood with shocked expressions on the other side. A white van zoomed onto the scene, almost mowing down her friends. Panic flooded her as her fate became clear. She kicked and screamed but the man's grip tightened. Even though she was no match against his strength, she refused to give up. As the van's back door burst open, Lila spotted a gunman training his weapon toward Cody. "No! Cody!"

The bullet drilled into Cody and seconds later she landed on the hard surface in the back of the van. The vehicle lurched forward, and they rocketed away. Her last thought: Cody was dead. Then her vision dimmed to black.

LILA'S EYES POPPED OPEN. Her breathing, in raspy staccato rhythm, filled the semi-dark room. Damp sheets clung to her body as she sat up. She shivered as the sounds of gunfire and screams dissipated in her memory. Hot tears snaked the length of her face as she rocked back and forth. The butterfly nightlight in front of her bed illuminated a small portion of the room. The light from blue and yellow wings sucked her in, creating a dizzying effect as her mind whirled through time. She counted in an attempt to control her breathing. In and out.

The count reached fifty before her heart slowed to a normal beat. When her body stopped shaking, she stared up at the ceiling. The argument with Cody last night had been her fault. He'd been concerned about her safety, and she'd treated him like he was the criminal. The nightmare had to be her subconscious reminding her how much danger those around her could be in. Hopping out of bed, she raced into the bathroom. She had to talk to Cody.

Twenty minutes later, she'd showered and dressed in jeans and a short-sleeved shirt. She rushed downstairs and ran straight into Cody in the living room.

"Uh, Cody. Hi."

He nodded and remained rooted to his spot. "Did you get some rest?"

"A few hours." She shifted. "I was rude to you last night. The press showing up sent me over the edge but that's still no excuse. I know you had my well-being in mind and I'm sorry."

His brows hiked upward. "You were completely out of line. I discharged my gun the other day. You owe me bullets." He remained stoic with arms crossed.

Lila met his gaze and erupted in a smile. "Jerk."

He grinned. "Takes one to know one."

Her grin dissolved. "I really am sorry. I needed to talk to my parents before things get worse. You know—warn them."

"Understandable." He moved to the window and peeped out the blinds before pivoting back. "Your SUV is out back."

"Thanks. I tutor kids at a church, but I'll be back before everyone gets here." She rushed past him on her way to the back door.

Cody caught up to her. "Full disclosure. I will follow you. Or I could just go with you."

She threw up her hands. "Fine, follow me. I don't want to answer questions if someone sees me pull up with you."

THE AROMA OF, candles, wood polish and old books tickled Lila's nose as she stepped through the heavy, wooden doors of Fox Street Christian Church. Muted lighting created an ethereal effect and wrapped a soothing arm around her. She ventured into the quiet sanctuary and took her regular seat, fourth row, left side.

Cody sat several pews behind her. Lila was surprised how comforted she felt with Cody near.

She'd been coming here for over a year. One summer day, she'd taken a walk during lunch, getting away from the office had been her goal. The church, a block away from her building, beckoned her inside. She attended church services on occasion but she much preferred to sit in quiet and reflect on life before tutoring started. Sometimes she allowed her mind to go where it wanted. Thoughts about faraway vacations, books she wanted to read, or any noncontroversial idea would traipse through her mind. She wouldn't allow bad memories to taint this place. Noise and activity commanded so much of her life that she relished the calm. However, today her mind wouldn't settle. The contents of the files on Fox7011 replayed in her mind. Unable to pinpoint how the church related to Jack's warning, she settled on wild speculation. Was a member of the church in trouble? Perhaps someone here had threatened Jack.

Large stained-glass windows refracted the afternoon sun in splintered rays. The pulpit rose upward and resembled a phoenix rising from the dead. Pictures depicting scenes from the Bible were painted on the walls and rows of candles were stationed at tables on either side of the sanctuary.

She often found herself here after a nightmare or a bad night. The church and the calm solitude helped ground her. Glancing at her watch, Lila pulled herself out of the pew and jogged downstairs for the math tutoring group.

Cody would wait in the downstairs lounge where some of the parents passed the time working on their laptops, reading, or socializing with other parents.

The basement classroom hummed with life and excited voices when Lila entered. Metal chairs scraped against the old tile floor and the aroma of fresh popcorn charged through the room.

"Ms. Caldwell!" one of the kids shouted from across the room.

"Hi, Ryan." She hugged the cute ten-year-old boy before he scampered off to his group. "Hi everyone."

A chorus of hellos were echoed back.

The Fox Street Christian Church Tutoring Program catered to neighborhood children but accepted anyone, free of charge. This church not only pulled from several low-rent housing areas but also bordered in another direction with more middle-class neighborhoods. Some of the kids attending the tutoring program were in foster care which tugged at her heart. As a child growing up in the same system, she appreciated the need to be treated as someone special, even if it were for a small amount of time.

"Everyone bring your chairs to our regular corner." Lila placed her bag near the chalkboard and settled into the circle of chairs.

For the next hour, Lila provided math help to her small group, today consisting of six students from both middle and high school. She always had a quick topic or a fun math game they tackled as a group before she provided each student with individual help on homework or test preparation. When the last child had left, Lila hung back. "I'll clean the room," she told the other two tutors. "I appreciate you taking my group when I was busy."

They nodded and vacated the room.

Twenty minutes later, Lila rushed out of the room and up to the sanctuary, slipping past Cody who was involved in a conversation with one of the parents. She hadn't told anyone about Jack's dying words.

Inhaling the earthy scent of fresh flowers, she neared the back of the church. Preparations for a wedding were underway. She crept around boxes of tulle and pink roses and headed upstairs. A tiny office and a small conference room were the first two rooms she passed. There were no signs to indicate a room number. As she neared the next door, a man she recognized as one of the janitors lumbered around the corner.

"Can I help you?" he asked.

"Frank, I'm looking for storage room 3B. I was told there were supplies inside I could use for the tutoring club." She stiffened. Would lying in church send her straight to hell?

Frank scrunched his nose then scratched his balding head. "Storage 3B was the old broom closet up in the bell tower. I can't imagine anything would still be stored there."

"Do you mind if I check anyway?" She cocked her head and waited.

Frank fumbled with his huge keyring, flipping through several keys. When he found the one he was looking for, he nodded. "Follow me."

When they reached the third floor, Frank showed her to the bell tower. "You don't want to be up here when they're ringing. I was here one day and almost went deaf, my dang ears were ringing for a week. Other than that, it's actually nice up here." He pointed to the set of three brass bells. "Those are originals, seventy-six years old. Were refurbished again last year."

While she appreciated the history lesson, she needed Frank to hurry.

They approached one door, but the key didn't work.

"Must be the other closet." Frank led her to the opposite side of the bell tower. This time when he inserted the key, the door swung open. "Here we are."

Lila peered inside. Bell oil, cleaning supplies, brooms, and shovels occupied the closet. In the corner stood several boxes. "Maybe this is what I'm looking for." She turned to Frank. "I don't want to hold you up. I'll close and lock the door when I leave." She flashed her biggest and nicest smile.

He hesitated. "Fine, just tug hard on the door to make sure it's closed good and tight. I'll be downstairs if you need any help." Sweeping a glance into the room, he scurried away.

Now that Lila stood in the closet, she blinked several times before heading to the boxes in the corner. The first box revealed Christmas decorations and the second box contained more cleaning supplies. The third box contained files. Lila's heart skipped a beat. The first folder contained information on the manufacturer of the brass bells, including information on care and maintenance. The next file contained similar information. Halfway through the box, she opened a file labeled LS. The next document sucked the air out of the tiny closet. She shoved the file into her purse, replaced the boxes, and shut the door.

Rushing down the stairs with the thick file, she spotted Cody. They made eye contact before she exited the church and jumped into her car. Once she'd traveled about a block from the church, her secured phone rang.

"Where were you?" Cody said.

"In a storage room. I have several stops to make." Lila glanced into her rearview mirror at Cody right behind her.

She drove to a library across town. Half hour later, she'd had three copies of the documents. She drove to another section of town where she had a storage unit.

Cody pulled up beside her and got out. "You have one, too?"

"Just like they taught us." Over the years, Alliance members taught them survival techniques. A storage unit with money, clothes, and another vehicle had been imperative. Lila also stored important documents related to The Order here. "With everyone coming I thought I'd bring the contents of the map box to the meeting. We've been over and over the information but maybe something will be useful." A locked safe stood in the corner. She entered the code and pulled open the door. Inside, she had important insurance documents, a Sig Sauer handgun, and about $15,000 in cash. She never knew when she needed to flee and stopping at a bank or using her ATM card may not be smart. While Cody sauntered to the front of the unit, Lila shoved two copies of the Fox Church documents inside the safe, grabbed the papers from the map box, and locked the door.

Although she hadn't had time to read through the entire file, what she read confirmed Lance's involvement. Now that she had the information Jack had possessed, she could easily suffer the same fate he did.

Once they were back in their cars and headed back to Jeb's, she stared through the windshield as swollen gray clouds opened up. The sunny day had disappeared, and the gloom matched her mood. She wanted more than anything to put Lance away. Images of her dead mother, shot in the head, raced through her memory. The callous way Lance had ended her life, without a second thought, exemplified his dangerous nature.

Relentless rain pounded her car, slowing what should have been light Saturday afternoon traffic. An accident on the highway had traffic ahead of her braking. Lila veered onto the off ramp to take the back roads around the lake to Jeb's. She glanced behind her and sighed. A number of cars and trucks were between her and Cody. By the time she got closer to Lake Burgess the traffic had lessened.

Large oak trees bordered the road and were in full summer bloom. Today, the rain-soaked trees created a drippy green covering making extra-large dollops of rain dive-bomb her car as if they were missiles. The rain picked up just as she rounded a bend in the road. Lila applied the brakes, but her car didn't react. "What the hell!" She pumped the brakes, and still nothing. Lila shifted into neutral and once again the move appeared futile. The car didn't slow. Perspiration snaked down her face as she searched for options to control the vehicle. She cut a quick glance at the speedometer. Thirty-seven miles per hour. With her gaze back on the road, she searched for a place to maneuver the car. The thick tree line didn't give her any space to negotiate an out-of-control vehicle.

She shot a glance into her rearview mirror. Instead of Cody behind her, she saw a large black truck.

Her pulse pounded in her ears as her car accelerated. How could that be? Her foot hadn't touched the pedal. Another sharp curve loomed ahead as Lila struggled to get the car under control. As the curve got closer, her car showed no signs of slowing down. Another vehicle approaching from the opposite direction could result in a devastating accident for both her and the other driver. Lila punched the horn, emitting a long wail from her car. Taking her hand off the horn, she gripped the steering wheel as the car entered the curve. In a flash, she lost control. She tried to guide the car past the trees. Missing two and scraping along a third, Lila spotted a clearing. Seconds later, her car passed the trees, and then headed straight for the lake.

Crashing through a metal railing in an instant murky, cool water rushed into the car as Lila struggled to release her seatbelt. She tried to control her breathing and rising panic. Grasping on to the seatbelt, she fumbled to unhook the latch.

Water rose to her waist.

"Come on, damn it!" She pushed and pulled at the release button. Slamming on all the buttons on the door console, she lowered as many windows as she could. Her phone. With frantic urgency she patted her seat but couldn't find the phone. She had only minutes before she would die. Jack's dying words hit her. *I was killed because of those documents.*

Would she follow? She pressed the compass pendant dangling around her neck, then remembered Cody. Had he seen her go into the lake?

Water rose to her chest, and she tried again to release herself. The seatbelt latch didn't budge. Her fate appeared settled. *Don't panic.* Then she recalled her training. Wrenching open the center console, she rooted around inside. A piece of metal scraped by her hand. With a sliver of hope, she grasped onto the seatbelt cutter and window hammer her father insisted she put in her car. In seconds, she'd sawed through the seatbelt but not before the water had risen to her neck. As she scrambled out of the seatbelt shreds, she took one huge breath. Green water engulfed her as she wiggled out of the drivers' side window. Her lungs screamed and her eyes stung. She kicked to propel herself up, trying not to think about what may be brushing up against her. Another kick and she felt the pull of something on her leg. Thick aquatic plants swayed below her trapping her legs in their vines. Lila jerked her leg, but her leafy captor didn't budge. Lungs burning, she continued to pull at the vine. With diminishing strength, her tugs weakened. She couldn't hold on. Water filled her lungs. Just as hope faded, the vine loosened, and an arm encircled her. Perhaps she was dreaming or maybe dying. Cody? She glimpsed a man, then her vision tunneled. Green water narrowed her vision, her chest burned as if lit on fire. Her body, suddenly heavy, relaxed. Just as her eyes closed, she caught a peek of a face bathed in a ray of sun.

Cody?

Chapter 15

For the thousandth time, Lance reread the letter.

My dearest Lance,

If you're reading this, then I've departed this life. Please know that even though I was hand-chosen to marry your father, I had a happy life. Russell, your grandfather, trusted me to watch over Ivan and mold him into a man capable of leading The Order. When I determined he was unable to carry out the duties in a way to make Russell proud, I shifted my energies to you. My son, you have been the light of my life and more importantly, the man Russell would have swelled with pride to call, The Grand Commander, Ruler of The Order. You possess the sentiment, capability, and heart to elevate The Order to heights unforeseen.

Your grandfather had the intelligence to prepare his descendants with not only the structure to build upon, but also the wealth to uphold and propel his vision. Before Ivan's death and prior to his brief stint as Grand Commander, I received a document from The Order council. The document indicated Russell was in possession of land containing natural resources worth billions. I am confident Russell would have wanted you to control this land. Russell kept the location of this property secret to prevent it from falling into untested hands. Although I don't know the location of this property, I'm convinced Ivan did. Please employ all measures necessary to find this land, your birthright. I'm sorry this is such a convoluted process, but your grandfather believed in signs and symbols. Ordo Ortus, my son.

With all my love,

Mother

With a finger, Lance traced over his mother's writing. Pia's loopy slanted penmanship brought back memories of her impeccable style. Although she'd bristle at the moniker, she'd be thrilled to be a grandmother. The moment she was shot remained imprinted in his memory, fueling his desire to strike back. He would seek revenge on those responsible for her death. They called themselves the Alliance. Picking them off one by one would be a just ending.

Lance hated over-emotional people, yet today he had a need to look back. Next to Pia's letter sat one of the diary pages of his great-grandfather. He stared at the highlighted phrase. *Only the weak apologize.* Lance considered Russell's motto, which was one of many wisdom-filled sentiments he'd found in the diary, like a special message only for him. How could this man father such a weakling like Ivan? When the time was right, he'd make his son read Russell's words. Puffing his chest, Lance swelled with pride at the thought of passing on the Grand Commander title to his son.

Shaking away his musings, he lifted the phone and sent for Peter Shaw.

Seconds later, Shaw entered Lance's private office and took the seat opposite him. He'd removed his suit jacket and held a glass of clear liquid. Peter didn't drink and usually had seltzer water. Men who were too afraid of alcohol didn't rate much in Lance's opinion, but he overlooked this shortcoming.

"Have you reviewed the documents again?"

Shaw placed his glass on the marble table next to him and twisted his antique gold Yale University ring. "Yes, I personally reviewed all three thousand pages. Like you, I found nothing."

Lance nodded and lifted the letter's attached document. He read the one sentence centered in the middle of antique parchment: *My writings hold the key.*

Russell produced thousands of documents over the course of his life, each intended to educate his ancestors. Lance had been through every document found in his parents' homes in Colorado and Switzerland. And now Shaw had confirmed his findings or lack of findings. "Anything from my Aunt Vivian's papers?"

Vivian Sinclair, Russell's only daughter and his father's sister, had been dead a number of years. She had succeeded Russell as the Grand Commander but had been killed as she spiraled out of control in a mental breakdown.

"We've found nothing useful other than all of her assets went to her daughter April." Peter crossed his legs and tapped his fingers together.

Lance scowled. "April was just as insane as her mother. I'm glad I killed her. She would have been a problem. Her daughter, Lila, foolishly refused possession of anything." Lance folded the papers and placed both documents back in the file. "Lila had a map box with artifacts and writings from my grandfather. Up until now I believed I had all the duplicate documents but now I have reason to believe that the box may hold an important clue to the whereabouts of an important property. As I've already instructed, Lila is the target."

Peter acknowledged Lance's comments with a brief nod. "On another front, we have every reason to believe Lila had time to speak with Jack Struthers before he died. I've explained my concern that he told her where the evidence of your misdeeds was located. Seems this young lady holds the key to your future."

Heat shot up Lance's neck. "I will not allow that little bitch to derail my destiny. Once I have what I need, I will see that she suffers before I kill her." He loosened his silk tie and poured a glass of brandy from the crystal decanter and settled on the pale green sofa.

Upstairs the newborn slept in his crib while his mother slumbered next door in her quarters. For her convenience, Lance had moved Delphine into the room adjoining the nursery. Regular nursing sessions occurred throughout the day and night and Lance didn't want his sleep interrupted every time she woke to feed the baby. Besides, her body still carried pregnancy flab, which was a definite turn-off.

"When I was in the nursery checking over the security measures, I peeked at the baby. Handsome boy you've got." Shaw said.

"He's definitely a Sinclair." Lance sipped his drink, the ice clinking against the expensive crystal glass. "Are you certain the nursey is secured? I'm a man of immense power, and I won't take any chances with the safety of my son. Also, put two more detail agents on Delphine any time she leaves the property."

Shaw nodded. "Absolutely. I've already handpicked two new guards for your wife's security team."

"Good. Now, I have a more sensitive issue to discuss." Lance channeled his Grandfather Russell. The old man had been right about his own wife and Lance would follow suit. "Delphine has safely delivered my son. She performed well during the pregnancy by maintaining her health and following both the doctors' and my orders. Soon, her use will expire."

"You mentioned other children once," Shaw said.

Lance flicked a piece of lint from his razor-sharp pants crease. "I have a *son*, and he will be my sole focus. Ivan fathered two children. As you know Sloane, Carson Maxwell as she calls herself, has taken a wayward path and chose to align herself with the enemy. She could have had the world at her feet, yet she insisted on running off. Now, she's set to marry your previous underling, that FBI agent Adam Forrester."

"I had heard they were engaged. Ashamed she didn't value her birthright."

"I don't want to risk having to deal with a child like my sister. By directing all my attention to my son, I will ensure he carries on my vision and the principles of The Order. They will not die with me. I will make sure Lance Junior has the best education and experiences all guided by me and me alone." Lance recalled happy times at his European boarding school. He had important friends and contacts all over the world, which served him well in business and personal matters. His child would have the same.

"Makes sense." Shaw rose and poured himself a glass of water.

"The baby needs his mother at the moment, but when the time is right, I will take the baby back to Switzerland. Delphine will not be accompanying us. I expect you to see that she will never pose a problem."

"Understood." Shaw drained his glass. "I'll be in touch with new updates." He exited the room.

Lance picked up a silver rattle. *Soon, my son, I will give you the world.*

Chapter 16

"Stay with me, Lila. You aren't leaving me." Cody held her close as he rushed through cattails bordering the lake. He reached an open area and placed her on the ground.

"Come on, Lila!" He listened for breath sounds. Unsure if he heard anything, he grimaced as he pumped her chest. "Come back to me, honey. We're not done."

Seconds later water erupted from her mouth, and she sputtered a cough.

Cody blew out the breath he'd been holding and cheered at the beautiful sound. He moved around to hold her head sideways to aid the expulsion of lake water pouring out her mouth.

Sirens screamed in the background.

Her eyes fluttered open "Cody?" she said in a weak voice.

"Yes, it's me. I'm here, baby. Hold on. Help is on the way."

She nodded then struggled to sit up. "I'm okay," she said in a raspy voice.

"I know." He wrapped his arms around her as her body shook. "You're okay."

She clung to him and nodded.

Relief poured through him as he spotted help on the way. An ambulance, a fire truck, and two police cruisers rushed toward them.

Within seconds, EMT's and firefighters were out of their vehicles.

The first firefighter to reach him, a tall man with a blue T-shirt with the name of the fire department on his left pectoral, bent next to Cody and Lila. "Is anyone else in the car?"

"No," Cody said. "She coughed out a lot of water." He relinquished her to the professionals.

"No hospital." Lila shook her head at a ginger-haired male EMT.

The EMT checked her vitals and pronounced them within normal limits. He turned to her, "Ma'am, you should go to the hospital to be safe."

Cody understood Lila's concern. She didn't trust easily, and he knew she'd probably recalled Carson being attacked in the hospital. "Lila, go. I'll be with you."

"Sir, are you all right?" the other EMT asked. "Looks like you got a nasty gash on your arm."

Cody glanced at his arm. He hadn't noticed the cut, which continued to bleed. A reddish tinge colored his shirt. "I'm fine."

"You probably need stitches, so you can hop a ride in the ambulance or follow us." The EMT moved closer, examined the cut, then placed gauze around his arm.

An officer rushed toward him. "Can you tell us what happened?"

Cody nodded. He leaned over the gurney Lila had been placed on. "I'll be right behind you." He squeezed her hand then turned back to the officer.

Just as the EMT's slammed the ambulance door closed, media trucks descended upon the scene. Cody turned his back, avoiding the cameras.

He explained what he knew of Lila's accident inside the police cruiser. The officer shielded him from the media while Cody got into his car. He also provided a police escort to the hospital.

Forty minutes, and thirty-two stitches later, Cody jumped off the hospital bed. He appreciated the level-one trauma center the hospital boasted about, but he needed to get going. The man-child doctor appeared intent on giving him thorough care. He instructed him on how to care for the stitches and when to take a pain reliever. Then a nurse entered with a document that repeated the same information. Cody had sighed but listened. The brief statement he'd given to the police probably didn't help much. He'd been following Lila all morning from her trip to the church, her flight across town, and then her harrowing drive into Lake Burgess. He'd seen a huge, black truck following her when she exited the freeway, but he couldn't be sure the driver had anything to do with her accident. Besides, he'd been so intent on observing Lila, he hadn't honed in on the license plate. All he could remember was that they were Texas plates.

He hadn't heard anything about Lila's condition and the lack of information magnified his worry. She left the scene talking but anything could happen

After the nurse completed her discharge speech, he scribbled his name on the paper and jumped off the gurney. "Thanks. Where is Lila Caldwell?"

"She's still in a CAT scan."

"I have a change of clothes in my car. Can I change and wait in her room?"

The nurse nodded. "She's in Room 12."

After stripping out of his wet clothes, he slid into sweats and a T-shirt then settled into a chair in Lila's room. Pulling out his phone, he entered a chat room. He didn't want to chance calling any of the Alliance members in public and he didn't want them learning about the accident in the media. Using his screen name, Stargazer, Cody logged into the travel chat room.

Took an unplanned swim in the lake today. Met up with LegalEagle and we're recovering from our activities. Will head out soon.

Cody checked area news sites. He read two small blurbs about the accident and thankfully neither mentioned their names. He returned to the chat room. CarolinaWave, who was Adam, had responded.

Great to know you connected with your friend. Hope you are rejuvenated from your rest. Currently in the air. Will tell the fam the good news.

He was satisfied Adam understood the context and would pass along the information to the rest of the team.

Ten minutes later, Lila was wheeled back into the room. The nurse settled her and reminded her the doctor would be in later, then retreated. Cody took a few steps, then his feet rooted to the floor as if the vines that had held her captive now ensnarled his legs. Lila lay wrapped in a blanket, her brown hair now dry and hanging in limp curls around her shoulders.

She gave him a weak smile. "Thanks for saving me."

Cody nodded, his voice also on a temporary hiatus.

Shifting in the bed, Lila pulled up the blanket and cocked her head.

Moving a step closer, he said, "You're welcome. I'm glad I was there. Are you sure you're okay?"

She huffed out a sigh. "The doctor examined me. Slight concussion. They want to monitor me for a couple hours, but I'll be going home after that." She paused. "What about you?" Her gaze landed on his bandage. "Your arm."

Cody moved forward until he stood next to the bed. "Thirty-two stitches. But it's fine."

Lila brushed a shaky finger across his injured arm. "Stings, huh?"

"Nah." He smiled. "The doctor numbed it. I'm sure it will burn like hell after the drug has worn off."

She pulled back and crossed her arms. "I see you changed."

"I finally took our friends' suggestion about carrying a go-bag. Certainly, came in handy today."

Lila adjusted her blanket. "I guess I'll have to bum some clothes from the hospital." Her voice shook.

Cody sat next to her on the bed and wrapped his arms around her. "You were a fighter. I think you would have freed yourself, even if I hadn't been there. We got lucky today."

"This was a close one. Sooner or later luck runs out." Lila stared ahead, clinging to her blanket.

Cody hated that she had to live this way. Worry about when the next threat will rain terror upon your life was no way to live. "You're a survivor. Don't forget that."

Before Lila could respond, a uniformed police officer stuck her head in. "Ms. Caldwell, I need to speak with you about the accident."

Cody jumped off the bed but remained at her side.

"Sure," Lila said, cutting a glance at Cody.

The petite female officer stepped into the room and introduced herself as Officer Nyland. She stood wide-legged, one hand on her belt, as her gaze swept over Lila. The officer wore her dark hair in a severe bun, which added to her no-nonsense persona. She glanced at Cody. "You may stay, Mr. Green." Then she turned to Lila. "I need to get your statement on what happened today." She pulled out a small notebook. "You were traveling east along Lake Burgess Road, is that correct?"

"Yes."

"Tell me what happened before you went into the water."

Lila gave her a full account of how the car failed to respond to her actions to decelerate. She explained how she searched for a place to crash, how she lost control, and ended with her attempts to get out of the lake punctuated by Cody's help.

"You were the woman who found the law partner just before he died, right?" Officer Nyland said, peering at Lila over her notebook.

"Yes."

The officer raised her eyebrows. "You're having a bad week. Do you have any reason to believe someone tampered with your car, perhaps in relation to the murder scene you happened upon?"

Officer Nyland drilled down to the crux of Cody's fears. Lila could be a target.

"I don't know but I have no reason to believe I'm a target." Lila's voice warbled, and she reached for a cup of water on the bedside tray. "I didn't see who killed Jack Struthers."

"Did you notice anyone following you? Maybe even someone you spotted earlier in the day?" With her writing hand in midair, she waited for Lila's answer.

A spate of coughing halted Lila from talking. After she had a few sips of water, she shook her head. "No. There had been an accident on the highway, so I took the back roads. Several vehicles did the same."

"Have you received any weird calls or noticed anyone watching your house?"

"No."

The officer froze as she listened to her shoulder radio.

Cody heard something about the tow truck arriving at the lake.

Officer Nyland turned back to Lila. "What about the vehicle? Have you had any problems or recent repairs?"

"No, my vehicle had been operating fine."

"How did you happen upon the scene, sir?" the officer said, glancing at Cody.

"I was following her back to a friend's house and saw her go into the lake." Cody's jaw tightened. At least he didn't lie.

Lila straightened in bed. "Cody is an old friend."

Officer Nyland narrowed her gaze, then nodded and stuffed her notebook into a pocket. "Ms. Caldwell, your blood alcohol level came back clear, so no worries there. We have crews at the scene pulling your vehicle out. We'll be in touch, but if you recall anything please contact me. I'll leave my card here." The officer pulled out her business card and placed it on the bedside tray. "You're lucky to have such a good friend." She gave Lila a reassuring pat on the arm then stepped out of the room.

"Now, I have a question." Cody pulled up a chair. "Do you know who caused the accident? Moments before you went into the lake, I saw a big black truck. Did the driver ram your car?"

"I remember a truck behind me, but I don't remember being rammed. The car seemed to have a life of its own. I couldn't control anything."

"Maybe the truck wasn't related to your accident."

Silence coated the room for a few seconds. "This was no accident." She pushed a stray hair out of her face.

Her hands trembled, and Cody couldn't blame her. "Okay." He didn't want to push her for more right now.

"I appreciate what you did," she said, her voice soft.

"My pleasure, ma'am." Cody affected a southern accent.

Lila rolled her eyes then laughed, a treasured sound he hadn't heard in years.

She shifted in the bed. "I don't mean to be a jerk."

"You realize this is the second time you've said that." He smiled then released a sigh. "I was worried. I thought I'd lost you. I mean...I thought your life was in jeopardy."

"Still here." Her voice shook, and she cleared her throat.

Swallowing, Cody stared into her bright hazel eyes. "I'm glad." He took her hand. Heat ignited from their touch. Perching on the side of the bed, he placed his arm around her. She leaned into him. The familiar connection he had with her permeated like a welcome drug. He expected her to pull away, but this time she didn't. Maybe she needed the comfort of someone after her near-death ordeal. He dared not believe she needed *him*. The thought of her rejection again would bring him to his knees. He'd never forget the sad, hurt look in her eyes, even after all these years. The sobs he'd heard from her room during that time tore out his heart. Yet, an hour later when they came face-to-face all traces of emotion were gone. Her stone-faced expression appeared and had never wavered—until now.

After a long minute, she shifted away. "My car is toast and so is my purse, cell phone, and the files. Do you mind if I use your cell?"

Cody fished his phone from his pocket and handed it to her.

Lila told her father about the accident and that she was fine. She answered several worried questions, then informed him that Cody had rescued her. Before ending the call, she begged him not to come to the hospital as she would be released in short order. Based on Lila's side of the conversation, he reluctantly agreed.

After handing Cody his phone, she stared at him. "What?"

"You told your father I was here. I can't imagine what he thinks of me." Cody could picture Mr. Caldwell's stern gaze, similar to his daughter's.

"I don't tell my Dad everything, but he got the gist of why we broke up. For the record, he always liked you. Even after the...incident, I think he was still rooting for you. And now that he knows you got me out of that car..." She shrugged.

"I didn't dive into that lake to win accolades from you or anyone else."

"I know."

He reached for the compass pendant all Alliance members wore. His fingers brushed against her collar bone, sending another electric thrill through him.

"Do you think the GPS function is dead?" she asked.

"Shouldn't be. We'll check with the guys later."

Lila stared at him with a tired expression. "I just need...some time."

"Sure. I'll be out in the waiting room when you're ready to leave." Cody stepped away.

She grabbed his uninjured arm. "Wait. Stay. Please."

Chapter 17

After promising the doctor she would follow up with her primary-care physician, Lila jumped off the bed. As she slid into a pair of sweats and a T-shirt the nurse had given her, she made a mental note to stop by and donate more clothes to the hospital.

Cody told her the media had arrived at the accident scene. Thankful the media hadn't tracked them to the hospital, Lila followed Cody to his SUV. She shivered despite the warm car, a bit unnerved to be inside a vehicle so soon after her plunge into the lake.

When he slid behind the wheel, she stared at him. "Before we head back to Jeb's, would you mind helping me with a few other things?"

"You want to run errands now?" Cody's voice rose in surprise and he met her gaze. "Everyone is due to arrive in a few hours."

She expelled a sigh. "Then I need to get a rental. Dad would loan me one of theirs, but if I go to the house, I'll never get out."

He blew out a frustrated breath and gave her an exasperated look. "You were just run off the road. Reid would skin me alive if I just let you loose. Your father, too."

"Let me *loose*? You make me sound like some uncontrollable

animal." Lila grimaced as she pulled on the seat belt. Although thankful her injuries weren't serious, she hated to think how sore she'd be by morning.

"I'm concerned about your safety. And you should be, too." With his jaw set, Cody started the engine and cranked up the AC.

Lila chewed her lip. "Forget the rental for now, but I need to pick up some files. These documents are extremely critical."

"What files? If this is about work, it can wait." Cody angled to face her.

She shook her head. "It's not about work, exactly."

"Lila, what the hell is going on? Your life was just threatened. Maybe it's time to come clean."

She laughed a bitter laugh. "Come clean? *You* want to talk about being honest?" Her head pounded, and her heart thumped. He'd hurt her and now expected to be her confidant? She hadn't been ready to face Cody again so soon and especially not after another near-death accident. Every time her voice warbled or her hands shook, she died a little inside. The last thing she wanted was for Cody to see her vulnerabilities.

Cody grimaced. "I guess I deserved that." He expelled a sigh. "Putting aside our past, can we focus on what happened today? The way I see it either you've had one horrible week of bad luck or you've been targeted. The officer at the hospital knew about you being a witness in the Struthers murder but didn't seem to know about the shooters at the safe house. We know the police were instructed to shut down the investigation. This whole think stinks and we'd be stupid not to think Lance is behind this."

"Don't you think I know this?" Her voice rose, filling the vehicle with a fragile grip on her emotions. She grasped the side of the seat, as if holding on for dear life.

"I know my presence isn't ideal, but for right now I'm here. I'm on your side. I'm part of the Alliance. We help one another handle situations like this. Everyone in the Alliance is coming here to support us. You can't allow them to put their lives at risk by withholding information."

She swallowed, her throat scratchy, as if she'd been screaming for hours. The intense pain in her head was like a crew of tiny construction workers ramming hammers into her skull. She leaned her head in her hand. "You're right. I'm sorry." Inhaling, she said, "I really need to get these documents."

"They are that important?" Cody asked.

"Yes."

"I'll take you wherever you need to go, but I'm not letting you out of my sight."

"Thanks, Cody." A medley of thoughts and theories clouded her mind. Who had caused her car to malfunction and go off the road? She hadn't seen Cody or anyone else following but her mind had been on the files. Chiding herself to be more cognizant, she stared out at the suburban scene whipping by. She'd had the documents Jack wanted her to find and they were directly tied to Lance. But how was Jack involved? She itched to review the files. Maybe a clue lay within the pages.

After retrieving a set of the documents from the storage unit and replacing her cell phone, Cody drove Lila to her house. As soon as they entered the house, Lila stopped. "Oh no!" Her house had been trashed. Contents of every kitchen cabinet littered the floor, along with broken glasses, and silverware. Her stove and refrigerator were displaced as if someone believed she had a hidden compartment behind them.

The map box. Her pulse launched into a full gallop.

Cody drew out his weapon and pulled her close. "I don't think anyone is still here, but we can't take any chances."

They stepped through the carnage on the kitchen floor and into the destruction in the living room. Every drawer had been ripped out and overturned. The sofa had been reduced to a mass of cushion stuffing and jagged pieces of material.

"Someone was angry," Cody headed through the living room and down the hall.

"They didn't find anything," Lila said stepping over a pile of destroyed books. She often burned candles to freshen the house, soothe her soul, and to enjoy the flickering flames. Today, the clean aroma of her candles had been replaced with something foreign. Her stomach flopped. The idea of strange people inside her home, her sanctuary, made her nauseous.

"They're long gone." Cody pointed to the patch of dried mud at the end of the hall. Half of a squiggly shoe tread imprint weaved through the hardened mound.

Lila rushed into the bathroom of her bedroom, her heart thrumming. Crouching in front of the sink, she opened the cabinet door. The intruders had tossed bottles of shampoo, lotion, and various makeup items onto the floor. She reached inside the cabinet and knocked on the back panel. Blowing out a relieved breath, she ripped off the piece of wood and revealed a safe. When she entered her code, the door clicked open and she withdrew a box.

"Is that the map box?" Cody stood behind her.

"Not the original but yes, it's a map box and contains duplicates of the documents inside the real one." Lila stood as they stared at the wooden box. "Do you think this is what they were after?"

"Possibly." Cody glanced around the room "Let's check your surveillance cameras."

Lila led the way to her office. "My desktop is gone." She blew out a sigh. "I don't keep anything of value on there. I only use it to check my cameras. We'll have to log in remotely."

"That's good. Anything else you want to check before we get out of here?"

Lila shook her head and sighed. "I just hope this ends well."

BACK IN THE CAR, Cody called Jeb and told him about Lila's accident and the break-in at her house. Jeb agreed they shouldn't go back to his house and gave them directions to an old farmhouse he was renovating. The house belonged to a friend who intended to sell it to Jeb, but they hadn't done the deal yet, so the property couldn't be traced to him. The house made the perfect location for the Alliance.

After buying food and supplies Cody pulled up to the two-story farmhouse. Soybean fields bordered three sides in the distance. Lila knew this place made for an attractive safe house due to the open space and the low-lying crops surrounding the property. They would be able to spot intruders from a distance. Cody stopped in front of a large five-bay garage. He jumped out entered a code and returned to the vehicle. The door rumbled up, and he parked inside.

Lila followed him into a gleaming kitchen with exposed wood beams, pine floors, and hickory wood cabinets. Although the exterior had paint chipping and a few drain spouts requiring repair, the inside of the house had been remodeled. "Wow, Jeb did a great job."

"He recruited me to work on a few things at his main house, but I've never been out here." Cody moved from the kitchen into the open living room.

"I need a shower." In one of the upstairs bathrooms, Lila stripped out of the sweats and stepped under the hot water, the spray soothing her battered body. As she washed her hair, twigs, dirt, and whatever else churned in Lake Burgess, circled down the drain. She counted numerous reddened places on her arms and legs, which would turn into ugly purple bruises soon. Stepping out of the shower, she wrapped a towel around herself. The warmth of the towel and the steam inside her bathroom made her want to remain in the small cocoon, shut off from the world—and Cody. She wiped away condensation on a section of the mirror behind the sink and stared at the cuts on her face. *If Cody hadn't been there...*

Sighing, she opened the door and stepped into her bedroom. She ambled into the room, turned, and jumped. "Cody! What are you doing in here?"

He had sprawled out on her bed, his long legs crossed, his hair wet from a shower.

"We need to talk. No more evasions. What the hell is going on?" Cody stared up at her, his eyes blazing. "You've got me driving you around, and you're fresh out of the hospital. Not to mention you are a witness in a murder investigation. Your life is in danger. Don't you recognize that?" He slid off the bed and placed both hands on his hips.

Lila scraped her lip between her teeth and held tight to her towel. "Of course, I recognize I could have died. I get that loud and clear. Three days ago, I was handling this alone. You waltzed into my life and now you expect me to spill my guts. I don't adjust that quick."

"Three days ago, you walked into a murder scene, two days ago the safe house you were inside was shot to hell, and hours ago you were near the bottom of Lake Burgess." Cody splayed his hands and shook his head. "I'm in this. We're in this together now."

She stomped across the room and began rooting through her bags. "I appreciate you stalking me because you were there when I needed someone but that doesn't give you the right to barge into my room and make demands."

Cody followed and stopped in front of her. His brown eyes drilled into hers. "Then what's going on? Keeping secrets is going to get you killed."

She slammed the drawer and pivoted toward him. "Are you kidding me? I just got out of the shower."

"I finally have your attention. What's going on with you?"

"I don't want anyone else to be killed! Don't you get that?" Her fists knotted as she held her towel. "I can't watch people I care about be hurt," she said, her voice lower.

"And you think *I* can?" He stepped closer. "On a constant loop, I relive that day in the tunnel when I thought I'd never see you again. I watched helpless as you were dragged away. I was there when Lance shot your mother, her blood splattered on you. I get it, Lila."

She'd been so caught up in her own nightmares that she hadn't thought that Cody might have a few of his own. Blowing out a breath, she stared at a fresh cut on her foot. The wound reminding her how lucky she'd been to get out of the lake with only minor injuries. She lifted her head and met Cody's gaze. "That comment about stalking was out of line. I'm sorry." She sank onto the bed and covered her eyes.

He sat beside her, close enough for her to feel his strong bicep brush against her arm.

They sat in silence for a few seconds, then Lila said, "I owe you an explanation."

"Damn right you do." His stern tone softened. "I don't want to be responsible for telling our friends you were killed."

She swallowed and with a shaky hand pushed a stray hair from her face. "Give me a minute to get dressed."

Fifteen minutes later, Lila emerged from her bedroom dressed in jeans and a yellow T-shirt, her bag in her hand. She inhaled the scent of coffee and found Cody leaning against the kitchen counter.

He handed her a mug. "Black with a splash of creamer?"

Shifting the bag containing Jack's files to her other hand, she took the mug and smiled. "You remembered."

"We drank a lot of coffee in college." He swiped his hand over his stubble.

Lila ambled into the living room and settled on the ivory-colored sofa positioned in front of a large, stone fireplace. "Alright, let's talk."

Cody sat one cushion away, angled toward her.

"As Jack was dying, he told me to find some files that he felt were critical. I was able to determine the documents were hidden at the church where I volunteer." She tapped her finger on the bag she'd set between them. "I haven't had a chance to read through each document, but they provide evidence of Lance's crimes. I have the original and three copies, with one now at the bottom the lake inside my car. I believe these files may give us the chance to see that Lance pays for his crimes. If we can get them into the right hands."

"Are you sure no one saw you with those files at the church or followed you when you left?" Cody said.

"I was alone when I found the files and you were right behind me when I left." She shook her head. "But then again, I didn't notice much about the truck behind me before I went into the lake. I can't ever allow myself to get that distracted again." As she opened her bag and drew out the files, her heart pounded as if she was about to open the holy grail.

Seconds later, the evidence lay before them. Photos, sworn statements, narrative accounts of Lance's kidnapping of Carson's friend,

Nina Prince, whom Lance had feigned interest in to lure Carson out of hiding. He even had a sick plan to poison Nina. There was evidence that he arranged for explosives to decimate Carson's research lab in Boston and that he called for the death of Rhoda Ellery, his own aunt and an ex-CIA agent who helped Carson flee her family. Everything was outlined in complete details within the files.

Page after page, even secret recordings, were laid out in graphic detail.

Cody huddled over the documents spread out on the square coffee table. "This is amazing but wasn't Lance's case dismissed?"

"Yes, the DA moved to dismiss the case, but if we can find another crime, within this documentation and get it to the right district attorney or even a federal prosecutor then we may have a chance of bringing Lance to justice." Hope rose in her voice, then reality crashed the party. "Finding someone willing to touch this could be difficult."

Cody crossed his arms. "Lance has made himself too powerful to cross and since the previous DA dropped the case, will anyone else want to chance this?"

"I don't know, but there's no statute of limitations on murder or attempted murder." Lila leaned forward. "Jack wanted me to find this file. He told me they killed him because of it and that I was in danger."

Cody hiked a brow. "Did he say who wanted him dead?"

"No. He wasn't in good shape, and after asking me to tell his family he loved them, he only had energy enough to warn me and tell me where to find these files."

"Based on what's happened the last few days, I'd say someone is awful worried you know something or have those files." Cody pointed to the table. "Don't you think it's too much of a coincidence that you happened to work for a man who was in possession of files that are damning to the one man hell-bent on hurting you?"

"Absolutely." Lila stood. "Hilary Foster and Walt Talcott are senior partners at HTP. They've asked me over and over again about what Jack said to me. I didn't tell them anything, of course."

Cody sipped his coffee, then set the mug on the table. "What does HTP have to do with Lance?"

"Those files represent the case HTP handled for Lance. Most of the attorneys are now gone, I think." Lila rubbed the bridge of her nose. "The Alliance knew about this before I accepted the job, but we thought there were still some partners with allegiance to Lance. So far, I don't have any evidence of that."

"I remember hearing about that," Cody said. "The question is who found out Jack had those files."

Lila shrugged. "The easy answer is Lance. But there's also the possibility that someone, namely someone at HTP, discovered Jack had the files and didn't want him to have a chance to disclose the information."

Silence hung as they were caught up in their thoughts.

Then Cody's cell buzzed. He glanced at the screen. "Our team is on the ground and should be here in less than an hour. I suggest we review these files. Maybe we'll gain some clarity."

Lila picked up the first document in the folder and studied the contents, handing off each paper to Cody after she finished. Nearing the end, she stopped. A note scribbled by Jack had been scrawled on a file. She recognized his slanted handwriting.

The note read. *Find Garvin Jennings.*

"Look at this." Lila passed the paper to Cody.

"Who's Garvin Jennings?"

"I'm not sure, but the name sounds familiar." Lila rose and paced the length of the room. "We have to find this guy."

Chapter 18

Cody entered the name in a search box. Seconds later, he said, "Five people come up with the name Garvin Jennings. Two with ties to Texas."

They quickly eliminated a Jennings in Iowa who died in 1991, a teenager in Georgia, and one in the military who'd been killed in action six years earlier.

Lila leaned back in her chair. "I don't see anything on these surface searches."

Turning to the dark web to cloak their presence, Cody and Lila ran searches for Garvin Jennings. Most people had a few hits on their name. Since they had no idea where in the world to look for the two Jennings, they started local.

"Found them. I've got one Jennings in St. Paul, Minnesota and the other in Toval, Texas, a small town on the outskirts of Dallas," Cody said.

Lila tapped her keyboard and second later said, "No social media presence, but if they are older men it's not a shock."

"According to the Algee town newspaper, Garvin Jennings won second place with his apple pie at their county fair last year. Algee is fifteen miles from Toval. Here's a photo of the winner with his prize-winning pie." Jennings was of medium height with a full head of white hair. Cody estimated his age to be late sixties or early seventies. He turned his laptop, so she could view the screen. "Do you recognize him?"

She stared at the photo then shook her head. "I've got a phone number for the other Garvin."

Cody didn't make a habit of rooting around on the dark web, but he had to admit the cloak of anonymity gave him relief. "We can make the call in the morning. I think that's all we can do tonight."

She nodded and stretched her arms. "I never asked about your family. How's your mom and Holden?"

"The same. Mom has diabetes now and refuses to take care of herself. There aren't as many men hanging around, so she bugs me for money." Cody shrugged. "Guess some things will never change. Holden is back after a dishonorable discharge from the Army. He has a son and an on-again-off-again girlfriend. He hasn't changed much either."

They were quiet for a few minutes then he said, "How do you like corporate law?"

She logged off her computer. "I'm pretty good at it."

"Being good and enjoying something are two different things."

"True. I enjoy corporate law. How do you like your job at Veridian?" She sipped her coffee and made a face—it had probably gone cold.

"I'm not sure if Veridian is a good long-term fit for me." Cody straightened in his seat. He'd discussed his work at Veridian with everyone else in the Alliance. Reid had heard rumblings that Lance was interested in buying the company. Lance's connection to Veridian had been established with his appearance at the benefit, but how deep did it go? Cody hoped his new position would provide the intel they needed.

~

LESS THAN THIRTY MINUTES LATER, Cody had hugged every Alliance member. Having them all here was more heartwarming than he'd anticipated. These people were his friends and due to his own stupidity, he hadn't seen several of them in over a year.

"I'm so glad you both got out of that lake," Holly's light-brown hair lay in a mass of curls around her pretty face. Her position as a child psychologist in the foster care division had brought her into Lila's life, and by default into his. Now that Holly was married to Reid, she had permanently become one of them.

"How are you?" Holly wrapped an arm around Lila.

"I have a slight headache and few body aches. It could have been a lot worse, but thanks to Cody, I'm here."

Lila met his gaze and Cody's heart seized. He hadn't wanted to lose his cool but maybe they'd finally turned a corner. *Maybe.* In his mind, he remembered how the curve of her body fit against him. But those days were long gone.

Marissa Tanner approached. "You're hurt." She touched his bandaged arm.

"I'm fine. Just a cut." Cody smiled at her.

"Do either of you want me to check you over?" Justin asked.

Dr. Justin Tanner was a trauma surgeon and Army Reserve physician. Prior to his marriage to Marissa, they became embroiled in The Order when Marissa's previous fiancé attempted to blackmail Vivian Sinclair, the Grand Commander at the time. After Marissa's fiancé was murdered, the couple were thrown into a battle with Vivian, who believed they had confidential intelligence about The Order.

Lila shook her head. "No, I'll be okay. The doctor at the hospital said I only had a slight concussion."

"If you aren't feeling better in a day or so let me know. Same goes for you, Cody."

"I'm glad you were there, Cody." Holly turned to Lila. "It's normal to feel shaken. We're all here if you need to talk."

"I know, thanks." Lila ambled into the kitchen. "We have sandwiches, fruit, and brownies for anyone who is hungry." She carried a tray of food into the living room, placed it on the table, and sat on the sofa between Holly and Marissa. "We have coffee and soft drinks, too."

Reid poured a cup of coffee, then stood in front as everyone gathered in the living room. "I know I speak for everyone when I say I'm relieved both Lila and Cody are okay." He faced Lila. "Why don't you tell us what's been happening, starting with finding the law partner."

Cody strolled to the back of the room, leaned against the wall, and crossed his arms.

Lila folded her hands on her lap. She met his gaze as an invisible connection flowed between them. Inhaling, she began the story and ended by telling them how she'd found Jack's files.

She stood, reached into a canvas bag, and retrieved several file folders. "These are copies of the documents Jack asked me to find. The original is locked in a storage facility and a copy is in the safe at my house." She handed each Alliance member a copy. "In these files are evidence and proof of the kidnapping and near-poisoning of Nina Prince, evidence that Lance ordered the murder of Rhoda Ellery, and conclusive information that he arranged for Carson's lab to be destroyed."

"Aunt Rhoda," Carson whispered.

Adam wrapped his arms around Carson. "We're going to get him," he muttered.

Cody had met Aunt Rhoda a few times. Rhoda Ellery had been Carson's mentor. In reality, the retired CIA operative, turned college professor, became more like her mother. The woman helped Carson change her name and escape her family. Carson was devastated when Lance's men killed her.

Cody cleared his throat. "Don't you think these files are a bit of an improbable coincidence seeing as the attorney Lila worked with, who seemingly had no connection to Lance's case, was in possession of files that could incriminate him? Why does this smell of a setup?"

Lila jumped up, plucking a carrot from the veggie tray. "I just remembered. Two weeks prior to his death, Jack had a meeting with a mystery person. I remember that day clearly because he canceled an important client meeting, claiming he had a serious personal issue to handle. Although foregoing a meeting was unlike him, I didn't think much of it until now."

"Maybe he did have a personal meeting," Holly shifted her gaze from Cody to Lila. "Perhaps a teacher conference for one of his kids, a doctor's appointment, counseling session with his wife. Maybe they were closing on a new house. The possibilities are endless."

"You're right. Except he always told his assistant where he was going. *And* Steve Dorman burst into my office that afternoon demanding to know where Jack had gone. Although Steve was Jack's counterpart in the corporate division, he never had cause to speak much to me, but that day stood out." Lila pointed with the uneaten carrot. "Steve was nervous, and I recall him stalking out my office saying he hoped Jack wasn't doing something stupid."

"We did background checks on everyone at HTP, but let's do another in-depth on Steve Dorman," Reid said.

"I met Dorman at the Veridian party," Cody added. "He was schmoozing with the Veridian bigwigs." Cody made eye contact with Reid and Adam. He hadn't told Lila about his own undercover status. "Reid? Adam?"

Lila cocked her head. "What's going on? Cody?"

Adam stood. "We have strong suspicions that Lance is trying to acquire Veridian. Cody is undercover at Veridian in hopes of gaining more intel on what Lance's plans could be."

"Have you made any progress at Veridian?" Holly asked.

Cody picked up a bottle of water and took a sip. "I'm on what they call the DDI team. The Deep Dive Initiative is one of the most secured and top-secret ventures within Veridian. A woman on the team put together a pretty good dossier on me and the other new recruit, Paul. I believe my cover is safe. If she knows of my connection to the Sinclair family, she didn't divulge it. I suspect they are doing some illegal surveillance. I'll know more next week and will report back."

Lila's eyes widened. "I'm one of Veridian's attorneys. I've been in meetings about Veridian acquiring other companies but at no time have they discussed *they* were being pursued." She paced the length of the room. "As their attorney, I have a duty to protect the company. Now that I have knowledge that Cody, one of their employees, may be smuggling out secrets, what am I supposed to do? I could get disbarred."

Reid nodded. "This is why we didn't want you to know. But now that both your lives have been threatened, we don't want either of you to be in the dark."

"I can't worry about my career." Lila ended her trek through the room next to Cody. "I'll always have a place in my father's company. If Veridian is as powerful as you say, and Lance gets his claws on that technology, he will be unstoppable. It's time to fight fire with fire."

Cody nodded. "I agree." As his gaze met Lila's, his heart lurched. He'd screwed up before, but he'd do anything to keep her from being hurt again. As images bombarded him of a teenaged Lila being tossed into a van, he clenched his jaw. Never again. He purged the image, knowing full well it was never far from mind. "Before we continue, I want to apologize for throwing a fissure into our group." He exhaled. "Lila and I talked, and we've decided to put our past behind us for the sake of this mission."

"I'm sorry, too." Lila steeled her back. "We never should have put this team in the middle. Our personal troubles belong on the backburner."

"Thanks, guys." Reid smiled. "Lila, review what you know about Lance's case and HTP's role, please."

"The attorney of record for Lance was his personal counselor, Archie Williams. We know Lance's legal team was led by a former HTP attorney, also Archie Williams, who died of a heart attack three years ago. Most of the other attorneys on his defense team, at least those known to the public, are either retired or dead, but there are others including those in the Justice Department who helped grease the wheels to keep any charges from materializing. Maybe the person Jack met with gave him the files, hoping he'd bring them to light or he consulted this person for more information. Although I can't prove it, I'm certain Jack wasn't corrupt. I believe he found out who at HTP was helping Lance and that got him killed."

"Seems plausible," Justin said.

"If you'll flip to the last page, you'll see a handwritten note."

Paper rustled as everyone turned pages.

"Who is this Garvin Jennings person?" Marissa asked.

"Lila and I did some research on Garvin Jennings," Cody said. "We believe we've located him right here in Texas, on the outskirts of Dallas." Cody explained how they found Jennings. "We need to talk to him." He glanced out the rear patio door, before turning back to the group.

Adam exhaled and leaned forward. "I'm not comfortable going in blind. We don't know anything about Jennings. News regarding a baking award isn't enough."

"I agree," Reid said. "We can't take unnecessary risks."

Lila's gaze shifted from Reid to Cody. "If Jennings is the person Jack met with, I can't believe he would tell me to find him only for it to be a trap. I believe we have the evidence that the state and Feds failed to use."

"Adam, is there any way you can get more information about Jennings?" Holly asked.

"I'll see what I can find. I'm looking forward to delving into this file." He tapped the folder.

Marissa scooted forward on the sofa and eyed Lila. "I don't mean to be a wet blanket, but do we know this evidence is solid?"

"I believe it is, but everyone needs to weed through the documents. Authenticated transcripts are included showing Lance told someone to plant the bombs in Carson's lab and also gave the go-ahead to abduct Carson's friend."

"My sister will learn she can't run from me. I am the Grand Commander and she will obey," Carson read the passage then sucked in a breath. "He's so evil."

Lila reclaimed her spot on the sofa. "There's also the curious reaction to Jack's death from some of the HTP partners." She explained Mr. Talcott's repeated warnings to keep her mouth shut, and Hilary offering her legal services. Lila even described the photo of Lance in Steve Dorman's office.

"How was it when you saw Lance at the benefit?" Holly asked.

"Shocking, like a gut punch," Lila said.

"I want Lance to pay for what he did." Carson massaged her temples as if warding off a headache. "He killed the woman who was more like mother to me than my own. He came within seconds of killing my friend, and he blew up my lab. Aunt Vivian almost killed Marissa and Justin; Reid, and everyone else was threatened by Ivan, and now Lance. His wife just had a son. I have no doubt Lance will pass on the principles of The Order to his son. We have to stop this pattern of evil. Please be careful everyone."

Cody pushed off the wall. "I agree with Lila—it's time to put our plan, Operation Chaos, into action. We need to put pressure on Lance and every member of The Order we can find. Expose them and watch them squirm."

Chapter 19

As night fell, the men checked the outside integrity of the house again while the women drifted together in one of the bedrooms.

Marissa sighed as she ended a call to her mother. "I miss Isabella, but my parents love having her under their roof." She swiped her phone for the latest photo of her two-year-old. Everyone gathered around the photo of the beaming toddler sitting on Justin's lap. Lila couldn't help but smile at the beautiful child who had Marissa's green eyes and Justin's light-brown hair.

The women discussed their jobs, married life, and weddings for the next several minutes. Lila listened but had no frame of reference. Entering that stage of life didn't seem in the cards for her.

Carson nudged Lila. "I saw the way Cody looked at you. Have you guys had a chance to talk?"

Lila sat on the floor and leaned against the bed "Not really. He tried. I thanked him for getting me out of the lake. I wasn't ready to talk. It was a humiliating time."

"He's definitely grown from a boy into man." Marissa grinned.

"It's obvious he still loves you, but how do you feel about him?" Holly plopped on the floor beside her.

Was it obvious? "Maybe we can be friends, but nothing more than that." Lila changed the subject to Carson and Adam's upcoming wedding. Thankful the women eased back into talk of dresses and cake flavors.

Minutes later, they quieted when a knock interrupted their conversation. Lila unfolded herself from the floor and opened the door. Her heart hitched when she faced Cody.

"Thought you may want these for tonight." He handed her two nightlights, one in the shape of star and the other resembling a cat.

Lila's mouth dropped opened as she stared at the nightlights then shifted her gaze to Cody. "Thanks."

He nodded and disappeared around the corner.

Lila shut the door and turned.

"Aww," her friends said in unison.

Marissa had a hand on her heart. A sappy grin splayed across Carson's face, and Holly nodded in approval.

"Shut up." But Lila couldn't stop a tiny grin from erupting. She hoped her friends didn't see that her heart had opened for Cody—just a little.

LILA SAT UP IN BED, grimacing as the expected soreness lit into her. After massaging her shoulders and rolling her neck, she climbed out of bed. She'd also expected nightmares to challenge her sleep, but thanks to exhaustion she'd slept without any terrifying intrusions.

After a quick shower and change, she ambled into the kitchen, she found Cody and Adam huddled over their laptops, coffee cups in hand.

"You look more rested this morning," Adam said.

"I am."

Cody glanced up. "Morning. Coffee is ready. I went out earlier and bought bagels and muffins. Help yourself."

"Thanks." She crossed the kitchen and poured a cup but with a shaky stomach she refrained from taking anything to eat. Seconds later, voices filled the kitchen as everyone else filed into the room.

With plates full, they gathered around the kitchen table with some sitting at the nearby island.

Adam placed his coffee mug on the table. "Cody and I did some digging into the Garvin Jennings here in Texas. Turns out he is a retired attorney who worked for HTP."

Lila furrowed her brows. "I searched the files and never saw Jennings on our roster of attorneys, past or current."

"I can't explain that, but we searched the Texas bar database and there he was." Cody closed his laptop. "We couldn't find a phone number but we have an address." Cody folded his arms over his chest.

"I should be the one to talk to him. I'm an HTP attorney and perhaps that connection will facilitate conversation. And I think I should go alone," Lila said.

A chorus of disagreement hit her.

Reid held up his hand. "It's too dangerous for you to go in alone."

"I'll go with her." Cody stood, ambled to the counter, and plucked a blueberry muffin off the platter. "Too many people could spook him."

"Agreed. But give Adam and me another day to look into this guy. We want as much intel on him as we can find before we play this card."

"I don't want to miss work today, but I can leave this afternoon," Cody said.

"Lila, are you up for this? You suffered a concussion, and I don't want you pushing yourself." Justin eyed her from across the room.

"I'm sore but my head is good." Lila turned to Cody. "What about you?"

"I'm good."

TWO HOURS LATER, Cody placed his right hand on the biometric

screen and lifted his eye to align with the retinal scanner. His credentials verified; the thick door slid open. As soon as he stepped into the
hive, he winced as the knocking on his skull started. Every cell inside
him screamed something about this place wasn't right.

"Hey, if it isn't the DDI's own superhero," Sher said with a grin.

Cody wrinkled his forehead and ignored her. He wasn't in the
mood for snide comments.

"Green! Rick and Tally want to see you," Paul said with a smug
smile. "They're waiting in Rick's office."

Cody suppressed a groan as he trudged toward Rick's office.

"Come in." Rick waved him into a chair.

Tally sat in the other chair, her long legs stretched out in front of
her. She didn't look up and instead focused on the papers in her
hand.

"I trust you had an enjoyable time at the benefit." Rick painted on
a grin that screamed fake.

Warning alarms blared inside Cody. "Yes, it was a nice affair. I'm
glad to help with the charity. I'll return the tux this afternoon." Cody
waited for the niceties to end.

"Good. And no problem on the tux." Rick sat back in his chair.
"How's your arm?" He nodded to the bandage.

Rick didn't ask how he'd been injured. His question implied he
already knew. "Just a few stitches. I'll live." Rick was going to have to
work for whatever he wanted.

"Good."

Tally straightened. "So, you're a hero, I suppose."

Cody lost patience with the conversation. "Why did you want to
see me?"

"We know you saved that woman who went into the lake." Tally
rejected beating around the bush, as well.

"Yeah. So? Some asshole caused the accident. I was there. I
helped. What's that got to do with my job here?" Hot blood boiled
inside him. Had someone been following him, too?

"You are part of a highly specialized team. We don't want our members maiming themselves or worse." Rick folded both hands on top of his desk.

"I'm fine." Cody wiggled his fingers. "I have no problem using the keyboard." Cody scooted up. "Am I under surveillance? I don't recall that in any of my employment documents. Perhaps I should contact an attorney."

Tally faced him, her eyes as black as Moby's hair. "Don't fuck with us, Green. We're extremely powerful. We just happened to catch the accident on one of our satellite feeds. Your license plate scanned in and alerted us. The news media was at the scene, plus everyone posts pictures."

"Don't fuck with me either." Cody stood and shoved his hands in his pockets to keep from reaching across the desk and slamming them both against the wall. "What I do on my own time is my business. I don't give a damn what kind of intel you have access to. If you can't give me privacy, then I walk."

"We live in a connected world," Tally turned her attention to a stack of papers on the edge of Rick's desk.

Rick shrugged. "Relax, Green. We're on the same side." Rick unfolded his fingers. "Get back to the hive. We have a special group project going on today. I think you'll like it." He grinned and leaned back in his chair.

Fifteen minutes later, Sher stood in the center of the hive. "I'm co-leading the experiment today. Case studies are on your desks. Rick says be ready in thirty."

"Are you up for the challenge?" Paul said, opening his energy drink. "I know I am."

I hate that guy. Cody shot him a glare then continued to his desk. He couldn't fathom what today would bring, but something told him to pay attention.

Moby scooted in, patted Cody on the shoulder, and then disappeared behind his desk.

Their primary desks were separated from the hive and included privacy walls. However, the desks within the hive were all open, lending to their group activities. Cody hated it already.

"Everyone, we need intel on subject SY324. You have twenty minutes." Rick strolled into the hive and pointed to a countdown timer which appeared on a massive wall-mounted monitor.

The loud ticking created a visceral feel of a countdown to doom.

Cody booted up his computer and spent five minutes studying his first case study. His fingers flew over the keyboard. As he collected data, he dumped the info into files. SY324 lived in Oklahoma City. He was forty-seven years old, married twenty years, with two children. Cody's pulse kicked up and perspiration beads dotted the back of his neck. Gathering information on people didn't sit right with him, but he considered that maybe the subject consented to this invasion of privacy or better yet, this was a completely fabricated person created for the purposes of testing Veridian systems.

When the timer beeped, Cody had a complete picture of SY324 from the number of times he attended church, how much he gave in donations, and the last time he went out for dinner to the type of lightbulbs he used in his bathroom. Cody hit the Send button and his report appeared on the huge monitor, along with everyone else's.

"Pretty good," Moby mumbled, eyes glued to the screen.

Rick glanced over the documents. "Print out your reports. I'll collect them by the end of the day." He assigned twenty more test subjects, and over the course of the three hours, they collected page after page of intimate data. Rick glanced over the material and within seconds, he said, "TG808. Sher."

She cracked her knuckles and attacked her keyboard.

Everyone turned to the monitor to observe the action.

Cody had no idea what to expect. He hoped TG808 didn't exist.

"What's your target area?" Rick hopped up on the table, his feet dangling.

Sher reviewed the data on TG808. "Idiot has a smart home. Furnace is about to malfunction."

"Good choice," Rick nodded.

Sher and her small fingers flew over the keyboard as everyone observed the numbers on the jumbo monitor. The screen split into two sides. One side showed the data from the smart home, including room temperature, security alarm status, which lights were turned on, what appliances were in use, water usage, and more. The other side displayed the subject TG808, an Arizona man currently lying on the sofa in a modest looking home. Suddenly the monitor indicated the furnace had clicked on. The temperature rose from seventy-one degrees to seventy-six within minutes. They watched as the temperature continued to rise. When the heat reached eighty-one, the man stirred.

Cody shifted in his seat. What the hell did this simulation have to do with anything? Were they out to prove Veridian ruled? This kind of intrusion and manipulation of an apparent civilian disturbed him. There had to be a law against this.

Paul leaned forward in his seat, a smile plastered across his face.

The heat climbed to eighty-four degrees, and the man popped up. At first, he appeared disoriented then he swung his legs to the floor. He wiped a hand across his forehead, jumped up, and then approached the thermostat. Cody observed him crinkle his forehead as he adjusted the setting.

"Crank it," Rick said.

Grinning, Sher carried out the command.

The number climbed to eighty-seven degrees, and the man continued to make attempts to correct the system. At ten in the morning outdoor Phoenix temperatures neared ninety degrees heading for a high topping one hundred. The man had to be in extreme discomfort.

Sher increased the temperature until it reached ninety degrees. The man stripped off his shirt and threw the garment on the floor, frustration seeping in. When the thermostat wouldn't budge, he phoned a heating and cooling company. His conversation came through on audio. The man groaned when informed that they wouldn't be able to service the unit until the next day. "I'm burning up. The freaking heat is on and won't shut off!" He tried opening the windows, but Sher had them locked down. After watching the man make several attempts to open the windows, Sher released them. As soon as the man opened the windows, his security system detected a breach and the wail of alarms commenced.

Paul chuckled. "This is classic."

Cody stared at the group. Moby averted his eyes as the remainder of the group had wide grins plastered across their faces. Were they a bunch of teenagers playing pranks? This was a Fortune Five Hundred company, and they were paying them big bucks to screw around with people.

After observing the man dance around, open windows, and turn on fans, Rick told Sher to back off. They witnessed the temperature gauge fall and the air conditioner kick on. The man huffed out a sigh.

"Okay, good work everyone. The next case study has been emailed to you. We have a huge test coming up."

Cody watched Rick saunter back into his office. Seconds later, he rose and stalked down the hall, stopping in front of Rick's closed office door. He inhaled and knocked on the door.

"Yep?" Rick opened the door.

Cody didn't wait for a further invitation. "Thank you for the opportunity, but I need to move on."

Rick closed the door and motioned for Cody to take a seat. "So, you got spooked by our little test."

He characterized Cody's decision to quit as if he were a weak-minded. Rick's attitude fueled Cody's anger, but he pushed the emotion away, not wanting to give Rick an ounce of ammunition. "I've been thinking of moving on for some time. I'm not sure Dallas is the place for me."

Rick sighed. "I'm sorry to hear that our city doesn't live up to your satisfaction."

"In light of the confidential nature of this unit, I will leave immediately." Cody scooted out of his chair. If they knew anything about him, they would expect him to bristle at the nature of this job. He couldn't risk not playing along.

"Ah, just a minute." Rick picked up his cell phone and appeared to text someone. Seconds later, the door opened and in walked Tally. Sighing, she took the chair next to him.

"There's always one who feels like they have a superior moral code." She smirked.

"You have a problem, Cody. I can't let you quit." With a set jaw, Rick busied himself cuffing the sleeves of his blue dress shirt with precision folds.

"What do you mean, you can't let me quit? This isn't North Korea. I have the free will to determine if I want to continue to work for this company and live in this city." Cody gambled on the fact that they'd believe he could expose their dirty deeds.

"And this isn't communist China either, but when you were drafted into our team, we had high expectations of you. Meaning, we decided your skills are advantageous to the goals of this unit." Rick glanced at Tally as if for support.

Cody sat straighter in his chair. The longer he stayed the more uncomfortable he became.

Tally stood and circled Rick's desk. She leaned over his computer and tapped on the keyboard. "I think I may have something that will change your mind." She perched on the desk and flipped the monitor around.

Cody's mouth went dry as the screen came to life. Footage of Lila and another woman sitting at a café displayed before him. He leaned forward. "Where did you get this?"

Tally shrugged. "This was recorded yesterday. Seems your friend, Lila Caldwell, enjoys Cobb salad for lunch."

"As you've seen, Veridian has the power to inject control in a subject's life. Lila is an up-and-coming attorney with a bright future. She even serves as outside counsel for Veridian, and we have strict rules about who works for us."

Cody continued to stare at Lila on the screen.

"I wonder what she'd think if the state of Texas suddenly revoked her law license?" Rick crossed his arms. "Or maybe a tragic accident? She works late. Perhaps she meets a shady character in her parking garage. I'm seeing a very violent man. Poor Lila won't have a chance."

"In a matter of minutes, I can dive into the dark web and come away with an assassin willing to take a quick job for a few bucks."

Tally met his gaze, then found the state of her nails required her full attention. "The bottom line is there are any number of scenarios in our arsenal. Of course, it's all up to you. All you have to do is remain in your job, continue to draw that handsome salary, and kept your damn mouth shut."

Cody jumped out of his chair. He balled his fists, the urge to pound Rick's face rising to a boiling point.

Rick leaned back in his chair. "The ball is in your court, Cody. See this *is* a free country and you have the option to walk away. The only problem is your friend, Lila may not fare as well."

He employed the last drops of willpower to remain still. "I'll play it your way."

Smiling, Rick nodded. "Excellent move." He jumped up and slapped him on the back as if they were old friends.

Rick and Tally can believe they have me by the balls, but they just made a new enemy. Cody wouldn't stand by and let Lila be threatened and neither would the Alliance. These kinds of strong-arm tactics would appeal to Lance. Now that he'd entered this deadly game of chicken, whoever backed down, lost, and losing could mean the difference between life and death.

Chapter 20

Infant wails cut through the quiet of Lance's private quarters. Slamming down the latest security report, Lance rose and wandered down the hall. The cries grew louder as he approached the three-room suite for mother and baby. Bypassing Delphine's room, Lance entered through the nursery door. The bright room featured soft blue walls along with wispy clouds painted on the ceiling by a professional artist Lance had commissioned. Antique white furniture trimmed in gold surrounded a circular crib in the center of the room. When Lance employed a decorator for the nursery, his only demand had been to decorate the room as if the baby were a prince. Lance, Junior represented the future. His son was the prince of The Order.

"Delphine, are you asleep? I can hear the baby down the hall." Lance smirked as his wife unfolded herself from the sofa and shuffled toward the crib. "Where is the baby's nurse?"

"I gave her the morning off. I should be able to take care of my baby without a nurse hovering. Other women do it," she said in her thick French accent. She glared at him as she collected the fussy infant from the crib.

With his heart swelling, Lance gazed at his son, currently

balling his fists as he wailed. The baby's face reddened, and his forehead scrunched in consternation about a need which had gone unmet for far too long. A perfect nose, intense brown eyes, and a full head of dark hair, strong Sinclair features, ballooned Lance's pride.

"I employed a nurse as a convenience. Forgive me. I thought you'd want rest. Have you forgotten the baby counts on your body for his sustenance?" Lance stalked to the window and stared out at the rear grounds of his southern California estate. The sun sparkled off the blue waters of his enormous pool. The yard, shaded by dense vegetation on the outer perimeter, also served to hide the iron fence around the property. He turned as a new set of cries wailed in tandem with the baby. "What is the matter?"

Delphine sniffed as she sank into a beige leather rocking chair. Loosening her robe, she guided one of her breasts toward the open-mouthed baby. "I feel so icky. My hair is limp, and my skin has such a haunted appearance."

Lance stared at her, then smiled. "You are the best-looking new mother I've ever seen." He sat on a chair opposite her and marveled at the sight of his son feasting on Delphine's magnificent breast. He figured he might as well receive some pleasure since he'd be forced to keep her around for several more months. "You're beautiful," he said in a whispered voice.

She beamed, then settled back in the chair. A French lullaby floated from her mouth and filled the room. After fifteen minutes, the baby was satiated and had fallen asleep.

Ignoring her earlier whines, Lance pulled her up and the robe fell open. He wrapped his arms around her and the baby she held. She really didn't look too bad. Her sexy curves had gone from model thin to Marilyn Monroe bombshell. "Let's go back to your room."

Delphine smiled up at him, her eyes pooling with adoration. "We can't. Remember the doctor said we needed to wait."

He snuggled her neck as the baby continued to sleep. "Smart boy. Even our son approves. You've done your duty to him, now do your duty to me."

"Lance, darling, you've changed my dull mood. Just to see you still desire me makes me feel like my old self."

He lifted the baby from her arms and placed him back in the crib. "Then let's go. We won't tell the doctor." He took her hand and led her toward her room.

She resisted. "My body is still healing. The doctor said six weeks. We're already down to five. It won't be long." She sidled up to him. "There are other things we can do. I'd love to fall asleep in your arms."

He pulled off her robe, fondled her breasts then pulled hard on her nipple.

Delphine shrieked as milk trickled down her chest.

His blood churned with anger and desire. *How dare she tease me.* "I've got no time for your games." Leaning in close, he said, "Don't ever think you have the upper hand." He picked up the robe and tossed it at her as he exited the room.

Two hours later, Lance wiped his brow then replaced his sunglasses as he descended the stairs of his private plane. The arid Nevada heat pressed down on him like a heavy woolen blanket. Right now, though, he preferred the uncomfortable weather to Delphine toying with him.

Casper approached, the sun creating a halo effect around his white-blond hair. He escorted Lance to the waiting SUV.

"Is everyone here?" Lance slid into the back seat.

"Yes, sir." Casper rode shotgun while another guard drove. Twenty minutes later, Lance followed Casper through a back door of a square three-story building north of the Las Vegas Strip. The building contained no markings and anyone passing by might believe it was abandoned. A perfect spot for the day's activities.

Lance entered an observation room with a two-way mirror, masking his presence from those on the other side. Rather than sit, he stood gazing at the man strapped to a chair in the middle of a large warehouse-type room.

Peter Shaw stood back from the man with his arms folded.

Lance hit a button to connect with Shaw's earpiece. "You may begin."

Shaw nodded and sauntered up to the man. "Barry. Nice to see you again. Now, where was it we saw each other last?" Shaw stared up at the ceiling as if to ponder his question.

With dull brown eyes, the man glared at Shaw. "Peter, you know damn well you served under me in the Chicago office," Barry said as his loose jowls jiggled. He didn't struggle against the binds. Perhaps he understood he'd be quickly overpowered, and his fifty-seven-year-old bones wouldn't last.

"That's right. And you walked around like you lived on a cloud. Now here you are and I'm asking the questions." Shaw circled like a vulture preparing for the kill. "You aren't the pristine agent you portrayed yourself to be. I decided to follow in your footsteps and go work for people who pay handsomely for my talents. Who did *you* work for?"

Barry focused on some unseen point ahead of him.

"I'm usually a patient man, but today, not so much." He nodded to a guard standing in the corner.

The large man stalked forward and in one quick swoop, punched Barry so hard he fell over in the chair. The guard yanked him up as if picking up pillow.

Blood streamed from a cut on the side of Barry's face. "I have grandchildren," he screamed.

"If you want to continue to play family patriarch, I suggest you start talking, or I can unleash Zeus here and see if he can convince you."

Lance didn't know the name of the large man, but his impressive muscles might require a promotion to his personal security team. He made a mental note to speak with Shaw about the man, because no one got close to him without a thorough vetting.

Barry nodded and lowered his head. "I worked for Ivan Sinclair."

Shaw walked to the other side of the room, his designer shoes tapping across the concrete floor. He placed a chair off to the side of Barry and sat, crossing his legs. "In what capacity did you work for Ivan?"

"I was his eyes and ears at the FBI. I alerted Ivan to possible inquiries into him, his close associates or his businesses while diverting attention away from some of Mr. Sinclair's pursuits that the FBI, or any legal entity, would find questionable." Barry's monotone voice filled the room.

Shaw remained quiet for a few seconds. "Your allegiance was to Ivan Sinclair and not the United States Government. Do I have that clear?"

"Same as you."

Lance observed a slight tensing in Shaw's body before he relaxed again. "How close were you to Mr. Sinclair?"

Lance crossed his arms.

"I met with him at least every few weeks, sometimes more. He consulted me on various legal and professional issues."

"What about financial?"

"Of course."

"Are you a member of The Order?"

Barry squirmed in the chair and shot a worried glance at Zeus. "In order to have that kind of access to Ivan..." He blew out a breath. "Yes, I'm a member of The Order."

"Ordo Ortus, Brother." Shaw held his gaze and allowed his words to linger before he spoke again. "You are aware that the current Grand Commander is Lance Sinclair?"

"Yes."

"Are you also aware that Mr. Sinclair is the CEO and Board president of Skies International and all its umbrella companies?"

"Yes, that's common knowledge."

"Then you'll agree that as CEO, Mr. Sinclair should be aware of important details about the business."

"Absolutely."

"I'm sure you'll agree that as Grand Commander, Mr. Sinclair should be privy to any and all confidential information related to The Order."

Barry swallowed hard. "Yes."

Shaw rose and circled Barry. "It's come to our attention that Russell Sinclair was in possession of a piece of land containing a valuable natural resource. Mr. Sinclair's grandfather would want Lance to take control of this property. We believe Ivan knew the location. As his right -hand man who, by your own words, had a close relationship with him, we believe you know the location of this valuable land."

Barry shook his head. "I don't know."

Shaw leaned in close to Barry. "Yes, you do."

"Peter, I would tell you, but I just don't know." Barry's eyes were huge orbs, made even larger when Zeus took a step toward him.

Shaw removed his suit jacket and with gentle care draped it over the back of his chair. He shook his head as his rolled up the cuffs of his shirt.

Barry squirmed as he shifted his gaze from Shaw to Zeus.

Ambling up to Barry, Shaw stared down at the man. Then in one motion he pulled Barry up by his collar. "My patience is on its last leg, Barry. You don't want to know what I'm capable of when I lose my calm." He slammed the man back into the chair. "Now, let's start over. Where is the property, which belongs to Lance Sinclair as the rightful heir?"

"I - I don't know." Perspiration coursed the length of the captive's face.

Shaw stalked to a workbench in the corner. He picked up a knife and sauntered toward Barry. "For a man in the intelligence business, you don't know much." Shaw stepped aside as the huge man deposited a wooden crate in front of Barry.

In a quick move, Zeus grabbed Barry's hands and bound them with duct tape to the crate.

Barry's eyes were huge, and his breathing came in short gasps.

Shaw narrowed his eyes, then swooped in and chopped off the index finger of Barry's left hand.

The man screams reverberated off the concrete walls.

"As an Order member you know how penance works. Now that I have your attention, where is the location?" Shaw bent over him.

Barry's head hung to the side as blood spurted from what was left of his finger. "I don't know."

In one exaggerated action, Shaw dropped the knife and slid a gun from his holster. He trained it on Barry. "Are you ready to answer my question? Where is the property that rightfully belongs to Lance?" He pushed the butt of the gun against Barry's temple.

Lance didn't think Barry's eyes could get any wider. Without taking his gaze off the scene in front of him, Lance signaled Casper for a bottle of his approved water. Seconds later, Casper handed him the bottle wrapped in a thin gold cloth. Lance took a sip and waited.

"I'm not going to ask again." Shaw's voice was barely a whisper.

Barry hesitated.

The sound of the gunshot boomed throughout the room. Even the mirror rattled.

Barry screamed as blood poured from the gunshot wound in his leg. "All right! No more!" He panted and grimaced. "I don't know the location. That's a fact." He inhaled. "But all I know is there is an emerald mine, worth billions. I briefly saw a note, written by Ivan or someone close to Ivan. I'm not sure which. The note said the girl is the key."

Shaw paced. "What girl and why is she the key?"

"The girl has some kind of document or item that will lead to the location."

"Again, I ask, what girl?" Shaw's voice was loud and demanding.

Barry lowered his head and closed his eyes. "The young girl with the tattoo."

Lance set the water on the ledge and inhaled. So, Lila was once again at the center of the puzzle. Thinking back to the scene at the Colorado mine several years ago, Lance recalled Lila's shock as he'd killed her mother. And moments later, Ivan's smug expression when he'd assumed his brief role as Grand Commander and had gained accessed to the millions of dollars in treasures unlocked in that mine.

If what Barry said was true, this emerald mine would dwarf the payout from Russell's last hidden treasure.

Lila is the key.

Lance crossed his arms. Now, he had yet another reason to deal with her. He would not allow this little bitch to destroy his world.

The intercom crackled with Shaw's voice. "Shall I proceed?"

He stared at the man who couldn't see him. "Yes." Lance turned to Casper. "Is my suite ready?" He checked his watch. Katarina's flight should have landed. Many decisions lay ahead but for now he needed a little playtime.

"Yes, sir. Your suite is ready, and Ms. Yurkov's plane landed fifteen minutes ago," Casper said.

"Good. Let's go." He tossed one more look at Barry, who stared at Shaw with hope. *Too bad.* As Lance stepped out the back door, he didn't look back when the sound of the gunshot followed.

Chapter 21

The firm had given everyone the option of taking time off before Jack's funeral the following afternoon, but Lila took advantage of the quiet to get some work done. Despite her fear someone in the firm was on Lance's payroll and could possibly be involved in Jack's murder, she still needed to put forth her best effort. Several other attorneys must have had the same thought because the offices weren't as deserted as she'd hoped.

At ten that morning, she glanced up when a knock sounded on her door and Gia poked her head in. "I need caffeine. Want to go downstairs?"

Lila pushed back her chair and logged off her computer. "Absolutely." She grimaced as she stood.

Gia stopped. "What happened?"

Lila gave her a brief explanation of her accident, ending with her stint in the ER.

"I can't imagine how much pain you're in. Why did you even bother coming in this morning?" Gia held the door open and followed her down the hall.

"Because I need to get this brief finished for Steve by tomorrow. Regardless of how I might look, I feel much better," Lila said.

Fifteen minutes later, they were seated at one of the tables overlooking the outdoor courtyard.

"You mind if I catch a ride with you to the funeral tomorrow? I still need to work through all the insurance hurdles." Lila stirred her chamomile tea, inhaling the fruity aroma.

"Sure. Are you going to be okay with the press there?"

Lila shrugged. "The focus should be on Jack as a man, not his manner of death."

Gia leaned in. "This morning I went to talk to Hilary about a case. Before I could enter her office, I overheard her in an intense conversation about you."

Lila swallowed. "What do you mean?"

Gia sipped her latte then set the drink back on the black marble table. "I assumed she was talking to someone at Dallas PD. She was yelling about your name being leaked to the media."

Now that Lila had more evidence pointing to a rogue element within HTP, everyone's motives were suspect. Hilary's sudden interest in her and her desire to represent her during the police interview took on new meaning. Mr. Talcott's repeated warnings not to talk to the media also concerned her. Yet, these activities could be out of concern for the well-being of the firm. Time would tell.

"You know, Hilary. She's the picture of intensity." Lila shrugged. She couldn't tell Gia her fear that someone within HTP could be a murderer.

WHEN CODY PICKED HER UP, Lila noted his grim expression. "Bad day?"

He pulled away from the building. "That's an understatement," he said, a bitter tone highlighted his statement. "We'll talk later." He kept his gaze glued ahead.

"Would you mind driving me somewhere?"

"I'm afraid to ask what you have in mind."

Forty minutes later, Cody pulled up to the curb of an expansive two-story European style house. "So, this is how a partner at a fancy law firm lives."

Lila stared at the house. "It's sad. Jack worked hard to get where he was. I've met his family, they're good people." She expelled a loud sigh. "I don't know what to say, but I promised Jack." She opened the SUV's door.

"You sure you don't want me to come with you?"

"No, I need to do this myself."

Lila rushed up the brick-inlayed driveway and climbed the stairs to the front door. Seconds later, an older woman with short gray hair swung open the door. "May I help you?"

After introducing herself, Lila discovered the older woman was Cheryl Struthers's mother. The woman showed Lila to a sunroom situated off the enormous kitchen and dining area.

"Lila, thank you for coming. Please call me Cheryl." Jack's widow had shoulder-length brown hair held back by a white headband. Tiny lines creased her face and her blue eyes held a tinge of red. Grief had a way of presenting itself and Lila found the pain of mourning had rooted into Cheryl's body.

"I'm so sorry for your loss. I thought the world of Jack." Lila settled on the beige sofa.

"The detectives told me you tried to save him. Thank you."

"I wish I could have done more."

Cheryl folded her shaky hands and placed them in her lap. "Jack was impressed with you. Although I know what a shock it must have been to find him, I'm sure he was comforted by the fact you were the last person he spoke to."

Lila cleared her throat. "Jack was thinking about his family until his last breath. He asked me to let you know how much he loved you and your children." She shifted, her gaze landing on the multitude of family pictures adorning the room. They had two teenaged boys who were obviously active in sports judging by all their football, track, and soccer photos. A lump formed in her throat as she viewed a photo of the foursome at the beach all dressed in white shirts and khaki shorts, smiling against a bright sun, a white sand beach, and sparkling azure water.

Cheryl dabbed at her eyes with a crumbled tissue, then reached for Lila's hand. "That means so much to me." Her voice hitched.

"It's the least I can do. Is there anything you need?" Lila covered Cheryl's other hand. She couldn't imagine the hole ripped into this family and the pain Jack's absence caused.

Cheryl sniffed and shook her head. "You and a few others from the firm are the only ones who seem to care. Walt Talcott came by but only seemed interested in going through Jack's things. Can you believe he wanted access to the penthouse? He said he'd have a professional go through and clean the unit for us, but I think he was searching for something. I refused and then he had the nerve to get upset with me."

"How awful." Tiny hairs on the back of Lila's neck pricked to attention. "I'm so sorry. Jack taught me that our work was important, but we can't be effective attorneys if we ignore the people we love." Lila leaned forward. "Please take care of yourself and family. If there is anything I can do, please call." Lila gave Cheryl's hand a squeeze, then placed her card on the table. "I can show myself out."

THE NEXT AFTERNOON held a schizophrenic feel—one moment full sun bathed the Dallas skyline, then the next rolling gray clouds materialized. Lila compared the weather to the happy and sad emotions flowing through her as she sat in a pew at the midway point of the enormous church. Jack would be pleased that the three-thousand-seat church was at max capacity, but Lila could imagine him commenting about what a waste all those flowers were.

As Lila glanced around the church, she spotted what appeared to be the majority of HTP employees filling the seats. Even at such a somber occasion, the HTP hierarchy played a role, with four full rows of partners seated in front of the associates and staff. In addition, she saw judges, state and federal congressmen, a few senators, and dignitaries from around Texas and the country. The funeral was a who's who among the rich and powerful. But among those power players, Lila also spotted a few pro-bono clients she and Jack had worked with.

As Lila and Gia settled among the associates and support staff, her phone vibrated. She looked at the screen and her heart hitched when she viewed the text from Cody.

You okay?

She smiled. *All good. Thanks.*

He responded with a thumbs up emoticon. Then he texted: I'll be right behind you today. ABS.

Lila read the text again as her belly fluttered. *ABS* among Alliance members meant always be safe. She needed the sentiment this morning. Something about Jack's funeral had set her on edge. Maybe seeing Jack's wife and family made her anxious. And what about Garvin Jennings? Would he show up to Jack's funeral? She would have to be alert to anything.

The din of the crowd quieted as Jack's family filed in. Her posture rigid, Cheryl held on to her two teenage sons. An older couple followed with the somber expressions of parents who'd lived to see their child buried.

"This is heartbreaking," Gia whispered.

Unable to find the words to express her thoughts, Lila simply nodded.

Death was such a final and abrupt goodbye. She stared at Jack's closed casket and pictured what her mother's funeral would have looked like if she'd grown up in a normal family. As it was, April had no services, and Ivan's had been a private affair. Even as Ivan's grandniece Lila hadn't rated, not that she wanted to attend. Aside from Reid and Carson, the rest of the family was one commitment hearing away from the psych ward.

One after another of Jack's colleagues and various VIP members of the community took their turns eulogizing the lost attorney. As the attendees appeared engrossed in the speeches, Lila recognized the detectives sitting at the rear of the church. She knew they were scoping out the crowd for signs from the unknown guilty party.

Lila spotted Cody standing with other late comers in the back of the church. She knew Reid and Adam were there, but she had no idea where. Good agents would blend in.

Almost three hours later, the services had moved to the cemetery. Lila and Gia stood near the back as the final words were uttered over Jack's casket. When the service ended, most people lingered, many offering condolences to the Struthers family while others mingled. So far, Lila hadn't spotted anyone who resembled Garvin Jennings.

As Lila and Gia stood in line to greet Jack's family, she spotted Talcott, Hilary, and Steve in conversation. Steve glanced up and stared her way. He nodded and for the first time Lila noted his shaken expression.

Minutes later, Lila stood face-to-face with Cheryl Struthers. No words were exchanged as the two women hugged. When Lila stepped away, she spotted Hilary and Talcott staring at her.

They wouldn't have approved of her visit to Jack's widow. Lila hadn't been called aside, so she assumed they didn't know. Blowing out a breath, she emerged from the open funeral tent.

Gia squeezed her arm then slid on sunglasses. "I need to show face to a couple of partners. Bastards are taking roll of who attended and who didn't. Be right back." Gia sauntered off.

Lila scanned the crowd and witnessed several handshakes and huddled conversations. A woman of advanced age stood next to her. Despite gripping a cane, she stood erect. Her shiny white hair tumbled in tiny curls around her head. "Jack was a good man," she said in a low, even voice.

Lila glanced down at the woman who measured up to her shoulders. "You're right. How did you know Jack?"

"Oh, I don't. But I admired his..." Her eyes drifted away as her voice quieted. A few seconds passed then she shook her head. "I admired his commitment to doing what's right." The woman placed her hand on Lila's arm, pressing upon her with surprising strength. "I know who you are."

The din of conversations around her dulled as the interaction became personal. The woman's brown eyes bored into hers, holding her attention. "How do you know me? Who are you?" With proper interrogation skills shoved aside, Lila hurled out more than one question.

The tiny woman smiled and tapped her cane again. "Maybe you'll remember. Your memories lay behind the surface and within your reach." They were standing in a grassy area and the cane pounding with the earth made a dull thudding sound. In rhythmic fashion, the woman continued to smack her cane against the ground.

Lila's gaze locked on to the cane. The wooden stick had green-and-white strips almost resembling the barbershop logo in another color. *Thump. Thump.* Her thoughts tumbled, landing her in murky memories of a long ago. *Thump. Thump.* Her eyes followed the up-and-down movement of the cane, acting as if it were a portal, but to what? The past? Thoughts continued to swirl, and Lila sensed she'd fallen down the rabbit hole. *Thump.* Colors swirled. *Thump.* The cane narrowed as the tip sharpened. *Thump.* The colors of the cane merged. *Thump.* Silver. Or maybe steel. *Thump.* A needle, the syringe holding a pale solution. *Thump.* Lila struggled to grasp on to something. Memories danced a wild wicked tango as images flashed before her. Instead of a cane crashing to earth, Lila focused on a sinister needle inching closer. Her pulse raced, and she longed to scream but no sound emitted. What was happening? The world tilted. Then nothing.

Lila's vision cleared and what had once been blurred images were now in focus. She could count the blades of grass. Bits of nearby conversations became sharp. Breathing in and out gave her confirmation she was alive. Lila glanced to her side. She now stood alone.

Searching the crowd, she didn't spot the woman anywhere. Her head pulsated as if a woodpecker had gone to town on her skull. Her gaze landed on Cody.

He cocked his head then moved toward the parking lot.

Seconds later, her cell buzzed.

She glanced at the text from Cody. *"You looked spooked. Meet later."*

"Lila, you okay?" Gia said walking up to her.

"Umm, yeah. I think." She shoved the phone back into her purse. "Did you see that little old lady with the green-and-white cane?" Lila pivoted in an attempt to spot the woman.

"No, not now." Gia opened her purse and dug around in her bag.

"You saw her earlier?" Lila placed a hand on her temple.

"Of course. She stood right next to you." Gia pulled her car keys from her bag and stared at Lila. "Are you sure you're okay?"

"I don't know." Lila shook her head. Once again, she peered over the crowd, but the woman had disappeared.

Memories lay behind the surface and within her reach. Lila shivered. What did the woman know about her fleeting memories?

An hour later, Lila entered her office. Through text messages, Cody tried to talk her into going back to his house, but she had a report to finish. She needed this job. Her position as outside counsel to Veridian may provide them with intel they could use against Lance. Gia had a dinner with her boyfriend's family that evening and most of the HTP employees didn't return to the office after Jack's funeral creating a quiet hush over the offices.

As soon as she sank into her chair, she eyed the lone window. Muzzle flashes, the whizzing of bullets by her ear, and clouds of furniture cushion fluff raining down on her penetrated her thoughts. She jumped up and pulled the shades, her office darkened enough with the gray clouds that she flipped on both the overhead light and her desk lamp.

After she'd completed her brief, she texted Cody to pick her up in two hours before turning to a legal research question. Steve expected her findings in the morning. An hour ticked by before Lila shifted her gaze from the computer screen. Rolling her neck, she sipped water as images of the day again trickled in. The grief on Cheryl's face, the wide-eyed shock on the faces of Jack's sons burrowed into her memory. If only she could have saved him.

The headache which had begun earlier raged on. She stepped out of her office and into an empty hall, trekking to the kitchen to make a cup of tea. On her way back to her office, she spotted Steve leaning against the wall. "Steve!" she called, catching up to him.

"Lila." Steve's red-rimmed eyes greeted her. He stumbled, then righted himself. His blue striped tie hung askew, and half of his shirt was out of his pants.

"I was coming to speak with you." Steve slurred a few of his words.

Alcohol-infused breath hit her in the face. "Whoa." Lila took his arm and helped him down the hall and into her office chair. "How about some coffee?"

He shook his head. "No. I need to talk to you. Jack is dead. His kids don't have a father."

She'd never seen Steve in this condition. Lila shifted a few steps toward the door, her muscles tensed and ready to react. "It's a very sad situation." She placed the cup of tea on her desk.

"Jack was good to you, right?"

"Yes, he was a great mentor."

"Yeah, great mentor." He leaned to the side in the chair and stared at his shoes. Steve's hair was always impeccable, as if he'd just stepped out of a stylist's chair. Now, a strand of his brown hair hung limp covering part of his face, creating shadows over his dull eyes. "How was your relationship with Jack? Did he talk to you about things going on here?"

Lila glanced into the hall then sat in the visitor's chair adjacent to him. She had no idea where Steve was going with this. "We talked about trends in law all the time and often discussed HTP cases outside our practice area."

Steve shook his head. "No, no. Did he talk to you about...unethical stuff? Illegal things?"

Did Steve know about the hidden evidence? Her heart rate ramped up.

He continued without waiting for an answer. "Jack was a good guy. Smart. When he found out about certain things going on here, he was very angry. He was a real attorney—by the book." Sniffing, Steve picked at a thread on his gray pants. "I never thought I would be an attorney." He grinned. "I wanted to be a rock star. I know it's so cliché, but I could play the guitar. I thought I was good and was going get all the women." He glanced up at her. "Sorry."

Lila splayed her hands out. "No worries."

"Anyway, Jack was such a good guy. No political favors or underhanded lawyering." He scratched his forehead then twisted toward her. "I'm the reason he's dead. I killed him." Tears traced down his face.

"Steve, what do you mean?"

"I told him. I was supposed to keep the secret. I didn't pull the trigger, but he died because of me. They killed him."

Lila scooted her chair closer. "Who killed Jack?"

Steve straightened. "I like you, Lila. You're smart. You'll go far. I'm going to tell you something I should have told Jack." He grabbed her hands. "Don't trust anyone."

With her pulse racing, she remembered the same words Jack had said to her. "Why?"

He pulled his hands away and stood, balancing himself by leaning on her desk. Wiping away the tear, he stumbled toward the door. "Danger. Danger," he mumbled.

"Steve, did someone at the firm kill Jack? Who shouldn't I trust?" Lila placed a hand on his back, trying to steady him.

He leaned against the wall. "Stay away from this. Too much danger. They are too powerful."

"Let me help you get home." Lila walked him to the door.

He shook his head. "There's nothing left. I'm staying here. Sleep it off. Nothing like a night in the lion's den." He slowly walked out and turned the corner.

Chapter 22

When Lila climbed into his SUV, Cody zeroed in on her grim expression. He expected her to be upset with Jack's funeral hours earlier, but he suspected something more troubled her. "Anything you want to talk about?" He glanced at her as he pulled out of the building's parking lot.

"No. I'm wiped out." She turned her head and stared out at the urban scenery whipping by.

Cody peered at her before turning his attention back to the road. Something was wrong.

Five long minutes of silenced elapsed before she spoke. "Thanks for picking me up. You've been really...decent during all this."

Decent hadn't been the description he'd hoped for. He swallowed. *I want her, plain and simple.* The crushing reality of knowing he wouldn't get what he wanted mimicked a gut punch. She sat only inches from him, but he couldn't touch her. Even thoughts of cold showers and baseball couldn't squelch his desire. Gripping the steering wheel, he wanted to throw a punch out of frustration. How life had changed because of one mistake.

He shook away the thought, refocusing on an area where they were in sync. "Did you notice anything weird at the funeral?"

Lila shifted in her seat, then angled toward him. "This whole day has been very weird. Do you mind if we don't talk about it right now? I need to think." She turned her head toward the window again.

Lila usually wanted to take her time and process a problem before talking it out. Cody had always given her the space she needed. "Sure." He started singing the song, "Closing Time" by Semisonic. Whenever she'd asked him for time to think, Cody would sing any song he could think of with the word "time" in the lyrics.

She glanced at him and smiled. "Good one." Laughing, she said, "I'd forgotten about your annoying habit."

"What annoying habit? I'm over here minding my business, giving you time to think." Cody grinned.

"Scratch that—I forgot how much of an asshole you were."

She smiled again, and Cody wanted to switch to a new song, "Hallelujah."

"It's a genetic trait." Cody nodded.

"Admitting it is the first step."

They had slipped back into their unique brand of banter. Cody didn't want to do or say anything to shatter the moment. Dealing with Lila was like trying to lure a skittish doe near a human.

"Remember the talent show junior year?" Cody asked.

"I'll never understand why Darryl thought serenading Brittany would make her fall in love with him. Especially when he couldn't carry a note." Lila chuckled.

"By that night she sure knew who he was." Cody merged onto the highway taking them away from the city.

Her smile dissolved as she rubbed her temples. "Remember our last years of high school and first few years of college? Even though the constant threat from Lance and The Order existed, we didn't seem to let the threats take over our lives. Now, everything seems more...dire."

"I meant what I said—I will do whatever I can to keep you safe. We may not be together any longer, but that doesn't erase the fact I still care for you."

She pushed a strand of hair away from her face. "Ever since we reacquainted, I've been thrown off with Jack's death and the two attacks. I don't have to tell you I'm angry...about a lot of things. I appreciate what you've done for me but, I don't know..." She inhaled and stared out the window. "I can't shake the feeling something even more horrible is about to happen."

THE ALLIANCE MEMBERS assembled in the living room of the farmhouse with takeout dinners. Lila would have preferred dinner from her father's restaurant The Ranch, but she couldn't risk leading the wrong people anywhere close to her family.

"Holly is on a conference call. She'll be down soon," Reid picked up a glass of tea from the table. "We didn't see anyone at the funeral resembling the man in the newspaper," Reid said. "But with the number law enforcement in attendance, we didn't want to announce our presence."

Adam dug into the carton containing roasted vegetable gnocchi. "My contact confirmed what Lila and Cody revealed—Garvin Jennings lives about thirty miles from here. He's seventy-two years old, married to Sheila Jennings, a retired teacher, no children. Grew up in Missouri." Adam shrugged. "This is all basic information, maybe a little too basic."

"His data has been scrubbed," Cody said.

"Looks like it, which makes Jennings all the more important."

Lila picked up a bottle of water and sauntered to the patio door. She gazed out into the backyard with half her mind on the conversation surrounding her and the other half on the woman at the funeral. Something stirred inside her, sparking a memory.

"I say we pay Jennings a visit tomorrow." Cody placed a slice of prime rib on to his plate, groaning after he took a bite. "So good."

"Are you sure that's a good move? We still don't know much," Carson said.

"We can't continue to play it safe." Cody set down his fork. "I understand you're reasoning, Carson, but it's time we kick our proactive plans into high gear."

"The lack of information *is* a red flag," Reid said.

Adam scooted to the edge of his seat. "With Cody's help, we discovered Jennings was once barred in Texas, New York, and Missouri. Went to law school in Missouri and ended up working for a local law firm after graduation. Dunkirk and Associates."

Lila whipped up her head. "Hold on. Dunkirk and Associates?"

Adam glanced at the paper he had in his hand. "Yes, that's it."

"Steve clerked there." Her heart pounded. "He's been acting weird. One minute he's the same jovial Steve and the next he's...I don't know—dark and brooding. In fact, I found him drunk this evening. He asked me a lot of questions about Jack. Even going as far to ask me what I knew about issues inside the firm? He said he was the cause of Jack's death. When I questioned him further, he began muttering about danger."

"What background information do you have on Steve?" Reid asked.

"Nothing that rang any bells, but there's something going on with him." Lila sat on a chair in the corner and rubbed the area of her arm containing the tattoo.

"We have Steve linked to Jennings and now his curious statements tonight. Lila review your file on him again and let me know if anything stands out based on this new information." Reid set his plate on the table and wrapped his arm around Holly, who sat next to him.

"Again, we need to pay Jennings a visit because..." Cody's voice trailed off. "What's wrong, Lila?"

She hesitated then bit her lip. "Something happened during Jack's funeral. I don't even know how to explain it." She jumped up and rounded to the back of the couch. "An elderly lady at the cemetery commented on how good a person Jack was. Then she said she knew me and began tapping her cane." Lila crossed her arms. "The tapping was more like rhythmic thuds against the ground. As she tapped, images flashed in my mind. I think they were memories. You know how you wake up after a dream and can't quite grasp what your dream was about?"

Cody nodded.

"The images or memories were like fuzzy pictures flashing through my mind. I couldn't see anything, but I remembered being afraid. Then just as suddenly as she started tapping her cane, she stopped. The next thing I knew, the woman was gone and I was talking to Gia."

"Had you seen the woman before?" Carson asked.

"No. She was tiny." Lila placed her hand at shoulder level. "She came up to here, and she had a green-and-white striped cane." As her voice cracked, she heaved her shoulders up. "The stripes looked like they could have been made with colored duct tape or paint."

"Did she say how she knew you?" Marissa crossed the room and placed an arm around Lila.

Lila leaned into Marissa. "No, but I wasn't afraid of her. I'm more concerned about the memories. All these weird things that have happened don't appear to be connected yet if they weren't it would mean a hell of a coincidence."

"Almost sounds like she was trying hypnosis. Justin, is that even a real thing?" Carson asked.

"It is real and can be a good therapeutic tool. However, employing the techniques of hypnotherapy during a public event isn't the best way to put someone under. Holly could probably speak more on it," Justin said.

"I don't have a good feeling." Cody approached her.

"This is getting dangerous." Carson sat on the edge of the sofa.

"It's worse than you know." Cody explained the threats leveled against Lila if he didn't continue working for Veridian. "They have the technology to dig into people's lives." Cody met Lila's gaze.

"So, they know about me...and you? I mean the Veridian people know we're acquainted?" She watched Cody bristle at the word "acquainted" and immediately regretted the word choice. Although they'd never slept together, they had planned to in Hawaii, so they were more than acquaintances.

"Yes, they know." Cody replied. "Veridian has the means to find out almost anything."

"This is crazy. They can't *make* you work for them." Carson jumped up. "The threat sounds like something Lance would do."

Lila nodded. "Carson is right. Cody, if you want to quit, don't worry about me. I'm armed, and I know how to use my weapon."

"I won't take any chances with your life. You've already escaped two near-death accidents. Plus, we need the intel on Veridian." Cody swiped a hand through his hair.

"Cody, do you think they were responsible for Lila's accident?" Reid asked.

"The threat came after her accident but it's hard to tell. Rick and Tally showed the footage of me carrying Lila out of the water. Then Lila and her friend Gia at a café. Scary shit."

"Where did they get the footage?" Lila wrapped her arms around herself. "The spot I went into the water was in a remote area. Why would there be cameras there? What the hell is going on?"

"I believe they were following me, probably with a drone. They said my license plate was flagged in their satellite images." Cody sighed and placed his hands on his hips.

"Do you think the threat was a strong-arm tactic, or do you believe they could carry it out?" Reid leaned forward, his elbows resting on his legs.

Cody told them about the types of testing his project team had been conducting. "Yes, I absolutely believe they'd make good on their threats." He turned to Lila. "I won't let that happen. Which brings me to another idea. I have a friend and former grad school classmate, Angie Spurlin. She dabbled in hacking years ago and is brilliant. She works at Veridian and we can trust her. I'd like to bring her in to help gather intel."

"I can't consider this without talking to Yvonne and running a background check," Reid said.

Adam blew out a breath. "Regarding Jennings—we need to talk to him."

"Cody and I are the logical choices to go in. He knows Veridian and I know HTP," Lila said.

Cody nodded. "I agree."

LATER THAT NIGHT, Cody stared up at the ceiling, trying to envision the night sky on the other side of the roof. Every constellation ended with images of Lila. He tiptoed out of the room and into the kitchen, then stopped dead.

Lila stood in the darkened kitchen, wearing a T-shirt and shorts.

Cody sucked in a breath, frozen as he watched her. Shapely legs extended out of the gray shorts reminding Cody of how he used to marvel at her silky-smooth skin. Her brown hair was tousled and fell in waves down her back. Sexy didn't come close to a description. He wouldn't be surprised if he was drooling.

Lila turned and their gazes clashed.

His eyes swept over the gap between her shirt and shorts, exposing a small section of her belly. Frozen in the moment, Cody forced his feet in motion and stepped toward her. "Didn't know anyone was up."

"I guess you couldn't sleep either."

"Nope." He stopped a couple of feet from her.

"It's all starting again. There something to living in denial, but when the bubble bursts, it's a hard landing." Lila adjusted her shirt, covering the small peek of stomach he'd think about for days.

"If you're not up for talking to Jennings tomorrow everyone will understand," Cody said.

Lila shook her head. "No, I'm going. We'll both be armed, and we'll have back up." She huffed out a big sigh. "Jack was a good man. If for no other reason, I'd like to see this through for him."

"What about you?" Cody moved closer. "You deserve to live a life where you don't have to look over your shoulder."

"I hesitated on moving here. I didn't want to put my family in jeopardy but then I thought I could watch over them if I was close.

Time will tell if that was a good move." She shrugged. "A lot of people have been hurt and killed because of my biological family. I don't want anyone else to be hurt. Including you," she added facing him.

Cody's mouth went dry and he wasn't sure what to say. Instead he reached out and caressed her cheek. A current sparked under his hand, igniting sensory receptors along the way. He moved even closer and wrapped her in his arms.

For the moment, time stood still as he relished the feel of her body next to his. In the quiet darkness they connected, reestablished a tether to one another. Cody had no way of knowing if this would last but Lila was in his arms now and it was all that mattered. "I missed you," he whispered.

Their lips met, and Lila appeared as hungry for the connection as he. He deepened the kiss and for a second, pure bliss showered him. Then she pulled back. Their eyes locked, confusion clouding hers. Shifting her head, she stepped out of his embrace and walked away.

Chapter 23

At nine the next morning, Cody slid into the drivers' seat of a blue, ten-year-old car borrowed from Jeb. The car lacked a navigation system and many of the bells and whistles most people desired. Funny how Cody had spent most of his life with advanced technology and now his life depended on old-school ways.

Lila ran past Reid and Adam seated in Adam's gray SUV, which matched his car in barebones electronics and climbed in next to him.

Lila and Cody both called off work for the morning, claiming personal issues they needed to attend to.

"Ready for this? Did you turn off your phone and remove the memory card?" Cody asked. He shelved the memory of their kiss. As wonderful as the kiss was, her walking away left him with more questions. But none of that could screw with his brain today.

"Yep." She reached into her purse and lifted her Glock. "I'm hoping neither of us will need weapons. Jack mentioned this Jennings guy for a reason. Maybe he has more information. The way I see it, if I'm going to be a target I want to know as much as possible about who may be targeting me, even if it's Lance."

He squinted in the bright sun and pulled away from the curb. "Understandable. Let's hope this pans out." He glanced over his shoulder and spotted Adam, with Reid riding shotgun, merging into traffic several cars behind.

Traffic was light by Dallas standards, so they crossed into the Toval city limits in under an hour. A wooden sign with bright yellow letters spelling out the town's name greeted them. Cody arrived at a white brick ranch-style house on a tree-lined suburban road. Red roses bordered the house and the scent of fresh grass smacked his nose. The driveway was devoid of cars.

"Adam's research indicates Garvin has a wife, Sheila, who is four years younger. We don't have much information on her," Lila said.

Cody placed a hand on her arm. "If things don't look right, we're out of there. Got it? We're not taking unnecessary risks." They'd decided on meeting Garvin during the day in hopes that the neighborhood would be less populated with people at work and school in case something should happen.

Lila nodded.

As they approached the door, Cody scanned the neighborhood. The street had little activity in the early afternoon hour. Halfway down the block, an unoccupied cable repair truck sat parked outside a house. He spotted Adam and Reid's vehicle along the curb about five houses away. Cody's gaze swung to the house on the right next to the Jennings' home. A tricycle lay on its side, the three wheels mud caked and still.

Cody focused on the house to the left of the Jennings' home. A curtain at the front window fluttered closed. "We have a nosey neighbor," he said.

They continued to the front door and Cody rang the bell.

Seconds later, the door wrenched open. "Can I..." The man stared at Lila.

Cody pulled her close and gripped the gun in his pocket. *What the hell?* The man stared at Lila as if she were an alien.

"Mr. Jennings?" Lila asked.

Cody sensed her alarm.

"Yes." He smiled. "You're Lila Sinclair." The man stepped back. "Please come in."

Lila didn't move. "I'm actually Lila Caldwell. How do you know me?"

Mr. Jennings nodded. "That's right. You have your father's last name." He leaned out the door and glanced up and down the street. "Do come in. Hurry."

Lila shot Cody a look of surprise then stepped inside.

"Who is this young man?"

"Cody Green, a friend." He hadn't been introduced as Lila's friend since they were kids, and he didn't like the title.

"Nice to meet you, Cody." Mr. Jennings extended his hand.

"How do you know me, Mr. Jennings?" Lila stopped in the middle of the living room despite the man waving them to the sofa.

A woman appeared from around the corner.

"We have guests, honey. Sheila, this is Lila and Cody," Garvin said.

Sheila shook their hands but turned her attention back to Lila, where her gaze stalled. Cody didn't understand their fascination with Lila and his guard remained on alert.

"Hello." Sheila stepped aside and shot a knowing glance at Garvin.

"Please sit," Garvin said. "I'm very sorry about Jack. Good man." He cleared his throat. "I know you're here for answers. I'm an old man. I know I don't have long on this earth, and I want to go out with no regrets."

Sheila expelled a loud sigh. She ambled to the large window facing the street and adjusted a clay pot filled with green leafy plants. While in front of the window, she shifted the blinds and shot a quick peek out. She guided the blind back in place then sat in the chair next to her husband.

Garvin smirked. "She doesn't like when I talk about my mortality. But death happens to us all." He shot a gaze toward the patio door, partially shielded by vertical blinds.

"How did you know Jack Struthers?" Lila sat, stiff as a board, on the blue plaid sofa.

The well-coordinated room contained matching blue chairs, and a blue-and-white area rug. Even the bookshelf in the corner held knickknacks in the color scheme. A vase with fresh cut flowers sat in the center of the glass coffee table surrounded by a splay of home decorating magazines.

"I'm a retired attorney. I was a partner at HTP. During my time there, the firm's name was Hirst, Comer, and Locklin. The last two guys are now dead and have obviously been replaced. So goes the circle of life. I knew Jack as a young, fresh-faced attorney. Bright and sharp, Jack displayed a knowledge of law that I've rarely seen."

"He had a brilliant legal mind." Lila folded both hands in her lap. "I've never seen your name associated with the firm."

"And you won't. I've been wiped clean as if I'd never existed." He turned to Sheila, who sat stone-faced, then his gaze went to the window.

"Mr. Jennings, you obviously know who Lila is and perhaps why we're here. Why don't you tell us what you know?" The constant glances toward the window and doors had Cody on edge. Why were the Jennings' so nervous? Rising, Cody peered through the window. Aside from the Speedstar Cable truck and Reid and Adam, the street was clear. "Are you expecting someone?" Cody said turning from the window.

Garvin displayed a strained smile. "No."

Cody sauntered across the living room to the rear sliding porch door and pushed aside the blinds a few inches. A wood fence with a rear gate surrounded the square yard. Lush green grass, a covered patio with an umbrella-topped table and a grill made up the typical back yard. He returned to the couch and took his place next to Lila. "Doesn't seem to be anyone lurking. I know the glances. You're worried someone is out to get you."

"You're a perceptive fellow. We've learned to live with a healthy sense of alarm."

Cody didn't believe him. Their behavior didn't resemble anything close to healthy. The Jennings' appeared to expect danger at any moment. As an Alliance member, he understood fear.

"My previous line of work created a less than ideal atmosphere when it comes to safety. I've been retired for several years." He grew quiet, and Sheila tiptoed out of the room.

"Have you been threatened?" Lila asked.

"No, not outright. But I can't be sure a threat doesn't exist."

Sheila returned with iced tea and cookies. "Please help yourselves. Those cookies were made from my grandmother's recipe."

Garvin patted his stomach. "She's a good cook. My only specialty is apple pie." After an awkward pause, Garvin knit his eyebrows and said, "I knew your Great Uncle Ivan. I worked as one of his attorneys. I know all about The Order, but I was an outside council, doing his dirty bidding under the employment of Hirst, Comer, and Locklin. I knew I was dirty, but the money was good, and I loved the perks. Use of the Sinclair planes, all-expenses-paid vacations, and more. I was a great attorney, and Ivan came to count on me." Garvin stood and picked up a photo from the bookshelf of he and Sheila on their wedding day. The bronze plate on the bottom read June 15, 1968. In the photo, Garvin dressed in a gray suit had his arm around Sheila who was in a knee-length, white wedding dress with a short veil across her face. Garvin pinched the bridge of this nose then replaced the photo on the shelf. "Ivan eventually took me into his confidence. He was worried about Lance, who was dangerous and impulsive." Garvin chuckled. "Funny how Ivan seem to know Lance would one day put himself in such a position where we'd have to use creative lawyering to save him."

Cody picked up a cookie, his mouth watering at the sight of the buttery wafer. He longed to take a bite, but he didn't trust them.

"Ivan didn't take well to any of the younger attorneys. He insisted on me taking care of his needs. Everything I did at the firm on behalf of Ivan or The Order was covered up. Only need-to-know personnel were let in on what we were doing. I created phony documents, suppressed evidence, you name it. Anything to grease the wheels for Ivan."

"I'm assuming your association with Ivan is how you came to know who I was?" Lila picked up a glass of tea from the tray but refrained from drinking.

"You're right. Ivan briefed me about you. He said you were bright and beautiful. He was right." Garvin returned to his seat across from the couch.

"Thank you. I had no idea Ivan could think such nice thoughts, especially since he locked me up in one of the rooms of his Colorado estate." Lila voice remained calm, even though Cody could tell impatience and anger lurked at the periphery.

Garvin nodded. "I understand. You have every right to be upset. I'm sure you've felt like a pawn your entire life. In many ways you were." Garvin rose and eyed his wife. "She deserves to know, Sheila."

The woman nodded, and her hand fluttered around her neck.

"First, I know about the files," Garvin said. "Jack must have instructed you to find them."

Lila remained quiet.

Garvin continued. "Jack found a portal we'd hidden within the company's computer system. He ended up discovering all the documentation, which would have put Lance away for life. There are certain people, including myself at the firm who ensured Lance would never serve a day behind bars. They made it all go away as if nothing happened. All the crimes, the lab explosion, kidnappings, murders. But HTP is only one player. We squelched the evidence, but others also had to do their part, and by that, I mean the FBI, the crime lab, prosecutors, the Justice Department, and police. It was a well-coordinated coverup. Jack found everything, including who the players are, and he could have gone to the police, but in doing so, he would've placed a target on his back. Turns out someone found out what Jack knew, and well...you know how it ended."

Cody sat back on the sofa, trying to absorb all this information. "You were a key player. How do you fit into this scenario now?"

"When Jack discovered the information, he came to me upset and concerned. By this time, I was tired of the secrets, lies, and lawlessness all for one family to gain power. Ivan was dead and working for Lance was no picnic. I had already walked away and given Lance my word that as an Order member I would remain quiet about what I knew. But I vowed to start the last sector of my life doing what's right.

Sheila and I never had children, but I started mentoring kids in the area. It feels good to finally be doing something positive."

Did he think teaching a few kids how to shoot free throws would excuse his role in covering for The Order?

Lila set the tea on the table. "Mrs. Jennings, I'm sure none of this has been easy on you either."

"No." Sheila trembled, her white hair shaking. She folded her hands in her lap and rocked.

"Why should we believe you? Why did Jack direct me to you?" Lila asked.

Garvin clasped his hands together in his lap. "When Jack discovered I was involved he was angry." Garvin sighed. "I told him not to go to the FBI, but he didn't listen."

"Who did Jack talk to at the FBI?" Lila asked, shooting a glance at Cody.

"I don't know but less than a week later he was dead." Garvin shook his head. "I told Jack that you'd be in danger if those files got out. He directed you to me because I have information that could save your life. I told Jack what I'm about to tell you." He rose, left the room, and returned with a small, black box.

Cody scooted closer to Lila as he braced for whatever would come next.

Garvin rubbed his thumb across the square box and then said, "Many years ago, Ivan told me about a secret island and emerald mine his father possessed. As far as I know no one but Ivan and maybe his top financial advisor, Morris Beak, knew the location. I'm sure you're aware that your great-grandfather, Russell enjoyed creating symbols and puzzles for everything. In that vein, the location of this billion-dollar mine is shrouded in secrecy. Before Ivan died, weeks actually, he called me to Switzerland." Garvin swiveled toward the window for a second before pivoting back to Lila. "You were once the key to what, in comparison, was a small treasure. You are now the key to this much larger one. The tattoo imprinted upon you as a child is once again critical. I don't know how, but I know it's important."

Cody leaned forward remembering how Lila's tattooed arm was

used to open the door to a vault inside an abandoned mine in Colorado. The code imprinted upon her arm unlocked the vault door. Why was Lila again the focus of the Sinclair's family psychotic games?

"As you can guess Ivan wouldn't give me the details, but I know Lance is very dangerous, and Ivan recognized that his son was on a perilous path. He wouldn't have wanted Lance to have access to this unlimited wealth." Garvin angled his head upward. "In some respects, I think he knew his own life was in danger. I can't imagine what Ivan must have thought as his own son and wife pushed him to his death from that airplane." Garvin shook his head then handed Lila the box.

She stared at the black velvet box before accepting it. "What is this?"

"About a month ago, I received a package and letter. I believe it's from The Order council instructing me to give you that box."

She opened the lid and gasped as she drew out an emerald plate, about the size of a square coaster. The sun streaming in through the window sparkled off the rock.

"I don't know if Lance knows about the island and mine, but I believe Ivan wanted you to find it. I assume this emerald plate is a clue."

Cody swiped a hand across his facial stubble. "The council wanted you to give Lila this emerald, but you did not seek us out. We found you."

"If you hadn't shown up here, I would have found you." He stood again. "As you know no one leaves The Order, but because of the work I did for Lance he allowed me to retire. Even so, Sheila and I live with the possibility that our lives are in jeopardy. I can't impress upon you enough—you are in extreme danger."

Cody's phone buzzed. He glanced at the device. Reid's text read: *"Take cover!"*

At that moment a fluttering sound erupted from the backyard.

Then bullets riddled the room.

Cody's gut seized then he dove to cover Lila as dry wall, glass, and couch stuffing exploded around them. He pulled his weapon as he shielded Lila with his body. Pulse pounding, he fired at an unknown assailant. Once the bullets stopped, he stared through what was left of the patio door. A weaponized drone, hovered. Just before the object lifted out of the sight, Cody recognized the green Veridian logo.

Chapter 24

F ive shots rang out from just above her. At first Lila thought the bullets were from the six- propeller drone, but they were coming from Cody. He fired out of the shattered patio door at the drone hovering outside. The silver flying object looked like an evil robot tasked with their destruction.

Lila squirmed out from under Cody. "Garvin! Sheila!"

She belly-crawled toward them across the floor. Sheila had collapsed on her side, her back to Lila. Scooting up to her, she turned the woman over. Blood oozed from two bullet wounds, one in her chest and one in her stomach. Leaning close, Lila pressed her ear to the woman chest. All she heard was the rapid thumping of her own heart.

Cody jumped up. "Lila, stay down. The drone is gone but there could be more." He raced to the door, peered up, and raised his weapon. Sprinting outside, he disappeared from view for a few seconds before he returned. "We're clear. Reid and Adam are covering the house. They saw the drone seconds before it started firing."

"Sheila is dead." Lila stepped over her to get to Garvin. He lay face up, blood seeping from several holes in his body, staining his pale skin a rusty red. Lila had counted multiple gunshots. One wound, above his right eye, and the other centered in his chest appeared to be the kill shots. Kneeling beside Garvin, Lila listened for a heartbeat but only silence returned. His eyes were open, and his left hand reached toward Sheila as if he were lurching for her when the attack occurred. "Garvin is dead, too. We need to call the police."

Reid stepped through the back door. "Are you guys okay?" With his weapon drawn, he surveyed the room.

"We're fine but Jennings and his wife are dead. I believe they both were targets." Cody took Lila's hand.

"You're bleeding." Lila stared at the trail of blood snaking down the side of Cody's face.

"It's nothing. I think I got hit by some flying glass. Are you hurt anywhere?" He cast a glance at her.

"No, I'm fine." She rubbed her eyes. Lila scrambled to the spot where she and Cody took a dive when the shooting started and found the box underneath a sofa cushion, now covered with white stuffing. With a shaky hand, she tucked the box into her purse "I can't believe Garvin and Sheila are dead."

Adam stood at the door. "The police are on their way."

"We're armed, Cody. The police are going to think we're responsible." Lila's heart hadn't stopped its staccato rhythm since the shooting started.

"We have the drone on video with shots fired. We're clear," Reid said.

"Don't mention the emerald." Cody continued to grip his weapon.

Reid wrinkled his forehead. "Emerald?"

Cody gave them a brief update. "No need to disclose the information to the police with the possibility Lance has people inside the department."

They crept out the back door and raced around the side of the house just as the first police car arrived.

Two officers approached, guns drawn.

The police separated all of them for questioning. After a trip to the police station to make a formal statement and undergo a check for gun residue, they were released. Lila shuddered at the memory of the detective staring at her. She couldn't decide if he believed her, but Reid and Adam with their FBI credentials helped bolster their claims of innocence.

Thirty minutes later, Cody pulled into a parking lot of a fast food restaurant, busy with the lunch time crowd.

Reid and Adam were still wrapping up at the police station.

Cody cut the engine and turned to her. "Are you sure you're okay?"

She nodded as her body shivered. "If Reid and Adam hadn't been there, I don't think the police would have believed we had nothing to do with Garvin and Sheila's deaths. We showed up and minutes later they're dead." Her voice broke.

He scooted closer and enveloped her in his arms. "When those bullets started flying, all I could think of was getting you out of there. First you nearly miss the murder of your boss, then you find yourself at the bottom of a lake, and now this..."

Lila settled into his arms, her head resting on his carved pectorals. She couldn't help the tremor that ran through her body. "I want this all to be over, but Garvin made it clear this is only the beginning." She shifted out of his embrace and took the box from her purse. She slid the top off the black velvet box and lifted the plate out then stopped. "I see some type of code." She pointed to the letters MSVVY engraved in tiny letters on the plate's surface.

Leaning toward the emerald, Cody inspected the plate. "What the hell does this mean?"

Lila turned the plate over in her hand, running her finger over the sides of the smooth emerald. "I don't know but a guess would say it is a clue to the mine's location." She set the emerald back inside the box.

"I'm sure this emerald is worth thousands, probably more." Cody took Lila's hand. "We'll talk to Reid and the others. I'm betting there are more clues in store."

"Something Garvin said has bothered me." Lila shut her eyes for a second, remembering Garvin's words. "Why am I involved? Why didn't Ivan have his associates contact Carson? She is his daughter."

"I don't know but you're the one with the invisible tattoo." Cody ran his finger across her arm.

"Garvin said my great-grandfather founded the mine. He couldn't know I would be born and then imprinted with this tattoo so maybe Vivian knew about the mine. That's the only explanation." Lila stared at a young couple exiting the restaurant and loading two kids into a minivan. Would she ever have that kind of existence?

"Make sense, but we're going to find out for sure."

"We owe it to Jack, and maybe even Garvin and Sheila to see this through." Lila stared at her arm. "I thought about removing this damn tattoo, but something stopped me." She turned her arm, palm side up and rubbed the roughened area. The Order, led by Vivian Sinclair, had imprinted her with an invisible ink tattoo, only visible under UV lighting.

"EBOP46," Cody said.

Lila nodded.

"EBOP46 the musical composition for *Scottish Fantasy* by Max Bruch. My great-grandfather Russell's favorite piece." She blew out a sigh. "I was seen as the chosen one simply because my birthday is May second. Grandmother Vivian saw the number seven when adding the number five from May as the fifth month to the day I was born. Even after all these years it's still hard to wrap my mind around their sick thinking. Now, here we go again." She stared out the window. "The Order blazed a trail littered with shattered lives and dead bodies. We have to end it."

Cody nodded. "We need to find the right person in the right position to take this evidence and they must be unafraid to prosecute Lance. I think we're getting close to kicking our plans into high gear."

Lila straightened in her seat "Garvin said Jack went to the FBI. He must have spoken with one of Lance's moles. The information definitely didn't make it back to Reid or Adam."

Cody picked up his phone and texted Adam. A second later, his phone pinged. "Adam says they are still with the police, but we'll meet later. Between the evidence we now have and the fact we could be in possession of information Lance desperately wants, we put ourselves in position to have the upper hand." He pulled at his scant beard. "There's something else. Did you notice anything about the drone?"

"Nothing other than the bullets flying."

"It wasn't a coincidence the shooting started right after Garvin gave you the box. The drone had the Veridian logo on the side. And the company is not in the business of selling drones."

"Veridian? Do you think they tracked us to Garvin's house or had them under surveillance?" Lila rubbed her sore shoulder.

"It's likely. My theory is Veridian or Lance don't know who knows about the mine and they need information."

"And when we showed up, they made their move." Once again Lila lifted the emerald out of the box, pulling the satin pillow along with the gem. A slip of paper lay in the bottom of the box. Lila picked up the paper and stared at two names: Morris Beak and Willa Dickerson.

Cody leaned over. "Garvin mentioned Morris Beak. Do you recognize the other name?"

Lila shook her head as she stared at the names. "No. I hope they are still alive."

A large white van rumbled into the parking lot, indicating the vehicle belonged to Roscoe the Painting Expert. Four men jumped out.

Cody stared at the vehicle and pointed. "See that van?"

Lila followed his gaze. "Roscoe, the Painting Expert?"

"Yeah. Reminds me of the Speedstar Cable van parked down the street from the Jennings' house. It wasn't there when we left." Cody locked his gaze on the van. "Speedstar Cable?" He turned to her, his eyes wide, then he picked up his phone and punched at the screen. Seconds later, he set down the phone. "I knew it! Speedstar Cable isn't in this area."

Her mouth dropped open. "Do you think someone from Veridian was operating the drone from inside the truck?"

"Maybe." Cody shot a look in the rearview mirror as he shifted the vehicle in gear. "Garvin was right to be suspicious. Whatever fears he had has now shifted to us. Although we could gain the upper hand, one false move and we'll all have bullets aiming for us."

Chapter 25

Cody rushed into the Veridian offices and made a beeline for the café. He needed a caffeine shot if he had any hope of making it through the day. A quick glance at his watch indicated he had a few minutes to spare before he needed to be in the DDI team area. With his cup of coffee, he stepped outside onto the patio dining section overlooking the lake on the Veridian campus. The water sparkled in the afternoon sun. A couple of joggers ran along the path next to the lake while another group practiced yoga, their green Veridian mats lined up on the grassy area near the lake. Veridian offered their employees ample opportunity for fun and exercise. Perhaps the top company executives found plying employees with perks encouraged loyalty and made their criminal deeds more palatable. Threatening Lila had taken their actions to a new low and now Veridian appeared directly involved in the drone attack.

He hadn't wanted to show up today, but he couldn't rock the boat when they needed as much information as possible. His disgust for Veridian had grown as bitter as the strong coffee he needed right now.

He hoped keeping Lila safe didn't equate to a fool's mission.

"Nice scene."

Cody turned to the voice behind him. Moby gripped a coffee cup and stared out at the lake.

"It's all bullshit. This fake nirvana." Moby turned his gaze to Cody. "By now you know that."

Cody pulled a chair out. "Cynical. Is that what a few years at Veridian will do for you?"

Moby shrugged and sat across from him. "In addition to the hefty salary, stock options, and free coffee." He raised his cup.

"Let's not forget their amazing knack for producing a tux which happens to fit perfectly." Cody didn't know who to trust. Moby could be an insider working on behalf of Rick and Tally.

"Can't forget that," Moby said. "As well as a few other highlights about working here. I've learned a lot." He drained his coffee cup and continued to stare out at the lake.

"How long have you worked for Veridian?"

"I came to the US from India for university about ten years ago. I've been at Veridian for four years. Even in that time I've seen lots of changes here."

Were those changes for good or bad? Cody didn't push him. If Rick and Tally monitored traffic cameras and police calls, then they surely could have cameras and audio surveillance in their own backyard.

"Is this all worth the sacrifice?" Moby whispered then cringed. He straightened and said a bit louder, "If you're a tech person worth any salt, Veridian is your dream company."

He probably wished he hadn't let that first comment slip. Cody observed the yoga teacher bringing her hands together by her chest before bowing. The class replicated her gesture then rolled up their mats and gathered their belongings. "There's something to be said for the simple life. Not that I would know." Yoga-induced calm and centered thinking didn't encompass the entire Veridian culture. Maybe Moby could shed some light on his worries.

Moby's gaze lifted to a corner of the building.

Cody followed and spotted a small camera panning the patio area. *What are they so nervous about?*

"We should head in. Wouldn't want to make the boss angry." Moby stood and gave Cody a prolonged look before heading toward the door.

~

"Are you up for the challenge?" Paul said as Cody slipped in to one of the open stations ten minutes later. "I know I am."

"Sure." *I hate that guy.* Cody shot him a glare then logged on to the system. He couldn't fathom what today would bring, but he needed to seem as if he was part of the team. "Hi Sher," Cody said.

She muttered a "hi" without looking up. "I'm co-leading the experiment today. Please pull up your case study. Be ready in thirty."

Stanley, the oldest on the team, scooted in next to Moby.

Cody studied the requirements of the case study. Text subject BR991. Medical history. He groaned inwardly then pulled up the database to find the test subject's real identity. His heart dropped as he stared at the name. Senator Bertram Reynolds. What did Veridian want with the senator from Louisiana?

Sher stood behind him. "Let's get moving."

Cody hacked into the senator's calendar and prayed this was all a simulation. Five minutes later, he had the name of Reynold's personal doctor. Then fifteen minutes after that, he lurked inside the electronic medical records for the senator. The 66-year-old wore a hearing aid and fractured his foot years ago. He had rheumatoid arthritis and congestive heart failure, for which he wore a pacemaker. According to his records, the senator had a surgical appointment in three weeks to replace the pacemaker battery. Cody's heart dropped.

"Times up!" Sher stood.

Rick sauntered into the hive and clapped his hands together. "We're about to embark on a special project, an inauguration, as such, for Cody and Paul."

Paul sat taller in his chair and stretched his fingers as if preparing for a computer battle.

Perching on the side of a desk, Rick said, "Financial."

Moby ran down the senator's bank account information, which included highlights from the last five years of tax returns and a review of his investment portfolio.

The prospects of the power within their grasps hit Cody. Veridian would harness this information and use it. They probably already had.

"Good, Moby. At what financial data point is the senator most vulnerable?" Rick stared at the senator's bank account balance on the large monitor.

"His investment accounts. He doesn't really monitor them. If I wanted to go undetected, I'd begin pulling money off those accounts. The senator also makes monthly deposits into another account, belonging to a Karen Boyd."

Rick nodded. "Paul, what do you have from a relationship stand-point? Any scandals?"

Paul hit a button on his keyboard, and his data popped up on the big screen. "Seems Bertram has a son that was *not* his wife's. The boy is twelve years old. The old man has been paying the mother, Karen Boyd a monthly allowance ever since the boy's birth and she has DNA evidence to prove parentage."

"Great work." Rick crossed his arms. "Definitely an exploitable weak spot. The senator is up for reelection next year. This tidbit won't play well with his constituents."

"I also have email messages where he threatened Ms. Boyd to keep her mouth shut." Paul flashed a salacious grin.

After Stanley gave his report on the senator's checkered career, Rick turned to Cody. "You're up."

As all eyes turned to him, Cody made a snap decision. "Dr. Oberlin is the senator's primary-care physician. The senator has a history of heart disease, rheumatoid arthritis mainly affecting his knees and back. He has profound hearing loss in his left ear, for which he wears a cochlear implant. Fourteen years ago, February twenty-second to be exact, at his Washington, DC, residence, he fell on the ice and broke his foot."

Silence blanketed the room as Rick stared at the monitor displaying the information Cody had gathered. "Is your analysis complete?"

Perspiration trailed down Cody's back. He feared where this case study would lead. Play along or protect the senator, were his only options. Cody's jaw tightened as he stared at the screen he hadn't shared. "There are other issues in his history."

Rick swung his gaze to Cody. "Your analysis isn't comprehensive. I'm aware that the senator may have had a cold or required medical services for some mundane bug." He allowed the words to hang in the air.

Cody met Rick's gaze. "HIPAA laws preclude this type of invasion."

"Veridian is *above* the law." Rick expelled a sigh. "The public has an insatiable thirst for transparency. View almost anyone's social medial accounts. They spew data like lava flows from an erupted volcano. *Going on a first date, wish me luck. Leaving for a seven-day Mexican cruise*, and here's the posted pics to prove it. *Have a strange growth protruding from my leg, what is it?* For any given year, we can run a query based on pregnancy announcements and roughly estimate the number of births that year. Users open the door to their lives with a wide grin and outstretched arms. Those tiny words of agreement no one reads but clicks in the affirmative gives us the mandate to know and analyze every aspect of human life. We owe them this, and you owe me a complete analysis."

Cody didn't care about Rick's passionate speech about why digging into the lives of others and manipulating them was an expected outcome of using social media. Yet, no matter what Cody did, the information would be collected and used however Veridian deemed. When he accepted the position and the challenge to go undercover for the Alliance, Cody considered the task a matter of a few people trying to stop a narcissist. Now, he actually had the fate of millions of unsuspecting people to fight for. The camera angling toward him and Moby earlier came to mind. If they were monitoring activity around Veridian, they were probably scrutinizing his computer and each key stroke. Sighing, he tapped his computer. "The senator has a pacemaker, model number 85P4T, serial number U3877R90."

Rick gave him a prolonged stare before sitting at a computer. Seconds later, data poured onto the monitor. The senator's heart function status appeared. "We are now God, ladies and gentlemen. With one click, I hold this man's life in my hands. Reynolds is currently on the floor of the senate chambers." Rick's fingers hovered above the keys. "I'm now inside his device. A couple of keystrokes and the senator will experience a sudden jolt. Perhaps a malfunction occurs which would emit a voltage high enough to short circuit his heart." Rick tapped his fingers together above his keyboard, now more lethal than a napalm bomb.

Cody held his breath. *What the hell is Rick doing?* All hope that these case studies were simulations, had evaporated.

"Fascinating," Paul said.

Moby shot Cody a worried glance.

"I get the power Veridian has." Cody scooted to the edge of his seat. "I get it. You don't need to demonstrate."

Rick shrugged. "Maybe you understand our power but *showing* you what Veridian can do may be a more valuable lesson."

The next monitor lit up with the scene from the legislative floor.

The vulnerable senator rose from his chair and slowly made his way to the podium.

Rick tapped at the computer keys and almost instantly the senator staggered and clutched his chest.

An aide rushed forward, but the senator waved him away.

Cody rose from his chair. "Back off!"

Rick didn't answer.

The senator regained his footing and began to speak. He shuddered, stopped, and cleared his throat.

"You're going to kill him," Cody said.

Sher stood and faced Cody. "Rick knows what he's doing."

Cody glanced at Moby, who gave him a slight shake of his head as if warning Cody not to put up a challenge. How could they stand here and let Rick kill this man? Cody advanced toward Rick, disregarding the consequences. "Back. Off."

Rick smiled and tapped a key.

The senator collapsed.

Chapter 26

When Lila entered the HTP offices, she rushed into her office and shut the door. She had a meeting with Steve and didn't want to bring attention to herself by not showing.

She leaned back in her chair and recalled the kiss Cody had given her in the dark early morning. The mass of emotions for Cody combined with the fear the police would decide she played a part in the recent string of murders plagued her. Closing herself off from the world seemed a good idea but wasn't going to happen today.

She opened a client file to study in preparation for a planning meeting with Steve in thirty minutes. Had he slept off his alcoholic binge? Her hand hesitated over the phone before she pulled away. She worked for twenty more minutes then picked up her desk phone. Steve might not be up for meeting her. She wanted to give him the chance to call off the meeting by phone to preserve embarrassment. Her call to Steve went unanswered.

Scooting away from her desk, Lila bounded up the stairs to the partner floor. As she neared Steve's office, his assistant, Peggy, cleared her throat. "Steve left a note on my desk giving explicit instructions that he does not wish to be disturbed. He must be awfully busy as I haven't heard a peep out of him."

Lila narrowed her eyes. "You haven't seen him today?"

Peggy shook her gray-haired bob. "No. And I came in early and haven't left my desk."

Lila grabbed the door handle.

Peggy advanced. "He doesn't want to be disturbed." Her voice was stern, as if she'd just caught Lila having a cookie before dinner.

"I think it'll be okay." Lila pushed opened the door and stepped in. Empty. Her gaze swept the vacant office. Where was he? She prayed he didn't get behind the wheel. She should have insisted on taking him home.

"That's curious. Where could he be?" Peggy asked coming up behind her. "He mentioned something about talking to Jim Dixon about a tax issue yesterday. Maybe he's up in Jim's office."

"Thanks." Lila headed one floor up to the senior partner floor to check with Jim. Arriving at Jim's office, his assistant glanced up from his computer. "If you're looking for Jim, he isn't in today."

"Thanks," Lila said. She continued past Jim's office glancing into any open office along the way. No sign of Steve. As she rounded the corner, she came face-to-face with Mr. Talcott.

"Ms. Caldwell. I've been meaning to call you up to my office." He stood with a coffee cup in hand, the scalp from his receding hairline shiny with perspiration.

"Hello, Mr. Talcott."

He waved her toward his office, a few feet away. Taking his position of power behind the huge desk, he placed his coffee mug on top of a gold coaster. "I saw an article about your unfortunate accident the other day. You're here so I assume you weren't hurt too severely."

"Only minor injuries." Lila stood in front of his desk.

"Any additional run-ins with the press?" Talcott wrapped his meaty hand around the coffee mug, his law school ring glinting off the sunlight filtering in through the window.

"No," Lila said.

"Good. I know I sound like a broken record, but it's vitally important for all HTP employees to remain out of the media when it comes to Jack's murder. We must allow the police to perform their investigation without our biased input."

"Maybe if someone from HTP spoke passionately about Jack then someone with information would step forward." As soon as the words escaped her mouth, Lila braced herself.

Anger flashed for a second in Talcott's eyes before his regained control. "Now, I see the fire Jack talked about. You have a valid point. However, the partners are all in full agreement about the no contact directive." He sniffed and narrowed his eyes. "Jack had a lot of confidence in you, and Steve has been pleased with your work. So far." He sighed. "HTP is a very prestigious law firm. You could go far here." He leaned forward. "But step out of bounds and you'll find yourself in Siberia."

Was he protecting himself or someone else? She held her shoulders back and maintained eye contact with Talcott. "I have no desire to speak with the media. I am interested in ensuring Jack's murderer is caught and will cooperate fully with the authorities, even though my information is limited. The last thing I want to do is impede an investigation or my position here. I hope that's acceptable to the partners." Lila kept her expression neutral, but inside she wanted to high five herself.

"Of course. We encourage your full cooperation with the detectives." He painted on a grin and stood. "I'll let you get back to work."

"Thank you." She turned toward the door.

"Oh, and Ms. Caldwell. If you remember any new details about the incident, I expect to be apprised of the new information." He rounded the desk. "We want to stay ahead of any new developments."

She pursed her lips then cleared her throat. "Of course." Lila exited the office, the raised hairs on the back of her neck sending a warning.

As she hurried down the hall, she spotted Hilary in the distance. With an inward groan, her first inclination was to turn around and take the long way back to her office. Instead, she steeled herself and kept going. Walking the partner floor was like navigating through a minefield.

"Lila, have you seen Steve?" Hilary placed a hand on her hip as if exasperated she had to speak with her.

"No." Lila hesitated, unsure if she should disclose that she had a meeting with him for which he was now late. Based on his condition last night, she hoped Steve was at home sleeping off his binge.

"I've called him twice today and he hasn't returned my calls." She blew out a breath. "If you see him tell him I need to speak with him. And inform his assistant that we're canceling the meeting with Gumfrey this afternoon. We won't go in unprepared." She pivoted on her heels, marched into her office, and slammed the door.

Lila trudged downstairs. She stopped at Peggy's desk to inform her of what happened on the partner floor.

"It's not like him not to call," Peggy said.

"I saw him last night. He was pretty broken up about Jack. Maybe he needed a bit more time today."

Back inside her office, Lila sank into her chair and put Steve out of her mind for the time being. Logging on to her computer, she ran a search for Morris Beak. Garvin said he was Ivan's accountant. Even though Ivan's US base was in Colorado, his accountant didn't have to be in the same location. The search failed to return anything useful. She logged into several national databases searching for an accountant with the name Morris Beak. When nothing came up again, Lila sighed. Although it was possible, maybe even likely Morris Beak would have retired from the profession, she still expected to see a crumb of his existence online. The fact she didn't find any information made her believe Morris Beak did indeed belong to The Order.

Lila moved on to Willa Dickerson. She found one article containing her name. Willa was one of three authors of a scientific article about the value of touch in helping children in pain from illness or undergoing medical treatments. Authored by three nurses, the article was published almost thirty years ago. She researched the other two authors and found loads of information.

The first woman died six years ago. The second author, Norma

Voss appeared to be the director of nursing at a small hospital in southern Arizona. Lila swung her gaze toward the clock. At one thirty Arizona time, Lila gambled Ms. Barnes would still be at work.

Lila fished her secured phone from her bag and made the call. After waiting on hold for a few minutes, Lila introduced herself. She informed the woman that Ms. Dickerson was her grandmother's friend and the two women had lost touch. "I promised my grandmother I'd find her friend, and I know I'm grasping at straws, but when I saw the article, I thought you might know of her current location."

"How nice of you. It's been years since I've talked to Willa." Norma's voice filled her ears with a gentle, soothing quality.

"Anything you can recall would be helpful." A surge of guilt powered through her for the lie, but life-and-death matters trumped honesty.

"Willa, Ruth, and I went to nursing school together at Johns Hopkins in Maryland. Ruth has since passed on. Poor thing. I'm about to retire, and as you can guess, I'm way overdue," she chuckled. "But about Willa... She married Edgar Dickerson after nursing school. We all got jobs at a DC hospital. I don't know much about him, but Willa was head over heels. Two years later, I got married, too, and we moved to Arizona. I learned later that Willa was leaving the hospital and following her husband to Virginia I believe. She was going to work for a family as a private nurse."

Lila jotted down the information. "Do you remember the name of the family?"

"No, I'm sorry I don't. I'm certain they were well off because she told me she and Edgar had their own cottage on the property."

Lila's skin prickled. There were cottages for Order members on the grounds of Babylon Hall, the Sinclair's original headquarters in Virginia. "Interesting. Is there anything else you remember?"

"Willa and Edgar had a daughter. She's also a nurse. I ran into her at a conference last years. She said her father had passed on and her mother had moved out of Virginia."

"Did she say where Willa moved?" Lila held her breath.

"Let's see. I believe she told me Willa moved to Texas, maybe it was Dallas. I'm sorry I can't be of more help. If you find Willa please let her know I'd like to chat." Norma said.

As Lila released a breath her pulse kicked up. *Dallas?* "I will. You've been a wealth of information." Lila thanked Norma and hung up. She tapped her pen on the notebook. Funny how people connected with The Order had ended up near Dallas. It couldn't be a coincidence.

She called Reid and relayed the information. He'd already started researching Willa Dickerson and Morris Beak but hadn't gotten far.

After hanging up, Lila called Peggy. "Did you find Steve?"

"Not exactly. I called security, and they told me Steve's car is still in the garage. They show he swiped into the building but never out. I'm getting worried."

Lila stood as she remembered a recent conversation with Steve. "I'll get back to you in a few minutes." She hung up raced out of her office toward the library. Zigzagging through the stacks of law books she stopped in front of the file room door. After punching in her code, she stepped inside.

"Brandon?"

He spun around, his face red. Brandon's tie hung askew, and his shirt sleeves were rolled up to his elbow.

Lila's gaze shifted to the pair of feet sticking out from the shelves. She advanced farther into the room and stopped again.

"I found him. Like this." With an unnaturally high pitch to his voice, Brandon scurried away from the body.

Lila stared at the dead body of Steve Dorman. Gel-like blood saturated his white shirt, riddled with angled slashes. She couldn't discern the number of stab wounds but judging from the amount of slashes in his shirt, someone had been intent on causing maximum damage.

She stumbled backward, unable to emit a scream. Death seemed a daily companion.

"He's dead." Brandon shook his head and ran out of the room.

Lila stared at Steve. *What were you trying to tell me?*

"What do we have here?"

Lila whipped around. Then the lights went out.

Chapter 27

Cody slapped on his helmet, slammed down on the clutch, and rocketed out of the farmhouse garage. Images of the politician gripping his heart paraded through his memory. The day had gone into the crapper, the only saving grace had been when Rick let up and the senator remained alive. The question of whether they'd hurt Lila required no further thought. He'd updated the Alliance on what happened, then escaped the house. The motorcycle hummed under his legs and the wind whacked against his darkened face shield.

The rural area gave him the needed space to open up on the empty road. He needed to be as far away as he could from Veridian and people. For several minutes, he and the bike were one, hugging the road and cutting through the atmosphere. The adrenaline surge satisfied a need to push boundaries. Cody recalled his first skydiving jump. He'd peered from the open door of the plane, then jumped. The thrill of diving from the plane to the thud of landing on earth, the experience filled him with an unmet need. As he slowed the bike, he made a mental note that he needed to search for a new skydiving club.

As he drove along, he compared the Texas scenery to what he'd become accustomed to in San Francisco. Hills, palm trees, fog, and close living. Although he missed life in California, he could get used to sprawling space, southern hospitality, and a lower cost of living. He could also get used to being with Lila. The kissed they shared had been seared into his soul. But what now?

Pulling over to the side of the road, he drew out his portable telescope and surveyed the Texas night sky. He spotted the constellation Cassiopeia within seconds. The colorful cluster, over nineteen light years away, gave him perspective. Everything seemed less important when he lost himself in the heavens. Everything but Lila. Only she could match and surpass the awesomeness of celestial bodies.

After a few minutes, he stuffed the telescope into his backpack. As he hopped back on his motorcycle, he stilled when his secured phone rang.

"Cody, can you pick me up from the police station?" Lila's panicked voice perked up his adrenaline. "What's wrong?"

"I'll tell you later, but I just need..." She paused. "Please come."

"I'll be there right there." Cody shoved the phone inside his pocket and sped out.

Breaking the speed limit, Cody shaved ten minutes off the thirty-minute trip. He pulled up to the police station and spotted Lila talking with some guy. Still dressed in what she wore to the funeral, black pants, white shirt, and black pumps, she adjusted the large bag hanging from her shoulder. She nodded then the guy hugged her. Something close to jealousy coursed through him as he gripped the handlebars of his bike. The man trudged off toward the parking lot and Lila glanced around. Cody waved her over.

She slowed as she approached him. "You finally got your motorcycle."

He swung a leg over and hopped off, holding his helmet under his arm. "I was out riding when you called. I didn't want to make you wait until I went back for the car." He stepped closer. "Are you okay?"

"Yes. Can we get out of here?"

He detached the second helmet and handed it to her.

Lila slid her bag across her body and put on the silver helmet. "Let's go."

Cody kept the bike moving at a respectable speed. He loved the feel of Lila's arms wrapped around his body. Her touch made him warm and spurred the desire to protect her from the world. A few days ago, he'd jumped into the lake to pull her from a sinking car, today he had no doubt he'd step in front of a bullet.

With her legs hugging him and her arms around his waist, Cody appreciated each second. She directed him to a country bar twenty miles from her house. As he took a curve, he felt her body stiffen and grip tighten. Once he was on the straightaway, he felt her grasp loosened. When he parked the bike, she jumped off and handed him the helmet.

Cody took her hand and led her toward the bar's entrance. A large gray cowboy boot flanked the front door offering no doubt about establishment's theme.

Crossing the threshold, he noted the interior of the bar resembled a log cabin with western wall hangings and a collection of cowboy hats and boots attached to the walls. Members of a band scurried about setting up in a corner while music blared from the overhead speakers. Televisions were mounted at each booth and throughout the bar. They were all muted and tuned to sports or national news stations.

"Your father owns a bar and grill, right?" Cody said as they slid into the booth.

"Yes, but I didn't want to run into anyone I knew. I've noticed this place, and they are always crowded so I figured no one would bother us." She fumbled with a napkin.

They ordered beer and when the waiter retreated Cody turned to Lila. "Why did I pick you up at the police station?" A modicum of relief shot through him that Lila was able to leave the police station. The grim look on her face told him the reason she'd been there was another devastating blow.

Lila twisted the paper napkin. "Steve Dorman. I introduced you to him at the Veridian benefit."

Cody nodded.

"He was murdered today. Inside the firm's file room. I got there minutes after his body was discovered. I was at the police station to give a statement." She abandoned the napkin and massaged the bridge of her nose.

Cody scooted up on the bench and leaned over the table. His heart raced as his jaw tightened. "Did you see who killed him?"

"No. From the looks of things, he'd been stabbed hours before he was found. Steve's assistant and I couldn't find him. When we determined he was still in the building, I had a hunch he'd holed up in the file room. I walked in and found Brandon standing over Steve."

"What do you know about Brandon?"

Lila shrugged. "He's kind of annoying, although I might be alone in that assessment. But he's a good guy, I think. Nothing came up on his background check. He was rattled when he found Steve." She traced a circle on the table with her finger. "Walt Talcott came into the file room after Brandon ran out. He didn't seem all that concerned about Steve. Then the lights went out and I almost died but I remembered the room is set to go dark if no movement is sensed."

"Based on Steve's interaction with you last night, we can assume he knew about the files."

"He knew he was in danger. But from who?" She expelled a sigh then quieted as the waiter deposited their beers then rushed to another table across the room.

"If they are killing people with knowledge of those incriminating files, then, Lila, you are in extreme danger." Cody glanced around the bar. He could find something suspicious about everyone. "The police probably haven't gotten far enough into the investigation to have a definite suspect." Cody tamped down his desire to jump over the table and take her in his arms.

She wrapped both hands around the mug. "One of the detectives commented that people around me have been dying. I called Reid and Adam. They are huddling with their boss, who may have to run interference and let the local authorities in on my connection to Lance."

"Risky call. We don't know if The Order has corrupted any of the higher-ups on the force. Doesn't end there." Cody leaned forward and lowered his voice. He told her about his latest test case. "Rick, my boss, came close to killing Senator Reynolds today by hacking his pacemaker. It's all supposed to be done in the name of testing Veridian's security. You know by pressing our system we can prevent the bad guys from doing harm but today involved hacking into the guy's pacemaker. Rick caused the pacemaker to fire. We watched the man on the monitor clutch his chest."

Lila's eyes widened. "What happened to the senator?"

"Rick finally let up and his heart returned to normal. I told everyone in the Alliance before I left for my motorcycle ride earlier. We have to stop this."

"How long has this project team been around?" Lila asked.

Cody sipped his beer. "About a year. Intel is hard to come by but I'm positive this wasn't the first time someone almost got killed. In fact, I'm betting someone already has. I intend to find out who's sanctioning this. The DDI team has extremely high security clearances, giving us access to the company's most sensitive information. Maybe I can find out more about what's going on."

"Won't snooping around send out red flags?"

He met Lila's concerned gaze. "I'm not going to do anything until I have vetted a way in and out." Cody shifted in his seat. "It's time to see who's playing for which team."

"You're talking about hacking into police servers?" Lila whispered.

"Maybe. I might be able to hack into Skies International, any accounts Lance might have, and the accounts of those in his inner circle."

Lila waited for a couple to pass their table before she spoke. "Can you do that without being detected?"

"Yes." Cody stopped talking as the waiter approached. He ordered pretzels just to keep the waiter busy. After the waiter left the table, Cody rubbed the stubble on his chin. "I'm not going to sit around and wait for one of Lance's men to grab you or worse. I spoke to the Alliance members last night. They are on board with my plan."

Lila shook her head. "I don't want you to become a target either."

"I'm already a target. We all are. But I promise I won't do anything until I have a clear plan." Cody leaned back as the waiter placed a bowl of pretzels on the table. When they were alone again, he said, "I've been asking myself, why Veridian chose you to threaten me with. Did they see us together at the charity event and figured we were...involved? Or do they know something deeper? Doesn't it seem too much of a coincidence that we've both landed in the world of Veridian Technologies?"

Several couples headed to the small dance floor as a slow country tune wafted throughout the restaurant. The band checked their set up and appeared ready for their gig.

"Reid and Adam taught me not to believe in coincidences, especially where the Sinclairs are involved." Lila ran a finger along the rim of her mug. "I guess I have reason to doubt most people."

Cody cringed inside. Did that include him? Of course, she doubted everything when it came to their nonexistent relationship. They hadn't discussed the past, yet they shared such a deep intimate kiss. She'd responded to the kiss so could he assume they still had a connection? He reminded himself to focus on their current life–and–death situation. Feelings would have to wait.

Lila pushed a strand of hair behind her ear, then shook it free. Her hair swung back, covering half her face and the ugly bruises on her collarbone. "I have an ethical duty to the law and to my clients." She rubbed her forehead. "The actions of your team are disturbing. I don't want to expose you and jeopardize Alliance goals, but what about the people they are targeting? Lives are in danger, Cody. We can't just sit on this."

"Even though we're sanctioned as an FBI covert operative team, we need to come to a consensus on how to handle this."

The piped in music ended, and the band's leader took the mic. He introduced himself as lead guitarist and singer for the group. He went on to introduce the rest of the band then they launched into their first set.

Cody focused on the cool, bitter liquid sliding down his throat. He appreciated the chance to focus on something else visceral other than staring into Lila's beautiful hazel eyes. His gaze moved down. She'd left the top three buttons unfastened, her compass necklace hanging in between two luscious mounds.

"I see you have another compass necklace."

She smiled and took hold of the compass pendant. "Reid is always prepared. I'm glad he ordered spares."

Lila's eyes lit up when she talked about Reid. She'd met her uncle as a teenager, and he'd helped her through some rough times. Aside from Reid, Cody knew that Carson her cousin, was the only family on the Sinclair side who'd rejected The Order.

"Reid is always spot on when it comes to Alliance matters." Cody glanced at the live band and the patrons dancing to their upbeat tune.

Lila leaned her head back against the booth. "You could have chosen to keep the Veridian threats from me. Why did you tell me?"

"I'll always been up front with you. Despite...our current status, you'll always be my best friend." He wanted to touch her, caress her soft face, but he fisted his hands on the table and held back the desire.

"Cody, I..." She held his gaze then shook her head. "I appreciate your honesty."

"I didn't do this to get a boy scout medal. I care about you." He let the words settle over her.

"So, what do we do now?"

You fall into my arms. He clamped his jaw shut, then said, "You have to be careful. More careful than usual. Veridian and your firm represent a serious threat. Stay away from anything connected to the internet. Veridian will use anything they can if they decide to go after you."

They each focused on the band for a few minutes before Cody

broke the silence. "I hope it wasn't too awkward getting stuck dancing with me at the benefit."

She stared at a spot on the table before glancing up at him. "I didn't expect to see you, much less share a dance. But you always were a good dancer." She smiled.

He shrugged. "I remember our first real dance. At Reid and Holly's wedding."

"Such a beautiful night." Lila met his gaze for a second before shifting to the dance floor.

"I would apologize but you're probably sick of the word *sorry*." Her sad expression tunneled inside him. How could he have been so stupid? He could spend the rest of his life trying to make up for his mistake, and he'd never succeed. Ruining the best thing in his life and hurting the one person he cared for more than anyone, ached like a gaping wound.

Lila shifted in her seat. "Let's chalk it up to fate and forget it."

A group of people entered the bar, raising the noise level as they chatted while pushing tables together to create room for the party of eight.

Cody's back stiffened, and he tightened the grip on his beer mug. From his position, he could only see her profile, but he knew it was her. Tally sat fifty yards from them. Her arrival couldn't be a coincidence. He had to think of way to get them out of there. Walking out of the front door would expose them. He tossed a twenty on the table. "Dance with me."

"Cody..." She shook her head then stopped when she caught his serious expression.

"ABS in question," he whispered. He stood and held out his hand.

She nodded and slipped her bag over her head, letting it lay across her body, then took his hand.

He led her to a spot on the dance floor nearest the band and back hallway, relieved Lila caught on to the game. As the band played, several more couples poured on to the crowded dance floor. Cody wrapped his arms around Lila and in an instant he was back in the past. He measured his life as his time with Lila and his time without her. He thought he'd been happy in San Francisco, but now he understood he'd only been surviving.

She rested her arms around his neck and soon they were pressed together. "What's going on?"

"Someone from my project team just walked in. She's my boss's right hand, and she's very dangerous. We need to get out of here ASAP but going out the front is a no-go." He peered at the group and saw Tally get up and head on to the dance floor with some guy about four inches shorter. He didn't recognize anyone in her party. Her intensity at work didn't match the raucous group surrounding her. Pulling Lila close, he spun so his back was to Tally. Thankfully, several couples had filled in the floor between them.

"I don't see a back door. We may have to go through the kitchen," Lila said.

They inched toward the hallway leading to the bathrooms.

Despite the issue of the cold-hearted bitch from his project team being near, Cody loved having Lila in his arms. The curve of her hips under his hands pulled at his attention. Forcing himself away from carnal thoughts, he searched for another way out. A waitress exiting the kitchen gave him their portal. "When the time is right follow me." He eased them closer then as the song wound down, he took her hand. Just as he was steps from the kitchen, a drunk patron collided with a waitress. Dishes and glasses crashed to the floor, scattering nachos and beer.

The band ended their song. In the brief period between starting a new song, Cody heard the serious voice of a newscaster coming across the television. He stared up at the screen and read the caption: *Senator Bertram Reynolds found dead in his Washington, DC, home. Apparent heart attack.*

Cody's heart drummed as if it would explode through his chest. He pulled Lila around the mess on the floor and raced toward the kitchen. Just as they entered the kitchen, he turned and saw Tally. Towering over the crowd, she stared at him, then raised her beer bottle in salute.

Chapter 28

"You guys okay?" Reid eyed them as Lila and Cody entered through the back door. He and Holly were seated at the kitchen table, laptops in front of them.

"Long day." Cody set their bags on the floor.

Holly stood. "Lila, I'm sorry about Steve. Do you want to talk about it?"

Lila hugged Holly. "There are some things you need to know, but Cody can go first. It's been an eventful evening."

Adam and Carson entered the kitchen taking seats at the table.

"Justin and Marissa had to go back to Virginia. They'll be back in a few days, sooner if necessary," Carson said.

Lila nodded. "In many ways I hope they stay there, protect little Isabella."

While Cody told them about the senator, Lila busied herself making coffee. She leaned against the counter as the coffee brewed.

"When I left work the senator was alive. Now, he's dead." Cody's jaw tightened. "During the case study, I pulled up the data from his medical record regarding this pacemaker. That's how he was killed. Rick caused the device to malfunction."

"This isn't your fault. You didn't hack into the pacemaker and kill the senator." Lila said. He put himself and his morals on the line to save her. Guilt snaked through her.

"Lila is right. You're there to stop this," Holly said.

"Someone had to authorize the murder." Cody gaze swung to Lila. "If they can kill the senator, they can come after you. I'm certain Tally was at that bar tonight to make sure I understood how powerful they are."

"You're in just as much danger," Lila countered. "Don't forget, you were reluctant to provide the data about the senator, which means they know you're not on board with their actions."

"Since we're sure Lance is connected to Veridian, these events may ultimately land at his door," Cody said. "To bolster that idea, my research shows the senator voted against several bills lobbied by two firms working on behalf of Skies International and Veridian Tech. I want to use Veridian Technology against them." Cody slid his chair closer to the table. "I've learned a lot about their system and the inner workings. I can mask myself and root around in the system. I'm convinced the hit list isn't a few random selections from Rick or Tally, at least not all of them. They are getting their orders from someone and it could lead back to Lance."

"I have confidence you know what you're doing. Don't make any big moves until we discuss, though. I'm going into the Dallas FBI headquarters tomorrow to update Yvonne Hewitt on the advancements of the task force. We've identified an Assistant SAC in the Dallas office who will be read into the task force."

"I'm glad you and Adam have someone trustworthy within the bureau to take our concerns seriously." Holly placed a hand over Reid's.

"Adam and I discussed the fact Jack approached the FBI." Reid raked a hand over chin. "We were able to trace a call made from Jack's phone into the Dallas FBI offices. Unfortunately, we didn't find any report of Jack speaking with an agent, which leads us to believe he ran up against one of Lance's people."

"Which put Jack in Lance's crosshairs," Adam added.

The discussion turned to Steve's death.

"Before you started at HTP, we ran background checks on everyone. Nothing sparked from Steve's review but I'm rerunning it, especially since we know he and Garvin Jennings crossed paths." Reid flipped his laptop around. "On another front, does this lady look familiar?"

Lila stared at a grainy photo of an elderly woman exiting a grocery store. She straightened. "That's the woman from the funeral."

"Yes, that's Willa Dickerson. I'm proposing you meet her in a public place."

Lila poured coffee into several mugs. "Maybe I should meet her alone."

"Too dangerous." Cody rose and helped her carry the coffee to the table.

"Cody is right. We don't know Willa Dickerson and even an elderly woman can be dangerous," Carson said.

"I have tutoring tomorrow. What about meeting her at the church? It's public and Reid and Adam can be there." Lila glanced around the table.

"That could work," Adam said. "Make the call and set up something for the afternoon." He narrowed his eyes. "Are you sure you're okay, Lila?"

"The bodies keep piling up. Where does it end?" Lila stared into her coffee.

By MIDNIGHT, everyone but Cody and Lila had retreated to their bedrooms. A mild thunderstorm rumbled outside, bringing back memories of the night she and Cody were attacked at the other safe house.

"Why don't you get some sleep?" Cody said, sitting on the sofa, legs outstretched on the coffee table.

Lila sat with legs curled under her in an overstuffed chair adjacent to the sofa. She couldn't tell him she feared nightmares, so she opted for another truth. "I can't get my mind to settle. Lance hasn't directly communicated anything to us. I'm certain everything leads back to him, but I worry about what's next."

Cody raked his hand over his scruff of beard. "Me, too, which is why we have to be proactive instead of reactive." He swung his legs off the table. "Jack, maybe Steve, are dead because of the suppressed evidence against Lance. Then we have the secret emerald mine and Lance's possible attempt to buy Veridian, but is there a connection between all these events?"

A sudden chill slithered through her. Lila pulled a blanket off the back of the chair and wrapped it around her shoulders. "Nothing in the files from Jack indicated he knew about the mine, the island, or Lance wanting to get his hands on Veridian." She gathered her hair into a ponytail using a hair tie she pulled off her wrist. "He's circling like a hawk waiting to swoop in."

"Let me show you something." Cody motioned to the bedroom area. "We won't talk about anything serious. I promise you'll like it."

Lila crossed her arms and stared at him. "Okay, Green, you've thirty seconds." She followed him to his bedroom.

"Only need ten." He shut the door, fumbled with something he pulled from his backpack, then flipped off the lights.

A second later the ceiling exploded in a myriad of stars and planets.

She gazed up. "Wow."

"Beautiful. Isn't it? It's not as awesome as the real thing but it works in a pinch. I often turn this on when I need to chill out and can't get outside." He grabbed a blanket and spread it out on the floor. Pointing to the floor, he lay down. "I hope it doesn't seem too juvenile." He grinned.

She hesitated as if weighing whether to go along, but then she settled next to him. "Not any more so than using nightlights."

"Speaking of nightlight, is this okay? I have a few more nightlights in my bag."

"No, I'm fine. Thanks." Her heart constricted at his concern.

As he pointed out various constellations and planets, she felt her muscles relax. For the moment, they were locked away from everything and everyone. They lay next to each with their arms the only contact points. Cody's voice had a calming effect as he talked about the constellations and stars. She had no idea he'd become interested in astronomy. Minutes later, he stopped. "Am I boring you?"

"No. I'm enjoying the show." She sat up and pointed. "What's that?"

"Sirius, which is the brightest star in the northern sky. It's one of the easiest to spot."

She turned and met his gaze. "It's beautiful." This time her voice sounded lighter, less constrained.

"Not half as beautiful as you."

Lila chewed her lip unsure of what to do.

Seconds passed then he cleared his throat and pointed out another constellation.

She settled back on the blanket and focused on the twinkling stars. The light from the projector and the stars on the ceiling illuminated Cody's profile. He rested with his arms clasped behind his head, his arm muscles bulging. She scooted closer as he continued to talk in soft whispers.

An hour later, Lila awoke in Cody's arms. She glanced down at her hands splayed across his chest. For a moment, she indulged herself, soaking in the safety and security of Cody's presence. For the first time in years, she felt truly safe.

"I didn't want to wake you. You appeared to be sleeping so soundly," Cody said, the low rumble of his voice reverberating in her ear. He moved a strand of hair out of her face.

"I'm sorry I fell asleep. I should go." She sat up.

"Don't."

Lila remained, indecision pumping through her brain.

"I'm sorry," he said. "About everything."

"You weren't supposed to talk about anything serious." Lila reclined again but resisted resting her head on his arm.

Cody turned sideways and leaned on his arm as the moon shimmered over his shoulder. "I've wanted you to know how sorry I am about how things ended. We don't have to talk anymore but I wanted you to know that."

Lila stared at the glistening stars on the ceiling. "You've been bending over backward to make sure I'm comfortable, plus you saved my life. I think the least I can do is listen."

He lay back down beside her. "I'm going to put it all on the table about what happened in Hawaii. You can respond or not."

She closed her eyes as thoughts of their graduation trip filtered into her head. She and Cody along with a group of their friends had rented a house in Hawaii the summer after their college graduation. On the third day of the trip, Lila got the shock of her life.

"I hurt you, and that's unforgiveable. I was drinking with the guys. Had a bit too much and the next thing I know I'm waking up in bed with Nikki Largent."

Cody's shocked expression, and Nikki's smug grin were imprinted in her memory.

"I still have no memory of that night." Cody shook his head. "I assume you never listened to the messages I left or read any of the letters I sent. I needed you to know that it all occurred because I had too much to drink that night and not out of interest in another woman." He sighed. "Still no excuse," he added. "You have every right to hate me."

"I was in shock after walking in on you and Nikki. At the time I didn't care to listen to your side of the story." Her heart hitched. She hadn't wanted to talk about Hawaii but now that they were, perhaps they could both move on. Lila swallowed. "Why do you think you can't remember that night?"

He shrugged. "I don't remember having more than a couple of beers. But it was hot and I hadn't had a lot to eat that day so I suppose a few beers could have affected me. One minute I was having drinks with the guys, then the next thing I knew I was waking up to Nikki and you."

The image hung in the air like a dead weight. Finally, Lila said, "I was angry, humiliated, and hurt. When I left Hawaii, all I wanted to do was get away. I moved out of my apartment within days of being back in Boston. I came to Dallas for the summer before law school. Being around my family helped." She paused and met his gaze. "I don't hate you."

Turning, he trailed a finger over the bruises on her neck.

She closed her eyes at his touch. "My entire existence has been a life-or-death situation. You shouldn't have to be worried about your life or career, but I'm thankful for what you're doing."

"You don't need to thank me. When we were teenagers, we vowed to always stick together. I dropped the ball once, but I'll never do it again. Regardless of our relationship status, I will spend my life doing what I can to keep you safe and bring down The Order." He pulled her into sitting position. Facing her, he stuck his hand out. "I'd suggest a blood brothers' oath but that's creepy and I don't want to be your brother. Let's just shake on it."

She laughed. "Now this is juvenile. What exactly are we shaking on?"

"Me vowing to do whatever I can to keep you safe."

She shook her head. "I'm not agreeing to that." She shifted, crossing her legs. "Since you're insisting on this teenaged contract, I have something to add. You will do whatever is in your power to keep me safe, but I will do the same for you, okay? I have the power to save your life, too, you know."

He raised his hands. "Far be it for me to second guess your badass abilities, especially after you started shooting while we were under fire. So, hell yeah, I'll shake to that. I'm not all macho about having a girl save my life." He grinned.

They shook hands.

With her hand still in his, Cody leaned in a gave her a featherlight kiss on her cheek. The contact setting his nerve endings on fire.

They pulled apart for only a second, their eyes locked on each other.

Bending his head, Cody met her halfway as their lips touched. He deepened the kiss and once again, she matched him with equal fervor.

When they pulled apart, they caught their breath.

A million emotions ricocheted inside her like a pinball machine on speed. "I'm afraid, Cody. I'm afraid for my family, the Alliance. And you. Things are happening, and one bullet could be the end of any one of us." With those words her emotions tumbled over and tears she'd always held tight, began to spill.

With the pad of his thumb, he wiped away her tears. "I won't leave you," he repeated.

She nodded and inhaled. "I'm a blubbering idiot." She lowered her head.

He lifted her chin and stared into her watery eyes. "A beautiful blubbering idiot." He leaned over and kissed her lips gently at first.

They were so connected she couldn't distinguish her heartbeat from his.

"I missed you." He mumbled when they came up for air.

"I missed you, too."

He pulled her on top of him, and she felt like she'd returned home.

"I want you."

Lila nodded and for at least one night, she let her emotions free.

Chapter 29

The next afternoon, Lila pulled open the heavy doors of the Fox Street Church and ambled into the sparsely populated building. The firm had been shut down while the police investigated Steve's death. In the meantime, HTP employees filled text messages and private social media discussions with expression of grief, shock, and sadness. Three emotions that were her constant companions these days. But then the prickly sensation on her cheek reminded her of Cody's whiskers brushing up against her last night. The memory of their passionate evening filled her with a new cluster of emotions. Joy, confusion, anger, and fear pulled her in all directions as if each emotion demanded her full attention.

In the basement, she rounded the corner and met a buzz of voices emanating from the study room. When the session had concluded, Lila packed away supplies as the other teachers filed out of the room. After locking up the tutoring room, she darted upstairs, sank onto a cushioned pew, stared at the ornate paintings, and waited. She shifted her gaze and caught sight of Reid and Holly entering the church. While Reid settled across the aisle several rows behind her, Holly approached the candle stand and lit a votive. She stood in front of the rows of candles for a few seconds before sitting next to Reid.

Adam remained outside while Cody sat one row behind her on the other side of the church.

A shadow darkened Lila's vision. She looked up and sucked in a breath. Willa Dickerson lumbered into the aisle and sat next to her. "Hello, Lila."

Lila eyed the cane, a dark wood one vastly different from the stick she'd used at the funeral. "Hello. Thanks for coming."

Glancing around the church, Lila spotted two women paused in front of the alter. When they moved aside, fragmented light shot through the stained-glass windows. The stillness of the room had been disrupted like a fluctuation in the time continuum. Lila shifted on the pew. Her friends were behind her and would jump into action if necessary.

"Willa Dickerson. Do you remember me?" She held out a wrinkled hand.

Lila shook the woman's hand, then scrunched her forehead. "I remember you from Jack's funeral, but should I have known you?" Tiny hairs rose on the back of Lila's neck as she spotted a revolver in the woman's purse. The fact that the Jennings and perhaps Steve, all possessed knowledge of the contents of Jack's files, and were all dead, made her nervous. Could a gun already be trained on them? She eyed the two women now ambling down the side aisle almost parallel to her pew.

Willa leaned on her cane. "Yes, you should."

Blowing out a sigh, Lila wanted to scream. "Ms. Dickerson, with all due respect, I don't remember you. What I know is you used some voodoo or hypnosis trick during the funeral. I don't enjoy being played with. How are you connected to Lance Sinclair and The Order?" Although Lila already had a loose grasp of the woman's connection to The Order, she wanted to hear from Mrs. Dickerson.

The woman tapped her cane on the floor as she maintained an intense lock on Lila's eyes. "I assure you there are no games here. Think."

"I presume you know that you could be in danger. I saw a weapon in your purse. Either you're here to use it on me, which I doubt because you likely would have already, or you're concerned about your own safety."

"Very astute."

"Mrs. Dickerson, how do you know me?" Lila asked, clamping her hands together. Anxiety and frustration washed over her. Apparently, she should know this woman, yet even though a slight whisper of something percolated just below the surface, she couldn't grasp the memory.

"Call me Willa." The woman stared at a point on the floor then lifted her head. "I knew this day would come. I will tell you what I know." She looked up, a sheen of tears in her eyes. "My husband Edgar was a member of The Order. When The Order was no more than a group of men getting together to play cards, Edgar's older brother joined. He talked up the group like they were the next best thing this side of the ocean. Edgar worked as a bellman at one of the most prestigious hotels in the Washington, DC, area. He was a simple man who performed his job with pride, but when Edgar met Russell and learned of an opportunity, he got excited."

Lila shifted and side-eyed Cody, relieved he sat near.

"Russell Sinclair spoke to Edgar about joining the group," Willa continued. "Seems he wanted him on his team. As a bellman, Edgar could get into rooms at the hotel and would be one of the first to know when dignitaries arrived in town. Russell wanted to up his station in life so rubbing elbows with the rich and famous was a priority."

"You knew Russell Sinclair?" Lila said.

"I knew the bastard." She winced and crossed herself. "I'm a nurse. I came to Babylon Hall as a young woman. Edgar was fifteen years older." She smiled. "The hotel was on the way to the hospital. I walked by every day. That's how I met my Edgar." Willa folded her hands in her lap and smiled, in an apparent happy memory of her husband.

"Did you know Mary, Russell's wife?" Lila asked.

"Yes, I helped deliver her babies. Poor thing. She was young, too, and Russell treated her poorly, as if she were a piece of property.

Once she'd completed her life as a childbearing woman, Russell had no use for her."

Lila pictured Lance with his newborn in the video message played at the Veridian benefit. He sat with a smug expression as he spewed lies about wanting to help other children. Lance was all about himself, but Lila's thoughts landed on the unseen mother of his child. Delphine and Lance always made a curious couple in her opinion. They were only seen at public events, making a show of how genuine their relationship was. Now that Delphine had delivered their child would Lance go the way of his grandfather? "How much do you know about Lance?"

"I've met him twice, and I'm sure he doesn't remember me. I represent the old days. Plus, I wasn't really on board with what The Order stood for. Edgar got wrapped up in being accepted into the group. He didn't consider that they were headed down a dark path." Shaking her head, she leaned on her cane and balled a fist against her heart. "He sold our house, and we moved into one of the cottages at Babylon Hall."

Lila still had many questions, but Willa's tearful expression made her remain quiet. Perhaps the woman *needed* to speak about her experiences.

"I hated living there. Fortunately, for me, since I came with a skill, they never made me commit to their silly doctrine. I cared for the people living at the estate, but most of the time I watched over Mary. By her second miscarriage, her mental state was dubious at best. Poor woman had been through so much."

"Did you know Jack Struthers?"

A long silence ensued as Willa closed her eyes. Lila thought she'd fallen asleep until the woman's eyes fluttered open. "Mr. Struthers called for Edgar, but he'd passed on by then. He even came to my house. I understood how ruthless The Order was and I didn't open the door. Jack said he found some information about The Order and wanted to speak to Edgar. Guess he didn't know my Edgar was no longer with us. Took me a few months to get the nerve to call him back. He came to my house again and he appeared trustworthy, so I told him what I knew. I was thrilled that perhaps he could finally bring The Order to justice." She sighed and shook her head. "Mr. Struthers was a decent man. I'm sorry he lost his life trying to do the right thing."

"Jack was special." Lila shifted. "How did he find Edgar?"

"I don't know."

"My grandmother was Vivian Sinclair. What do you know about her?"

The old woman stared ahead, both hands resting on the apex of her cane. "I helped deliver Vivian. In many ways she was worse than her father. Amazing how people can get sucked into such a twisted ideology." She cast her gaze downward. "After Russell died, Ivan contacted many of his father's closest friends and confidants, at least the ones he knew about. As I'm sure you know Russell separated his children, choosing to focus on developing Vivian as the Grand Commander. I remember the day he sent Ivan away." Her voice trailed off for a few seconds. "Although Edgar only held a cursory position on the perimeter of the controlling council, he'd received a call from Ivan. They had several conversations and a couple of times Ivan paid for Edgar's travels to meet him. My husband never told me what those conversations entailed. However, weeks before he died, he made me promise to deliver a box to you. Edgar's involvement in The Order meant I was involved. They made me do a lot of things I'm not proud of." With shaky hands, she reached into her purse and drew out a small black box. She held the box in her lap.

Once again Lila scanned the church for trouble. Not seeing anything alarming, she focused on the box in Willa's lap.

"What else did they ask you to do?" Lila said, her voice soft.

Willa shook her head and pulled a tissue from the pocket of her gray sweater. Tears pooled at the edges of her eyes. "Not now."

"You mentioned Garvin Jennings. Do you know a Morris Beak?"

Willa's face blanched, and she used her right thumb to rub the space between her left thumb and forefinger. "Garvin and Morris were Edgar's friends. Women were not allowed to know much about The Order back then, and Edgar kept his friends at arm's length from me, but I got to know Garvin pretty well. His wife, Sheila had a miscarriage, too. Poor thing. They never had any children. Garvin was an attorney and a smart man. I couldn't for the life of me understand why he'd get involved in something like this. But Morris Beak." She shook her head. "The two men were complete opposites. Mr. Beak was in finance or banking. Very intense. He was a young man when Edgar and I still lived at the compound. They put him through school. In those days, a lot of the young men were granted scholarships. In return, they were expected to use their expertise for the good of The Order. The scholarships garnered loyalty."

"I guess that's one way," Lila said.

"Morris Beak was as loyal as they come. He came along toward the end of Russell's life but quickly gained favor. Last I heard he moved his allegiance to Ivan. By default, I assume he honors Lance as his boss, although Beak is an old man now." She pursed her lips and shook her head.

"What else do you know about Beak?" Lila forced herself to slow down.

Willa grew quiet, then said, "There were rumors. He's a very dangerous man. Get as far away from Morris Beak and anything related to The Order and Lance Sinclair as you can."

Lila chose her next few questions with care. As an attorney, she'd learned the art of deposing a witness. "Did you and Edgar have family in the area?"

"My parents died a year after Edgar and I married. Went one after the other. I have a sister, but she's been gone now close to ten years. Edgar and I have a daughter." Her face brightened. "She lives in Iowa with her family. She's a nurse, too. Her husband is a good man, and of course, I'm over the moon about my grandchildren, two girls and a boy. I hope to be there this Thanksgiving, if I make it that far." She pursed her lips.

Willa was right to be concerned for her life.

"Sounds like you and your daughter have a special relationship." A stab to her heart reminded her she would never know the special feeling of a mother-daughter relationship. "You must miss your husband. How long has he been gone?" Lila hoped to keep her talking for as long as possible. They needed answers, and Willa represented their only hope.

"I miss him terribly. Other than the questionable decision to follow Russell Sinclair, Edgar was a great husband and father. He died of cancer a year ago. One day he was here and the next gone." She patted glistening tears from her eyes.

"I'm sorry, Willa." Lila nodded toward the object in Willa's hand. "That box, what does it mean?"

"This box has been sitting inside a drawer ever since Edgar asked me to make the delivery. On his deathbed and he was still thinking about Order business." She sniffed. "I don't know what the contents means," she handed the box to Lila, "but be careful."

"Garvin Jennings gave me a similar box." Lila opened the lid and wasn't shocked to see an emerald plate inside. She quickly spotted the letters PZ PU on the plate.

Willa eyed the emerald and shook her head. With sad eyes she said, "He's dead, isn't he?"

"Yes, he is. He and Sheila were killed moments after he handed me the box."

She nodded. "Months before Edgar died, he made me promise to deliver this box if he couldn't. He made this request with tears in his eyes. I believe he knew of the danger. Two weeks ago, I got a letter delivered to my home. It didn't come in the mail." Once again, she reached inside her purse, but this time, pulled out a piece of paper and handed it to Lila.

Lila opened the folded paper. The note read:

Now is the time for your mission. Deliver the box to Lila Caldwell. You have three weeks from the date of receipt to carry out this assignment. It is imperative she receive this box. Once you make the delivery, beware. There may be others wishing you harm.

Hugo Castille

Heart thumping wildly, Lila reread the note. Why her? And why now? "Who is Hugo Castille?"

Willa shook her head. "I don't know."

"Can I keep this note?"

"Yes, take it. I don't know anything else other than what's inside that note. If Edgar hadn't pressed me to do this, I would have taken my chances. I hate being a messenger for The Order, but my family could be in danger."

"I understand, and I think you did the right thing." Lila dropped the paper inside her bag. She sensed Willa's fear and was concerned for her safety as well. "You've done your job. Can you visit your daughter earlier than planned?"

Willa shook her head. "I won't put them in jeopardy. I hope that the potential for danger eases in a few weeks, so I can make that visit. If I sense a threat, I won't go." Turning to Lila, she placed a hand on her arm. "For some reason, you hold the key."

"The key to what?"

Willa glanced at the emerald stone in Lila's hand. "That's obviously a clue. Whoever compelled me to deliver this message must want you to figure it out. Think, child. Your memories are there, just under the surface. Use them." The woman expelled a heavy sigh as her shoulder slumped. "I'm tired. It's time I go home."

Lila hesitated, but rationalized she'd get better cooperation under Willa's terms. "How did you get here? Can I take you home?"

The woman shook her head and smiled weakly. "I'll be okay. If not, I've lived a good and long life. I've made my share of mistakes, but I hope I've made my peace." She stared ahead at the altar and made the sign of the cross.

"Please, be careful," Lila said.

With the aid of her cane and Lila's assistance, she stood. "Think." She tapped the cane three times.

"You tapped your cane at the funeral." Lila pinched her eyebrows. "I started to remember...I think. Did you hypnotize me?" She looked at the woman.

"No. I know nothing about hypnosis. During my time at Babylon Hall, a large part of my nursing duties involved caring for babies, children, and pregnant women. Most of the women chose to have their babies on the property. Rhythmic sounds can help with anxiety and pain management during labor. I started thumping a stick on the floor during the process of childbirth or to help a colicky baby. Newborns like the sound of heartbeats but the tapping was close enough. It didn't help everyone. I sensed tension in you during the funeral. I thought it might help."

Lila stared at her. "There are memories I can't quit grasp now. What do you know about me?"

"I'm tired now. We'll talk again later." Willa stepped forward, then stopped. "Be dauntless." She ran her wrinkled hand over Lila's arm, then ambled out of the church.

Chapter 30

L ance sliced through the water on his fiftieth lap in his California beach home's oversized pool. The Mediterranean-blue pool water reminded him of his villa in Cap d'Antibes. Soon, he'd take the baby there. He pulled up to the side and gripped the greenish-blue tile, dipping the back of his head into the water.

Delphine. Disgust and desire. His feelings for her vacillated between the two emotions but last night he'd made the decision to kill her. She would be of no use soon. The pediatrician told him the baby should receive mother's milk for at least six months. As beautiful as Delphine was, Lance couldn't stand the thought of her for another few weeks. He had his people locate a woman, in good health who'd be willing to sell her breast milk. Lance agreed to pay top dollar. Nothing but the best for his son.

"I woke up and you weren't there. I missed you." Katarina sauntered toward him topless as if she were on a European beach.

Ah, I miss the topless beaches of Europe. Katarina's breasts sparkled in the mid-morning sun.

"I needed to think." He climbed out of the pool and wrapped a plush towel around his neck.

"Stress isn't good for the skin," she encircled his neck and planted butterfly kisses along his collarbone.

Lance replied with roaming hands and a physical appreciation for Katarina's assets.

His cell phone buzzed on the lounge chair, breaking the passionate scene. Lance pulled away. "I have to take this call. Wait for me inside."

Katarina nodded and sashayed into the house.

Lance tore his gaze from her glorious ass and answered the call he'd been waiting on. "Shaw, what do you have?"

"Lila and her boyfriend visited Jennings. We let them get away. The Jennings kill went as planned. We're still running down your father's close associates and have almost completed the rest of our target list."

"Excellent," Lance said. "I want everyone afraid to talk to them."

"What about the old woman? Our men spotted her in a conversation with Lila at Struthers's funeral."

"I want her alive for now. Good work with the senator. Son of a bitch got what was coming to him. All he had to do was make sure Skies got the UN contract. Senator Harper stepped up. I'll make a note to donate to his next campaign. Also, I have a special recon I want you to conduct." Lance tightened his fists as he gave Shaw the details.

"As the Veridian DDI contact, I'll be sure to express pleasure with the team. Expect to hear from me soon on the recon." Shaw hung up.

No one could trump him. This would end all resistance. His family and their friends had caused enough trouble. Their intrusion would be crushed. But he'd make sure they suffered first.

Lance considered the old Order mantra. *Ordo Ortus, Order Rising.*

Chapter 31

Cody shifted in his seat again and glanced up at the wall clock inside the DDI team offices. Although staying holed up at the farmhouse with the Alliance appeared to be a better, safer option he needed to be at work to find out as much as possible. In a couple more hours he could get back to Lila and the team, who were reviewing all they'd learned from Willa Dickerson, and looking for Morris Beak.

Pivoting to his screen, Cody stared at the blinking cursor and huffed out a sigh. He had a job to do.

He hadn't seen Rick and Tally all day. Perhaps they were laying low after murdering the senator. So far, none of the team members had said a thing about the senator's death. He looked up from his screen. Although shielded by a dull gray cubicle partition, Cody stared in the direction of his coworkers on the other side. How could they live with themselves? Maybe the senator had been the first death. Maybe they believed the other scenarios were only tests or perhaps they were being threatened, too.

He'd been working on a report, which on the surface appeared to be nonlethal. The project covered itself with legitimate security pursuits, but the tests that crossed the line were pure evil. He couldn't be sure how the information in his report would be used, so he kept some areas intentionally vague. Keeping his job was a priority for the sole purpose of bringing down The Order, Lance, and Veridian.

Cody attached his report to an email and sent it off to Rick. Staring at his own calendar, which thankfully was devoid of meetings for the day, he clicked on Rick's. Some of the managers chose to open their calendars so their teams could always find them. Rick wasn't one of them. Neither was Tally.

As some of the team filtered out for the day, Cody stayed behind. He expected his every keystroke was being monitored so he had to be careful. Wading into the inner workings of Veridian would be like dodging bullets in a war zone. For now, he stayed within areas appropriate for his position. Cody ventured into the common directories on the company's intranet. He perused various files and if anyone had been tracking his keystrokes, they'd believe he was looking for employee information. He checked the company's clinic hours, the cafeteria menu for the rest of the week, and read a few articles on Veridian's community service pursuits. Venturing into department public folders, he rooted around, already familiar with some of the projects. He didn't expect to find a folder entitled "evil deeds" but he wanted to know as much as possible about Veridian projects. With the company hierarchy on his screen, Cody studied each department. The DDI, as expected, wasn't listed. Each DDI member had been designated under special teams in the employee directory and they all fell under the authority of Robert Gumfrey, CLO. He'd never met the man or been told he ultimately reported up to him. Cody planned to research Gumfrey this evening.

Waiting until he heard nothing on the other side of his partition, he printed off a copy of his report then jumped up. On his way through the hive, he plucked the report off the printer. The room remained empty. He marched up to Rick's office and twisted the knob on his door. When it opened, he ambled in with the report. All areas of the project team area were monitored by surveillance cameras and Cody expected Rick's office was included. On first glance, the office appeared like any other, but something had to exist which would gain leverage on Rick. A large L-shaped desk sat in the center of the room, with the two guest chairs in front. Off to the side sat a bookcase with three shelves and a set of cabinets at the bottom. Cody longed to inspect the inside of the drawers, but such a bold act might come back to bite him. A face-down picture frame sat on the edge of Rick's desk. Cody hadn't seen the frame in previous visits. He slid the report on Rick's desk, knocking over the frame. Cursing, Cody bent to retrieve the object. He flipped it over and stared at a smiling Rick with his arm around a woman and two little boys, grinning in front of them. The foursome wore winter attire and posed in front of a sign that said WELCOME TO ZURICH, SWITZERLAND. Scrawled in the left corner, someone had written Rick, Stacy, Frankie, four, and Sammy, seven. Rick had a family? He replaced the picture, shut the door quietly, and sauntered down the hall.

Chapter 32

As soon as Cody entered the farmhouse, Lila longed to rush into his arms but stopped when she glimpsed his dull expression and the woman standing beside him.

He met Lila's gaze then said, "Everyone, meet Angie. She and I are good friends from grad school. We both work for Veridian."

Smiling, Lila shook her hand. She remembered seeing Angie at the Veridian charity event. Her first thought had been she and Cody were a couple, but as she'd watched their interaction, she concluded they were indeed just friends. Their easy friendship made Lila long for the days when she and Cody shared a comfortable relationship. Could they get there again? Was that what she wanted?

Reid crossed the room and shook Angie's hand. "We are a covert FBI task force. Each of us here have been personally affected by The Order. Some of us are connected to this by blood and others have been thrown into to the fight by our relationships. This isn't your fight. If you choose to continue, none of us can guarantee your safety but we could use your computer skills."

All eyes turned to Angie, who appeared a bit shocked at the attention. "I appreciate the warning. I've known Cody for a few years now.

He was there for me when I needed someone. I'm in. Plus, I'm sure you've already performed a background check on me."

"Smart." Reid nodded. "You're now read into, meaning accepted into, our mission. Welcome to the Alliance."

"Sounds badass." She flashed a grin then sobered. "But I understand the serious nature."

"Welcome to the team." Adam shook her hand, then smoothed back his jet-black hair.

Carson greeted her and waved everyone to the table. "We didn't get anything fancy, just pizza."

"Perfect," Angie said following Holly.

"Lila, can I speak with you?" Cody took her hand and led her into the bedroom.

As soon as the door closed, he gathered her into his arms. "Are you okay?"

"No." She sighed. "I can't help but think about the warnings I've received. I think we're getting closer. To something."

"We're going to end this. I promise." His gaze speared into her as his ran his hand up and down the length of her arms.

"You can't make that promise," she said, her voice soft.

Cody focused on the floor then looked at her. "Maybe I'm jumping the gun, but I don't want to lose you. Even if we aren't together, I'll always want the best for you." His jaw tightened. "I hope you believe that."

Lila held on to him. "I believe you but all of this...us back together. I don't know."

"We don't need to rush." He touched her chin then lifted her head as leaned in to kiss her.

Her head swam with conflicting emotions. The kiss held a dizzying effect while her head sifted through all the reasons she should shut this down. Maybe there would be a time she could devote to sorting through her feelings, but with the growing danger surrounding them she couldn't focus.

"I want to take you away from all this." His voice was low as he moved a stray hair away from her face.

"I'd settle for a night when I'm not looking over my shoulder."

A knock sounded followed by Holly. She stuck her head in. "Sorry to interrupt, but we need you guys out here."

When she and Cody settled in at the table, Holly smiled and patted Lila's arm as she handed over a plate.

Holly had been rooting for her and Cody's reunion for several years. Lila had no idea where she and Cody would end up, but having a friend like Holly would help, no matter what happened.

Reid pulled a slice of pizza from the box. "We need all hands on deck. Justin and Marissa are arranging their schedules and should be here shortly." He turned to Angie. "Did Cody update you on our situation?"

She set down her fork. "Yes. I had heard rumblings about The Order and Lance Sinclair years ago but when there weren't any arrests, I figured there was no truth to the rumors."

"Which is exactly what Lance wants everyone to believe," Carson said.

Angie shook her head and glanced at Cody. "Hard to believe we're working for the enemy. I had no idea Veridian was evil, but you know what they say about absolute power."

Reid nodded. "The Englishman, Lord Acton. *Absolute power corrupts absolutely.*" He turned to Lila. "Why don't you update everyone."

Lila explained the strange conversation with Willa Dickerson. "She told me how she came to live at Babylon Hall and her husband's involvement with The Order." Lila told them about Willa's cane and how she used it to calm her patients. Rubbing her temples, Lila furrowed her brows. "A memory is there, prickling on the fringe. It's like after you wake up and you know you had a dream but the memory is just out of reach."

"Don't put too much pressure on yourself." Reid patted her shoulder. "Do you have the map box?"

She nodded, looking up at him. "I scanned all the documents and have stored them in multiple places." She pulled on her bracelet. "I have a copy on this flash drive. I also have the actual map box with me."

Cody turned to Angie. "Lila found a map box containing her great-grandfather's diary and other documents related to The Order. It's been helpful in deciphering some of the codes and complexities of the organization." He finished one pizza slice and reached for another.

"We need to find as much information on Morris Beak as possible. Willa warned me against meeting him, but I believe he's critical to finding out about the emerald mine and secret island."

Holly moved a stack of papers. "There are so many moving parts. I'm still trying to understand why all this about a secret emerald mine and island has come up now. Ivan has been dead for several years."

"Willa didn't understand. And now we have two emerald plates locked in a portable safe. She got a letter, delivered to her by courier, instructing her to give me the emerald plate. The sender is someone named Hugo Castille. She didn't know him. Neither do I." Lila pulled the note from her purse.

"No one else touch it." Reid rushed into the kitchen and returned with a plastic bag. With the bag in hand, he pushed the paper inside. Then leaned over Holly's shoulder as they read the letter through the bag. When they finished, he handed the note to Cody. "Anyone recognize the name Hugo Castille?"

Everyone shook their heads.

"I'll have this analyzed. Maybe we can get some fingerprints. This directive came from someone and it's not Lance," Reid said.

"We've started working the Morris Beak angle." Adam closed an empty pizza box.

Angie wiped her hands on a napkin. "What do you want me to do?"

Cody placed a half-eaten pizza slice on his plate. "We're going to hack into Veridian and get some answers."

Angie pushed one of her braids aside and tapped her fingers together. "You just said that in front of an FBI agent."

"I'm not worried about your past. We've all had to make some ethical decisions. Everyone here will understand if you don't want to take the risk," Reid said.

"Cody and I have already discussed this. He wouldn't let me come here until I made a choice. I'll admit to a history of hacking, but I'm a white hat now. I'm choosing to look at this as performing a public service. If only from the aspect that Veridian can't abuse their power." Angie stretched her arms. "Let's do this."

Two hours later, Angie and Cody sat at the table with their laptops. They'd set up a secured internet connection and mounted safeguards to mask their identities online while everyone else studied the documents and files from the map box.

Cody's fingers tapped at the keyboard. "I'm in the dark web, which is like the deepest core of the internet. I'm using a TOR browser which ensures my anonymity."

"It's been a long time since I've been here," Angie said, her fingers flying over the keyboard. "But I see some of my old friends."

"I thought everyone was anonymous," Holly said, peering over Cody's shoulder.

"A lot of us go by aliases." Angie cocked her head. "Meet Glamzam."

Lila grinned. "Cool name."

Angie shook her head and made a show of tossing her braids around. "Thanks."

Cody rolled his eyes. "Hey, Glam, I'm in. Everyone knows Veridian is currently a publicly owned company, but right away I'm finding rumors about a group called Stonegate who want to acquire it and take the company private. Does the name sound familiar?"

Lila tapped her fingers on the table. "No. What about you, Reid?"

"I'm not aware of Stonegate, but I can do some checking." He set aside a document and pulled out his laptop.

"Maybe I can find out." Sitting at the table and opening her laptop, Lila logged into the HTP network. Minutes later, she pulled up an electronic file labeled Stonegate. When she opened the file, she stopped when a warning flashed. *Unauthorized Access.* "Damn. I can't get in. But the fact there is a file indicates HTP has done something on behalf of Stonegate." She rubbed her eyes, then tried another avenue. "I'm not finding anything about a company called Stonegate. Everywhere I look is a big dead end."

"I can't shake the feeling that we're swirling around in the middle of a huge shit pile." Cody rubbed his eyes and sat back against the chair.

Reid stood and began to pace. "Let's review. Jack contacted the FBI about important evidence and a week later he's dead for what we can assume is having the hidden evidence against Lance. In addition to Peter Shaw, the corrupt ex-FBI agent working for Lance, we know there are a number of other agents with allegiance to The Order. Garvin Jennings and his wife were killed by a weaponized Veridian drone moments after handing Lila an emerald plate with some type of code on it. Willa Dickerson received a note compelling her to also hand off an emerald plate to Lila. Neither Garvin nor Sheila mentioned a note."

Reid stopped pacing and placed his hands on the back of Holly's chair. "As far as we know Willa Dickerson is still alive. Yvonne is working on placing someone to guard her outside her house. Then the latest death is Steve Dorman's on the HTP premises."

Lila's heart jumped a few beats as she consulted her laptop. Several clicks later, she inhaled. "Veridian stock, as of today, is trading at a little over $100 a share. Acquiring companies usually pay at least a 20 percent premium over the current stock price. If Stonegate were to acquire Veridian, they'd have to shell out billions. Assuming that Lance takes ownership of the emerald mine and it's worth as much as Jennings indicated, that money would significantly boost Lance's position to acquire Veridian."

Cody rose from his desk chair and glanced out the patio glass door. "If Lance gets Veridian, he will own the world. Veridian has over two billion users. They have government contracts, both with the US and internationally. They have access to information in schools, universities, technology, and other companies. Most people don't even know this company's reach. The Deep Dive Initiative will be child's play."

"We can't let that happen." Carson pointed to Russell Sinclair's open diary. "I found references to what he called 'his island insurance plan,' but so far nothing to indicate a location." She studied the diary, then flipped the page. "Wait. I found something, 'The Caduceus holds the secret. A tetrad of plates of green will show the way.'" Carson reread the passage.

Reid leaned over her shoulder and stared at the diary page. "Caduceus. Caduceus," he said scratching his head.

Holly glanced up from her position on the floor. "A caduceus is a wand with serpents intertwined around the staff."

Beaming at his wife, Reid nodded. "You're right." He paced the length of the room then stopped. "Hermes, the Greek god of trade and wealth, carried a caduceus. Hermes is sometimes referred to as the trickster. Also, in Roman history the caduceus is carried in the left hand of Mercury, the god of financial gain, commerce, messages, merchants, tricksters, and thieves."

"What's with this guy? He's a walking Google search engine," Angie said, staring at Reid.

"You'll get used to him," Lila said.

Cody glanced at Angie. "The Order was started by Russell Sinclair, Lila's great-grandfather. He based The Order around the number seven. Their logo contains a heptagon and seven symbols are imbedded in their core principles."

"Most everything related to The Order is shrouded in symbols and cryptic messages." Holly swept her curly brown hair up into a ponytail. "The leader of The Order is called the Grand Commander and each one has continued to use secret messages and symbols."

Adam opened a portable safe in a corner of the room and drew out the emerald tablets. "Plates of green."

"The emerald tablet of Hermes." Reid pulled up a photo on his laptop and pointed. "Actually, the text on the emerald tablets is said to be authored by Hermes Trismegistus who is associated with both the Greek god Hermes and the Egyptian god Thoth. The emerald tablet is an ancient artifact that is purported to contain a powerful formula for achieving personal transformation and bring about the evolution of our species. Around 400 AD, in order to protect the tablet, it was buried somewhere in the Giza plateau, which is near Cairo, Egypt."

"Cairo? Near the Great Pyramids and the Sphinx?" Lila asked.

"Exactly."

"What does all this have to do with the secret island and emerald mine?" Holly asked.

Reid studied the two plates then placed them together. "We've dealt with symbols associated with The Order in the past. I believe each small tablet contains a portion of larger clue." He pointed to the tablets that when placed next to one another contained the letters MSVVY and PZ PU. "Tetrad means four. We don't have them all."

Lila rubbed her temples. "The piece of paper that fell out of box Garvin gave had only two names: Willa Dickerson and Morris Beak. We have Garvin and Willa's plate and we can assume Morris Beak has the third plate. So where is the fourth plate?"

"I got a bite." Angie leaned toward her screen. "Someone talking about Stonegate. Seems it's a small investor group." She continued to tap her keyboard. "The contact didn't know where it was incorporated but knows the name of one of the board members. His name is Peter Shaw."

Chapter 33

She hated the dark. She'd been taken from her bed in the dark of night. Her eyes had been closed when a strange man with garlic-scented breath scooped her out of bed and taken her for a long car ride.

She wanted to cry but what was the use? No one would help her. Inside the room, she huddled under a wool blanket which smelled like mold and thought about her friends. Did they miss her? She'd stopped trying to figure out what day it was. Days and nights didn't matter here. Perhaps her class had already taken the annual fourth grade field trip to the zoo. She'd begged her foster mother to pay the five-dollar fee so she could go. Her foster mother finally agreed and on the last day to submit the permission slip and money, Lila, with swelled pride, presented the envelope to her teacher, treating the simple task as if she were paying for a trip to the moon. Despite her vow not to cry, tears leaked from her eyes. Did anyone miss her?

Lila sucked in a breath. No more tears. The blanket had become her lifeline. Sometimes she wondered if she were dead but as long as she could feel the scratchy wool, she was alive.

Minutes or hours later a clanging sound signaled an arrival. She gripped the blanket, drew in a breath, and waited.

"Lila," a voice called.

She expelled a sigh. The lady was nice. She had a gentleness about her which Lila on instinct decided she could trust. Maybe. Still, she drew the blanket closer and didn't answer.

"Lila, you need to come with me." A light flashed in her eyes, blinding her so she turned away.

A light touch grazed her shoulder. "I won't hurt you."

But there was something to fear.

"Come child. You'll get me in trouble, too, if I don't deliver you."

Strong arms guided Lila out of the bed and through a door. A few more steps and darkness turned to light. She shivered in the thin nightgown. They were in a long, narrow hallway, overhead lightbulbs leading the way.

"Where am I?" Lila said, her voice hoarse. She glanced at the woman. With her dark hair pulled back in a bun and a pale blue shirt with matching pants, she appeared like the nice nurse at her doctor's office. But she worked for them.

Lila's heart rattled inside her chest as they stopped in front of a door.

The woman turned and kneeled in front of her. "I wish I could help you. Be dauntless." She squeezed her hand, and Lila didn't want her to let go. For the first time in a long time the kind eyes of an adult gazed at her. But when the door opened, she whimpered when the woman pulled away.

Lila shuddered and skittered close to the woman.

The man sneered and yanked her away, dragging her into the room. "Brat." He hoisted her up and roughly tossed her onto a metal table. The odor of tobacco crashed over her, making her gag. She hated the smell of tobacco, which reminded her of grumpy foster father number four. Now, another grumpy man applied leather restraints to her arms and legs. Terror dripped through her body.

"Don't hurt her!" the woman said.

The man whipped around. "Shut up."

Eyes wide, the woman stepped to the back of the room.

Two more men entered. The older man stood in a corner and folded his arms, as if overseeing whatever was about to happen. The young one rushed to her side, peering at her through thick, square glasses.

Lila stared at the men. She forced herself to keep her eyes open. Study these men. She'd be able to tell the police what they looked like after she was rescued.

Lila grimaced against the restraints then moved her gaze to the mean man. Two disgusting hairs protruded from his bumpy nose. Dark brown hair and even darker eyes made him look sinister.

She shifted her gaze to the younger man with the square glasses. Brown hair framed his face and a fresh, reddened scar sat above the top of his glasses. With his white dress shirt, sleeves rolled up to his elbows, Lila didn't take him for the fighting kind.

The door flew open and a blonde woman entered. Something familiar stirred. She'd never met this lady but something about her...

"Hello, daughter," the blonde woman said.

"You're...you're my mother?" Confusion blanketed her.

"Yes. Do you remember me?" With a gentle touch, the woman moved a strand of hair from Lila's face.

"No." Lila's entire body stilled, as if she were caught in suspended time.

"Such a pretty child." Cocking her head sideways, she continued to stroke her hair.

"If you're my mother, why did you give me away?" Lila had been told she was left at a fire station or hospital, but she wasn't sure which.

"I had to. But now you are very important to my future." She leaned in closer.

Another older woman entered the room. She carried an air of authority, like the stern principal at her school. "You had your time, April," she said.

April's eyes blazed then softened. "Thank you, Mother."

This woman was her grandmother?

"You may begin," Grandmother said.

The mean man pinned down her arm and rubbed a solution on her forearm.

Lila stared in horror as he grabbed a needle. The long metal point glinted in the light.

Then she screamed.

"Lila! Lila!" Cody rushed into the room. "Are you okay?"

Drenched in sweat and out of breath, Lila jerked up in bed. For a moment, the surroundings were foreign, then after blinking a couple of times she remembered she'd fallen asleep in one of the bedrooms at the farmhouse. "I'm okay." Humiliation washed over her. She hadn't wanted Cody to see her like this.

Cody kneeled in front of her. "You're not." He wiped away tears she didn't know existed. He held her face in his warm hands. "You're safe."

She shook her head. "Please go away." Her body trembled, as if she had no control.

"Lila, you are safe and I'm here." He rubbed her arms.

"Just go away, Cody." Her voice broke and more tears flowed. Why wouldn't he leave? She'd been handling these nightmares alone for years.

"Nope. You don't have to go through this alone."

She shut her eyes. But just as in her nightmare, simply closing her eyes never removed the situation. When she opened her eyes, Cody remained in front of her.

He stood and flipped on the television although he kept the volume low. The blue light soothed her.

"I'll be right back." Seconds later, he returned with bottles of water. Setting the bottles on the table, he dragged a throw off the end of the bed and placed the blanket around her. "Better?" He asked climbing into bed next to her.

She stared at the blanket, this one soft with the faint aroma of a dryer sheet. "Umm, give me a minute." While attuned to everything going on around her, Lila sat gazing at the floor. Counting helped to calm her and normalize her breathing. When she reached fifty, she stopped and took a sip of water.

Television voices droned on in the background against the cadence of the air conditioning.

He pulled her back into the crook of his arm as he leaned against the bedframe. "I didn't know what to do after I witnessed your first nightmare. After a while, I spoke to Holly about it. She suggested I give you space and not make a big deal. She didn't think you'd want to talk to anyone."

Lila nodded. "Holly was right. I would have hated you hovering over me and trying to help. Plus, I decided I couldn't disclose this to anyone."

"What about now? I hope I'm not making things worse."

She thought a moment then shrugged. "I don't talk about my nightmares with anyone. I haven't been in a relationship, and when I'm with my girlfriends, I make sure to sleep by myself. It's embarrassing."

"You've been through a lot. Don't be embarrassed. Besides, it's just me." He grinned then his expression grew serious. "Do you want to talk about it?"

The door burst open. Holly and Reid, weapon in hand, stood in front of them.

"Are you okay?" Reid asked, his gaze sweeping the room.

Holly slipped around Reid and sat next to Lila on the bed. "What happened? Do you want to talk?"

Holly kept her hands folded in her lap, which prompted a silent thank you from Lila.

Concerned stares aimed at her tear-stained face made her want to shrink into the mattress. Swallowing her pride, she pulled the blanket around her. "The dream helped me remember what happened after I was kidnapped. I was held somewhere, maybe Babylon Hall. April was there and Vivian, who oversaw the application of my tattoo." She pointed to her forearm. "But the woman who escorted me from the room I was kept in...was Willa."

Cody stiffened. "Are you sure? What's her agenda then? Still working for The Order?"

Lila shook her head. "I don't think so. She was scared. I don't believe she really wanted to be there. She told me that her husband, Edgar, joined The Order but she didn't subscribe to their beliefs. Instead, she worked as a nurse. She even helped Mary with her pregnancies."

Reid stepped farther into the room. "What makes you sure that Willa is the same woman in your dream?"

"In my dream, or memories, just before she delivered me to that room, she told me to be dauntless. Willa said the same thing at the church. I know it's her." Lila twisted the blanket.

"Given what happened to Garvin and Sheila, I'm going to swing by Willa's house. Whichever side she falls on, we don't want to lose her." Reid backed out of the room. "Holly, why don't we get breakfast started?"

Holly nodded and patted Lila's hand. She tiptoed out of the room, closing the door behind her.

Cody placed his arm around her. "Are you sure you're okay?"

She smiled. "Jogging down memory lane always makes me anxious."

"I want to earn your trust again. I want you. I want us." He expelled a loud sigh.

Remembering Nikki's smug grin plummeted her thoughts. The moment Lila had entered the room, Nikki's gaze was on her. Languid, her hair tousled, Nikki had slithered out of bed. Nude, she'd ambled across the room and grabbed a towel, seemingly oblivious to the horror splayed across Lila's and Cody's faces.

Lila stared up at Cody. His brown eyes were kind. Despite his one slipup, he'd always been someone she could count on. As if someone gave her an invisible push, she reached up and kissed him.

He appeared stunned as first, then he returned her kiss with more enthusiasm than Lila had been prepared for. Her stomach clenched as Cody pulled her closer.

Seconds later, he pulled back. "Although I don't want to stop, I also don't want to take advantage of this moment." He brushed his thumb across her check, then stepped away.

She wanted to scream. Her body wanted him, but her mind urged her to run.

Chapter 34

Cody made a U-turn and headed back to the farmhouse. He'd intended to go to work but a call from Reid changed his plans. When he burst in the door, strained faces looked his way. "What happened?"

"Lila received a call on her work phone. A man claiming to be Morris Beak is requesting to meet Lila alone in the park today."

Lila sat with her hands folded at the table next to Holly.

Cody swiped a hand through his hair. "What time do we leave?"

"*We* aren't leaving. He said come alone so I'm going alone." Lila crossed her arms.

"I'm afraid for her to go alone. This could be a setup," Holly said.

"I agree. Do you even know the park?" Cody placed his hands on his hips.

"Not exactly. I've been there once or twice. Reid and I have mapped out a plan. He'll be close, if anything should happen. Adam and Carson will be monitoring the situation at the park, too." Lila stood and crossed the room. "Cody, we need this lead."

Adam took a chair at the table. "We were tailing Morris but the last known address we had for him was in New Jersey."

"We don't know much about Morris Beak other than Willa warning you away from him." Cody paced the room.

"We didn't know a lot about Garvin Jennings, either, but we went." Lila matched his gait. "You know I'm right. If this means we're one step closer to bringing Lance to justice, then it's worth the risk." She stopped and faced him. "I don't need your approval, but I'd like your support."

Cody sighed. "Alright, what's the plan?"

AT TWO THAT AFTERNOON, Lila pulled into the small parking lot of the Orange Creek Park in a rural section of town. Bright sun blinded her for a second before she shifted in the seat.

"Testing," Reid's voice leapt from the inconspicuous earphones hidden by her hair.

"I hear you," Lila checked her weapon, slid it in her running pouch, and stepped out of the car. She placed the pouch around her waist and clicked the bar into the buckle to secure it. As she entered the park, she noted signs which pointed to the jogging path. Dressed in workout pants and a T-shirt, Lila looked ready for a run. She twisted her torso, using the stretch to scan the park. A few mothers with kids enjoyed the playground, which was tucked into a corner of the park adjacent to three sets of basketball courts and a small pond with a family of geese swimming near the bank. Lila didn't spot Reid or Adam, but once again she knew they were present.

Cody approached wearing jogging attire, as well. As he spoke into the radio, he ran past her. "I didn't spot anything suspicious. There is a tree line behind the meeting spot I'm concerned about. I checked the area and so far, it's clear."

"I'm positioned a few yards south, which will give me a better view of the tree line," Adam said over the radio. "We have a thermal detection scope on my rifle. If anyone surfaces behind them, I'll know it."

Cody stopped jogging, leaned on a nearby tree, and shot quick glance at Lila. "Give the signal if you sense anything. I'll continue to make several passes, but if you need me just signal." He pushed off the tree. "ABS." He took off down the path.

Always be safe. She inhaled, eyeing his muscular ass through her sunglasses as Cody disappeared around the bend. Shifting her view, she said, "Is the camera clear?"

"Affirmative," Adam replied. "We can see everything in front of you." Her sunglasses held a small camera, monitored by Reid and Adam.

Angling onto the jogging path, Lila broke out in a light jog. When she reached the half mile point, she slowed. A few feet from the marker were a set of benches in front of a thick mass of trees and bushes. The curve of the path made it difficult for anyone to get off a shot from a distance. Beak had chosen the perfect spot for a clandestine daytime meeting.

As she neared the meeting location, she watched as a man walking from the other direction came into view. Dressed in khaki pants and a black shirt, the man lumbered over to the bench and plopped down. He wore large, thick glasses and crossed his arms over a distended belly. Thin brown hair peppered gray and crow's feet around his eyes suggested he was in his sixties. Bushy eyebrows angled downward, made him appear perpetually angry.

"Are you Morris Beak?" Lila asked approaching the bench.

The man glared at her. "I'm not Santa Claus." He kept a hardened gaze on her. "Sit down. I'm sure as hell not going to talk to you from over there."

Lila stiffened but she sat on the other end of the bench. A puckered scar above his left eye which extended above the frame of his glasses drew her attention.

"I'm Morris Beak. I've been waiting for you, Lila."

Lila cocked her head. "Why? What do you want?" She rested her arms across her lap, the weapon inside the pouch pressed against her.

"You were always defiant." Morris emitted a sneering chuckle.

"You want answers? Ha. Get in line. Asking too many questions gets you killed. Like your friend Struthers."

"You knew Jack?"

"Never met the man. I *do* know he played secret superhero and got himself killed. At least, that's what I hear." Morris shrugged. "Could be all bull."

"What kinds of questions was Jack asking?" Lila turned toward Morris, to give Reid and Adam a better view of the man.

"How the hell should I know?" He blew out a breath. "I wasn't there."

Lila kept one eye on Morris and the other on potential threats within the park.

Morris appeared just as nervous with his gaze tracking their surroundings as if he expected trouble.

Lila studied the man. He wanted her to believe he was in control, but his actions told her otherwise. Morris was afraid and probably with good reason. Lila froze as the low hum of an aircraft approached. With memories of the weaponized drone attack, she shifted her hand toward her weapon, even though Reid and Adam had long range rifles trained on the area. She relaxed a fraction when she spotted the plane above them.

Morris eyed Lila. "You know who I am, don't you?" He grinned, showing off yellowing teeth.

Again, Lila stared at the scar above his left eyebrow, puckered and a shade darker than his skin. In an instant she was transported back to that room and the anxious younger man who'd stood over her. Anger bubbled up into her throat. "You were with Vivian Sinclair and my mother, April, when I was kidnapped and tattooed." She glared at the man she held partially responsible for the childhood trauma.

She ran a finger over the raised brand on her arm. People thought she was a freak. That day at the museum during her junior high year when an ultraviolet light lit up the tattoo had her classmates buzzing. EBOP46, which stood for her grandfather's favorite symphony, Scottish Fantasy, blazed from her arm. From then on, she'd taken steps to make sure the tattoo remained hidden.

"I remember you standing by as they branded me. I was a child. How could you let them deface my body, all in the name of your stupid ideology?"

"They paid well and offered the respect I deserved. I destroyed people in the name of The Order." He folded his wrinkled hands and lifted his head in regal fashion.

"You must be proud."

"Damn right I am." He glanced toward the wooded area then focused on his hands, shoulders suddenly slumped forward like a man depleted of air. "Now I've been put out to pasture. Your cousin Lance is a Class A jerk. I was loyal to The Order, but my star shone brightest under his father's tutelage. My allegiance to Ivan became a black mark after his death." He lapsed into a coughing fit. When he quieted, he leaned over the bench and spat. He straightened then pulled a gold case from his pocket.

Lila's hand crept closer to her weapon. When she saw him slide a cigarette from the case and light it with a matching gold lighter, she relaxed. He probably shouldn't be smoking especially with that hacking cough, but it was his life.

She spotted Cody jogging by but gave no indication of trouble, so he continued past them.

Morris took a few drags on the cigarette, causing swirly plumes of smoke to ghost upward. "I gave them everything," he continued. "Everything. What do I have to show for it—no wife and no children to carry on a legacy. Nothing." He stopped and stared at her. "I was once feared. People would shake when I came into the room. *That* was power."

"Get to the point. Why did you contact me?"

"I got my last orders. Move to Dallas and wait. It's been a long three years." He puffed more on the cigarette, closing his eyes as he inhaled the toxic fumes.

"So, Lance exiled you, so to speak?" Lila angled more to escape the cigarette smoke.

Morris shrugged. "I didn't know at first. But like a loyal Order subject I am, I complied without question."

"Lance asked you to move here?"

"Does it matter? I was ordered to move here. But to answer your question, I don't think Lance was behind it. I received a letter. My guess is it's from Ivan's estate. Then I got another letter over a month ago instructing me on my 'final act' before I was 'retired'."

"Do you still have that letter?"

He shot her an are-you-kidding look. "I'm in finance so, of course, I keep meticulous books. I document everything. Even as a young kid, I had Russell's ear. I appreciated the old man. Instead of ignoring me because I was so young, he listened. When he died, I wasn't sure what was going to happen, but Vivian, his daughter, kept some of us on, especially those in key positions. But many didn't last long. Vivian was...intense...crazy. I can appreciate intensity but crazy is quite something else. So, I left and went to work for Ivan." Morris watched the cigarette burn, then dropped the butt on the ground. "I don't know why Russell chose Vivian to lead rather than Ivan. Vivian, while willing to make the hard decisions, proved unpredictable at best."

"Would you be willing to let me see that letter?" Lila asked.

Morris inhaled and ignored her question. "I've spent the majority of my life surrounded by the Sinclair family as a member of The Order. My father left my mother when I was a child. Mother did her best to care for me and my sister, but it was never enough for me. I met Russell at the men's tailor shop. My mother worked there as a seamstress. When I saw the wad of money that he pulled out to pay for custom-made suits, I knew I wanted in. I ran away and joined The Order as a teen. I saw Russell as a father figure even though he died shortly after I came to Babylon Hall. I was committed and willing to do anything, including taking part in the kidnapping of a little girl." He stared at Lila. "Don't think this is an apology. Your kidnapping was necessary. Sacrifices must be made. We are only pawns in the larger picture." His voice trailed off as if he were caught up in his own memories.

"What about a company called Stonegate? Have you heard of it?"

Morris stalled, his eyebrows hiked upward for a moment, then he shook his head. "Never heard of it."

Liar.

Lila swept a gaze across the room/park. So far, she hadn't heard the whipping sound of an approaching drone.

"Do you know about an emerald mine located on an island?" Lila asked.

"It exists. I don't know where, but I've seen financial documents about the mine. It's worth billions. I also know a will is hidden somewhere. Find it and you may control the mine." Once again, Morris shot glances at the woods and surrounding areas.

"Who's will?" Lila followed Morris's gaze. This guy was nervous, and she needed to be on guard.

She caught sight of Cody nearing the bench.

Morris swiveled toward her and grinned, displaying a crooked row of yellowing teeth. Ignoring another question, he said, "Might as well get this show on the road."

Cody pulled up short. He bent to tie his shoe, stalling for time.

Morris pulled a small container from his pocket and bit down on a large pill. Then he drew a large envelope from inside his jacket. He stared at the envelope with a bulged section in the middle. "Sacrifice." Tears formed in the corners of his eyes.

Lila's pulse jump-started. What kind of medication was he taking? She gave a slight shake of her head as Cody appeared to contemplate moving in her direction. She didn't want to spook Morris.

The old man ripped open the envelope and shoved a black box and piece of paper into her hand.

The weight of the box mimicked the ones she'd already received. The third emerald plate had to be inside.

"Now, I've completed my orders." Morris lurched forward, grabbed his chest, and fell to the ground.

Chapter 35

Hot water sluiced over her body as Lila closed her eyes. She'd longed to get back to her own house, but even in the familiar surroundings of the farmhouse, the feelings of comfort had evaded her.

She adjusted the temperature once more, unable to get the water hot enough to wash away images of Morris Beak's self-destruction. The police found what they believed was a second cyanide pill in his pocket. He'd only needed one.

As Lila scrubbed her face, she remembered Morris Beak as one of the men standing by while Vivian had her tattooed. Had everyone in that room understood what the tattoo meant? If Vivian comprehended the meaning of the tattoo, then did that mean she knew where the treasure was? Vivian had long been dead when the climactic scene in the Colorado mine occurred. Perhaps she lost her life before she had time to act upon it. But April had acted, and Lance had killed her inside that mine. Now, another mine bubbled to the forefront, this one worth even more.

Climbing out of the shower, she dried off and dressed for the office. She longed to skip work, but Hilary had texted her about their meeting at Veridian. Business didn't stop. Maintaining the Veridian account may be more imperative now. HTP had a public relations issue with two of their partners killed in the last few weeks. Steve's official cause of death wouldn't be released for a few days, but the multitude of knife slashes and blood told a conclusive story.

In the living room, she found Cody staring out the front window. His hair, wet from a shower, lay slicked back. "Any bad guys out there?" She didn't intend to sound flippant, but she'd grown tired of the fight.

"All clear."

Carson and Holly entered from the kitchen.

"Are you both okay?" Carson said, her gaze shifting between Lila and Cody.

"I'm fine." Lila slipped into a sweater. Despite the heat outside, she couldn't get warm. "Getting tired of talking to the police." Although an investigation had to ensue, the detectives had told Reid and Adam they expected Beak's death to be ruled a suicide.

"What's our next move?" Cody moved away from the window and stepped closer to her.

Lila picked up her laptop bag. "I have a meeting at Veridian with Hilary and Robert Gumfrey. I can't flake on this. Besides, I want to push him a little by asking about Stonegate. I'm certain Morris knew about the company although he denied it. Maybe Robert does, too." She wanted to crawl in bed and sleep for a week, but sleep would have to wait.

Reid entered and settled at the table in front of the emerald plates laid out there, the latest one from Beak included. "I hate for you to be back out there, but I agree, we need to push this."

"I'll take you." Cody placed his arm around Lila. "I want to go back into the Veridian system. If I can get into Rick or Tally's email, then maybe I can find out who's calling the shots. The official hierarchy has them reporting up to Gumfrey."

"I'll try to get more information out of Gumfrey. Any news on the letter from Hugo Castille?" Lila asked.

"We couldn't get any prints off the letter. We've also searched for Hugo Castille but hit a dead-end." Reid stared at the newest emerald tablet, stamped with the codes: DPSS, AOL(2). "While you guys are at Veridian, I will take these tablets to a geologist in the area. I'm hoping the gems can be traced to a specific region." He placed each plate back in its box then turned to Lila and Cody. "Be careful."

Five minutes later, Cody and Lila entered the farmhouse garage where Cody's vehicle was parked. He gathered her into his arms.

Lila closed her eyes, soaking up his strength as if he were the water to her sponge. Enveloped in the cocoon of his arms, she felt safe and desired. For a second, she lay her head on his chest, the thumping of his heart calming her.

Lila lifted her head. As their lips touched, Lila clung to him as if she would never see him again.

When he pulled back, he studied her. "Asking if you're okay is a dumb question, but I'm asking."

"I don't know. I feel like we're getting closer to something huge. Is Lance doing this? Is there someone else in The Order making a go for power? According to Reid and Adam, Lance disbanded the council, and I believe all of the original council members are dead." She shook her head. "We've just watched three people die. I don't want to do this anymore, but I have no choice. If we don't fight back, someone else will surely die." Her voice was barely a whisper, and she hated being afraid.

"I'd love to take you away somewhere, if only for a few days."

Lila nodded. "It would be nice not to think about this." She inhaled Cody's masculine soap scent. If only time could be suspended. They could stay like this and not worry about the world.

AN HOUR LATER, Robert Gumfrey's assistant led Lila and Hilary to a conference room on the executive level of the Veridian offices. The executive offices were sleek and modern with splashes of their logo colors of electric blue and brilliant green scattered about. Lila took a seat next to Hilary at the conference table. The assistant took their drink orders as they waited for Veridian's chief legal officer.

When Robert lumbered into the room, he flashed a quick smile. "Good afternoon, ladies." He shook their hands and took a seat across from them. "I'm sorry to hear about Steve. His presence on our legal team will be missed."

Lila eyed the man with suspicion. Although he spoke the words, sincerity didn't reach his eyes. Per Hilary's request, she said very little during the one-hour meeting; rather, she listened intently for any information regarding Stonegate or Lance Sinclair. As expected, there was no mention of either. If another entity were preparing to acquire Veridian, then that business issue would fall into the purview of HTP services. As the chief legal officer, Robert would be heavily involved, yet he said nothing. In fact, this meeting was to discuss Veridian buying another small company. Their actions didn't align with a company on the verge of being taken over. Perhaps Stonegate hadn't played their cards, and Veridian executives didn't know what was coming. The Alliance obtained the information via the dark web, so the accuracy of the intel remained uncertain.

As the meeting neared conclusion, she decided to test the waters. "Mr. Gumfrey, what is Veridian's stand on the rumors that the company could be acquired by another entity, Stonegate, LLC?"

The room quieted as if the air had been sucked out. Robert's brown eyes darkened. "Young lady, I don't know where you heard that rumor, but it's incorrect. When you have a company as large and important as Veridian, there are bound to be inaccurate reports, especially from other up-and-coming groups determined to derail us. In the future, if you expect to continue in your role as outside council, I suggest you shut out rumors and gossip."

Hilary appeared equally appalled. "I assure you, Robert, Ms. Caldwell's question is out of line and something we'll discuss later. Although, not an excuse, we've all been affected by Steve's death."

"Then perhaps this meeting should have been rescheduled," Robert said, adjusting his suit jacket.

"I meant no offense. I simply wanted to understand how to address other companies you are acquiring should the topic arise." Lila noted both Hilary and Robert's reaction appeared overblown. In other dealings she'd experienced with Jack, discussions about rumors and public relations would not be off-limits.

Robert pulled in his flash of anger and stretched his mouth in a thin smile. "Very well." He closed the file in front of him and rose from his chair. As they exited the conference room, Robert said, "Nice meeting you again, Ms. Caldwell."

"You as well," Lila said. She followed Hilary and Robert out of the conference room, disappointed she couldn't find a way to bring up the secret project team.

He signaled for his assistant. "Marcia will escort you back to the lobby." Then Robert turned to Hilary. "Have you met our new VP of marketing?"

"No, I haven't." Hilary flashed her megawatt only-reserved-for-important-clients smile. Then she glanced over her shoulder, grin fading. "Lila, I will touch base with you later about those action items." With Lila officially dismissed, Hilary followed Robert down the hall and around the corner.

Marcia smiled. "I got a call from Cody Green and he said he'd meet you at door 3G in the parking garage. Follow me."

Once they were inside elevator, Lila smiled at Marcia whom she estimated to be around forty. "How do you like working for Veridian?"

"It's the best job I've ever had. The pay is good, and the perks are great." Marcia pushed the button for the ground floor.

"Wonderful. I suppose you see a lot of high-profile people coming in to see your boss and the other executives."

She nodded, her short bob shaking.

"I was here for the charity event the other night. Lance Sinclair spoke via video. Have you ever seen him here in person? He's married to that beautiful actress, Delphine Renaud, right?" Lila dropped her phone inside her purse.

"I worked behind the scenes, but I saw Mr. Sinclair's video message. I bet he and Delphine have a beautiful child." She glanced up at the elevator panel as the car descended.

"No doubt."

Marcia cocked her head. "About a year ago Mr. Sinclair visited Veridian. He spent some time on the fifth floor rubbing elbows with the executives, then I think he got a tour. We rarely give tours. Too many restricted areas."

Lila's heart pounded. Despite the information proving nothing, she knew they were on the right track. The elevator came to a stop and the doors slid open. As their heels tapped on the shiny marble floor, they entered the cavernous lobby atrium. Marcia pointed out things already obvious to Lila such as the post office, coffee bar, and bookstore. People milled about or sat at tables scattered around the large atrium. They continued through the atrium and then angled left to a smaller corridor. They moved along the unoccupied hall past a few darkened conference rooms.

Marcia led her up two flights of stairs then came to a stop and pointed to the sign labeled PARKING STRUCTURE 1. "Door 3G will be straight ahead."

Lila smiled and thanked her then pushed open the door, obviously free to travel this stretch unaccompanied. She kept to the center of the roadway as much as possible, moving to the side when a vehicle approached. Dark parking garages always gave her the willies. A chill slithered down her spine.

Only a parking garage, a very public one. Get a grip.

She eyed the multitude of surveillance cameras scattered around the garage. The presence of the cameras didn't bring about the expected relief. As she moved farther into the garage, she passed door C and stopped. Did she hear something? She whipped around but saw nothing. Did the lights dim even more?

She picked up the pace, then stopped as something dawned on her. Cody had been aware of her dislike of dark places, even to the point of placing nightlights in her room. Why would he send her through a dark parking garage? She turned and began to run back toward the building. Pulse racing, her footsteps slapped against the concrete.

Seconds later, a van roared around the corner and stopped. Three men alighted and with lightning-quick speed, one of the men grabbed her around the waist.

She dropped her purse and swung, trying to break the hold. Air swooshed in her ears and her skin prickled as if every nerve ending stood at attention. A large hand covering her mouth cut off her scream. He pressed so hard she thought he'd break her teeth. The scent of body odor wafted into her nose as she heard the creek of the van door wrench open. With the heel of her shoe, she stomped down on his instep.

"Bitch!" The man yelled in pain and released her.

"Leave me alone!" She jetted away before another man grabbed her by the hair. He tugged hard, gripping a fist full, causing her to fall to the ground. She grimaced as white lights flashed before her. Drawing in a breath, she pressed the compass pendant as the man tossed her inside the van.

Someone loomed over her. A quick prick to her arm then everything went dark.

Chapter 36

Jogging through the exterior door of Veridian's coffee shop to the outdoor patio area, Cody plopped into the chair across from Moby. "I need to talk to you." He'd been observing Moby from his first day on the DDI project. Although he couldn't be sure, his instincts told him Moby wasn't like the others.

"Hello to you, too." Moby stirred the light brown liquid.

Leaning across the table, Cody lowered his voice to just above a whisper. "Have you ever heard of Stonegate?"

Moby shifted in his chair but kept his focus toward the pond. "I learned recently that a group of geese are called something different depending on where they are." He pointed to the geese lazily paddling by. "A group of geese in the water are called a *plump*. A *gaggle* of geese would mean they are on land while a *skein* means a group of geese in flight."

Cody sat back in his chair. Might as well let the man get out this bit of trivia, no matter how useless it was to him at the moment.

"See their feet paddling in the water? Reminds me of the swim lessons I took as a child. No matter how hard I tried or no matter what stroke I used, I always ended up treading water. Stuck, unable to propel forward." He sipped his coffee. "I'm tired of treading water. I have a wife now, and she's expecting our first child." His voice was low as if coming to the conclusion in a moment of introspection. "I'll tell you what I know but not here. Let's take a walk."

Cody tamped down his impatience. He needed to get as much information as soon as he could. Every moment they delayed on this another person could die, and he suspected those victims would be people he cared about. Jumping up, he matched pace with Moby as they made their way to a path circling the pond.

When they were well away from any Veridian building, Moby cleared his throat. "This place is evil. I was happy before I moved to the DDI team." He grunted out a bitter laugh. "When I got the news I'd been "promoted" to a special project team I thought I'd hit it big. I made more money than I thought possible, and I finally had the means to buy a new house. We have a yard, three-car garage, and room enough for a couple more kids." Moby stopped and kicked a rock. The stone tumbled down a short embankment and plopped into the water.

Cody remained silent. Reid and Adam once told him to allow people who want to talk uninterrupted time.

Moby shrugged. "Then I learned what the DDI really did. I struggled with my conscience for a few weeks then I went to Rick and submitted my resignation. He wouldn't accept it. Told me once you're a DDI team member, you're always committed to the team. When I insisted, he threatened my wife and my younger brother who was about to come to the States on a student Visa." He shook his head. "They told me if I went to the authorities or spoke to anyone about this, they'd kill my wife and destroy my brother's chances of coming to America."

Cody spoke up. "You did the right thing. Rick and Tally are dangerous."

Nodding, Moby began walking again. "They have these meetings off-site. Sometimes they are gone for days at a time."

"Do you know who they are meeting and where?" Cody's gut clenched. This could be something they could use.

"No. I tried to hunt for information, but I didn't want to go too far and be exposed." He glanced around then shifted closer to Cody. "They are at one of those meetings now. I saw Rick with luggage a few days ago. I'm assume this is one of the long meetings."

"Why are you telling me this? How do I know you're not working with Rick and Tally?" Cody squinted in the sun.

"My family has been threatened. My wife is pregnant now, but she had an earlier miscarriage. I blame the stress of the threats. I shouldn't have told her, so I take the blame for that."

"I'm sorry, Moby." Cody understood the soul crushing weight of guilt.

"Maybe it's not too late for you. If you see an opportunity to get out—run. My fear is we'll all end up behind bars one day."

Cody considered the potential fallout for the DDI group when Veridian was exposed, and he had no doubt they would be brought to justice. Unable to give Moby any encouraging words, he remained quiet. Moments later a group of employees out for a walk approached and Cody and Moby headed toward the building.

Fifteen minutes later, they entered the DDI offices, each heading toward their desks. Cody settled in his chair, pulled up his computer screen, and ran a search for Peter Shaw. If someone confronted him about the search, he'd deal with the fallout then. Shaw wanted everyone to know he'd been named VP of Security for Skies International, which Cody understood meant he'd kill at Lance's command. Nothing came up on the various social medial sites. Cody dug deeper and found a credit card charge for a gas station near Las Vegas. Pulling traffic camera footage and using facial recognition software, he spotted a black SUV with Shaw riding shotgun. He couldn't make out the driver or the passengers in the back seat. The SUV appeared to be in an industrial area but after a few seconds, the vehicle turned out of camera range. Cody sighed and hit a button to exit out of the system. Additional searches turned up nothing more.

Cody shot a glance at his desk phone, which he instructed Lila to call after her meeting ended. By this time, Lila's meeting had lasted close to an hour.

His computer alerted, letting him know he had an email.

Glancing at the sender, he knit his brows. Who was URGENT? They had strict firewall procedures so if this email hadn't been deemed safe, he wouldn't have received it. He opened the email and read the short message several times. *Cody, urgent project. Click link and follow directions.*

Without a name attached to the email, he could only assume the sender had to be Rick or maybe even Tally. Sher hadn't said anything about a special project before she left. As he weighed his options, he faced the screen when another URGENT email arrived, this time from Rick.

Please follow the link. I need this project completed ASAP.

He stood. "Anyone else get an urgent project?"

When he received no answer from his teammates, he circled through the area to discover he was alone.

Returning to his desk, he clicked on the link and braced for the next DDI horror show. A second later, his screen filled with a familiar scene. His mother's house in Virginia? Then suddenly the scene pivoted to a man dressed in jeans and a MIT hoodie. He had shaggy brown hair giving him a youthful appearance.

"Hey, Cody. Kyle here. Remember me?" The man grinned into the smart phone camera.

Cody cocked his head and studied Kyle. "I don't know you."

"Yeah, you do. We were in ethics together at MIT." He waved his hand. "Don't worry about it, man. We have a few people in common, but they don't exactly run in your circles, if you know what I mean." He shrugged. "Anyway, a friend is interested in some information we believe you have."

Dread burrowed into Cody's bones as his pulse hitched. He leaned closer to the screen. "Who are you?"

"I told you. Kyle."

"Who sent you to my mother's house?"

Kyle threw his head back and laughed. "Do I really need to answer that question?" He climbed the crumbling concrete stairs and leaned against the house, just out of sight of the door and the front living room window where the shades half covered the window in a droopy slope. "We need some information we believe you have. Give us the location of the mine."

Cody froze, his throat suddenly dry. "What are you talking about?"

"You know damn well what I'm talking about, but perhaps seeing your mother would spur your memory."

"Stay away from her," Cody hissed into his computer. He gripped the side of his desk as his mind flooded with possible ways to respond. Shifting in his chair, he hit a button to record the interaction.

Kyle held the phone at arm's length in selfie fashion. "Where is the emerald mine?"

Cody shook his head. "I don't know." Although he didn't know the location, Cody knew Kyle wouldn't believe him.

Kyle smirked then made the sound of a buzzer. "Wrong answer." He rang the doorbell.

Seconds later, his mother, with disheveled hair, answered the door. "Can I help you?"

"Mom, don't let him in the house," Cody yelled. But when Tina Green slumped against the doorjamb what little hope this would end well evaporated. She'd been drinking.

"Mrs. Green, my name is Kyle. Your son Cody and I were class-mates at MIT. May I come in?" Kyle had slapped on his boy-next-door persona but even a bad impersonation would win his mother over.

His mother grinned and opened the door wider, stumbling as she stepped back. "Come on in." She smoothed down her rumpled shirt.

Kyle stepped in and said, "I hope you don't mind. I have Cody on the line. We made a bet I couldn't find the house."

The camera swung around allowing Cody to view a portion of the small living room. The console television which hadn't worked in years sat against one wall with a photo of him as a toothless kinder-gartner. A photo of his older brother, Holden, as a long-haired teenager occupied the other frame. The camera's focus lifted and settled on Tina.

"I guess you won." Tina giggled as she fingered a strand of fake pearls.

"You hear that Cody, I won." He flipped around the camera. "Mrs. Green, say hi to your son."

"Hi Cody. You know I'm still waiting on that money you promised." Tina's grin dissolved as she stared at him.

"Mom, don't say anything else to this guy." Cody jumped up and scanned the area for his coworkers. Silence greeted him. Rare for everyone to be gone. Where was Moby? He slammed back down in his chair. How could he get his mother to understand? And where was Holden? His brother could usually be found parked on the sagging faded blue sofa. Today, of all days, he chose not to be there.

"Now, is that any way to treat your friend?"

"Tsk tsk, Cody." Kyle turned to Tina. "I recently came into a large sum of money. Since your son has been delinquent in helping you, I'd be honored to give you a couple hundred bucks."

Tina's mouth dropped open. "Kyle, what a generous offer. I have diabetes and the medication is very expensive."

"We're not friends! Mom, don't take any money from him. This man is dangerous." Cody's blood pulsed in his veins, threatening to explode as his worst fears rose.

"Honey, you're being paranoid. Kyle seems perfectly harmless and wants to help me."

"Do not listen to him." Cody gritted his teeth as he willed his mother to have a bit of common sense for once. He could hear her offering to make him a cup of coffee, as if this hired gun had stopped by for crumpets and conversation.

Cody snatched up his desk phone and called Reid's secured phone. Reid answered the call, and Cody whispered not to talk then he placed the phone near his computer. Cody considered tracing the man's digital footprint, but he knew he'd hit a wall. Lance and his people were too smart to be easily tracked.

"Mom, I'm begging you not to talk to this asshole," Cody said. Yet money commanded Tina Green's entire existence. She'd sold out Cody before, and she'd do it again.

"My son is a bit overly cautious." Tina placed her hands on her hips and leaned toward Kyle. "He's making a lot of money at Veridian down in Dallas."

Cody heard a shuffling noise then the man's voice oozed in his ear. "Hey buddy, your mother tells me you work for Veridian. You must be on top of the world working for such a great company. I've even heard good things about your work. I ran into Senator Reynolds and he had some concerns about Veridian. A shame he's dead now." He shook his head as if broken up about the senator's demise.

"Leave my mother alone. She doesn't know what kind of swine you are nor the trash you work for."

"Is that any way to talk to an old friend? Your mother is a beautiful woman, and I'd be happy to help her." He turned his focus back to Tina. "Your health issues are concerning. I happen to have some special insulin. It's much cheaper and longer lasting."

"Mom, don't take anything from him!" But she'd disappeared into the kitchen.

The camera flipped back to Kyle.

Cody jumped up and leaned over his desk. "Get the fuck out her house now or I will..."

"What? You're over a thousand miles away. And I have money and meds." He reached into his bag, pulled out a syringe filled with clear liquid, then lowered his voice. "Tell me where the mine is and maybe she'll live."

"I don't know! I don't know where the damn mine is. My mother is innocent. Let her go."

"Wrong answer. Say goodbye to Mommy." Kyle flipped the camera once again and sauntered in the kitchen.

"No. Don't. She's innocent." Cody pounded his desk, as two pens rolled to the floor.

"Here's your coffee, Kyle." Tina placed the cup on the table and smiled. "Did you have a nice conversation with Cody?" Tina's voice had that I'm-trying-to-impress-someone tone.

"Thank you, Tina. Unfortunately, I can't stay."

"That's too bad. But what about the money and the insulin?" She puffed out her lips as if she were a pouting three-year-old.

Cody shut his eyes.

"A son should help his mother." Kyle stepped closer to Tina.

She shook her head. "I can't control Cody, who'd rather be rude than welcome an old friend."

Tina spoke loudly to emphasize her point.

"Yes, that is too bad. Roll up your sleeve." Kyle turned the camera to focus on Tina.

She sat at the kitchen table and shoved up the sleeve of her sweater.

"Mom, please don't do this."

"I need medication. I haven't had my insulin in three days." She blew out a sigh.

Cody traced over his mother's image on the screen as Kyle pumped what he suspected was some type of poison into her. A few seconds later, Tina slumped in her chair then fell to the floor.

Muscles twitching, Cody stood. "You won't get away with this." He seethed. At the moment, he wanted to destroy anything, and anyone related to The Order.

Kyle switched the camera back to him as he cocked his head. "Oh, but I have. My employer sends his condolences." The connection went dead.

Cody ended the call with Reid and forwarded the footage to his personal email. He ran out of the DDI, grabbed his cell, and called Reid again.

While talking to Reid, Cody sent him the video of Kyle's visit.

Reid had already called the authorities in Virginia. "There's a chance she's still alive."

Cody's mind swam with dark conclusions, the light of goodness and fairness dimmed to the point where he could no longer envision an Alliance win. But he couldn't go there. Even if he lost his life, he had to stop Lance and The Order.

Jamming the phone into his pocket, Cody bolted through the building. *I have to get to Lila.* He raced across campus to the executive building. Lance had likely killed his mother. Blood boiling, his rage ramped up the perspiration dripping from his face. The image of his mother on the floor of their kitchen replayed in his mind. If he ever saw Kyle or whatever his name was, he'd rip his limbs from his body one by one.

Entering the executive building, he ignored curious stares from employees as he rounded the corner and skidded to a halt. He'd never been up to the executive floors, and he didn't expect to get far. Before visiting the fifth floor everyone had to gain admittance from a dedicated receptionist on guard in front of the special elevator.

"May I help you?" a dark-haired woman said, looking down at him from her perch.

"I need to see Lila Caldwell." Cody leaned over the tall reception desk. "She's an attorney with Hirst, Talcott, and Painter. She's in a meeting with Robert Gumfrey. It's urgent." He winced at the use of the word and flashed his Veridian badged hoping the gesture would speed up the process.

She emitted a sigh then picked up her phone.

Cody pushed off the counter, pacing as she had a brief conversation someone upstairs.

"I'm sorry but Mr. Gumfrey is no longer in the building. If she had a meeting with him, then that meeting has concluded. There are currently no visitors in the executive suites." She flashed a curt smile then returned her gaze to the computer screen.

Cody stepped back and hit Lila's speed dial button on his cell phone. When he got no answer, his skin prickled. Where was she?

Once again, he approached the receptionist. "Did you see Lila Caldwell exit the offices?"

She exhaled and glared at him. "Who?"

He punched at his phone screen and held out a photo. "This woman. Did you see her leave?" He didn't care that he'd raised his voice. He needed to find Lila. Now.

The receptionist leaned closer. "Marcia escorted her out. I overheard them talking. I think Marcia was taking her to the parking garage."

"Can you ask Marcia?" As alarms sounded in his head he gripped the cool stone reception counter.

Just as she picked up the phone, she glanced over as the elevator door swooshed open and a woman stepped out.

"Oh, Marcia. This gentleman has a question for you."

The woman nodded and turned her attention to Cody. "Can I help you?"

"Lila Caldwell had a meeting upstairs today. You escorted her out. Where did she go?" Cody swallowed then lifted his badge. "We're friends. I work here and gave her a ride."

Marcia nodded. "She said her friend texted her to meet him at door 3G in the garage."

"Thanks." Cody shot out of the lobby toward the parking structure. Why would Lila go into the garage? When he reached door 3G, he stopped. There were only a couple of vehicles in the area, all unoccupied as much as he could tell.

"Lila!"

His voice echoed off the concrete walls, returning to him with an eerie vibe. Every nerve fiber screamed a warning. He retraced his steps, then stopped when he spotted something on the ground. Bending, he picked up a purse and a visitor's badge. His heart thundered as he flipped over the badge. He zeroed in on the visitor's name. LILA CALDWELL.

They had her.

In a matter of minutes, he'd lost his mother and the only woman he'd ever loved.

Chapter 37

With her eyes shut, Lila tried lifting her head, but her skull felt as if it weighed fifty pounds. Dragging her eyes open, she stared at the ceiling, a white blur. Blinking several times, she cleared her vision. Something appeared off. The ceiling vent was gone. Shaking her head, she remembered she'd been at the farmhouse. She shifted her gaze, searching for the nightlights. They were gone. Why would Cody remove them?

Then her gaze fell on the bars to the side of her.

She bolted up.

Where am I?

Scrambling to her feet, she grabbed the cold metal bars. The room beyond the bars resembled an office with several computers lining one wall and a large monitor in front of the cell. She didn't see anyone, but she spotted the eye of a camera perched on the wall and aimed at the cell. How did she let this happen again? Memories flooded back. She'd been walking in the garage at Veridian when a van pulled up and a couple of men grabbed her. She still wore the clothes she'd worn to the meeting, but her shoes and purse were gone. Lance had to be behind this. Confusion shifted to anger.

The compass necklace still hung around her neck. She pressed the pendant and prayed her friends would find a way to help. Although she had no idea what time it was or how long she had been here, she knew Cody wouldn't stop until he found her.

A whimper sounded behind her. She pivoted. A small mound in a corner of the cell shifted under a white blanket. Lila hurried to the source of the sound. The mound shifted, allowing her a glimpse at strands of white hair. Lila slid back the blanket and gasped.

Willa.

The old woman opened her eyes and met Lila's gaze. A grimace appeared then she shook her head.

"Willa, it's me Lila. Are you hurt?" She helped her sit up, observing her for signs of distress.

"I -I'm all right. I think." She rubbed her head and blinked several times.

"Are you sure?" Lila scanned the cell for water but spotted nothing.

"Yes. They got you, too. Buggers came out of nowhere." She leaned on Lila as she stood, smoothing down her blue sweatshirt. Willa's shoes had been removed, as well.

"Do you know where we are?" Lila's head rang and the dizziness continued, but she hoped she could help Willa, if necessary. As soon as the thought surfaced, she wanted to laugh. She'd been unable to prevent her own kidnapping so how in the hell could she help Willa?

"One minute I was making tea and the next two hooded men burst through my door. I'm surprised to be waking up." She wobbled.

Lila held on and led her to the back wall where she helped her sit. Then she returned to the bars, peering out to locate anything that would tell her where they were. She stalked the length of the cell, approximately six feet long, to get a better look at her surroundings from each point. Coming up empty, she pulled on the bars on the off chance they weren't locked in. Nothing budged as expected.

"Lila, sit. Save your strength." Willa rested her head against the concrete wall.

"Lance did this," Lila said through gritted teeth.

"He's desperate, which makes him even more dangerous." Willa coughed and braced a hand on her stomach. "But you are just as powerful as he is. You can rise above this."

Lila shook her head. "I don't know. I want this to end, but I don't know if my efforts will be enough."

"You know more than you give yourself credit for. Come here." Willa held out her wrinkled hand.

Lila released the bars and sat next to Willa. "Cody and the Alliance will come for me. I'm afraid people I care about will be hurt or worse."

"Remember what they did to you?" Willa took her hand and tapped. Her finger made a soft, rhythmic tapping along Lila's hand. "They took away your childhood."

The concrete floor of the cell reminded her of the hard, steel table they'd placed her on. Leather straps had bound her limbs. She wanted to scream but a cloth had been slapped around her mouth. Salty tears escaped her eyes. Why? Had the simple fact she was April's daughter been enough to warrant their behavior?

Her body stiffened as she recalled the needle coming toward her. Over and over needles impaled her arm. The man, held at gunpoint, spoke to her with his brown eyes. He didn't want to do this. She heard him say at one point, *she's only a child.* But the man holding the gun urged along his actions. As they marked her with ink, she heard Vivian talking to the other men in the room, but she reached a point where her tears dried, and her young mind went to another place. She imagined a world where she had loving parents and maybe siblings and a dog. Where she didn't live in fear. Where people wouldn't jump out of the shadows and whisk her away. Did that world even exist?

Now, Lila stared at the woman on the cell floor beside her. "You were there?"

"I didn't want to be. As the only nurse in the facility, I was compelled to be in attendance. By this time, Vivian's mental capacity had sunk to a new low. I suspected she was delusional. I caught her on many occasions talking to her dead father and that black horse she was so devoted to." Willa's eyes pooled with unshed tears. "You were so small and confused. I wanted to scoop you up and take you away. I was afraid we'd both be killed if I acted." Tears ran down her face. "Remember what they did to you. Vivian was unhinged, but Lance is a psychopath."

"You said I was the key to finding the mine. How?"

She ran a finger over the invisible tattoo they'd inked on her arm so many years ago. "I wish I knew."

Lila sighed. "Is all this really because my birth month and date equal seven? My great-grandfather didn't know about my existence?"

"Russell was no more of a deep thinker than my little toe, but he presented to his followers as if he had a pipeline into knowing the future. I don't believe he had any foreknowledge of you. I was around when April came back shortly after you were born. When Vivian discovered your birthdate equaled the number seven, her psychosis took over and she proclaimed you were the *one*." Her shoulders sagged. "I'm sorry my Edgar got mixed up in all this."

"How well did you know Vivian?" Although Lila had met her grandmother on a few occasions, she couldn't say she knew her to any degree.

"As much as anyone could know Vivian. When Edgar and I moved to Babylon Hall, your grandmother came to me. She was wild with fear because she was pregnant. Russell had already told her that for a woman to be a strong leader she was not to have children. He felt children weakened women, gave them an albatross. Vivian never told me who'd fathered her child, but it wasn't too hard to figure out. I'd seen the way Vivian looked Harold Silva, one of your great-grand-father's advisors. I believe they were truly in love."

Lila had never heard anything about her grandmother that made her human or resembling anything like a woman capable of love. The few times she'd seen her, Vivian had been vicious and control-ling. "What did she want with you?"

"She wanted me to help her conceal her pregnancy, deliver the baby when the time came, and then smuggle the baby out. A friend had agreed to take the child."

Willa continued to hold her hand. The connection warmed Lila's heart. She prayed she'd be able to get Willa safely out of this cell and to her family. "Vivian took a big risk."

"Thankfully, Russell was so preoccupied with Order business that he didn't suspect Vivian's pregnancy. I have no doubt Russell would have had her killed and the child. When the time came, I delivered the baby in the tunnels of Babylon Hall. Vivian didn't bond much with the child and wanted me to take the baby girl soon after. I felt sorry for both Vivian and her daughter."

"What about Harold? Did he know about the baby?"

"Harold knew about the baby. To keep up appearances, he only saw the child for a few minutes before I delivered April to Vivian's friend." She quieted, appearing lost in thoughts of long ago. Then she straightened. "A couple of years later, Vivian returned with the same plan when she found herself pregnant again. This time the plan didn't work so well. Russell found out about the pregnancy. He was livid. When he demanded to know who'd fathered the child, Vivian lied and told him a local boy. Russell forced a name out of her and had the innocent boy killed, then demanded that Vivian kill her baby upon its birth."

"I'm sad to say I'm not surprised. My uncle Reid was that baby and I can't imagine life without him." Lila said. The grisly facts about her family no longer stunned.

"It just so happened that another woman on the grounds had recently had a stillborn. Vivian took her fetus, preserved the baby, and planned to use the body to show Russell she'd killed her baby when, in fact, she'd given the baby away. But the plan went awry, and Vivian's baby ended up on the side of the road."

"Reid told me the story of his birth. He was deeply affected by the notion of being tossed away," Lila said.

"It's a horrible way to enter the world." Willa's rheumy eyes filled with sadness. "I couldn't help Vivian's babies, but I thought in some small way I could help you. Such a precious thing you were."

Willa continued the light tapping on her arm, the motion somehow soothing.

Yet, with each tap, Lila floated closer to the past. Morris Beak's sneer materialized and. Lila saw Vivian standing over her like an impenetrable sentinel, then someone else appeared. She remembered the woman who enveloped her in a warm, delicate embrace, with the faint scent of cinnamon. Then a soothing singing voice blanketed her with a soothing song Lila had never heard before. As if she were inside a safe cocoon, Lila curled into the woman.

Tearing herself back to the present, Lila stared at Willa with newfound deference. "I remember." She glanced at Willa and whispered. "You were there. In the dark room with me. You sang to me and comforted me after they tattooed my arm." Tears pooled in her eyes.

"Yes, honey. It wasn't much but I did what I could. By that time Edgar and I had a daughter of our own. I couldn't be a good mother and allow you to suffer. I only wish I could have rescued you." Willa held on to her arm.

"Thank you. I pushed those memories away but now I remember. You helped me survive and you showed kindness I didn't know existed." Lila hugged her, clinging to the goodness inside the woman.

When they separated, Willa said, "I want you to remember everything."

"Do you know something? If so, you need to tell me. Maybe it can help us get out of here." Lila glanced around, relieved not to see anyone.

"Edgar didn't know Lance, but he knew Ivan. All I know is a few months before Ivan died, he changed his will." Willa grimaced and rubbed her shoulder.

"Garvin Jennings said Ivan wasn't happy with the way Lance had been conducting himself and changed his will. Morris Beak also mentioned the will." Lila moved Willa's hand and took over the massage. "What if Ivan left everything to Carson? The mine would be hers. If we can get that will, she can assume ownership. If Lance gets that will, he will destroy it and take possession of the mine. We *have* to find that will."

Willa shook her head, her voice in a low whisper. "I agree. Find the mine and will as soon as possible. For your sake and everyone else's."

Lila continued massaging Willa's shoulder. "Thank you. You don't know what your kindness means to me. I will do anything in my power to get you back to your daughter. I promise."

Willa caressed her face. "I believe you will. Don't give in. No matter what. I'm an old woman. If I don't make it, tell my daughter and my grandchildren I love them."

"We're going to get out here. You deserve to be with your family. I will find a way."

"Be careful." Willa placed a hand on top of Lila's.

Lila jumped up and inspected the perimeter of the cell. She didn't spot any means of escape. Turning her attention outside of the cell, she approached the bars. Without a weapon, she'd have to rely on her brain.

The clicking of footsteps on the concrete floor sounded outside the cell. Lila scrambled back to Willa, held on to her hand, and waited.

Lance sauntered in, followed by two guards, and stood in front of the cell. "Hello, Lila. I'm sorry these accommodations aren't what you're accustomed to but if you cooperate, I will see that you are moved to more suitable quarters. I'm a busy man so I'll get down to business. Where is the emerald mine?"

"I don't know. Now let Willa go." Lila glared at the man with whom she shared a portion of DNA.

Lance chuckled. "You always were bold. You're in no position to make demands." His expression darkened as he crossed his arms, drawing close the flaps of his gray designer suit jacket. "You need to learn your place. Your beloved Jack Struthers learned that lesson the hard way. Even though he was a partner in a law firm, he still had a place and it wasn't to poke his nose into things he had no business."

Lila rose and approached the bars of the cell. "Jack was a decent man." Swallowing, Lila gritted her teeth, doing everything she could to keep from crying.

"A decent man who poked his nose into things he should have left alone." Lance shrugged. "He had to be silenced." Lance stalked closer. "You have witnessed my power, yet you still have no idea how ruthless I can be. You probably believe you've been making your own decisions. That you got that fancy law firm job all on your own." He grinned.

Lila's knuckles whitened as she clung to the bars. "You arranged for me to work at HTP? Why?" Lila refused to grant him the satisfaction of an outraged reaction, instead she remained calm—at least on the outside. Lance didn't know she and the Alliance had done their due diligence. She'd focused her job search during her last year of law school on HTP with the understanding that Lance's criminal attorneys had an affiliation with HTP.

"Simple. I wanted you close, so I could manipulate your career." He shrugged. "Until I was ready for my final revenge. My lawyers were from HTP and did a hell of a job securing my freedom. They're in my pocket, one might say. In addition to performing any legal maneuvers and keeping an eye on my overzealous cousin, their sole job was to destroy the evidence. Obviously, they failed, and will be dealt with, but your precious Jack found it." Lance pulled out his phone and stared at the screen. Not lifting his head, he said in a bored tone, "Your mentor needed to die."

"You killed Jack." Her voice rose as she stared at man who exemplified true evil. The admission didn't surprise her but hearing Lance's confession stung.

Lance stepped closer to the bars. "I've been watching you. Could have killed you myself a few times but I needed you alive. Once again, where is the emerald mine?"

Lila shook her head. "I. Don't. Know." She held her breath as her arm containing the tattoo itched, as if her limb independently understood its role.

He stepped back and nodded to a guard.

Lila's pulse raced, and her muscles twitched in anticipation of what would happen next.

Seconds later, one guard opened the cell, and another rushed in and pulled Willa up. She protested but was no match for the man.

Lila lunged toward the guard, but he aimed a gun her way. His glare inviting her to make him fire.

He backed out of the cell with Willa and the other guard locked the door again.

As the guard held on to Willa, she stopped fighting and stood still, her eyes tired but focused on Lila.

Lance folded his arms. "Where is the mine?"

"Stay strong, Lila," Willa said.

"Shut up!" Lance said, as he drew a gun from his jacket. He pivoted to Lila. "Now, where is the island containing the emerald mine? It's my birthright and I want it. Now!"

"I don't know!" Her heart pounded with fear. For a moment indecision clouded her thinking. Although she didn't know the location, should she make up something? She discarded the idea. Any information she disclosed could be verified in minutes. They'd be worse off.

Willa must have picked up on her thoughts. She gave a slight shake of her head and mouthed, "no."

Lance blew out a breath. "You were always difficult, strong-willed." He turned to Willa. "Do you know the location of the mine?"

She steeled her back. "No, I do not but if I did, I wouldn't tell you."

Lance's jaw tightened then he reared back and smacked her so hard she crumbled to the floor.

"You asshole. Leave her alone!" Fury fueled Lila as she gripped the bars. "Willa!"

The old woman groaned but remained on the floor.

Lance motioned to a nearby guard.

The monitor in front of the cell wiggled to life.

Lila's heart dropped as she stared at the screen. She swallowed as the picture cleared. Firetrucks and emergency vehicles surrounded a building fully engulfed in fire. Lila searched for something familiar then as the camera panned out, she gasped. Flames shot from the roof of The Ranch, her father's flagship Dallas restaurant. Her heart dropped. "You bastard! Was anyone inside? My father? Patty?"

Lance only stared at her, his eyes almost black. "Our little movie isn't over." He lifted his finger and pointed to the monitor.

Lila shifted her gaze back to the screen as the picture moved from the restaurant to a scene even worse. Her parents' house crumbled as angry red-orange flames licked up the side and out of the roof. *My family. Were they gone?* Tears snaked the length of her face, but not in grief but white-hot anger. "You're a monster!"

The scene then shifted to an empty warehouse with concrete floors and walls. The camera panned to the left and, from a distance, Lila could make out four chair legs. Then the camera lifted and zoomed in. Air left her lungs behind a jungle scream. Tied and bound to the chairs were her father, Patty, Jenna, and Brent.

"I own you." Lance stalked closer to the cell. "This is only a preview of what I will do if you refuse to cooperate. My power is all consuming and you, Lila, will experience a wrath no one ever has." He stepped back and yanked Willa up from the floor, aiming the gun at Willa's head. "I will kill her."

The old woman winced but met Lila's gaze. "Be dauntless. Remember."

"Lance, let her go. Willa has nothing to do with this." Lila pleaded; her fingers numb from the strong grip on the bars.

"Where is the mine?" His voice deep and menacing.

Concern turned to fear. "For the last time, I don't know." She gritted her teeth.

"Too bad." He pulled the trigger.

Willa fell instantly. Blood seeped from the wound on the side of her head. Her open eyes staring upward.

Lila's ears thrummed with the echo of the gun while everything else in the room was silent.

A monitor remained focused on the scene showing her parents, Jenna, and Brent sitting with wide-eyed expressions of fear.

"One of them will be next unless I get what I want. I'll leave the monitor on, so you can chew on your decision."

Footsteps faded.

Lila sank to the floor, alone with images of her captured family and the deceased corpse of her friend.

Tears clouded her vision. She had no power to help her family or Willa. Staring up at the ceiling, she suppressed her sobs. She'd cry later. Then suddenly another memory surfaced. Lila sat up.

Palmarius. I know where the mine is.

Chapter 38

The Alliance registered Lila's distress call from her compass necklace and Reid and Adam arrived at Veridian in record time. They called in FBI evidence collectors and local police to investigate the garage.

Cody told them all he knew about Lila's visit to Veridian and that he hadn't sent her the text to meet him. He paced while he talked, fists clenching and unclenching, holding his anger in check by a pinpoint margin. Lila was taken under his watch. How could he have let this happen again?

They called Marcia to the scene and she reiterated what she'd told Cody—that she'd escorted Lila to the parking garage and pointed her to door 3G. "I didn't see anything, but I didn't go into the garage."

"Hilary Foster, another attorney from HTP was in the same meeting with Lila and Robert Gumfrey. Did Ms. Foster leave at the same time?" Adam asked.

Marcia shook her head. "Ms. Foster remained behind to speak with Mr. Gumfrey but only for a few minutes. She had a car pick her up outside the private entrance to the executive suites. I overheard her say she was headed to the airport."

Adam nodded. "Thank you, Marcia."

With concern in her eyes, she said. "If I'd known that young woman was in potential danger, I would have alerted security." She turned and walked back into the building.

"Speaking of Veridian security, where the hell were they? They have cameras everywhere to prevent shit from happening." Cody scanned the scene again.

"We spoke to them," Adam said. "They weren't alerted to anything and the cameras were down in this area. Didn't catch a thing."

"That's a lie." Cody glanced past Adam. "Where is the security guy?"

Reid stepped closer to Cody and spoke in quiet tones. "We know it's a lie. This whole thing stinks but we'll have to deal with it in our way." Reid placed his hand on Cody's shoulder in an attempt to calm him.

"What about my mother?" Bile rose in Cody's throat as he remembered his mother slumped in a heap on the floor. Tina had always been in motion, always prepping herself for male attention. To see her motionless broke his heart.

"We're working on it," Reid said before one of the techs called him away.

While Reid and Adam worked the scene of Lila's kidnapping, Cody slipped away. He stalked through the halls of Veridian. Slamming through the doors of the DDI, he glanced around the offices. Cody found Moby at his desk. "Is Rick back?"

Moby pivoted in his chair. "He's in his office." He knit his brows. "You okay?"

"No." Cody reversed his steps and headed to Rick's office. As he got closer, Cody felt the blood pumping through him, fueling his muscles and his rage. Not bothering to knock, he burst through the door.

Rick snapped up his head in shock and confusion. "Cody, what the hell."

In two steps Cody was in front of his desk. He leaned over and grabbed Rick by his blue designer collar. "Who are you working for?" He dragged Rick across his desk, spilling pens and papers on to the floor.

Eyes large, Rick struggled but Cody's grip was no match. "I don't know what you're talking about."

Cody pulled him the rest of the way across the desk displacing the remainder of the desk's contents to bring Rick face-to-face. "Bullshit. I'm going to ask you one more time—who are you working for?"

Rick inhaled. "Veridian."

Cody reared back, and his fist landed on the side of Rick's face.

The impact sent Rick reeling backward to the floor.

Cody stood over him. "My mother was most likely murdered minutes ago, and I witnessed the footage on my DDI computer," he said through gritted teeth. "We both know nothing will get through the system unless you or Tally want it to. I no longer give a fuck about this job or your well-being so you'd better talk."

"I can't give you the information you want." Rick rubbed his jaw as blood seeped from a cut beside his mouth.

"What does that mean?" Cody yanked him up and slammed him into a visitor's chair.

Rick swallowed. "It means I don't know who's pulling the strings. You may or may not believe this but I'm a victim, too. Yes, I'm paid well, but if I don't produce, my family's fate is in jeopardy."

Cody glared at him. "You gave that up awfully quick." He suspected a possible setup, so he needed to choose his own words with care.

"I'm frustrated. I don't know how much longer I can do this." Rick lowered his voice as his shoulders slumped.

"My friend, Lila Caldwell, is missing. They grabbed her in one of the Veridian parking garages. You have any information about that?" Cody stood in front of Rick and crossed his arms.

In the scuffle the photo of Rick's family now lay face up. Cody bent and picked up the photo. "Nice looking family. There's no positive ending for you if you continue to work for them. They"—Cody pointed at the photo—"will never be safe. I know these people and what they can do. You do, too." He placed the photo next to Rick. "I'm sure Tally or whomever already knows I'm here or soon will." Cody shrugged. "It's war now. For the sake of your family, I hope you land on the right side." He stalked out.

TWO HOURS LATER, with Angie riding shotgun, Cody arrived back at the Alliance farmhouse. The situation had gone from critical to Chernobyl nuclear when Cody found out that Dan Caldwell's restaurant had been torched along with the family's home. He'd raced to the house and was relieved when the woman next door told him no one had been home. The firefighters confirmed the fact, but the house sustained catastrophic damage. Cody's relief turned to fear when reports filtered in that the family was missing.

According to her GPS tracker, her last known location was a mile outside of Veridian then nothing. Had her abductors discovered the GPS pendant? Lance had started a war, but Cody would give his life to end it.

As soon as he entered the house, Carson and Holly rushed toward him.

"Any word about your mother or Lila?" Holly said, embracing him.

"No, I'm waiting on Reid and Adam to arrive with an update." He pulled Carson into a quick hug. "I tried to warn my mother. She wouldn't listen."

"That had to be horrifying," Holly said. "What about Lila?"

Cody shook his head. "Lance has her. They snatched her inside the Veridian parking garage. Angie will help me hack into their security cameras, which I don't believe were down."

Angie and Cody set up their computers and got to work.

Cody shut down all thoughts of his mother as he focused on finding Lila. They had to find her. His gut clenched. As he and Angie worked, he heard Holly and Carson speaking in hushed tones on the other side of the room. Lila should be here. How much did one person have to suffer?

Adam and Reid stormed into the room.

Cody jumped up. "Any news about my mother?" Cody's heart seized as the unthinkable surfaced.

Reid swallowed, glanced at Holly, and stepped toward Cody. "I'm sorry. She slipped into a coma. The doctors couldn't save her. Only an autopsy will verify but it sounds like an overdose of insulin. The authorities have been unable to find your brother. Based on your description, we're trying to find out who this Kyle guy is." He shook his head.

Holly and Carson gasped.

Cody sucked up a breath grappling for air that had suddenly disappeared from the room. He raked a hand through his hair. "For all her faults as a mother, she was innocent and didn't deserve this. This is my fault. I've warned her before to be cautious of strangers popping up and asking about me, but I should have reiterated it with all that's been happening recently."

"I'm sorry, Cody." Adam pulled Carson close. "You can't blame yourself. The fault lies with the guy who injected her and the man who ordered it."

Holly rubbed Cody's arm. "Adam is right. Don't pile blame on yourself. That kind of thinking is toxic, and we need you. Lila needs you."

Reid placed his hand on Cody's shoulder. "Lance will pay, one way or another. We will get him."

"What about Lila?" Cody asked. He held his breath.

Reid shook his head. "No further hits from her GPS locator."

"I need to call Holden. My brother should hear this from me." Stepping outside, Cody was smacked with a gust of wind. Nature's presence did little to clear the jumble of thoughts rolling through his mind. He slid out his secured phone and punched in Holden's number.

A second later, a sleepy voice answered. "Who's this?" Holden said in lieu of hello.

"It's Cody. I have some news." He opened his mouth, but the words refused to come out.

"I don't have time to listen to dead air. What'd you call me for?" Holden said, his voice gruff.

Despite their less than brotherly relationship Cody wasn't sure how to break the news. He chose the straightforward route. "Holden, mom is gone. A man posing as my friend gained entry to the house and injected her with what may have be an overdose of insulin."

"You mean Mom is dead?" Rumbling and crashing noises erupted through the phone. "Who is this guy? I'll kill him."

"He said his name was Kyle, but I doubt it was his real name." Cody paced around the patio, oblivious to sweat streaking down his face.

"So, this is your fault?" Holden's words were slightly slurred indicating he'd been drinking or drugging.

Cody stopped moving and closed his eyes. Despite warnings from Adam and Holly, guilt sludging around his chest seized hold and twisted. "I can probably get you, your daughter, and her mother into a safe house."

Holden let out a bitter laugh. "You got our mother killed. I'm sure as hell not going to take any help from you. I can take care of myself and my own damn kid."

Holden's words hit the intended target as Cody's gut clenched. "Be careful, Holden. This Kyle person promised Mom money and medicine. If someone offers you money, please get as far away from them as possible." Cody blew out a breath. "The coroner will do an autopsy. I'll be in touch about the arrangements." He hung up and leaned against the house. Holly was right, he needed to focus. He couldn't do anything else for his mother, but he had a chance to help Lila.

Cody entered the house and rushed into what was now their command center. "Any progress on the Veridian CCT footage?" He balled his fists. Every minute Lila was in the hands of Lance was a minute too long. He'd failed her once and now, here he stood bathed in failure again. Right under his nose, she'd been taken while he watched his mother murdered. With every breath, fear tore through his heart. He refused to consider how Lila's story might end. His mother was already dead. He collapsed into a chair and grabbed his laptop.

"Getting there," Angie said. She tossed him a look of concern. Her fingers flew across the keyboard, the clicking noise creating a hollow thrum in Cody's chest.

Reid glanced up from his laptop. "I checked the GPS coordinates from Lila's compass necklace. She pressed the panic button inside the garage then again three blocks south of Veridian headquarters."

Cody opened his laptop and logged into the GPS system. Even though Reid checked her coordinates, he stared at the blip indicating Lila's last location. Where did they take her from that point?

Holly sat next to him and sniffled. "I can't believe they got her again."

Reid placed a hand on her shoulder. "If the intel is out there, we'll find it."

Seconds later, Angie stopped, flipped her a braid over her shoulder, and leaned closer to the monitor. "I've got something."

Everyone rushed to her side and peered over her shoulders.

"I'm in the Veridian system. Here's the footage from the parking garage."

Cody stared at the seventeen seconds of tape. Lila rushed through the parking garage then suddenly stopped and ran back toward the building. "She must have realized I would never send her through the parking garage to meet me." He swiped his hand over the rough whiskers sprouting on his cheek. A white van zoomed into the frame and two masked men jumped out. Within seconds, they had Lila. She fought back and got in some good kicks and punches, but it was over when one of the men injected her. Cody's heart hitched as he watched her collapse. He prayed the liquid inside the syringe was only to subdue not kill as his mother's lifeless body came to mind.

Angie replayed the video.

Cody focused on the men. There were no distinguishing marks or anything notable on their clothes to give him an idea who they worked for, but he knew Lance was behind this. Slamming his fist on the table, Cody jumped up and stalked to the other side of the room. "How could I let this happen again?"

Adam placed his hand on Cody's shoulder. "Don't do this. Blaming yourself will only cloud your thinking and we need you to help us find her. Focus on Lila and getting her back."

Cody nodded then sank into a chair in front of his computer. Minutes later, he pointed to the screen. "This is a listing of all registered aircraft belonging to either Lance Sinclair, Veridian, or Stonegate. There are thirty aircraft on this list. Out of the thirty, nine are in the air."

Reid raced back to his laptop. "Give me some of the tail numbers. I'll start running these down."

"I'll help," Angie said.

Cody, Angie, and Reid worked in silence for the next half hour while Marissa and Carson monitored Lila's GPS signal. Adam was at the Dallas FBI offices with Yvonne attempting to coordinate an FBI effort.

Reid emitted a loud sigh. "I've got nothing."

"Nada for me," Angie said.

"Try aircraft associated with Skies International," Reid said.

Cody repeated the inquiry based on Skies and the results remained the same. "Nothing." He slapped the table and jumped up. "She's out there." He whirled around. "Maybe they didn't file a flight plan."

Reid cocked his head. "If they remained in the US, maybe. If they are going international, they would have to file a flight plan."

"Could the plane be registered to anyone else?" Angie pulled a clear tumbler from her backpack. She sipped a bright orange-colored concoction.

"I don't know. Check Pia and Ivan Sinclair, even Carson, under her birth name Sloane. Ivan is dead but might as well throw him in the mix. Just to cover all bases." Cody stared at the computer screen. There had to be something more he could do.

"Hold on. Here's a light jet registered to a Hilary Foster. The only reason I bring this up is the address matches the PO Box listed for Stonegate."

Cody scratched his head. "Hilary was at the meeting with Lila and Robert Gumfrey earlier today."

Almost in an instant, Angie flipped her monitor to face Cody. "She look familiar?"

Cody stared at a photo taken at the Veridian charity ball. A woman dressed in red sat at one of the VIP tables. Hilary grinned as she leaned close to Veridian executives and another HTP attorney, Steve Dorman. "Steve Dorman. That's the guy Lila introduced me to. He was found dead at HTP a few days ago."

"What does Hilary Foster have to do with Stonegate?" Reid popped the tab on a can of Coke. "I'll call Adam. He'll search the FBI databases."

"I found the plane." Angie pointed to a small depiction of a plane sitting on an amoeba shaped island. "The jet flew to Miami. It was on the ground approximately an hour before heading southeast and landing on an island in Columbia."

Using the plane's coordinates, Cody searched for the location. "I see an island, but I can't find any other information." He sat back in his chair. "I'm going in through Veridian. Might as well use all their resources for something good."

"Mask yourself online," Angie warned as she turned back to her own computer.

"Will do." Minutes later, Cody pumped his fist. "That's it. Palmarius Island. Owned by Stonegate. Palmarius Island is about twelve nautical miles off the coast of Columbia. From satellite images, the island looks to contain at least three structures. One belongs to the mining operation and the other two appeared to be private residences."

"I've got a live feed. This Hilary woman made a fatal mistake. She turned on her phone. I hacked into her device." Angie pointed to her screen. "We're seeing through her phone's camera. She's leaving the airport."

Reid leaned over her shoulder. "There's a street sign. The Stonegate Mine is five kilometers away from Hilary's location."

Cody who stood next to Reid, watched as the screen went black. "She turned off her phone, but we got what we needed."

Angie tapped at her keyboard. "Here's the mine." Images of men carrying raw, uncut emeralds occupied her computer screen."

"Great work. Get as much information as possible," Adam said.

Returning to his laptop Cody switched to another screen. "Wait! I found another plane. This one is registered to Skies International and is out West." As he stared at the tiny blip on the screen, he turned when another beep pulled away his attention. Cody stared at data suddenly coming in from Lila's tracking device, which matched the plane's location. His heart pounded. "Lila is at Blue Vista in Colorado."

Chapter 39

The Colorado mountains were always a source of inspiration. As Lance stood at the window of what once was his father's office, he recalled the moments before Ivan's death. Lance smiled as his mind replayed the shocked expression on Ivan's face, seconds before he plummeted from the airplane. His father had underestimated him. Now, Lance stood on the summit with ultimate power coursing through his veins.

Lance crossed the room. Sitting behind Ivan's desk hadn't evoked a single emotion, other than victory. His father had been weak—too weak to lead The Order. Sure, he'd been a decent businessman, but commanding The Order to new heights of wealth and power would take more than slightly above-average business skills. The new era of The Order had to be led by a man willing to make tough decisions. Willing to kill those standing in the way. Even if it meant those who shared his DNA.

Lance hadn't been back to Blue Vista, his father's Colorado estate and the location where he conducted US operations, in many years. He thought the location appropriate to bring Lila. After all, he'd killed her mother here. Seemed fitting he'd kill her here, as well.

The desk phone chirped. He'd given instructions not to be disturbed so this had better be important. Lance pressed a button.

"Sir, Mr. Shaw is on the line for you. He says it's important." one of his personal guards said.

"Put him through." Lance folded his hands on the desk.

"Lance, I have news. We performed a thorough sweep of the Dickerson house. We found a document indicating Edgar, that's the old woman's husband, was to deliver a package to Lila. The paper appears to be a copy. The person who initiated that exchange is someone at HTP."

"Anything on the sweeps of the Jennings and Beak homes?" Lance stood and ambled to the bookshelves to the right of the desk.

"We found the same document in the Jennings' house but Beak's house was clear."

"Do you have a name of the person at HTP?"

"Not yet. We're still tracking down the information," Shaw said.

"Get me those documents." Energy surged within Lance. He was close. "What do we know about the death of Steve Dorman?"

"My sources indicate he died of multiple stab wounds. Someone at HTP has a secret. If we're dealing with a defector, we need to plug the hole ASAP before something more critical is unleashed," Shaw said.

"I'll handle this one. How are our newest visitors?"

"We scooped them all up at the house before we torched it. As you saw on the video feed, they are under heavy guard. We caught an older man watching the house. We gave chase and one of our guys caught up to him. Turns out the old man was stronger than he looked. He got away, but our sources indicate he may be a private investigator by the name, Jeb Barker. He's a friend of Cody Green's."

"Find Barker and kill him. I want no loose ends." Lance slammed down the phone. He longed to end all this and kill Lila and her family, but he needed his cousin to find the location of the island mine. After he had the information, he no longer had use for her. In fact, he'd already instructed Shaw to place hits on every member of their so-called Alliance. The Grand Commander of The Order would not be defeated.

Lance drew out his personal cell and jammed his forefinger on one of the buttons to connect with the head of his personal detail. "Have my jet ready within the hour. I'm going to Dallas." He would take care of the HTP issue himself.

Chapter 40

Cody drove one of the two SUV's. One the way to the executive airport, his cell buzzed. After reading the screen, Cody punched the phone to connect. "Jeb."

"I have some news. Can I meet you?" Jeb said, his voice hurried.

Cody pinched his eyebrows together. "Meet me at the executive airport."

Ten minutes later inside an airport hangar, Reid ran through last minute checks of a private jet while the others checked their gear.

Justin and Marissa rushed into the hangar and Carson gave them a brief update.

Adam shoved his phone into his pocket and turned to the group. "Dan Caldwell's restaurant is a complete loss. The good news is no fatalities. Same as the Caldwell house. Still no sighting of any members of Lila's family. Also, Willa Dickerson's daughter contacted the Dallas PD. Her mother is missing."

"Lance." Carson whispered and clutched Adam's hand.

"All I need is five minutes alone with him." Cody stalked the length of the hangar. He stopped as a car he recognized as Jeb's, pulled up to the open bay. "He's okay," Cody said holding out his hand as several members pulled their weapons. When Jeb limped closer, Cody stepped back as he took a second look at his friend. "What the hell happened?" Dried blood dotted Jeb's face, his left eye had swollen, and Cody spotted several bruises on his arms.

"I ran into your friends. I'm okay." He waved a hand through the air. "I have some information you'll find interesting." Jeb sank onto a bench near the wall.

"Some of you may remember Jeb Barker. He's close friend and private investigator. We can trust him." Cody nodded.

"I got roughed up some, but it looks worse than it is." He shifted in his seat. "After Lila went missing, Cody asked me to check on her family. As I pulled up to the house, I saw a truck in the drive. At first, I didn't think anything of it, but when four men with guns got out, I knew it was trouble. A few minutes later, I saw flames inside the house and the family being herded into the van. Before I could do anything, a mountain of a guy dragged me out of the car. I got in a couple of punches," Jeb pointed to his face, "and so did he. Thanks to the neighborhood security guard, the fight didn't last long. I'm still kicking myself that I couldn't grab my gun." Jeb wiped the sweat from his face with a small handkerchief he fished from his pocket. "Unfortunately, the van with the Caldwells took off. I managed to get a partial plate."

"Let me guess, it was stolen," Adam said.

Jeb nodded. "I had a buddy at DPD confirm that the van had been reported stolen two days ago. The van's owner also reported that his security cameras recorded the heist. According to him at least one of the culprits had a jacket patch that said SKIES INTERNATIONAL."

Cody blew out a breath. "It's definitely Lance. Any ideas where he took them?"

Justin wrapped a protective arm around Marissa. "Maybe we'll get lucky and Lila and her family are together in Colorado."

"Maybe." Adam said.

"Thanks, Jeb. I appreciate what you've done." Cody said.

"Are you sure you're okay?" Justin said. "If you feel weird in any way, let me know."

"Will do." He stood. "Let me know if there is anything else I can do to help find Lila and her family."

Adam approached Jeb. "Cody has told us a lot about you. Thanks for your help. We could use some extra muscle."

Jeb straightened, his eyes bright. "Wherever you need me."

Seconds later, another small jet taxied into the hangar. Four men exited. An older man with a white Navy ball cap Cody recognized as Oscar, Reid's former flight instructor. Oscar had been their pilot when they were on another life-and-death jaunt thanks to The Order. A large muscular man everyone called Bobsled, who'd also accompanied them on other Order missions, exited the plane, as well. Following Bobsled was a man with a noticeable limp whom Cody recognized as Gabe. Like Bobsled, Gabe had a military background. He'd lost a leg in combat, but his prosthesis didn't slow him down. The last man to deplane shocked Cody.

"Is that who I think it is?" Carson squinted. "Evan?"

Reid stared in the direction of the men. "I recruited more help."

"Carson, it's good to see you again. I'm here to help." Evan removed his white baseball cap emblazoned with the RED SOX logo.

Cody had met Evan a few times while he lived in Boston. He had a crush on Carson but had tamped down his feelings when she and Adam got serious. Evan worked for an IT company in Boston and had a knack for tracking people.

Carson nodded. "We need all the help we can get. Thanks for coming, Evan."

Cody turned to Oscar, Gabe, and Bobsled. "Good to see you all."

Reid stood in the middle of the group. "We've been preparing for this for some time. Our plans are in place and we all know what to do. Don't take any chances. I don't have to tell any of you how dangerous Lance and his people are. Stay safe." He turned to Jed. "Marissa, Holly, and Gabe will brief you on the flight. Bobsled is coming with us."

Reid and Justin hugged and kissed their wives.

"Let's meet on a secured call tonight," Reid said.

Gabe nodded and clapped Reid's back. "I'll keep them safe." He turned and lumbered toward the plane.

Cody hugged Marissa and Holly before the women trailed Oscar and Gabe to the other plane. Swallowing a lump in his throat, he climbed the stairs to Reid's plane. He prayed they weren't too late.

Chapter 41

Lila had no idea how long she lay in the corner of the cell. Her body, numb and still, curled into itself. Fog clouded her mind as if her thoughts waded through swampy waters. She lifted a heavy arm to wipe her face, suddenly realizing she'd been crying. The moisture on her hand was the only sign she still functioned.

Willa's words played in her mind. *Be dauntless.*

How could she? Willa's fate had rested in her hands and she'd died. Would her family's fate take a similar path? If she'd had the information Lance wanted, would Willa still be alive? Her mind scanned several scenarios as if she were a computer program and each sketch ended in Willa's death. Could she trust her conclusions? She shifted so that Willa's body moved out her field of vision. A second later, she forced herself to turn back. It was her fault the woman lay in a lifeless heap the least she could do was face her. "I'm sorry." Sobs shook her body and her vision blinded with tears. Her soul, speared with grief, had to endure. At least for Willa's sake.

Be dauntless.

How? How was she supposed to get herself out of this cell? How was she supposed to save her family? If Lance came for her family, he'd certainly come for the others. But Cody wouldn't stop until he found her. The thought of him lifeless like Willa or her father, Patty, or her siblings cut through the muck. She had to fight.

She added Willa's death to her long, sad list of memories to fuel her rage. Death and the fear of death of those she cared most for had to provide the ammunition to defeat Lance and The Order.

First, she needed to get out of this cell. She focused on the black orb watching over her. "Hey!" She waved her arms and waited for them to come.

REID ANGLED out of the clouds and moments later, he skated the aircraft on to the runway of the small airport twenty miles outside of Denver.

Before the plane came to a stop, Cody jumped up, ready to burst out the door.

Adam placed a hand on his arm. "Calm down. We don't want to make mistakes by being too antsy." His expression softened. "I've been where you are. She's in your skin and you want rip to shreds anyone who touches her."

Cody inhaled and placed his hands on his hips. "I hurt her once, but we're finding our way back. I can't lose her again."

Carson stood. "We're getting her back alive. I won't accept any other conclusion."

Reid exited the cockpit. "Oscar just radioed. They will be on the ground in Los Angeles in about an hour." He met Justin's gaze. "I have full faith Gabe and Jeb will keep them safe."

Bobsled nodded as he stood. "Neither Gabe nor I take too kindly to people messing with one of ours."

Reid turned to Evan and Angie. "Bobsled and Gabe have been along on this ride since the beginning."

"The Order killed our friend and fellow soldier, Cas, so they have as much skin in the game as any of us. We don't leave anyone behind." Justin picked up his phone.

"I've already texted Marissa and Holly reminders not take any chances," Reid said as Justin nodded but sent off a quick text anyway. "We'll review everything on our way."

The group split up into two vans as they sped toward Blue Vista. Adam drove one of the vans with Reid, Cody, Carson and Bobsled inside. Justin operated the other van with Evan and Angie, their eyes glued to their laptops while they worked.

Climbing higher along the mountain roads, Cody stared at the gray sky merging with the white-tipped peaks. Blue Vista, Ivan's Colorado estate, sat below them. Ivan had a fear of heights, which Cody found ironic given the man died when his son tossed him out of an airborne plane, so he constructed his estate in the gap between two mountains. Cody stared at the twisting mountain road as they climbed higher to enter the back of the estate. Images of the scene inside the Babylon Hall tunnels slammed into his thoughts. He stiffened as he recalled in the midst of bullets flying, Lila had been thrown in a van and spirited away.

"...are you listening, man?" Adam asked.

In the back seat, Cody swallowed. "What were you saying?"

Reid shot him a worried glace from the front passenger seat. "Are you sure you're up for this?"

"Absolutely. I have to get her out of there." Cody checked his weapon. Over the years, they'd stockpiled supplies for an operation like this, but Cody hoped the situation would never arise.

Minutes from Blue Vista, Adam and Justin parked the vans on the side of the road as everyone checked their two-way radios.

Evan pointed to his screen. "I'll have the way clear as soon as you get there but wait for me to give the go-ahead."

"Have the packages been received?" Cody asked Angie.

With her laptop on the seat, she turned and studied the screen. Smiling, she said, "Hope this mansion has good plumbing. The target will be shitting bricks any moment now."

"Fantastic." Cody wanted Lance's world disrupted with as much disorder as possible.

As evening settled in, Cody could make out a few clouds dotting the dark sky. He hoped the darkness would provide adequate cover. The chill in the late-summer Colorado air, energized him. He zipped his jacket, ready to attack. Flexing and unflexing his fists, Cody paced back and forth. Lila had been missing for over twenty-four hours. He stared at the expansive house. *Hold on, Lila. We're coming.*

"We're fifteen minutes out." Reid strapped on his backpack and turned to Cody. "We are not going in guns blazing. We all understand what you're feeling but put it on ice. We have to play this smart."

Cody nodded. "I'm cool."

Carson squeezed his arm as she moved next to Adam.

They left Justin to guard Evan and Angie in the other van still parked on the side of the mountain road. Adam wanted Carson to stay behind, but she insisted on coming with them. She'd lived in the house and knew the layout inside and out so the decision for her to accompany them made sense.

As they passed the unmarked road leading to Blue Vista, Carson pointed. "Stay on the main road. Up ahead a service road should angle to the left but continue past it. They will have surveillance cameras along that route. There is another road that leads to our entry point."

Adam complied, turned down the narrow road, then stopped behind a clump of pine trees.

Reid spoke into his radio. "We're ready to move."

Evan responded, "The path is cleared."

They trudged along the edge of a tree line. Cody kept his focus ahead, eyeing the perimeter of the property and the large electrified barbed wire fence.

When they neared the property line, Carson motioned for them to follow her. "There is a gate for large equipment to enter the grounds."

Adam nodded and took the lead.

True to Carson's word, Cody spotted the gate with an attached keypad. A bright light above the gate would bathe them in a spotlight. They'd have to hurry through and hope like hell they didn't run into the guards. Cody whispered into his radio. "Any chance one of you could take out this light above the gate."

Seconds later the light went out and a metallic click emanated from the lock heralding in hope they'd be able to pull off this rescue mission. "Thanks, Evan," Cody said, thankful Evan and Angie appeared enthusiastic about being drafted into the Alliance.

Adam held up his hand for everyone to pause. He listened to his radio and nodded. "Angie took down the remainder of the security in this sector. She pushed an alert on the other side of the estate, which sent a number of guards to investigate."

Evan's voice crackled across the radio. "Surveillance cameras stalled. You have fifteen minutes."

"Let's get our asses in gear, get our girl, and get the heck out of Dodge," Bobsled said adjusting his weapon.

Adam pushed open the gate and signaled for the group to follow. "Watch your six."

After everyone slipped inside and took cover behind a maintenance shack, Adam motioned for them to wait.

Carson pointed. "The door straight ahead is a secondary service entrance used for pool maintenance. It will lead us into the indoor pool complex. Once inside, the second door to the right leads down to the lower level where we believe Lila is being held."

Cody scanned the area for guards.

Two rounded the pool complex, wearing their standard dark green uniforms.

"Two guards ahead," Cody said.

As one of the guards neared the group, Bobsled jumped out of the shadows and, in one stealth motion, grabbed the guard and immobilized him. The man sank to the ground.

The other guard pivoted, shock registering on his face.

Cody lurched. Implementing his martial arts training, he debilitated the man, dragging him to the ground. He'd sleep for a while. Brute strength would have to be enough to combat the guards, for now. They didn't want to announce their presence by using their weapons, but Cody remained ready to use his gun if necessary.

"Bobsled and I will cover your six." Reid's gaze met Cody's. "Be careful."

The group arrived at the service door minutes later.

"Evan and Angie should have the security system disarmed and the doors unlocked," Adam said. He pushed open the door. "We're in."

Cody blew out a breath when they weren't greeted with a blaring alarm or armed guards firing upon them. The odor of chlorine surrounded Cody as they crept into the pool complex. Four dim lights lit the area, but the waters of the large Olympic sized pool were dark and motionless. They tiptoed across the gleaming tile floor.

Carson led them to another door. As she reached to open the door, Cody heard voices. They scrambled behind a stack of lounge chairs in a dark corner. Two guards neared them as they discussed a recent boxing match, unaware of the intruders.

"Do we need to check the prisoner?" one of the guards said, shifting the conversation.

The other guard shrugged. "Brenda and the new guys are down there. Let them handle it."

Then animated voices erupted over their radios and both men rushed out the door.

Cody rose, and the group continued through the door. The staircase was dim with just enough light to see the steps in front of them. When they'd reached the bottom of the stairs, Cody raised his weapon and pressed against the wall

Then the first bullet flew.

Chapter 42

Lila dropped behind a desk and grabbed the gun from the female guard she'd overpowered. The other guard, standing across the room, had been watching over her trip to the bathroom but when he responded to some kind of alert via his radio. Lila took advantage of his distraction. She jumped on the guard they called Brenda, and in seconds had her on the ground, unconscious. Mentally thanking Carson for insisting she practice martial arts, Lila readied herself to take on the second guard.

Her muscles tightened as a bullet whizzed past her and slammed into a wall. A moment of shock registered when she spotted the guard firing in front of her but not *at* her.

As she reached for Brenda's Glock, she felt a hand clamp around her wrist. She grimaced as another guard yanked her up. He must have come from another room in the back.

"You're not going anywhere."

The man stood only inches taller, giving her optimal targets. She lifted her leg and reared back, striking the center of his knee cap.

His body buckled and he loosened his grip.

Lila spun around and with the heel of her hand struck his nose.

Blood spurted as the man grabbed his face, dropping his weapon.

With bullets still lobbing in the opposite direction, Lila raised her leg, reading to aim for his groin, but he recovered and caught her foot. He pulled out a knife and in quick motion stabbed the meaty flesh of her thigh then pulled her to the floor.

Gritting her teeth, Lila suppressed a scream. She ignored the pain as the man lunged for her.

With her other foot, she struck his nose again. A crack and his howl of pain had her cheering the small victory.

He reached for her but, in seconds, she had him in a choke hold. As he passed out, she dropped him to the floor with a thud.

Limping out of reach, she pulled the knife from her leg. A fresh bolt of pain shot through her. Instead of tossing the knife, she stuck the weapon into the belt of her skirt.

She picked up Brenda's gun and belly-crawled toward the action on the stairs. In hopes of getting a better idea of her situation while not being seen, she scrambled under a desk. The stairs ahead appeared to be the only means of escape and they were currently blocked with gunfire. Her pulse raced inside her ears like a gush of water, but she kept her eyes trained on the scene ahead.

She inched up, squatting as she glared at the guard. A clear shot of the guard emerged. Lila aimed and fired. The man screamed in agony as the bullet blasted his leg.

Another shot from the stairwell injured his hand causing him to drop the gun.

A pause in the gunfire presented Lila with the opportunity to flee. Although she had no idea who was on the stairs, she prayed it was her cavalry. The guard was down thanks in part to an unknown shooter, so she shot up and took her chance.

On her way to the staircase, she scooped up the weapon the guard dropped. When she reached the stairs, she almost stumbled when a man turned the corner.

Cody!

Relief washed over her.

"Lila! I hoped that was you who took out that guard." Cody took her in his arms then pulled back. His gaze shifted down. "You're hurt."

"What are you all doing here?" Her eyes widened when she spotted, Adam, Carson, and Bobsled.

"Getting you out of this hellhole." Cody marched over to the injured guard, and with one punch, the man grunted and fell over.

"Can you walk?" Carson asked, hugging her.

"Yes, but I'm dripping blood, which is going to leave a trail," Lila studied her leg.

Adam squeezed her shoulder before turning back to assess the room. "Is that Willa Dickerson?"

Lila nodded. "Lance shot her."

Bobsled pulled a bandage from his jacket pocket and made a crude tourniquet on her leg. "Don't mean to be rough, but we need get out of here."

"Thanks, Bobsled."

Adam spoke into his radio. "Need a little help with our exit plan. ASAP." He kneeled in front of a guard and yanked the radio from his shoulder clip.

Lila didn't know who was on the other end, but she followed her friends back up the stairs. Just they reached the top, she heard a muffled explosion. The lights flickered. "What's going on?"

"It's our exit plan." Cody pulled her down as Adam and Reid peered around the corner.

Through the radio Adam stole from the guard, Lila heard excited voices indicating intruders at the front gates as well as the back perimeter. A call for a large contingent of guards to those locations crackled through the radio.

Adam took Carson's hand and waved them on, and Lila shot out of the door and into the pool complex.

She expected warm humid air associated with an indoor pool but instead a cool blast of air greeted her. The windows were frosting over.

"Looks like Evan and Angie took out the furnaces."

They followed Adam and Carson down a small hallway where they stopped at a door.

"All clear." Lila recognized Angie's voice over the radio Cody had clipped to his shoulder.

They bolted out the door. The cold ground shocked Lila who still wore no shoes. She admonished herself. She could have grabbed Brenda's shoes before leaving. Although likely the wrong size, she'd at least have protection for her feet.

The group slipped out of the gate and raced toward the tree line. Lila expected bullets to follow but they ran without issue. After they emerged from the cover of the trees, Lila released a breath when she spotted a large van idling along the road.

Adam climbed into the drivers' seat and as soon as everyone was inside, he angled off the road. He kept his speed at the limit.

"That seemed a bit easy," Reid said from the shotgun position. He turned. "Lila, are you okay?"

Cody slid a blanket over Lila's shoulders as he cast a worried look at her wound.

"My family. Lance has my family!" Despite the blanket, she shivered as perspiration chilled with the blast of the air conditioner.

Carson sat on the other side of her and took her hand.

Adam shot her glance over the seat. "We know. Yvonne has been alerted. Once we're clear here we'll switch to searching for your family."

"Did Lance or any of the guards give any indication where they are being held?" Reid asked.

"No. He showed me video of them tied up in what looks like a warehouse. They could be dead by now. Lance killed Willa. When I woke up, she was in the cell with me. She made me promise not to give in to him, even though I didn't have the information he wanted. He wants to know the location of the mine."

Carson squeezed her hand. "We'll find your family, but right now we need to get you out of here."

Tears flowed. "I couldn't save Willa. I can't lose my family, too."

Cody adjusted the blanket. "Carson's right, we'll find them." He glanced at her leg. "We need to get Justin to look at your leg."

"Damn it!" Adam slowed as the other van came into view. He'd driven with their headlights off. "The guards are here."

Lila glared at the truck in front of them. Three guards shot at the van as Justin traded fire. Her heart seized as she witnessed the danger her friends were in. Adding their peril to her family's, and she feared someone else might not survive.

CODY DREW his gun as Adam pulled over.

Reid studied the scene through night vision goggles. "Justin is holding them off for now. The guards don't know we're here." He lowered the goggles and readied his weapon. "But if they call in backup, we're going to be outnumbered." Reid turned toward Cody. "Stay here with Lila and Carson."

Cody didn't argue. He didn't want to leave Lila's side.

"Be careful, guys." Carson stared at Adam as he and Bobsled jumped out and followed Reid into the woods.

Cody hopped into the driver's seat, picked up the goggles, and scanned the road behind them. So far, no other vehicles were in sight. Then he turned the goggles to the scene a football field ahead of them. Reid, Bobsled, and Adam neared the van. Several shots were fired and after a couple of minutes the guards crumpled to the ground. Each rolled in agony with the pain of lower extremity wounds.

Evan and Angie appeared unhurt as they climbed into the van. Reid jumped into the drivers' seat, Bobsled took shotgun, and Adam shoved into the back.

Cody engaged the van and raced toward the scene. When they neared the other van, Bobsled reached out the window and motioned them to follow.

"Hurry. They may have called it in," Adam's voice boomed from the radio.

Seconds later, Cody spotted a Jeep in his rear-view mirror. "We've been spotted," he said into the radio. Cody glanced at Carson. "Get ready."

Carson and Lila picked up their weapons and angled toward the back.

"Here they come," Carson said into her radio. "There's four of them."

The first bullet slammed into the passenger side mirror.

"Lila, Carson get down!" Cody sped up, staying behind Adam in hopes of shielding them from the gunfire.

"I'm good." Lila aimed and fired.

She hit one of the shooters on his side. The man slumped over the rear window, the gun falling from his hand.

"We're moving beside you to take care of these guys," Reid shouted through the radio.

"No, it's too dangerous on this two-lane road." A vehicle coming from the opposite direction could cause a serious accident.

The Jeep raced up behind Cody, slamming into their bumper. At the same time their back window exploded. Cold air rushed into the vehicle. Cody gritted his teeth. If he didn't do something they'd either be run off the road or the bullets would get them. Another bullet whizzed into the van zipping between Lila and Carson and smashing through the front windshield.

Reid's voice crackled through the radio. "There is a curve up ahead with a runaway truck ramp. Follow the ramp and we'll take care of them. Can you handle that?"

Cody gripped the wheel as the Jeep rammed them again. "No choice." He floored the van putting distance between the Jeep. "Tighten your seatbelts and hold on." He caught a worried look from Lila.

"You got this," Lila said as she held on to Carson's hand.

Cody eyed the curve in the road and slowed a bit. Holding tight to the steering wheel, he maneuvered the curve and angled onto the dirt ramp. Dirt and rocks rattled underneath them as Cody struggled to slow the van without skidding out of control.

The Jeep whipped by them and seconds later the echo of more gunshots erupted followed by a plume of smoke. Cody's heart pumped as he brought the van to stop. *Please let that be the bad guys.*

Chapter 43

"That was intense. Is it in poor taste to say I'm totally pumped?" Angie's brown eyes shone bright, as she boarded the plane with the rest of the Alliance members.

"Nope." Bobsled high-fived her. "We didn't lose anyone and kicked some bad guy ass."

"I need to sit," Evan said scrambling for a seat, his face blanched.

Justin handed Evan a bottle of water. "Drink."

Evan nodded, whipped off his Boston Red Sox baseball cap, and twisted off the bottle top.

"Evan and Angie—you both did great," Reid said. He turned to Cody. "Helluva job." He clapped a hand on Cody's shoulder. "We shot the driver, and the Jeep went into the ravine."

Adam wrapped his arm around Carson. "Good job, everyone."

As soon as Lila collapsed in the seat, Justin approached, kneeling in front of her. He unwrapped the tourniquet and examined her leg. "The bleeding has slowed, and no major blood vessels were hit. The wound is deeper than I'd like so you'll need stitches."

Lila leaned her head against the seat and shut her eyes. "I can't stomach the thought of another needle."

"The good thing about being a combat doc is I can stitch you up quick." Justin winked and reached for his medical bag.

"Wait!" Lila straightened and turned to Carson. "Is there any chance there is a warehouse on the grounds of Blue Vista?"

Carson shook her head. "There wasn't when I lived there."

On his way to the cockpit, Reid stopped. "Before we left Dallas, I researched building permits for Blue Vista and didn't come across anything. Plus, we checked satellite images. We don't believe your family is here."

You remember Evan?" Cody said to Lila as he grabbed his computer.

"Yes, thank you. Both of you." Lila addressed Evan and Angie.

Cody turned on his computer then glanced up. "Reid, can we stall taking off for a few minutes?"

"We're good for now. We're still fueling up and waiting on clearance anyway." Reid crossed his arms. "Why?"

"If they have anyone worth their salt, they would clamp down after Lila's escape, so we need to get through their firewall ASAP." Cody said, staring at his computer screen.

Angie's fingers hovered above her keyboard. "What am I looking for?"

"A video uplink," Cody said. Less than five minutes later, Cody pumped his fists. "Bingo." He flipped his laptop around.

Everyone gathered around and viewed the image of Lila's family bound to chairs in the middle of a large concrete room.

"Can you get a bead on where this is coming from?" Adam asked.

Evan, already at his computer, said, "I'm on it."

"Does this scene look any different? What about individual members of your family—do they appear weakened or injured?" Reid asked, eyeing Lila.

"The scene looks the same. I guess." She bent closer to the screen. "The sweat stains on my father's shirt appear larger."

"Okay, that's good. Shows time progression." Reid sat next to Lila and placed his arm around her. "You did good."

"Thanks, Reid."

"While they're working, I'll sew up your leg," Justin opened his medical bag.

Cody shot a glance at her. He wanted to hold her hand, but he needed to focus on his task.

"Where are Marissa and Holly?" Lila asked, wincing as Justin cleaned her wound then shot numbing medicine into her leg.

Carson sat next to Lila and held her hand. "The plans we've been working on all these years are in place. We were about to initiate our own counteroffensive against Lance but with your family still in danger, we're holding off. Holly and Marissa, along with Oscar and Jed, are in LA."

"Los Angeles?" Lila said.

"Remember what Willa said about Lance getting rid of Delphine when she was of no use? We're trying to pull Delphine away. We have to persuade her to leave with the baby before it's too late," Carson said.

Cody drew in a breath, thankful Lila was safe and now in Justin's capable hands. The cruelty of The Order continued to amaze him. For Carson, Lila, and Reid to rise above their family and fight back showed true grit and fortitude.

Justin glanced up. "Any word on the LA operation?"

Reid headed to the cockpit. "As soon as we're in the air, we'll make contact."

Justin nodded as he continued stitching. When he finished, he handed her a bottle of pills. "Antibiotics, just as a precaution. I don't want you getting an infection."

"Thanks, Justin," Lila leaned her head on Carson's shoulder.

Ten minutes later, they were in the air and Carson updated her on the progress they made finding the island.

Lila nodded. "While I was in that cell I recalled, as a child, hearing Vivian speak about Palmarius Island so we're on the right track."

CODY FOCUSED ON HIS WORK. If they didn't find Lila's family, she'd be broken forever. He returned to the video footage, rerunning the tape over and over. "I think I have something." He zoomed in on an image. As everyone crowded around him, he pointed to a corner of the room.

"Looks like takeout food boxes," Carson said.

His fingers tapped the computer with lightning speed. Seconds later, he sat back. "They are in a town called Prager, Oklahoma, population 24,514."

"The receipt." Adam nodded.

Angie perked up. "The receipt on top of that takeout box is from a place called Lonnie's Burgers. The only Lonnie's Burgers in Oklahoma is in Prager. The food order was called in at 6:02 this evening."

Evan stretched his fingers. "I'm hacking into the traffic cameras." Minutes later, he said, "Got you!"

Cody moved next to Evan. He shifted to allow everyone to view the footage.

"See that unmarked white van? It pulls into Lonnie's parking lot." Evan pointed to the screen.

Cody observed a man jumping out from the driver's seat and returning five minutes later with three large bags of food. He drove out of the parking lot and out of the camera's view. Evan pulled up another screen showing the van again. Another camera picked up the van and Cody watched as the vehicle made a turn.

"I can't find the van on any other cameras," Evan said. "But I captured the license plate. It's from Texas."

Adam jumped up and headed toward the cockpit. "I'll coordinate with Reid and Yvonne."

Cody pulled Lila close. He hoped they'd make it in time.

LILA'S EYES snapped open when the plane bounced on to the runway.

"Hey, you're safe." Cody closed down the laptop he'd been working on and wrapped his arms around her tighter.

For a moment Lila believed she was back in the cell staring at Willa's body. Then her breath caught. "My family."

"We're in Oklahoma. Evan was able to get into their closed-circuit cameras. They are still alive, but we lost the connection about a half hour ago."

Lila released the breath she'd been holding. "But they were alive. We need to go."

Justin stood. "We have our team. Lila, you need to stay here with Cody. You're emotional and hurt." He placed a hand on her shoulder. "We know what your family means. We'll do our best to bring them back."

Carson stood and embraced her. "For what it's worth, I've been relegated to the plane, too. We'll sit and wait together." Carson stepped back and took Adam's hand.

Reid emerged from the cockpit as he slapped a weapon into his holster. "Yvonne's team just landed too." He turned to Lila. "Try to stay calm. I'll keep you updated." After hugging her, he pivoted. "You guys ready?"

Bobsled stood like an unmovable tree. "I'm ready to kick ass."

"Evan and Angie, you're our eyes and ears inside the warehouse. Let us know if so much as a mouse runs across the room," Adam said. Then he leaned down and kissed Carson. "I'll be careful." He winked. "We have a wedding in our future."

"Stay off that leg, Lila," Justin said, before he followed the others off the plane.

Cody rushed ahead conferring with the rescue group.

Lila rung her hands together. "They all have to come back safe." She sank into the seat. "My parents, Jenna, and Brent—they're innocent. Same as Willa. I tried to save her but..."

"I know you wanted to help Willa. I don't know how Lance and I are siblings. He has some type of evil dark matter flowing through him. Probably comes from our mother." Carson emitted a bitter chuckle. "Doesn't feel right calling her mother. Pia supported everything Lance did. After Lance killed Father and my Aunt Rhoda, I understood he had no redemptive qualities. I want him behind bars and in a place where he'll never see the sun. Where he can't hurt anyone else." She shook her head and focused her gaze downward.

Lila took Carson's hand. "Adam is going to be okay. He's a good agent with great instincts."

Carson squeezed Lila's hand and nodded. "We need to stay positive."

"There isn't a group of people I'd trust more than those guys." Cody sank onto the seat next to Lila and snaked an arm around her.

Even though she felt safe in Cody's arms Lila understood the feeling wouldn't last. It never did. She rose and lumbered to other side of the plane where Evan and Angie had set up their workstations. "Any changes?"

Angie glanced over her shoulder. "So far we haven't been able to establish the connection." He brown eyes softened. "I'm sorry Lila."

"I know you and Evan are doing everything you can." She sank into the closest seat. They have to be alive. Anger and fear roiled in her stomach, as if she'd ingested a sip of bitter alcohol.

Cody took the seat next to her. "They are twenty minutes out." Again, he wrapped a protective arm around her shoulders.

Stay positive. But the sentiment couldn't distract from the gnawing in her belly.

A second later, Evan glanced up from his screen. "I got a connection."

Cody, Carson, and Lila rushed to peer at his screen.

Lila's heart dropped as she stared at four empty chairs. "Where are they?"

Chapter 44

Lance entered the banal room of a chain hotel in a suburb of Dallas. How they could advertise this as *luxury* escaped him. He whipped off dark sunglasses and a Dallas Cowboys baseball cap, tossing the items on the cheap wood-grain table. Staring at the older man in front of him, he stepped farther into the room, moving past the bathroom entrance and stopping short of the king size bed. "I'm not happy."

Folding his meaty hands, Walt Talcott sat in the dull brown wing-back chair with his shoulders slumped. "I was expecting one of your subordinates."

Lance's gaze swept the room before settling on the old man. "Some tasks I still like to do on my own."

"I'm sorry about the latest mistake." Talcott stared at the law school ring squeezing his meaty finger.

"I'm a man of actions, not words. I expected the evidence to be destroyed. My mistake was trusting you to handle that. You and your colleagues had done such an exemplary job of handling the legal matters. I assumed this tiny task would be simple."

Talcott shifted in his chair. "When I discovered the breach, I took care of it. Steve dabbled into matters having nothing to do with him.

He made copies of the files and sent them anonymously to Jack Struthers. I killed Steve Dorman, so the issue has been resolved. I assure you, I have the firm and all my employees locked down."

Lance stared at the man. He hated when men begged, even if it was for their lives. "I've paid you and your firm millions. In return all I've asked for was a rigorous defense and proper disposal of the dubious evidence upon which the Feds based their weak case." Lance folded his arms.

"I took care of it Lance. There's nothing to worry about."

"Stop!" Lance shoved his hands inside his jacket, the cool metal of his weapon resting inside the holster, ramping up his desire for revenge. "You wouldn't have had to *take care of it* if you had disposed of the files immediately. But I don't think you had any intention of getting rid of those files. I know how you think. You wanted those files to use for your own purpose. You intended to blackmail me."

Talcott swallowed, the skin of his flabby jowls jiggled in response. "No, Lance, I had no such intention."

Lance slid the gun, equipped with a silencer, from his pocket. "Give me the location of the mine."

Talcott's eyes widened then he expelled a sigh. "The mine is on an island called Palmarius, off the coast of Columbia." He lowered his head.

"Good boy. Too bad you forgot I'm the Grand Commander." The bullet slammed into Talcott's skull, blowing brain matter against the far wall. *"Ordo Ortus."*

Lance grinned as he strolled out of the room. *Feels good to rid the world of the naysayers, but my purging isn't over yet.*

Chapter 45

The bedside clock read seven twenty. Sun rays splintering through the blinds confirmed morning had risen over the Texas farmhouse. Cody squirmed in the chair in the corner and sighed as he set down the phone. He'd been trying to reach Holden and for the third time he'd received no answer. Was his brother avoiding him or had one of Lance's operatives found him? The last image of his mother played through his mind. He'd never shake the sadness that her last thoughts of him were teamed with disappointment. Leaning back, he rested his head against the back of the blue overstuffed chair and stared at Lila's sleeping body. *At least she's safe.*

After Reid and the team confirmed the Caldwell's were not inside the warehouse, they'd returned to the plane defeated and concerned about the family. Another hour later, they'd received intel that a plane registered to Lance had left Oklahoma airspace shortly after they'd landed.

He pulled out his laptop and rubbed his eyes. Time to see what's going on at Skies International, the company supplying Lance's main source of income. Skies, a large umbrella company had several subsidiary companies with diverse products and services. After logging in, his fingers hovered over his keyboard, as he reviewed his line of attack. He'd already research the top executives and pinpointed a new assistant for the VP of Finance. The unsuspecting assistant clicked on the link she thought was from human resources. Her action gave Cody what he needed to get inside Skies. He set his trap and got out.

Lila stirred, then bolted up. "Any news?"

Her hair, tousled around her skull, created a sexy image. How could he think such thoughts at a time like this? He climbed into bed next to her, pulling her close. "Lance's plane landed in Florida. We are trying to track them from the airport."

"You believe they are still alive?" Lila's eyes were filled with unshed tears.

"Yes, everyone does. They could have killed them at the Oklahoma warehouse. We think he may want them as bait or leverage, especially since you said he wanted the location of the emerald mine." Cody cupped her face. "We're going to find them and bring them home." His gut twisted. He'd do anything to see her smile and make her feel safe.

She nodded and wiped at her eyes. "I'm sorry I lost it last night. You know how I hate crying."

"No one blames you." He swallowed. How could he tell her about his mother's death while making assurances her family would be safe?

"What's wrong?" She stiffened. "I know you, Cody. Tell me."

He swiped his hand through his hair. "My mother was killed yesterday by one of Lance's men. We think he gave her an overdose of insulin."

She slapped her hands across her mouth in shock. "I'm so sorry, Cody. And you're here dealing with me. What can I do? Do the authorities know who the man was?" She angled toward him.

He shook his head. "There's nothing you can do. The police are investigating but we both know what Lance is capable of. The best thing we both can do is bring him down."

Lila scooted off the bed. "I don't have the right words. I'm...sorry.

Are you okay?" She placed her hands on her hips. "Of course not. But you're here helping me. Shouldn't you be back in Virginia with Holden, making arrangements?"

Cody pulled her into his arms. "I've spoken with Holden, warned him about the danger, and tried to get him into a safe house. He refused. An autopsy will have to be performed so my mother's body won't be released until that's completed." He shook his head. "There's nothing for me to do. The only thing I wanted from her is the identity of my father. That likely won't happen unless there's some kind of documentation in the house. Once things settle, I'll go through her things. Holden can have the house." Conflicting emotions stunted further conversation between them. Overwhelming sadness combined with anger and disappointment. His mother was gone, taken by someone hired by a man with a twisted world view. Yet, his mother had had a chance, albeit a slim one, if only she had listened to him, but she'd been so quick to believe him a deadbeat son. The knowledge she went to her death with that thought had already burrowed in his heart. He forced the thoughts out of mind. Keeping Lila safe and getting her family back had to take precedence.

Lila met his gaze before reaching up and kissing him. "I'll take a quick shower and join you and the others."

AFTER A QUICK SHOWER Lila stood alone in the bedroom. Her gaze moved to the map box, sitting on the bedside table. She sat on the bed and stared at the box. There had to be something inside the diary to help them decipher the codes on the emerald tablets. She'd read Russell's diary from start to finish several times. Each pass she'd discovered something new. Inspecting the diary, she flipped through the pages, examined the back cover, then ran a finger over the spine. Nothing new popped out at her. With a sigh, she placed the diary back inside the box. Pulling out a map, she studied the layout of Babylon Hall. The same familiar attributes stared back her, so she placed the map back inside the box then lifted the container. The decoupage map covering the box gave the container a vintage feel. As she set the box down, her thumb rubbed against a rough area. She peered closer. Pulling at the bottom of the box, a section of the container clicked. Lila gasped as a mechanism released and a tiny door slid open. She eyed a sliver of green from a thin compartment on the bottom of the box. An emerald plate popped out similar to discharging a disc from a computer.

She stared in shock at the emerald plate before racing into the living room. "I found the last emerald plate!"

Everyone gathered as Lila laid the tablet next to the others. This plate had the code, JHIPU. Lila explained how she found the plate. With the last tablet in place, the tetrad of emerald plates was complete.

"Good work. With all that was going on, I forgot to tell you. The geologist indicated that based on the deep color these emeralds were most likely mined in South America, most likely in the area of Columbia, which fits our location. Regarding the map box—it's been in your possession since you were fifteen which means Russell, Vivian, or maybe even Ivan placed the plate inside." Reid crossed his arms and studied the newest tablet. "The code on this one says MSVVY."

Lila leaned over the table. "What does this mean?" She didn't expect an answer.

"Can we run a search on each code? Maybe that will tell us something," Angie said, grabbing her laptop. "That's what hackers do—decipher codes." She glanced up. "At least that's what I've heard." Seconds later, she said, "I've got nothing for MSVVY."

Evan pointed to another plate. "DPSS. Department of Public Social Services doesn't seem a likely match."

Angie continued to stare at her screen. "I doubt AOL means the web portal. And it repeats, so whatever it means there's two of them."

Justin set his glass on the table. "The only thing I can think of related to PZ is patient zero."

"Nothing for JHIPU, either," Evan said.

"None of this appears related." Cody picked up the newest plate and turned it over.

"Wait! I see something," Reid said. He turned one of the emerald plates to the side and pointed. "There is a tiny number on the spine. This one has the number three."

Lila picked up another tablet. "This is number two. Could this be The Order of the tablets?'

"I think so." Reid lined each tablet up according to the number and studied the codes.

Carson expelled a breath. "I'm so tired of all the ambiguity. Secret islands, codes, symbols. When will it end?"

"I agree with you, Carson, but we deciphered the clues last time. We'll do it again." Cody nodded.

"Decipher." Reid lifted his head, his eyes wide. "It's a cipher." He stared at the emerald tablets. "I need paper."

Lila handed him a notebook.

He wrote out each code. "Someone pull up an image of the alphabet."

Nodding, Evan shoved his laptop in front of Reid.

"A cipher is a secret way of writing a code." His gaze traveled from the paper to the screen. "That's it." He lifted his head. "ROT1 is a simple letter substitution cipher. You would replace the letter with the next letter ahead."

"Plate number one corresponds to AOL. Using ROT1 would mean *aol* stands for *bmp*." Lila shrugged. "It still makes no sense."

"That's because the rule for *this* cipher isn't one, it's seven," Reid said. He wrote: "The will" on a pad of paper. At this point everyone understood. Minutes ticked by and they stared at the complete code.

Chapter 46

"The will is in the cabin floor," Cody repeated the phrase. "Even the code has seven words."

"We'll get the coordinates of the two private residences on the island," Adam said.

"Russell mentioned an island cottage in his writings." Lila tapped the diary. "We have to get to that island. It may be our only bargaining chip to get my family back."

Reid's phone rang. He scooped up the device and retreated to a corner of the room as everyone got quiet. When he returned minutes later, he said, "That was Yvonne. We think Lance is in the area."

"Do you think my family was moved to Dallas?" Lila bit her lower lip.

"No, we don't believe so. But we have learned that Walt Talcott was murdered this morning in a hotel fifteen minutes outside Dallas. One bullet to the head."

"Mr. Talcott is dead?" Lila scooted to the edge of her seat on the sofa. "Talcott worked for Lance. He must have done something to anger his boss. I'm not surprised. Talcott's reaction after Jack died had been weird. I understand that partners had to be concerned about the firm, but that appeared to be the only thing he was concerned about, aside from his repeated warnings for me not to talk about Jack to anyone." Standing, Lila trudged to the other side of the room, staring out into the expansive yard. "What about Hilary Foster? Where is she?"

Adam gave Lila a brief update on Hilary.

Lila rubbed her forehead. "The background check on Hilary when I started with HTP showed nothing, but she's been more distant. Her disappearances from the office have been more frequent in the last few months. The talk around the firm is that she's having an affair. Lots of speculation about the man being a celebrity or someone in politics."

From the open kitchen Marissa divided a pitcher of strawberry smoothie into several glasses on a tray, then ambled into the living room. "Hilary's presence on the island indicates she's connected to someone in The Order. The question is who this Hugo Castille is, and is he the one running the show?"

"Angie and Evan are working on the Hilary and Hugo angle. I hope they'll have something soon." Reid accepted one of glasses from Marissa.

"If I'm pivotal to this mystery, as others have said, then this damn tattoo must provide a key to something." Lila extended her arm.

Cody joined Lila near the window. He placed a protective arm around her.

Adam paced back and forth. "It has to be the will. But why would Ivan go through the trouble of hiding his will on an island no one knew anything about?"

"He didn't want Lance to gain possession of the mine." Reid moved closer to the screen. "Carson is his daughter. Maybe the will gives the mine to her."

Carson emitted a sarcastic grunt. "My father wasn't exactly thrilled that I had no enthusiasm for The Order. He focused on Lance to take the helm, so he would likely will my brother the mine. As far as I know, he hadn't had a falling out with Lance prior to this death which means he wouldn't have had time to change his will to cut my brother out."

"But when we were inside the Colorado mine, before Ivan's death, I saw the way he looked at Lance. Ivan didn't have the look of a proud father." Reid crossed his arms. "He could have suspected Lance had plans to off him."

Lila picked up a bottle of water and twisted off the top. "Lance has access to Blue Vista, the Swiss mansion, and all the business locales. He would have had all of them searched. The one place he has no access to is the island. Even if we got the will and Ivan gave everything to Carson, Lance would be sure to contest it. We'd have to authenticate the will." She may not be the most experienced attorney, but this legal battle could mean life or death for her and those she cared about.

"Not everything makes sense though." Cody crossed the room and studied the photo of Palmarius Island.

"Cody is right. Let's back up a minute." Reid tapped his fingers together. "A lot has happened, and it all seems connected but there are holes in the story. Start with Lila finding Jack Struthers near death."

Lila tapped her fingers together. "He told me to find the documents and not to trust anyone. The documents were the suppressed evidence that could have put Lance away for life. The documents led me to Garvin Jennings, but Morris Beak and Willa Dickerson sought me out. Each gave me emeralds and were instructed to do so in a letter from Hugo Castille. Now, they're all dead, including Jennings' wife."

"Lance killed Willa but that was to put pressure on Lila. Why would he risk killing Beak and Jennings so soon if they had information that could help him find the mine? Hugo could be a messenger but he's key to this mystery." Justin stood, stretched, and took one of his wife's smoothies.

"This morning I ventured back to the dark web and managed to get a little intel on Stonegate," Cody said. "I don't have much but it's a small company formed out of Delaware four years ago."

"Why Delaware?" Carson asked.

"Many companies, even Fortune 500 ones, incorporate out of Delaware because of the attractive business and tax laws," Lila said.

"Exactly." Cody took a sip of water. "I haven't been able to find anything on the corporate structure, other than a list board of directors' titles with no names. There's lots of buzz about Stonegate's desire to buy Veridian but not much else."

"Just before Steve's death, he mentioned something about people being too powerful. HTP is already involved in this but they could be more intertwined than I first thought." Lila rubbed her forehead as her mind whirled back to the events of the last few weeks. "I need to go to the island. It's the only way."

Cody shook his head. "It's too dangerous."

"The lives of all of us and our families are at stake. Reid, you said yourself if Lance gets ahold of the mine and purchases Veridian, he will be more powerful than anyone can imagine. This has to end, and we have to be the ones to end it."

"I hate to agree with you because you're talking about an extremely dangerous mission, but you're right. We need to get to that island," Adam said.

"I'm going with you." Cody took her hand. "But how do we get on the island without being seen?"

Reid tapped the computer screen. "I think I have a way. The mining operation runs in shifts. A ferry from the mainland to the island arrives at certain points during the day to drop off and pick up workers. Unfortunately, it's too dangerous for all of us to go."

"Can you get us on that ferry?" Lila's heart pounded with the idea of finally doing something to bring down Lance and get her family back. "Then, enact Operation Chaos. I know it's a risk with Lance having my family, but at the same time this move will put us on the offense. This way if something happens to my family everyone will know who's responsible."

Chapter 47

The ferry slowed and pulled up to the wharf. Workers gathered their belongings and headed toward the exits. Lila pulled her hood lower across her face, adjusted her backpack, and merged into the crowd with Cody next to her. The mild steady rain had been a lucky break. Many of the workers wore hooded windbreakers so Lila and Cody blended in well.

They made their way onto the gangplank, following the workers to a low, one-story building.

"I hope these IDs work," Lila whispered. She considered the main building looming and the expectation that all workers clock in. She gripped the fake ID and suppressed an inappropriate giggle. She'd never been one of those teenagers who got ahold of a fake ID in order to get into the bars or buy beer, but here she was sneaking into an emerald mine with one. The Alliance had spent hours discussing the best way onto the island and everyone agreed that slipping in with the miners and workers on the island would be the best way to avoid detection. But only if their IDs worked.

"Angie assured me they would." Cody swept a glance at Lila before shifting his gaze ahead.

Lila lifted her hand to adjust her communication earpiece hidden by her hair then thought better. She and Cody both were fitted the earpieces to maintain contact with the rest of the Alliance members currently running the operation from a boat off the coast of Palmarius Island. Gabe, Holly, Marissa, and Jeb had returned. They'd spoken with Delphine about the urgency to get away from Lance. She'd been resistant at first, but in the end Holly and Marissa appeared to have convinced Delphine of the danger she might find herself in. However, so far Delphine still remained reluctant to leave.

Cody and Lila inched forward until their turn came to walk through the metal detector then they would slide the ID through the card reader. Lila pasted on a bored expression and stepped through the scanner. They didn't have weapons on them because they'd expected this type of scrutiny, yet her body stiffened.

The guard stared at her, his gaze traveling the length of her body. "You must be new."

She bobbed her head. Even though she brushed up on her Spanish on the flight over, Lila didn't want to engage in a long, detailed conversation. Remaining silent was her best option. When the light turned green, she released the breath she'd been holding in measured beats, cognizant of appearing too relieved. Next, she slid the card through the reader and once again held her breath. Seconds elapsed like years. If she was caught, she had no idea what the officials would do to her. A bell buzzed, and the red light lit green. Relief burst through her like water erupting from a geyser. She stepped through, praying Cody would breeze across, too. Seconds later, he stood next to her.

"We made it over one hump." He leaned in. "Stay close."

Lila gave him a slight nod, pressure already building again. Between Reid and Angie, they were able to get the schematics for the island. Although, the document was a few years old, it was all they had.

A massive sign in Spanish and English loomed ahead, WELCOME TO THE STONEGATE MINE. Lila slowed and stared at the wooden greeting. Even though they'd discovered the name of the mine prior to arriving, the words displayed in large letters gave her pause. Her great-grandfather founded The Order that had started this entire deadly thirst for power. This emerald mine was their latest find, but what other secrets lay hidden?

"Are you sure your leg is okay for this?" Cody's eyes were full of concern.

Lila tore her gaze from the sign. "Too late for that. Let's go."

They weaved into a group trekking down the hall, following them down a staircase to the ground floor. The group headed to cafeteria buzzing with change-of-shift conversations while Lila and Cody moved past the large room. Spicy meat and the aroma of fried food wafted from the cafeteria. On any other day Lila would have been interested in testing the local cuisine but in the wake of her family's disappearance, food didn't rate high on her list. At a swift pace, they moved through the corridor, passing photos of the mining operation process along the way. They stopped in front of a door at the end of the hall.

Cody pushed open the door and they entered a loading dock area. He pulled her behind a tall stack of crates so they could survey the area.

Lila eyed the crates labeled as bottled water, granola bars, and fruit among other items. Based on the schematics she'd studied, she knew the mining supplies were stored at another location closer to the actual operation.

Lila spotted two men on the other side of the dock. They scooped up a few boxes and disappeared through another door into the main building.

"How's it look?" Cody said into the hidden earpiece.

Reid's voice echoed in Lila's own earpiece. "Surveillance is down. You have three minutes."

"Where's our contact?" As soon as Lila whispered the words a lone Columbian man appeared in the dock area carrying two black backpacks.

Cody stood and took her hand. They approached the man.

"*Plátanos*," Cody said.

"*Plátanos, amigo. Vamos!*" The man shoved the backpacks at Cody, waved them away, and raced out of a side door.

Yvonne and Reid used their FBI resources to find a contact at the mining facility. They'd settled on the code word bananas, *plátanos* in Spanish, in case someone overheard them. The interaction would appear as if they were hungry employees.

Cody and Lila strapped on their new backpacks, crouched low, and ducked out of a back door. They darted into the dense forest.

Once they were about a football field from the facility, Cody stopped. He opened his backpack and pulled out a gun and a can of bug repellent. "We'll need this. We also have a lightweight tent, a GPS tracker, maps, food, and a phone. The GPS tracker will remain off most of the time and phone is only used if necessary."

"Understood." Lila, breathless from their sprint, swung her backpack around and drew out her gun. She shoved the weapon into the backpack's side pouch. After covering herself in bug repellent, she slid on a wide-brimmed hat and sunglasses.

"Did our delivery boy arrive?" Adam's voice came through their earpieces.

"Affirmative," Cody replied as he applied the repellent and put on his baseball hat and sunglasses. "We're outside the facility. We're signing off for a few hours until we get closer."

"Be careful, guys." Marissa's voice came over the line.

"We will." Lila stared up at the massive trees. The light rain trickled like a soothing fountain across the leaves and large palm tree fronds. A humid earthy aroma replaced the greasy cafeteria scents.

Cody checked his watch. "The cabin is five miles from here. We should be able to get there in less than two hours, but we may be slowed by terrain and the weather. First, we stay together. But, if for some reason, we get separated, I want you to stay put, if possible. Call for help using the communication link but if it isn't working turn the on phone or use your compass GPS tracker. Don't chance going to cabin alone. It's too dangerous." He handed her a map and a compass. "Don't lose this." He moved close and placed his hands on her hips. "Promise me you'll adhere to this?"

Concern emanated from his brown eyes. *Nothing could happen.*

Right? Frightening scenarios ripped through her mind, but she pushed each one away. Positive thinking. "I promise but I'm confident we'll both make it to the house, find the document, and then get out. Everyone has been through enough." She checked her shoelaces, which evoked images of her family tied up and afraid.

They took off at a brisk pace side by side.

Lila inhaled the earthy scent of the rain-soaked vegetation as they slowed before tackling a hill. She estimated they'd covered a couple miles, but the rough terrain and rain slowed their progress. They crested the hill, and Lila's breath caught. In front of them was a huge waterfall cascading into a rocky stream. In addition to the rain, the steamy spray peppered them.

Cody pulled out a canteen and gulped down the water. "If we weren't on a mission, this would be an ideal place to camp out." He squinted. "According to the map, there should be a land bridge nearby."

Lila glanced around. "There." She pointed to a mossy strip of land a football field away. She raced forward, ready to cross the bridge. As she took her first step, she stumbled as the ground below her crumbled. She screamed as she scratched at vines and rocks to gain a foothold. A glance downward had her heart tumbling into her stomach. That same waterway she thought was so beautiful minutes earlier now threatened to consume her body in its rocky waters.

Then Cody's hand clamped around hers. "I've got you." He yanked her up and they both landed in a heap.

Blowing deep breaths, Lila stared into Cody's eyes. His arms remained around her and she clung to his chest.

"Are you okay?" Cody asked.

"I,..I...y-yes."

"Damn it, Lila. You could have died. You can't take these kinds of chances. You don't know this territory. *I* don't know this territory." His brown eyes blazed, and his jaw tightened.

She expelled another breath. "You're right. I'm so focused on getting this document and bringing down Lance that I've been careless. I'm sorry—running on adrenaline. All this death and I'm afraid we won't find my family in time..." She shook her head."

"I know but we both need to be careful." He pushed a strand of hair away from her eyes. "I don't want to lose you."

This time her heart skipped a beat for another reason. "It would have sucked to fall to my death." She rose up on her elbows and kissed him.

He returned the kiss, then pulled back. "As much as I'd like to stay here like this, we need to get you cleaned up and press on." He stood and held out a hand to her.

"Cleaned up?" She took his hand and stood.

"You have a small cut on your arm." He lowered his backpack and in seconds unpacked a first aid kit. He cleaned the cut, applied antibiotic cream, and then covered the wound with a bandage. "All set. Let's go."

After hiking to the stream, they climbed up the banks. When they reached the other side, they noticed the rain and fog had settled in. Even though Lila considered herself in good shape, she huffed along as the hike proved challenging.

Cody grinned and wiped rain from his face. "Hiking isn't for the weak. Normally, I'd suggest hiking poles, but we don't need the extra equipment."

"I'm officially impressed." She pulled her hood tighter. "How much farther?"

"It's due south. But I think we should stop. The rain and fog make it too dangerous to continue. We can't risk another near fall." He circled the area and then pointed. "This is a good spot to set up camp for the night."

"Here?" Lila glanced up at the darkening sky, made darker with the clouds and trees.

"Yeah." He set his backpack down and pulled out supplies.

After they assembled the tent, Cody turned on the radio. "We need to stop for the night. The weather conditions are too risky."

"You guys gonna be okay for the night?" The concern in Adam's voice came through the radio.

"We'll be fine." Lila wasn't sure she agreed, but she didn't want her friends to worry even more. "What's the status of Operation Chaos?"

"I spoke to the reporters we'd targeted and sent them the data, plus informed whoever would listen that your family is missing. The articles are set to run tomorrow," Carson said.

Cody's eye lit up. "Once we have the will and Lance's dirty deeds are exposed to the world tomorrow, we might have the upper hand. If anything happens to the Caldwells, Lance will have to be investigated, no matter who he has working for him."

Lila's heart knocked inside her chest. She wouldn't allow herself to think this tactic could fail.

"Stay safe," Reid said.

Lance glanced at the surroundings. For the first time she considered just how dark the rainforest was. There would be no light.

"I wish I could make a fire. Through our limited surveillance there doesn't appear to be patrols through the rainforest, but we can't risk detection." Cody pulled out a lantern and in the dim light, motioned for her to sit next to him.

Her gaze swept across the dark trees which took on the appearance of black-clothed faceless men with branches for arms wielding long swords. She scooted onto the blankets. Cody's familiar scent, a mixture of light sweat and his spicy deodorant, caught her attention and worked to calm her anxiety. She shifted closer as a cacophony of forest sounds exploded around them.

"We'll be fine. I'm sure the animals will stay away." Cody grinned as he opened a thermos of hot noodles. He handed her a thermos, then opened another.

Lila reached for a fork and stirred the noodles, the savory aroma waking her empty stomach. "How did you know I was concerned about animals?"

"You're snuggling. You don't snuggle." He shoved a forkful into his mouth.

"I can snuggle." She held her fork in midair. "I'll admit it crossed my mind. What about snakes?" Her voice rose as chirping and buzzing echoed in the background.

"We're good." Cody continued to eat.

His nonchalance annoyed her. "We are in the wilderness. I did some research. There are probably jaguars, poison frogs, caimans—those crocodile-like animals—and all kinds of venomous snakes and spiders." She lowered her voice. "Maybe even anacondas." Despite the humidity of the rain-drenched forest, Lila shivered. "Whatever is out there probably doesn't like visitors and may be very hungry."

"Just keep your distance and don't provoke them and you'll be fine."

"Not helpful." Lila poked her fork into the noodles. Surprised they were actually good, she speared more on her fork.

"I did some research, too. I studied the topography, the trail to the cabin, and the animals likely to live here. I won't let anything happen to you." He placed his thermos on the blanket and turned. Cupping her face, he stroked her cheeks. "We're going to survive this, then go back to Dallas. I promise." He leaned in and kissed her then dug into his backpack and presented her with a canister of pepper spray.

She smiled. "Thanks."

After they finished their meal and they hadn't been attacked by rabid animals with a taste for humans, Lila relaxed more.

Cody gave her a smile. "For the record, I think you're handling this like a champ. I know you're out of your mind with worry about your family. Lance is going to be rocked by our move."

"I keep telling myself that this will be over soon, and we'll have my family all back safely but then I remember what Lance did to Willa and..."

He covered her hand. "I'm sorry about Willa."

Lila hadn't expected to talk about the woman. "Willa was...she was special. She didn't deserve to die. She brought my memories to life. So much of my childhood was lost in my mind. I guess I chose not to remember."

"I'm glad you were able to get some of your questions answered."

"Those memories are difficult, but I feel better having a full account of what happened." She folded her hands in her lap. "Everything boils down to power and money. If we don't stop Lance, we know the cycle will continue, possibly with his son." She glanced at Cody. "I feel sorry for that baby and Lance's wife."

"We'll stop him. But we need to be careful doing it."

Lila stared at the lantern's bluish glow. "How many more people have to die?"

Cody pulled her close and kissed the top of her head. "For now, look up."

She shifted her head and through a clearing, she saw an explosion of stars fanned out before them. "Wow. I don't think I've ever seen that many stars."

Cody stretched out on the blanket and pulled her down next to him. "See that one. It's the Southern Cross, or the Crux Constellation."

With her head on his shoulder, she snuggled closer. "Tell me more."

"The Southern Cross can only be seen in the Southern Hemisphere and because the long bar of the cross point to the south pole, the constellation is used as a navigation tool." He pointed. "The four stars of the cross are Acrux, Becrux, Gacrux, and Delta Crucix. There is actually a fifth star but it's hard to see."

"Beautiful. So serene." She shifted her gaze to him. "Cody, I care so much about you."

He angled toward her and took her face in his hands. Shifting a strand of hair from her face, he kissed her.

Lila responded to his kiss with enthusiasm. Memories of kissing Cody had never left her, but this kiss held new meaning.

Cody pulled back. He took their bowls and utensils, rinsed them with water, and put them inside a drawstring bag. He strung the bag up on a nearby tree away from their tent and grabbed the lantern. He returned to her and took her hand and pulled her inside the tent. He flipped open a flap in the tent's ceiling, revealing a mass of bright stars twinkling down on them. "Now, we won't be in the dark." He unrolled their sleeping bags.

Lila smiled, and tears trickled down her face. Cody was always thinking of her.

Cody kissed her, and they lowered on top of the blanket.

"You are so beautiful. I'd die trying to part the seas for you. Don't ever forget that."

Lila's heart soared. Under the twinkling stars, she found a new home in Cody's arms.

Chapter 48

The next morning, Cody woke with a smile and Lila in his arms. The earthy aroma of the forest mixed with her familiar vanilla scent spiked his libido. He tamped down his passion and tapped her arm. "Hey, sleepyhead." She stirred. Cody had never seen anything as beautiful as Lila at this moment. He pulled her naked body into a spooning position and cupped her breasts in his hands.

"Wow, I like this alarm clock." Lila tossed a sexy smile over her shoulder.

He kissed her neck and groaned. "I don't want to move."

"Me either but we've got to get to the house and get off this island." She sighed and flipped over on her back. "Why is there always a *have-to*?"

"One day, I'm going to take you on a trip. We'll go anywhere you want." He shifted and leaned over her.

She placed a finger at her chin. "Hmm. I always wanted to go to Singapore."

"Singapore? Why?"

"All the pictures. The city seems to be a mysterious and energetic place with lots of beauty and history."

"Done. We're going."

"Okay, Mr. Moneybags. That's an expensive vacation." She toyed with his pectoral muscles and for a second, he forgot the topic of conversation.

"I minored in finance. Remember when I put money in Bitcoin?"

She nodded, her eyes lighting up. "It paid off?"

"Yep. Big. So, *we* can afford a trip to Singapore." He ran his thumb along her jawline. "I'll do anything to keep that beautiful smile on your face."

"Thank you. But more than anything I just want you and everyone to be safe." She stared at his chest. "You said *we* can afford Singapore. Are we a *we*?"

"I hope so, especially after last night."

"I like that." She planted a quick kiss on his lips then jumped up.

AFTER BREAKING DOWN CAMP, they both turned on their communication devices.

"We're leaving camp and heading toward the cabin. Anything we need to know?" Cody said.

"All is quiet in your sector," Reid said. "The ferry will be coming into dock soon with the morning shift, but we don't have any threats coming your way."

"Any news on my family?" Lila asked.

"We tracked a Skies International plane from Oklahoma to an area in southern Florida. We'll know more later today," Reid said.

"Please let me know something as soon as you can."

Cody glanced over his shoulder, making a mental picture of what had become their special spot.

Lila also glanced back. "I wish I could take a photo, but I know we can't risk turning on our phones right now."

"It's nice to know we're both sentimental saps." He nudged her elbow then took her hand.

She smiled as they started their trek toward the cabin.

Thirty minutes later, they entered a clearing, arriving at another waterfall. Cody peered over the rocky edge, catching a rainbow above the two-hundred-foot drop. Trees and vegetation bordered the plummeting water.

As they searched for the best route over the water, they came upon a different clearing. Cody paused. "Did you hear something?" His intuition prodded him.

"No, why?" Lila asked. Her eyes were wide.

"I don't know. Maybe it's nothing." He shifted his gaze upward. A bird with a severely pointed beak that he recognized as a kingfisher, lifted off a branch, its blued-hued wings fanning outward. He remained quiet, listening for something else. Then the unmistakable sound of helicopter rotors flapped in the distance. "Someone is coming."

He pulled Lila back and attempted to push them toward the tree line but before he could something splintered into a tree.

Bullets.

Cody pulled her to the ground as bullets peppered down. A yellow helicopter hovered above them with a gun-toting man firing from aircraft's skids. Cody covered her as best he could. If they didn't get to the forest, they'd both be killed.

"Stay down!" Cody pulled his gun from his holster as bullets slammed into the ground inches from them. He lifted and fired. "We are under attack!" he said into the radio.

The helicopter pulled up and shifted, dodging his bullets then returned.

No way he could hold off the barrage of bullets.

"We're trying to get to you, but our boat is forty minutes out," Reid said.

Lila wiggled. "My gun!"

Before Lila reached for her weapon, she screamed as a round of bullets rained down in front of them.

A second helicopter arrived spraying more bullets.

They ran in the only clear direction, which moved them back toward the waterfall.

"They're trapping us!" Lila screamed.

Cody swept the scene. He spotted another way out. "Lila. Move with me. A land bridge is up ahead. We missed it earlier because of the heavy vegetation. If we get across and into the woods on the other side, we might have a chance."

She nodded.

The second the men stopped shooting from the helicopter, they ran for a large tree which was yards from the land bridge. Just as they reached the tree, they dodged for cover as more bullets rained down.

Panting, Cody pulled her tight against him. "I'll try to cover you. When I say go, run as fast as you can. Keep running. I'll catch up."

Stunned eyes stared back at him. "We should stay together."

"We'll never make it. If I occupy them, you can get across. I'll be fine." Although true they were dealing with one less shooter on their side, Cody's hopes for escaping unscathed were fading.

She hesitated, then nodded. "I'll get to the other side and start firing."

"No, keep running. Don't worry." He glanced up. Based on his estimation, the shooter would have to change magazines soon. "I'll be right behind you." He returned her gaze. "I love you. Go!"

As Lila raced away from the trees, Cody aimed at the helicopter and fired. The shooter reengaged. Bullets slammed into trees and bushes all around him. He chanced a look and spotted Lila reaching the land bridge. He prayed the earth would hold her. Turning his attention back to the helicopter, he continued to fire. Then fear froze in his gut as the shooter began firing at Lila, now halfway to the other side. Making a quick decision, he stepped out from behind the tree and aimed at the shooter, drawing his attention away from her.

Bullets nudged him closer to the edge of the cliff. He shot a brief glance at the fifty-foot drop. "Run, Lila!" He yelled, urging her away from danger. His chest tightened as he implored her to move faster. He couldn't lose her. "Stay away from her!" He fired off more shots. Then a bullet pierced his arm and he stumbled. His gaze locked onto Lila's for a second before he tumbled over the edge.

Chapter 49

Reaching the other side of the falls, Lila turned. She aimed her weapon, but just as she fired, she screamed when a bullet smashed into Cody. He stumbled back. Her world stilled as Cody plummeted off the edge.

"Cody!"

She emptied her gun as the helicopter rose higher and fluttered out of sight. Her weapon thudded to the ground, and her vision narrowed. Lila raced to the cliff's edge and peered down. Mist from the nearby falls mixed with tears, impeding her vision.

"Cody! Cody!"

Her screams were met only with the roar of the falls. She had no idea how deep the water was, but she had to get down to bottom of the fall's rocky edge. Could he have survived? She sunk to the ground as sobs wracked her body.

What seemed like faraway voices shouted at her. "Lila! Run!"

She couldn't pull her focus from the falls as her heart plummeted over and over just like the water rushing over the cliff.

The *chop chop* of helicopter blades jolted her away from the edge followed by more screams in her earpiece.

"Lila are you there?" Reid's voice, full of concern, streamed into her ear.

"I'm here." She wiped her face as the shock of her situation settled. "Cody went over." She refused to think anything worse than that.

Then she spotted a couple of men rappelling from the hovering aircraft.

Keep running.

Cody's words echoed in her mind. The mantra of her life burrowed into her body like a field tick embedding in her skin.

"We spotted the helicopters. Get out of there! Now!"

If there was an iota of a chance Cody had survived, she had to try.

With one last glance at the gushing water, she rose, scooped up her gun, and raced away from the scene. She passed trees and bushes which bore the results of the gun battle moments earlier. One man had rappelled from the helicopter on the other side of the falls and there could be more.

Her heart hadn't stopped beating in staccato rhythm.

"I have to find Cody." Lila spoke more to herself than to the Alliance members monitoring the situation from a boat off the island's coast.

"No, Lila. Keep moving away. We're tracking you," Carson's voice echoed in her earpiece. "We're working on a way to get to you without starting a shootout. Hold on."

Please be all right. Cody's face before he plummeted off the cliff dominated her thoughts. *Please be all right.* The phrase played on a loop in her head as she raced through the forest. She slowed and leaned against a tree as her breath erupted in raspy gasps. Seconds elapsed then she straightened and angled back toward the falls.

"What are you doing, Lila?" This time the voice belonged to Holly.

"If he's hurt, I can't leave him."

"Okay, honey. The shooters are..." A crackle in her earpiece cut off Holly's voice. Lila prayed interference caused the outage and not an attack. When she reached an area with a manageable slope, she skidded down the incline, falling on her butt most of the way. At the bottom, she popped up, yet her shoes slid on the rocky moss-covered bank. She scanned the water, which appeared deeper than she'd imagined.

She listened for signs of him, her breath held. She ran several yards down the bank, mud caking her on shoes. Part of her breathed relief that she didn't come across his body, while the other part panicked that she hadn't found him.

Maybe he survived and was looking for her. She opened her backpack and stared at the phone. If she turned on the phone her location could be compromised. Cody had warned her to use the phone only in an emergency. Her finger hovered over the ON button. *What if I inadvertently expose Cody as they are tracking my signal?* As Lila paced mud squished beneath her feet, but she didn't care. All she wanted was Cody. He said he loved her. Despite all the hurt in their past, she knew in her soul she'd never stopped loving him. Everything else now paled in comparison.

She dropped the phone into her backpack, climbed back up the embankment and sank to the ground. Cody had told her to continue on if they got separated, but how? How was she supposed to leave? Tears flowed again and she didn't bother to try to control them. Lila had never felt more alone in her life. A green iguana sat on the branch of a nearby tree. As Lila wiped her face, she noted the iguana didn't appear frightened of her. Perhaps he, too, was numb to the world. She forced herself to get up. Spinning around, she searched for the man who'd exited the helicopter.

She started walking—remembering Cody's last instruction to keep running. Half an hour later from a spot at the top of a hill, she caught sight of the single-story log cabin, set in the middle of a clearing. Her heart kicked up, but she studied her tattoo and hoped once again the mark led her to what she needed. More than anything she wanted Cody to appear. Maybe he was waiting for her.

Attempts to reach the Alliance and Cody again resulted in dead air. Pressing her compass pendant, she hoped they would receive her coordinates.

She trudged down the hill as her feet sunk in the doughy grass. Sweat trickled down her face. At the bottom of the hill, she ducked behind a tree and stared at the house. A wooden porch with a roof overhang, wrapped around three fourths of the house. There were no vehicles in sight, no helicopters in the air.

Speaking into her radio, she told the Alliance members she'd made it to the cabin. Crackling static drummed into her ears. Her heart dropped as she considered the worst. Had the Alliance boat been ambushed?

Lila scurried toward the wooden front porch steps. She stared at the combination lock. After trying several combinations, she entered her birthdate and the lock clicked. She pushed open the door a few inches and listened for sounds. Hearing nothing, she pushed opened the door farther and slipped inside.

A large stone fireplace dominated the living room. She moved to the fireplace and waved a hand over the logs. Although she sniffed the odor of burnt wood, the remnants of a fire were cold with a thick layer of ash.

She scanned the room. After a cursory check of the two bedrooms and one bathroom she concluded she was alone. With concerns for her safety placated, Lila reentered the first bedroom. *The will is in the cabin floor.* After a thorough search, she came up with nothing. A search of the second bedroom yielded the same results. She searched the small bathroom before returning to the kitchen.

Exhausted, Lila plopped on the faded blue and yellow rug in the center of the kitchen floor. As she leaned against a cabinet, she spotted a creased area of the rug. She pulled back the dusty rug and gasped. A tiny gap between two of the floorboards provided the method to pull apart the floor revealing a hidden compartment. Inside the compartment sat a square briefcase-shaped safe. With her heart pattering, Lila pulled out the safe. Retrieving her phone from her backpack she turned on the ultraviolet light Cody rigged on her device. She extended her arm next to the safe and aimed the UV light at the invisible tattoo. The code illuminated onto the safe's sensor and the lock clicked.

"Unbelievable," she whispered. She extracted a set of papers. The deed to the island and Ivan's will. She flipped through the papers, noting Ivan had created the will under a sound mind and body. The will indicated Ivan wanted all of his property to go to Carson, Reid Patterson, and her. Her mouth dropped open. She expected the will to name Carson as the sole beneficiary. Flipping to the last page, her heart dropped. The will had been signed by Ivan. In accordance with estate law, two witnesses were required. The first signature was Dirk Gustason, his longstanding advisor. The second name was Hilary Foster.

Hilary? How did Ivan know Hilary?

Lila stared at the signatures then folded the papers, shoved them into her backpack, and rose.

As she took a step forward, she halted when the back door burst open. Two men rushed in. Lila whipped around and slammed the safe into the temple of the man nearest her. He yowled and went down. She turned and extended a roundhouse kick to the taller man's groin.

"You bitch!" He cupped his privates and fell backward.

The first man recovered and came at her again. He grabbed her around the neck and pushed her against the wall. The man towered over her and probably outweighed her by close to a hundred pounds. His large hands squeezed her neck as she struggled to get loose. For a second, she flailed then she remembered her training. Gasping for air, she wouldn't have long. She reared back as far as she could and aimed for his nose. The gesture grazed him.

The man thought her feeble attempt funny.

The other man yelled, "Stop! We're not supposed to kill her!"

The man holding her dropped his hands.

Lila slid to the floor, coughing and sputtering for air. Her pulse raced and anger lit her belly. She jumped up and kicked the man in the knees.

He screamed and smacked her hard. Slamming to the floor, Lila grimaced in pain. She pushed her compass pendant again, hope fading she could hold her own for much longer.

The smaller man hauled her up and covered her face with a cloth. She inhaled a sweet scent, then she felt herself fall.

Chapter 50

Wild images danced before her. Green iguanas turned into dinosaurs. Innocent birds flapped their wings and morphed into flying monsters. And Cody fell to his death over and over again.

Then she woke up.

At least she thought so. Darkness surrounded her. She bolted up. *Where am I?* For a moment, she thought she was dead but pain radiated across her skull awakening her senses. With hands extended, she slapped against the air. Nothing. Then a cold, damp wall greeted her. Was she in a cellar or maybe a cave? The thought of being buried alive or left for dead chilled her. Closing her eyes, she hoped for a new reality. When she opened them, she winced when the horror remained.

Cody. *Where are you?*

She closed her eyes again, willing him to appear.

Slapping at her waist, she groaned. Her gun was gone. Her backpack and the will gone, too. Raspy breathing startled her until she realized it was her own choppy breaths. She banged the wall. When she heard nothing in return, she sank to the ground. Hard rocky dirt pierced her palms.

I have to gain control. She started counting. Every few numbers, she inhaled then exhaled to a beat. Over time, her breathing slowed. She forced herself to concentrate on counting and to block out everything else. When she topped fifty, she exhaled a final time, then swallowed.

Now what?

She stood and raised her arms. Her fingers didn't touch the ceiling, so she relaxed a little knowing her space might not be as cramped as she first thought. With her hands extended outward, she counted her steps between the rocky walls. Nine steps covered the distance. She recalled the conversion and calculated about twenty-three feet spanned the width of the enclosure. Reid had taught her the math for a situation like this.

The first time she was locked away in a dark room, she'd been eight years old. When they came for her, she'd endured pain she hadn't anticipated. The memory of being strapped to a table and injected with needles over and over again haunted her.

As a teenager she'd been abducted from the tunnels of Babylon Hall and thrown into a room at Ivan's compound in Colorado. The room had been lit with one dim bulb, which cast scary shadows onto the walls. Alone and shaken, she'd spent her time worrying about Cody, Reid, and Holly. Now, once again, she'd been shut away, left to ruminate about the fate of those she cared for most.

With her heartbeat ramping up again, Lila splayed her hands on the ground and inhaled and exhaled several times. She slapped the floor. Counting and deep breathing exercises wouldn't get her anywhere.

If Lance didn't know the location of the island, who had captured her? The name Hugo Castille entered her thoughts.

The sound of crunching rocks kicked her pulse into high gear. Lila hunched on her feet, ready to fight.

Minutes later, the door wrenched open and sunlight flooded in. Lila squinted in the sudden light, then attacked.

Chapter 51

L ance paced the cramped mining office. "If that little bitch, Lila gets her hands on that will, then they can contest it. But, I'll win. My sister, Sloane, changed her identity so everyone will believe she's only out to usurp my birthright as the oldest *and* as the only heir to stand by the family. Reid has never been recognized by any of us and neither has Lila. She hooked her boat to her father, Dan Caldwell." Lance stalked around the desk. "I'd prefer not to engage in a legal battle or worse yet, a courtroom brawl."

"Lance, the old man is dead." Peter parked himself in a metal chair with a thin black cushion. "You have nothing to worry about."

"You're right but I have to make sure all loose ends are eradicated. I ended that weasel Walt Talcott's life, after he told me about the island. I'll admit I never thought that blowhard had the information. Seems he was savvy enough to blackmail an older Order member, Morris Beak out of the information."

"You have great instincts, Lance. Before you killed your father, you and your mother Pia forged a new will that gave you everything. I have no doubt we'll get this latest will." Peter's phone buzzed, and he drew the device from his jacket pocket. After a brief conversation, he lifted his head. "My men are bringing in the document."

"What about Lila?"

"She's locked in the underground storm shelter." Peter rose at the knock on the door.

"Good. Leave her there. She can rot in that hole."

Casper opened the door and allowed in two men.

Lance stared at the men, one a huge guy with a tree trunk neck. They had cuts and bruises on their faces and arms. "She fought back."

The huge man stepped forward. "That tramp came at us and…"

The smaller man held up his hand and flashed his partner a frown. "And she's contained. We have the document." He handed the set of papers to Peter.

"Good work. Dismissed." Peter gave the documents to Lance, then answered another call.

Lance read through documents then glanced up. "Damn him!" He slammed his hands on the cheap table. "My own father cut me out of this will." Anger boiled in his gut. Neither his nor his mother's name appeared in the will. Once again, he peered down at the document focusing on the date. It had been signed two weeks before his father's demise. Had Ivan discovered their plot? Didn't matter. Ivan was dead. He tore the paper in half. Problem solved.

"…are you sure?" Peter said into his phone. "Stay on it." He shoved his phone into his pocket and turned to Lance. "We've got a problem."

Chapter 52

Lila raced toward the man, aiming for his knees. Her vision was off due to being locked in the dark for so long.

The man scooped her up with ease as she continued to attack.

"Lila, I'm here to help!" the man yelled.

Stunned, she stopped. With her hand shielding her eyes, she stared. Something about the voice rang familiar but a large hood shielded his face.

She turned and glanced back at where she'd been. Thick brush half covered a rusty metal door of what appeared to be a storm shelter. Shifting her gaze, she spotted the cabin about fifty yards in the distance.

He put her down with a thud. "Let's go."

"Where is Cody?" Her voice was raspy, and she cleared her throat several times.

"We need to go." The man took her arm and pushed her toward a black truck parked behind the cabin.

"I'm not going anywhere with you! Let go of me!" Lila struggled against his grip.

"If you don't want to go back in that storm shelter and be left for dead or worse killed right out, then you'll come with me." He huffed out a deep sigh.

Who is this man? Rising, her muscles ached from multi-mile hike across the island and being stuffed in the shelter. Sweat zig-zagged down her back, and her skull throbbed. The last time she ate had been breakfast with Cody before they left their campsite. Had that been earlier today? "Who are you and who do you work for?" Lila held her ground. Although the man could strong-arm her, he remained still.

"I don't work for Lance, if that's what you're thinking."

"You know Lance?" She blinked several times to clear her vision.

"Yes, now let's go before his men come back."

Again, she tried to get a glimpse of the man, but the hood impeded most of his face. He was tall, almost the same height as Cody. Judging by the way his jacket filled out, the man had bulk. Her intuition urged her forward. She swallowed hard and trudged a few feet to the rear of the house.

When they neared the truck, he swung open the door of the pickup. He pushed her into the front seat of the cab. "If you fight, I'll be forced to handcuff you. Do you understand?"

She nodded.

Starting the truck, he shot out of the gravel drive and up a hill. In seconds, they were on a treacherous path with a rocky cliff on one side and a tall fence with electrical wiring on the other. Even if she wanted to jump, there were no options for escape. "Again, who are you and where are you taking me?" If she couldn't bail out maybe she could talk her way into bettering her situation.

"It's a short drive."

This time she detected a slight European accent but couldn't pinpoint exactly where. She searched her memory for his name.

An iron gate, barely visible due to the massive green vines, slid open ahead of them. The man drove through and followed a curvy road bordered by a thick tree line. He made a turn and a sprawling two-story U-shaped house lay ahead. Lush green grass, colorful flowers in pristine gardens, and towering palm trees with their fronds blowing in the wind dotted the grounds. A wide portico framed a set of brown double doors which Lila suspected led to pure opulence. Despite the luxurious house, Lila braced for the evil inside.

The man pulled to a stop and adjusted his hood.

Lila stared at the house. The man said he didn't work for Lance, however, she didn't expect anyone to tell her the truth. But if this place didn't belong to Lance, then who? Her heart sunk. She might have just sentenced her family to death. Maybe she shouldn't have insisted Carson proceed with outing Lance and The Order. Had her decision killed Cody? She sucked back tears. She wouldn't allow Lance nor anyone else to witness her pain.

The man circled the truck. When he reached her side, he opened the door. He took her arm with a firm yet gentle grip, guided her to the front door, and nudged her inside.

The interior matched the island greenery, with plants and stone fountains on each side of the entryway. Gleaming bamboo floors and lazy circulating ceiling fans added to the relaxing resort-like atmosphere.

The man continued to hold her arm as he led her through a large living area with a wall of open sliding doors leading to a covered patio. A swimming pool with water matching the blue-green ocean that lay beyond the patio. On the other side of the pool, she saw a grassy area leading to a steep cliff, which met the ocean water below.

They moved toward the patio and Lila stopped. A man sitting in a chair with his back to her settled into her field of vision.

The hooded man pushed her forward.

She stepped outside, and the man turned.

"Hello, Lila."

Her mouth dropped open as her blood stilled. "Ivan?"

Chapter 53

I van Sinclair rose from his chair, using a wooden cane for assistance.

A full head of white hair and a few wrinkles around his eyes were the only signs of aging—aside from the cane. His eyes had changed. Gone was the fierce dark evil she'd once witnessed. Instead, he gazed at her with kindness.

Kindness? Not possible.

Maybe this wasn't the man she thought. She repeated, "Ivan?"

"Yes, it's me."

A woman stepped out of a door near Ivan, placing her hands on the man's shoulders in an intimate gesture. The woman shifted and once again Lila's jaw dropped.

Hilary Foster smiled. "Hello, Lila."

"Hilary. What are you doing here?" She recalled her signature on Ivan's will and the woman's sudden interest in her.

Ivan moved around the chair, leaving the cane behind. "I'm glad you're here. And you already know my wife."

Lila shook her head in confusion. "What are you doing here? I mean, you're supposed to be dead. I-I...we...we thought you died." She swallowed and glanced past Ivan. She expected guards to rush out any moment and throw her into a cell. She tightened her muscles.

"I know this must be confusing. Your questions will be answered." He approached her. "You must be thirsty and hungry."

Lila stepped back and checked her surroundings again. The man with the hood stood to the side of her.

"Berta!" Ivan said.

In an instant, an older woman appeared wearing light blue pants and shirt with an apron tied around her waist. "Yes, Mr. Ivan?" she said with a Columbian accent.

"Please bring some beverages for my special guests."

She nodded and disappeared inside.

"Guests?" Lila said.

"First, know I'm not here to hurt you. I applaud your arrival."

"You found *me*, so do you know where Cody is?" Whatever Ivan or Hilary had to say paled in comparison to finding Cody.

Ivan waved a hand. "I will answer every question you have but—"

"I saw the will. Why is—"

Ivan held up his hand. "Lila, I will answer your questions. I promise."

At the sound of footsteps, she whipped around. "Cody!" She jumped and raced into his arms. "You're alive! I went to look for you."

He held her tight. "I know, baby. I'm here, and I'm fine. Are you okay?" He pulled back and studied her.

"I'm fine." She turned and lunged toward Ivan. "Did you and Lance send those helicopters after us?"

Cody grabbed her. "Lila, no! Dirk helped me. Ivan isn't working with Lance."

Dirk? He'd been Ivan's right hand for years. Dirk was the one who'd shut her in that room at Ivan's Colorado estate. Today, he'd been the one to free her from the underground shelter. Lila recalled after Ivan had been killed, Dirk worked for Lance. However, after Lance tried to kill Carson, Dirk had taken off. The FBI couldn't find him. Perhaps, his allegiance had always been to Ivan.

"Lila." Dirk nodded then slid off his hood.

Lila shifted her gaze from Ivan to Cody. Before she could say anything else, she heard footsteps behind her. Reid, Adam, Justin, and Carson rushed to join them.

"Are you both all right?" Reid said, hugging Lila and Cody.

Lila turned to Carson who stood staring at Ivan. "I can't believe this."

Ivan approached her. "Sloane." He reached out to her, but she stepped back.

"Dad? You're alive. Where have you been all this time?" Carson's pained expression tore at Lila's heart.

"I'm sorry, Sloane. It was imperative I handle things in the manner I did. I'm sorry I hurt you." Ivan pulled Hilary close, holding her hand. "Please meet Hilary. She's been by my side for years and integral to my survival. As well as Dirk," Ivan added.

"Dirk." Carson pivoted toward him.

"Hello, Sloane. It's good to see you." He stepped back against the house, standing rigid like the sentinel he'd always been.

"It's actually Carson, now." She turned her attention back to Ivan.

"I'm aware of your name change but you'll always be Sloane to me." Ivan nodded.

"Hilary, you've lived here with Ivan all this time? Were you responsible for Jack's death?" Lila gripped Cody's hand as thousands of questions peppered her brain.

Hilary shook her head. "Ivan and I have known each other for quite a while and were married about a year ago. We don't always live here. As you know, I have active cases requiring my attention. I have a house in Dallas, and we have another in Switzerland." She continued to hold Ivan's hand. "Lance is guilty of Jack's murder, in addition to others. Our firm represented him and then suppressed the evidence."

"You let Jack take the fall?" Heat crawled up Lila's back. "Why didn't you take the evidence to the authorities?"

"I liked Jack. Had I known he had the evidence, I would have tried to keep him safe, but I didn't know. Lance had a large criminal defense team. Not until Jack was murdered did I come to suspect that

Steve had smuggled the evidence out of the firm." She ran her fingers up and down Ivan's back

"But you were on Lance's criminal team." Lila looked at Hilary with fresh eyes. The hard as nails attorney now appeared like a schoolgirl enamored of her first crush.

"I consulted on Lance's defense team to monitor him. I, we"—she glanced at Ivan— "knew Lance would never be brought to justice. But we wanted the evidence so that we could, one day, expose him. After all, when he tried to kill Ivan...when he pushed him from that plane, he of course, became someone Ivan could no longer trust. When I discovered another set of those files were missing, I knew someone else in firm was either working with Lance and took the files as insurance or was working against Lance and had plans to disclose the evidence. Now, we know Steve evidently gave Jack the evidence with specific instructions to hide the documents. Apparently, Steve wanted the files in case he ever needed them but knowing Steve, he didn't want to know where Jack hid them. He's sort of an out-of-sight-out-of-mind kind of guy. But when Jack was killed, Steve knew he needed to find the evidence."

Lila emitted a loud sigh as she rubbed her forehead. "So much deception. Was Mr. Talcott part of the coverup?"

Hilary nodded. "I'm aware of his death. With both Jack and Steve dead, Walt knew the heat would be on him."

Carson stepped forward, but Adam placed his hand on her arm. "How did you survive being pushed out of that airplane?" Carson asked.

"I'll get to that."

"Reid, you're awfully quiet," Ivan said.

Reid swept a glance across the outdoor room. "Taking in the environment. I can't decide if you're full of shit or not."

Ivan reared back his head and laughed. "You are the ever-present surveyor." Then his demeanor grew serious. "I've been faced with death. At that moment, I reevaluated my life and didn't like what I saw." He sighed. "I made some serious mistakes." He paused and turned to Lila. "I'm very sorry about the way your life started and for the pain I caused you and those close to you. I'm not asking for forgiveness. I'm not sure I deserve that." He stared over her head at the ocean waves crashing onto the rocky shore creating a frothy spray, then he faced Carson. "I haven't been the best father to you. I'm sorry. The fact you had to flee and change your name... On one hand, you impressed me with your tenacity but on the other hand, I'm deeply saddened you had to make such a drastic decision." Ivan turned his gaze to Adam. "So, this is the man who's captured your heart."

"I know the sick things done in the name of The Order. You shouldn't be allowed to see the light of day." Adam's eyes blazed.

Justin stepped forward. "Many people have been killed and hurt. Do you believe saying sorry means you're forgiven?"

Ivan dipped his head. "I know it's not so simple, Dr. Tanner."

Carson stared at her father. "Is this about revenge or to regain power?" She shook her head. "Doesn't matter. You're wasting your time. Father, I witnessed some of the atrocities you and others engaged in all in the name of The Order. You imprisoned Lila. And she was our blood." She spoke as if she ingested something bitter, her blue eyes giving off an icy glare.

Lila slid her hand toward Carson and her friend gripped it with gusto.

"After the shooting broke out and Lila and Cody disappeared, we got a message requesting our presence. Why did you send for us, Ivan?" Reid asked. His lips flattened into a thin line, and he held his jaw was rigid.

Ivan swallowed and tapped his fingers as if contemplating his next move. "I've been monitoring you all and the situation for some time. I expected some type of activity, but I must applaud your proactive response. Everyone deserves to see how this ends. I've gone through a transformation of sorts. I will agree that I was ruthless and evil. And Sloane, you are correct, power is a dangerous drug more addictive than any substance. The more you have, the more you want. Then I learned a truth which shook me to my core—my wife and my own son would kill for that power."

Lila shot Cody a worried glance. Events were happening so fast.

She knew everyone was considering exit options. Dirk brought her in through the front, which contained a heavily fortified gate and what appeared to be an electrified fence. But if Ivan were to be believed, they had nothing to worry about. She didn't trust him, and she suspected neither did any other Alliance member.

"What about Morris Beak, Garvin Jennings, Willa Dickerson, and my mother? Do you realize they are all dead?" Cody held both arms at his sides, his hands curling in a fist.

"Yes, I do. In the case of Willa Dickerson, her husband, Edgar, was part of my inner circle. I sent the directions to these individuals years ago to contact Lila when the time was right. I needed to heal from my injuries and wasn't capable of dealing with any of this. Then as I got stronger, I became aware of Lance's plan to acquire Veridian. I knew that if he got ahold of the mine as well, he'd be unstoppable." Ivan settled in his chair, with the help of Hilary. "As far as your mother, Cody—I'm sorry. In the heat of battle, we must expect collateral damage. Same goes for the Caldwell family."

Lila stepped forward, her body shaking with rage. "Ms. Green and my family had nothing to do with this stupid fight. If you have any hope of gaining a sliver of respect or forgiveness, you could start by sounding like you give a damn."

Reid threw up his hands. "If your desire was to stop your son, then why not step out of the shadows, contact Carson or any of us, and let us know what Lance was up to?"

"Would you have believed me? Would we have become allies? Besides, as silly as it sounds, I wanted to prove to myself that I was just as savvy as *my* father. He discounted me. Just as my sister tossed you aside, Reid."

"People are dead because you played another game, Father." Carson said softly.

"And I'm sorry. No one knew I was alive. If my secret was exposed, then Lance would've kicked his plans into high gear. I wanted Hilary on the Stonegate board to monitor their progress."

"We know Lance killed Willa Dickerson and Beak committed suicide. Did Lance kill the Jennings'?" Adam pulled Carson close.

"Lance knew there was another player. I had to remain dead. My son had feelers out on several people, including Beak, Jennings, and Dickerson to find the other puppet master. He killed the Jennings to send a message to the person pulling the strings—me." Ivan leaned on his cane. Although his physical abilities appeared diminished, the ferocious determination in his eyes remained.

"You're Hugo Castille," Lila said. The last puzzle piece clicked into place.

He nodded.

"Lance has a team working for him at Veridian" Ivan continued. "He had a taste of the power he'd have if he controlled Veridian."

Cody took a step forward. "The DDI. I was on that team."

Hilary nodded. "Many of the upper-level executives are Order members."

"What are you trying to prove, Ivan? You're now one of the good guys?" Reid said.

Dirk appeared once again. He moved with the stealth of a jaguar on the hunt then whispered something to Ivan. After a nod from his boss, he retreated.

Ivan stood. "I have another guest."

Chapter 54

A familiar voice boomed through the house seconds before its owner stepped on to the patio.

Lila jumped up and ran toward Lance standing at the door in his usual smug manner. She reared back and walloped his nose. "Where's my family, you bastard?"

Cody charged after Lila. If anyone laid a hand on her...

Lance took a knee as blood spurted from his nose. "Bitch!" He rose and reached for Lila, but Cody's fist met the side of his face.

"What the hell?" Lance glared at the scene, dabbing at the blood pouring from his nose.

Ivan stood. "Hello, Lance."

Lance's eyes widened. "How can you be alive?" He stood and stepped closer to his father, confusion clouding his eyes before he stiffened. "Whoever you are, I want my wife and child returned to me now. I came alone as requested by a man named Hugo Castille who indicated my wife and son had been taken. If I don't see Delphine and my son immediately, I will rain down my wrath like you've never seen." Lance lifted his head as if to show he maintained control.

Ivan shook his head. "You and your mother thought you killed me. I am very much alive and have been living under the name Hugo

Castille. You see, I discovered your plan to kill me months prior. I got notice that my will had been altered when I hadn't made any changes. I knew then what you were planning." He picked up a set of papers from the table and waved them. "This is my current will. I have evidence that you committed fraud to change my will making you the sole beneficiary."

Lance laughed bitterly. "You are considered dead. You have no power, and you'll be looking at your own fraud charges. I'll make sure."

"I made you believe that all those papers were legitimate, even my death certificate. You aren't the only one who can manipulate a situation."

Lance glanced at the group. "I suppose you're all are in on this?"

Reid shook his head. "Nope. We're just as surprised as you."

"I knew you tried to kill our father," Carson shot daggers at Lance.

"Who the hell cares what you think, Sloane? I suppose you believe that when our old man actually does kick the bucket, you and your buddies here will get everything."

Sloane shrugged. "I really don't care what's in his will. I don't want anything to do with him or the money."

Reid moved toward the door. "Lance you have a chance to do something right for once. Call off the dogs and tells us where the Caldwells are."

Lance whipped his head toward Reid. "Your media blitz didn't work. You'll never get your family back, Lila." He turned back to Ivan. "Now, give me my wife and child."

Delphine stepped through another door followed by Marissa, Holly, Justin, and Bobsled. She held the baby as she eyed Lance. "Hello."

"Finally. Let's go, Delphine."

"I'm not going anywhere." She held her head high. "I know you were going to kill me and take the baby."

Lance stalked closer to Delphine and pointed. "You know nothing. How the hell are you going to listen to this man? He probably has brain damage after he fell out of an airplane."

"Correction, I was pushed out of an airplane. But I'd prepared. My men were following in another plane. When you tossed me to my death, one of my men with a parachute picked me up. Very risky move but it worked." Ivan smiled. "I went back to Europe for a while, then I built this place."

"I want my son," Lance almost spat the words.

Delphine jumped back and smiled. She shot a glance toward Holly and Marissa as if drawing strength from them before turning back to Lance. "You'll get nothing. This baby isn't yours."

"What the hell are you talking about, Delphine?" Lance's always pristine hair hung limp, as if his hair follicles, like his power, had also been weakened.

"Say hello to your brother." Delphine flashed a satisfied grin.

Ivan puffed out his chest. "With the blessing of my wife, *I* impregnated Delphine. We were blessed to create a beautiful son. *My* son."

Lance lunged toward Ivan.

Hilary screamed as the two men tumbled over one another.

Groans erupted from Ivan as he fell to the ground with Lance on top of him.

Dirk rushed to Ivan's side and lifted Lance up, tossing him aside as if he were a toy.

Lance popped up, his eyes full of rage. "I'll kill you. You won't survive this time! I'm the Grand Commander. You were weak."

"I outsmarted you and lived. Who's the weak one?" Ivan struggled to stand before holding out his hand. "But you're my first born. I will have mercy."

Lance stared at his father's outstretched hand. "I am on the pinnacle of power and wealth and you want me to concede to you?"

"Let's end our family feud. I'm sorry, son."

"I learned from Russell. Only a weak man apologizes." He curled his lips and spat at Ivan's feet. "Your weakness disgusts me."

Sloane stood next to her father. "For the sake of this innocent baby. Don't let him grow up in this hatred. Tell us where Lila's family is."

Lance laughed with a bitter tone. "You both are fools. Mother was right. I deserved to be Grand Commander. I can't believe I share DNA with you." Lance charged toward Lila, grabbing her around the neck and jamming a knife at her throat. He pulled her past the pool toward the cliff's edge.

Marissa pulled Delphine back. "Take the baby and get inside."

"If she takes another step, I'll slit Lila's throat."

Delphine's eyes widened. "Lance!"

With his heart lodged in his throat, Cody raced toward Lila. "Let her go!" He had no doubt Lance would kill her. Cody stepped in front of Reid, Adam, Justin, and Bobsled who'd followed him.

"Don't be a hero. I will kill her." Lance tightened his grip on Lila. Then he smiled. "Just like I killed your mother. It was so easy. You know better than anyone what you can learn when you dive into someone's history."

Cody's heart tumbled in his chest as rage rose. "You won't get away with this."

"Looks like I already have." Lance pulled Lila farther away from them, past the pool and into the grassy area about fifty yards from the ledge. A small wooden fence stood as a paltry barrier to the rocky shore below.

"Killing Lila will serve no purpose," Ivan said, still rooted to his spot.

Lila grimaced as the knife lay parallel to her neck.

Cody met her gaze. Despite her situation, Lila appeared calm. With her hands on Lance's arm, she moved to widen her stance.

Lance shifted the knife. "Be still or I will cut you."

She was getting in position. Cody needed to give her the chance to pull out Lance's grip and throw Lance off balance. Reid inched up behind him. They only needed a second but so did Lance.

Carson stared from Lila to her brother then stepped several feet to the side of her brother. "Lance, the authorities will be here any minute. Let Lila go, and we can talk."

From the corner of Cody's eye, he saw Dirk draw out his weapon. Dirk couldn't get off a shot without hitting Lila or Ivan. He was in a better position to hit Lance.

"Don't come any closer, Sloane!" Sweat poured down Lance's face. He emitted a maniacal chuckle. "You didn't want to talk before. You took off. Our mother died of a broken heart after you rejected her."

"She died trying to protect you. I left to survive. To have a life," Carson said.

"*You* killed her! You killed my mother with your desire to bring me down." Spittle flew from his mouth. "Lila and this so-called Alliance have been on a mission to topple me. If I have to kill each of you one by one, I will. I saw you, Sloane, on the television spewing lies."

"Let's talk now." Carson maintained Lance's focus on her.

In the split second, Lance's gaze shifted, Reid slapped a gun into Cody's hand. The cold steel gave him hope he could save Lila.

"No! You left and didn't want to talk, so why should we now?" Lance turned the knife and with the tip drew blood on Lila's neck.

Lila winced but didn't move.

They were standing uncomfortably close to the ledge, a couple hundred feet from the bottom of the waterfall. A fall wouldn't be survivable.

Once a well-put-together, smooth-as-ice person, Lance had dissolved into an out-of-control maniac with a knife.

Carson held her hands out. "I'm sorry about Mother."

"Listen to your sister, son. All the power and money in the world won't bring your mother back." Ivan leaned on his cane.

Cody stared at Lila. With her eyes, she signaled to the left. Cody tensed. They had no other choice. He gave her a slight nod. He'd prefer to use his hands and go to work on this dude. All he needed was five minutes. Instead, he chose his target and waited for Lila to act.

Carson shot a glance behind her. "Let Delphine take the baby inside and we can talk."

Lance shook his head. "Delphine, don't you move. The old man couldn't impregnate anyone."

"It's hot. Let me take the baby inside where it's cooler." Delphine pleaded with her husband.

"I told you to stay put! I don't give a damn about what happens to you, Delphine. I'll kill you all and take the child." Lance's voice boomed across the yard and bounced off the canyon behind him.

With fear in her eyes, Delphine nodded. She pulled the baby closer to her chest and adjusted the blanket. The baby stirred and began to whimper.

"Son, you were raised on the ways of The Order. Loyalty is a trait we hold dear. You may have inspired loyalty among your followers but what about to your father. I was the Grand Commander when you committed that egregious act of overthrowing me in every way." Ivan held Hilary's hand. "This woman has shown commitment you can't begin to comprehend. She stood by while I impregnated another woman, for the good of The Order."

Cody wanted to grab Lila and get as far away from these psychotic people as possible.

Lance loosened his tie. "I'm in control. I'm the better one. Grandfather would approve and so would Aunt Vivian. I don't need nor want you in my life. I thought I'd killed you before, and I didn't suffer a minute of regret."

Lance's hateful words didn't appear to penetrate Ivan as he remained steady and upright.

The baby went from soft whimper to all out cries. Delphine tried to calm the infant without success.

Cody maintained eye contact with Lila.

As the baby's cries grew louder, Lance continued his downward spiral. With the pointed blade, he skimmed the knife along Lila's throat creating tiny cuts along the blade's path.

"Shut up!" Lance screamed.

Ivan inched close, pushing Sloane back. "It's over. Let Lila go. Penance is your next course of action as a disloyal subject of The Order."

"Never." In one motion, Lance reared back and plunged the knife into Lila's arm.

She yelled then thrust her elbow back striking Lance in the neck. When Lance reacted to the assault, Lila dived left.

Two shots rang out.

The force of the bullets caused Lance to stumble back but he grabbed on to Lila's ankles, pulling her half over the edge.

Cody rushed to Lila. "I've got you." He clamped his hands around her arms and pulled.

Lila's gaze connected with his as held on to him. "Cody!"

"I will not let you fall. I promise." Cody blocked out the dizzying effect of the ocean crashing against the shore and long drop from their dangerous position.

As the Alliance circled around Cody to help, Ivan approached. "Son, this is your destiny. It was always you who should fall to your death, not me." Ivan leaned over. "Let her go."

Cody pulled Lila up with Lance hanging on. Holding on to her, he stumbled back on safe ground. "I've got you," he whispered.

Then a wild scream penetrated the atmosphere.

Cody twisted around just as Lance grabbed hold of Ivan. "No, Father. If I must die, then so shall you." Lance pounced and they both disappeared over the edge, their cries cut short seconds later.

Hilary screamed as she raced toward the edge. Collapsing at the precipice, she dissolved in tears. "Ivan, no!"

Cody turned back to Lila. Blood poured from her wound. "I've got you." He repeated as he pressed his hand over her wound.

"Are they gone?" she said.

"Yeah, you're safe."

She nodded then closed her eyes.

Chapter 55

Pain radiated through Lila's arm, but she relished the ache because it meant her heart continued to beat. She placed the last of her personal items in the cardboard box and stared at the empty office. Had she ever been truly happy, at HTP?

Gia sauntered in and perched on the side of her empty desk. "I'm going to miss you around here. But I understand why you're leaving."

Lila gave her a weak smile. "I learned a lot, and I don't regret taking this job, but I can't stay here."

"We all may be looking for new jobs when the Feds finish their investigation." Gia rose and closed the door. "According to the grapevine, it's bad. Suppressing evidence, corruption, murder. Who knows what else? Thankfully, at the moment, the dirty deeds were limited to the senior partners, but with Talcott and Steve dead, shit may roll downhill. And where the hell is Hilary?"

Lila inhaled. "Hilary has her own set of problems. Turns out she was working with her husband Ivan Sinclair. She won't be going anywhere for a very long time."

"How are you holding up?"

Lila shrugged. "Walking the line between fatigue and excitement. The last week has been exhausting but my family was rescued in

Florida without anyone being hurt so I'm beyond grateful." After Lance's death and the swarm of FBI agents and international authorities investigating The Order, members were falling over each other to cooperate, hoping for a reprieve from prosecution. Between quitting her job, endless rounds of questioning with the authorities, and processing all that had happened, Lila vacillated from joy to worry to relief. She dropped two phone chargers into a box. "Thanks for all of your support. Having a friend like you has definitely helped. So, what's up with you and Jimmy?"

Gia extended her hand, a mid-size diamond sparkled on her ring finger.

Lila's eyes widened. "When did this happen? I'm so happy for you guys." She hugged her friend.

"Right after the Veridian ball. I didn't want to tell you because so much was going on." She smiled down at the ring. "I'm really happy. We've got no plans yet, but you better believe you'll be standing right beside me when I take that leap." She grinned, wiping away happy tears.

"I wouldn't want to be anywhere else." Lila hugged her again then inspected Gia's hand.

"What about that emerald mine and the island you mentioned?" Gia asked.

Lila sighed. "The authorities shut down operation, but the initial paperwork revealed the mine had been purchased by my great-grandfather, Russell Sinclair. After Russell's death the mine went to Ivan and his sister, Vivian. After Vivian's death, Ivan owned the entire mine and island. The authorities authenticated Ivan's will. Reid, Sloane, and I are not thrilled to be the rightful owners. Hilary didn't ask for a cut because she'd been promised Ivan's other assets which were valued in the millions. Turns out Hilary is Delphine's aunt. Along with Ivan, they concocted the idea for him to impregnate Delphine in order to get back at Lance."

"Wow, that's some twisted family drama for you." Gia scrunched her face and tossed a dead plant in the trash can. "What about you and Cody? Sounds like you guys have bonded."

Lila thought back to their magical time under the stars and smiled "We're good. Better than good."

Gia emitted an uncharacteristic squeal. "We're two badass attorneys with hot men. Call me later." She hugged Lila then disappeared around the corner.

Lila surveyed her office once more, picked up the last box, and then turned off the lights. Sadness filled her. She could deal with moving on, but the lives ruined because of her family hurt. Did Russell Sinclair have any clue the destruction his sordid vision would have?

Thirty minutes later, she pulled into the parking lot of her father's bar and grill, Tribe. The restaurant Lance destroyed, The Ranch, had been demolished and her father was working through plans to rebuild. She smiled as she gazed at the building. Her family waited for her inside. She said another silent thank you that they were all alive and assembled to celebrate a new beginning. As she neared the door, she spotted a sign reading CLOSED FOR A PRIVATE EVENT.

Cody stood at the door dressed in jeans and V-neck shirt. Her heart lurched as he grinned.

"I missed you," he said, embracing her. After they pulled apart, his brown eyes landed on Lila and her belly fluttered. Cody had always held a special place in her life. Once as her best friend and boyfriend, then the man who'd hurt her, and now the man who sat center in her heart.

"You just saw me this morning." She laughed.

He checked his watch. "That was seven hours ago." Leaning down, he kissed her.

"How was your last day?"

"Great. Rick, Tally, and even Sher were too involved in meetings to save their asses to think about me. And the entire project team quit. The authorities are having a field day lobbing charges at the company and Veridian executives. I'm glad to be done with that episode."

"Did you get a chance to speak with your brother?" Lila hated that Cody's mother was another of Lance's victims.

"I think her death has sobered him. I made the last of the arrangements. We decided on a graveside service. The police in Virginia arrested the guy posing as Kyle." He pulled out his phone and handed her the device. Before we go in, I need to show you something."

Lila read the email from Nikki twice before she glanced up at Cody. "You never slept with her."

"After all the arrests associated with The Order, she confessed someone paid her to claim we slept together all those years ago. Unfortunately, our relationship was another casualty of The Order." Cody ran a hand through his hair.

"I should have believed you. I should have had more faith in us. I'm sorry." Lila covered his hand.

"I don't want to live in the past. It's over. Tonight, is about celebrating." Cody brushed a kiss across her lips. "Then later we'll have our own private celebration."

"I like that plan." Her heart fluttered with anticipation. "So many changes I feel like I need time to absorb it all."

Cody grinned and began to hum the song, "Time in a Bottle" by Jim Croce.

Laughing, she gave him a playful shove.

As they entered the private room, Lila's eyes lit up. Everyone jumped up when they entered. Lila wiped tears away as her entire family surrounded her. In addition to the Caldwells, everyone from the Alliance was there, including Jeb.

Her father approached, with Patty, Jenna, and Brent close behind. "We thought you could use a celebration dinner." He turned to face everyone. "Thank you all for your love and concern for my daughter and my family. You all are special people and will be a part of our family forever. Congratulations on bringing down The Order."

Patty and Jenna served champagne to everyone.

Dan raised his glass. "Here's to love, family, and sleep!"

Clinking of glass and shouts of "here, here" echoed throughout the room.

"I'm so thankful for all of you." Lila bit her lip. "I will never forget those who lost their lives because of The Order." Faces of lost loved ones flashed through her mind as she embraced Reid.

Reid nodded. "That's why we're here." He pulled out a chair for Holly then took the one next to her. "Adam and I have a few updates. We were frozen out of a joint investigation with the CIA and other departments into Lance and The Order because we were deemed too close to the subjects. I hate we were left in the dark, but I understand."

Adam took Sloane's hand. "Hilary has been indicted on a number of charges and she's talking up a storm. She knows the operation and has been a valuable source in bringing charges against others."

"As we speak, Peter Shaw and several others have been taken into federal custody. Thanks to Cody, who planted some secret software into the Skies International system, Evan, and Angie, unlocked database giving us the complete history and roster of Order operatives and members."

Holly turned to Lila. "I'm so glad you're all safe." The two women embraced. "I'm thrilled for you and Cody."

"Thanks." Lila turned to Carson. "How are you?"

Carson's brilliant blue eyes sparkled with tears. "My family bought into the notion they were superior to others. In some respects, I'm sad they had to lose their lives, but I wouldn't have wanted anyone else hurt. At one time, I had a great relationship with my father. He exhibited signs of compassion. I remember hearing so from some of the employees during my time growing up in Switzerland. Maybe in time, I can separate his evil deeds from the sliver of goodness within him."

Adam wrapped her in his arms.

Justin, who held Marissa's hand cleared his throat. "What will Delphine do now?"

Reid shook his head. "There isn't anything to charge her with. Poor judgment isn't grounds for arrest. Delphine and the baby will be going back to France this evening."

"Adam and I visited her this morning." Carson said. "She promised to give us regular updates about the baby. I still can't believe that baby is my half-brother. He now has a chance for a normal life."

Marissa placed an arm around Lila. "You and Cody have quit your jobs. What's next?"

Lila grinned. "My father has offered us positions with Caldwell International. I'll be working under the CLO, and Cody will be director of Information Security."

Dan beam. "I finally got my wish. I understand you wanted to go out on your own and you needed to do what you could to bring down The Order, but I love having your legal skills under my roof. And Cody, thank you for coming on board. We're lucky to have you."

"You're lucky to have them both," Jeb slapped Cody's shoulder and winked at Lila.

"We have something to show you." Cody pulled up his sleeve then did the same to Lila's. "Matching tattoos."

Everyone crowded around. The code Lila had been imprinted with as a child had been turned into stars alongside the phrase WITH TRUTH AND LOVE THE STARS SHINE BRIGHTER.

"I didn't want to live with that tattoo any longer. The mark had once been a permanent reminder on my body. Thanks to Cody and all of you, I have a new life. Now we're really free." She wiped away tears as she glanced from her arm to Cody's.

Cody pulled her into his arms. "We're together now and that's all that matters. I love you, Lila."

She smiled, and for the first time, looked to the future with excitement. "I love you, too."

EPILOGUE

The iron gates of Babylon Hall stood like jagged edges of broken glass, sharp and formidable, but crippled at the same time. The Alliance stood just beyond the gates, each member lost in their own thoughts.

Lila took Cody's hand. He looked handsome in the suit he'd worn to his mother's funeral hours earlier. "You okay?"

"Strangely, yes. Although there was nothing in my mother's papers to indicate who my father is, I'm okay. I have you, your family, and our friends. That's my family."

Adam embraced Carson. "Are you ready?"

She nodded and led the way through the gates.

On a slight hill the ruins of Babylon Hall rose. Windows had been removed and most of the interior of the grand mansion had been gutted. Cranes and men in yellow hard hats stood waiting for the go-ahead.

"This place is evil. So much pain and bloodshed. This is really over. Lila said.

Cody squeezed her hand.

Reid wrapped his arm around Holly. "And we're all safe."

As the investigation continued, many of the properties would be liquidated or sold, including the emerald mine. Babylon Hall would be the first to go. The companies, including Skies International and Veridian Technologies, had been stripped of most of their power and business status. Sloane, Reid, and Lila took the Sinclair money and set up funds for Order victims.

The foreman approached. "We're ready when you are."

Justin wrapped his arms around Marissa, who patted her tear-stained cheeks. Reid and Holly turned to face the house. Carson stared at the ruins as the cranes began to demolish the building.

Cody cupped Lila's face then kissed her. Drawing back, he whispered, "You're free." He handed her an envelope.

"What's this?" She opened the envelope and drew out two airline tickets to Singapore. She lifted her gaze and grinned. "Really?"

"I told you I'd take you wherever you wanted. No time like the present. I will always light the dark for you." Cody wrapped his arm around her.

As the crane demolished the last wall of Babylon Hall, Reid smiled. "*Ordo Ortus* is dead. Order Rising has fallen."

ALSO BY LISA CAVINESS

Thank you for reading Order of Truth. Reviews are important to authors. Please consider leaving one!

The Order Series (listed in reading order)

Order of Fear

Order of Malice

Order of Rage

Order of Truth

ACKNOWLEDGMENTS

This book would never have been published without a few fabulously smart and kind people. Thank you to my beta readers, especially Jillian Jacobs who read and reread this book. Thanks to my editor, Nan Reinhardt, who's patience, words of encouragement, and keen eyes are a blessing. A huge thank you to Susan Cambry for your input. Thank you to my amazing and talented cover designer, Alexandra Corza. And as always, thank you to my family. Love you all!

This book is a work of fiction and while I have taken strides to mirror reality as much as possible, any mistakes or liberties taken with the facts are my own.

ABOUT THE AUTHOR

Lisa Caviness is an award-winning author of romantic thrillers and suspense novels. She loves dreaming up story ideas where her characters are pushed to their limits during dangerous and blood-tingling adventures before finding true love. She also has a deep interest in science. After college, she worked as a registered nurse before starting a career as a clinical project manager in medical research. She has lived in Boston, Massachusetts and now makes her home in Indiana with her husband, kids, and a sometimes affectionate black cat.

Subscribe to Lisa's newsletter for updates on new releases, giveaways, and more! Lisa's Website and Newsletter Signup

www.lisacavinessauthor.com